PRAISE FOR *DEADLY LOVE*
BY BRENDA JOYCE

"The steamy revelations . . . are genuinely intriguing, and just enough of them are left unresolved at the book's end to leave readers waiting eagerly for the series' next installment." —*Publishers Weekly*

"Joyce carefully crafted a wonderful mystery with twists and turns and red herrings galore, then added two marvelous, witty protagonists who will appeal to romance readers . . . Add to this a charming cast of secondary characters and a meticulously researched picture of society life in the early 1900s. I can hardly wait to see what Francesca and Rick will be up to next." —*Romantic Times*

"A delight!" —*Reader to Reader*

CHARTER

8 8696

DEADLY
Affairs

BRENDA JOYCE

St. Martin's Paperbacks

DEADLY AFFAIRS

Copyright © 2002 by Brenda Joyce Dreams Unlimited, Inc.
Excerpts from *Deadly Pleasure* and *Deadly Desire* copyright © 2002 by Brenda Joyce Dreams Unlimited.

ISBN: 0-312-98262-3

Printed in the United States of America

St. Martin's Paperbacks edition / April 2002

St. Martin's Paperbacks are published by St. Martin's Press, 175 Fifth Avenue, New York, NY 10010.

10 9 8 7 6 5 4 3 2 1

ONE

"What do you think of this one, Miss Cahill?"

Francesca Cahill stood as patiently as possible, no easy task. She glanced down at the shimmering piece of apricot-hued silk fabric that Maggie Kennedy was holding up. "Why, that one is just as lovely as the others," she said. Was it already nine o'clock? Had her father noticed that one of his morning papers was missing? Vanished, as it were? And would they ever be finished with this fitting? Francesca had two classes to attend uptown at Barnard College, a very exclusive institution dedicated to the higher education of women, in which she had secretly enrolled— and, thus far, not been found out by her mother, who abhorred the thought of her younger daughter ever being labeled a bluestocking.

For being an intellectual—and a Reformer with a capital *R*—could only interfere with Julia Van Wyck Cahill's plans to successfully marry Francesca off—and the sooner, the better.

Francesca sighed loudly.

"This blue suits you, too, Miss Cahill," Maggie murmured from where she knelt at Francesca's feet. Francesca remained in her undergarments, with pins, a pincushion, and a measuring tape scattered about her.

"Please, Mrs. Kennedy, 'Francesca' will do," she said with a genuine smile, glancing down at the redhead.

Maggie returned the smile tentatively. "So you wish for

the blue? I would do it as a day ensemble for you. The fabric is a bit stiff, and would be most flattering in a fitted little jacket and a skirt."

"That's perfect," Francesca said, hardly caring. By now, surely, Andrew had gone down to breakfast and discovered that he had only the *Times* and the *Tribune* to peruse. Good God. Had she been insane to allow those reporters an interview last Tuesday while at the Plaza? Apparently her pride had overtaken her common sense. But hopefully no story would come out of that interview now. Yesterday's news had been filled with the details of the Randall Murder, but no mention had been made of her name.

In spite of the fact that she had solved the case.

"Would you consider a Chinese red for an evening gown? It is a color most blondes cannot carry off, but you are so golden, it would be lovely on you," Maggie said, standing.

"Oh, I do love red," Francesca said.

Maggie looked at her oddly, as if sensing that she hardly cared about the ten new gowns she was ordering.

"I mean, I have a passion for red," Francesca said, wincing a bit. It was hardly true, and after both the Randall Murder and the Burton Abduction, the color red now reminded her of blood.

Maggie walked over to Francesca's immense canopied bed, which was covered with fabric samples. The bed dominated a large and beautiful bedroom and faced a seating area and a fireplace. She fingered the various silks, wool, and chiffon.

Instantly Francesca was alert. "Is anything wrong, Mrs. Kennedy?"

"No." Maggie faced her, clutching a stunning piece of dark red fabric. "I was so surprised when you actually called and told me you needed so many new garments."

Francesca smiled brightly. "My mother will be in heaven when she learns I have finally taken an interest in my wardrobe," Francesca said, and that was the truth.

Maggie looked at her. She was a faded redhead who had once, undoubtedly, been stunning, but a life of hardship had made her look fifteen years older than Francesca, who was twenty. Francesca guessed she was perhaps twenty-three or -four. But she had four children, and the eldest, Joel, who was eleven, was Francesca's new assistant. She had recently hired him, as he had been indispensable in solving both the Burton Abduction and the Randall Murder, and he had even gotten her out of two life-threatening predicaments. He knew almost every inch of the city's underbelly, especially the Lower East Side—as she certainly did not. He had even taught her how to bribe a person in order to gain important information. "Joel speaks about you constantly, Miss Cahill. He does admire you so," Maggie added.

Francesca smiled. "He is a wonderful boy."

Maggie did not smile in return. "He is often in trouble with the police."

"I know." Her own smile faded. "But he is not bad. Not at all. Quite the opposite, I think."

Maggie seemed relieved. Francesca wondered if she knew the extent of Joel's activities. He was a kid—a child pickpocket—and the police had his photograph in the Rogues' Gallery. "I am glad you think so." Maggie held up the dark red fabric. "You will be the belle of the ball in a gown made from this brocade."

Francesca looked at the bold fabric—it hardly suited her character, which was serious and intellectual, and although she had accepted every fabric sample thus far shown, she hesitated, thinking about Rick Bragg, the city's police commissioner. Her heart skipped a little. She hadn't seen him since Tuesday, when they had spoken intimately on the steps of the Plaza. "Do you really think I can carry off such a seductive color?" she asked, sobering.

"Oh, yes!" Maggie cried, her eyes brightening. And

when she smiled like that, the years of hard work seemed to fade from her face, and she looked young, vibrant, and pretty.

Francesca knew she should not imagine wearing such a gown for Bragg's sake. After all, they were friends, and nothing more. They could never be anything more—he was a married man. Of course, his wife was a horrid and selfish creature who lived in Europe with her various lovers; Bragg hadn't seen her in four years. He didn't want to see her. He supported her selflessly, while she spent his every hard-earned penny, not caring one whit that a man in public service earned a moderate income. Thank God she was abroad, Francesca thought with heat.

She had never met Leigh Anne. She hoped never to do so. But she despised her, and she did not care if she was being unjust.

"Maggie, I know this might not be possible, but there is a party next week, on Thursday. My brother's fiancée, Sarah Channing, is having a ball in honor of her cousin, Bartolla Benevente. Apparently the countess is newly arrived in the city and—"

Maggie smiled. "You know I work at night. I think I can have the gown ready for you, but we must plan on a final fitting Wednesday morning."

"Really?" For the first time since Maggie had arrived for the fitting, Francesca felt genuine enthusiasm. She could imagine the look in Bragg's golden eyes when he saw her descend the stairs in that bold red gown. In fact, she felt more than certain he would not be able to take his eyes off her. "The gown should be rather daring," she said.

"It must be backless and low-cut," Maggie said briskly. "I have a pattern that would be perfect. Here, let me show it to you." She walked over to her worn leather valise.

Of course, Francesca knew that she must not think this way and she must not care if he admired her in any manner, much less in that dress. Still, it was easier to command herself to think a certain way than to actually do so. She sighed, suddenly and immeasurably saddened.

"Are you all right?" Maggie asked softly, the pattern in her hands.

Francesca smiled. "I am fine." She glanced at the bronze clock on the marble top of a bureau. God, it was nine-twenty now. She had to leave for school shortly. "Is that it?"

Maggie held it up. "This is the bodice. It is rather low, but I can make it higher. I can also put two tiny sleeves on it if that would make you more comfortable." She held up another piece of the pattern. "The back can be made higher as well."

Her heart skidded uncontrollably now. What was she doing? Thinking? "I rather like it that way," she said, flushing. Would she be able to be so daring?

And had Bragg seen the *Sun*? Had he seen what that cur, Arthur Kurland, had written about her? And how had Kurland known about her role in the solving of the Randall Murder? He hadn't even been present when she had given all those reporters an interview!

Maggie tucked the pattern pieces away. "Well, I am done for now. You have ordered two suits, two skirts, three shirtwaists, two day gowns, and one evening gown. I should love to match shoes for you, Miss Cahill," Maggie said earnestly.

Francesca was about to tell her to do whatever she wished, when there was a knock on her door. Before she could even answer, the door opened, and her sister, Connie, walked in. Instantly the beautiful blonde's eyes widened in surprise as she stared about the room.

"What is this?" Connie asked, looking from Francesca, to Maggie, to the items on the floor, and then to all the fabrics scattered on the canopied bed. She was almost identical to Francesca in looks; they were often mistaken for twins. Connie, however, was twenty-two, and her hair was a champagne blond, her complexion ivory. Francesca's skin was several shades warmer in hue and her hair a rich, honeyed gold. Otherwise, their features were very similar: wide blue eyes, perfect high cheekbones, a small, sloping nose, and full rosy lips. Universally they were considered to be beauties.

"I am having a fitting," Francesca said, hoping her sister would not let this particular cat out of the bag. "I have ordered a few dresses from Mrs. Kennedy. Con, Mrs. Kennedy. Mrs. Kennedy, my sister, Lady Montrose."

Maggie blinked at Connie, who, unlike Francesca, was extremely glamorous, not to mention that she had married an Englishman and gained a title. Connie stood in the doorway in the most stunning pale blue suit, one delicately pin-striped. It was only nine in the morning, or rather about half past, but she wore three delicate strands of blue topaz in a choker around her neck, the brooch in the middle a cameo. Her glorious hair was pulled back and pinned securely at the nape; she wore a matching hat with two dried flowers adhering to the brim. Even her gloves, which she carried, were a powder blue kidskin and stunningly stitched. A huge yellow diamond ring winked from her left hand. Her skirts revealed the frothy French lace of her expensive petticoat.

"Hullo," Connie said with a pleasant smile. She shook her head. "You have ordered gowns, Fran? What is this? A transformation of character? Has there been a full moon or some such thing? Or has sleuthing permanently damaged your nature?"

Francesca gave her an annoyed and warning look. "Mama has asked me to order new gowns for at least a year," she began.

"I do believe it is more like two," Connie returned, serene.

"I simply have not had the time," Francesca started.

"Or the inclination," Connie finished.

"I had been intending to order a new wardrobe for quite some time," Francesca said, becoming annoyed.

"Oh, when? Before school, after sleuthing, or while sleeping?"

"Ssh," hissed Francesca.

Connie laughed at her. "Oh, this is good, Fran, truly well and good. I cannot wait to find out what—" She stopped. Her gaze went to the red fabric on top of the pile in Maggie's hands. "You have ordered *that*?"

Francesca folded her arms across her breasts. "Mrs. Kennedy assures me it will be stunning."

"I begin to see," Connie said, arch. "It is *Bragg*."

"It is not," Francesca said, heated and aghast. She glared. "Con, by the way, Mrs. Kennedy is Joel's mother."

"And I do have to get going," Maggie said, looking from the one sister to the other. "I sent a note to my supervisor, telling him I was sick this morning, but I promised him that I would be in at noon. I'd like to order these fabrics before I go into work," Maggie told Francesca. Maggie worked by day at the Moe Levy Factory. By night, she sewed for private customers at home. Her diligence amazed Francesca no end. In fact, she did not need *any* new gowns. But she was determined to somehow help the Kennedy family.

"Thank you so much for the fitting, especially at the last moment," Francesca said, walking Maggie to the bedroom door.

"No, thank *you*, Miss Cahill," Maggie said warmly, smiling just a little. It erased the tiny lines around her eyes.

Francesca clasped her elbow. "Please, do call me Francesca. I should like it so."

Maggie hesitated. "I will try, Miss Cahill," she said. And she flushed.

"That's all right," Francesca said, and she watched as Maggie left.

Connie stared at her sister. She was not smiling now.

"Do not begin!" Francesca erupted.

"Very well, I won't. But I do hope you are not becoming a peacock for a *married* man?" Her gaze remained unwavering. "I know how stubborn you are, Francesca. Please, please tell me this is not about Bragg."

"It is not," she lied, a little. "We are friends." And that was the truth. "That is all there is, and all there can ever be," she said firmly. It hurt when she spoke. But with the hurt there was now resignation. In the past few days she had come to accept what could not be changed.

Or had she?

For he would never divorce his wife. He was too honorable, and his political aspirations were too great.

Francesca shared those aspirations for him.

"Well, if you are not strutting for him, then this must be a charitable endeavor," Connie said, eyeing her cautiously.

Francesca sighed. "I give up. She works so hard to support her four children—"

"Say no more. I thought so." Connie walked over to her and hugged her, hard and surprisingly. "You are the kindest person I have ever known."

"Con"—Francesca took her hand—"are you all right? How . . ." She hesitated. "How is Neil?"

Connie took a deep breath and looked away. "He is fine." She smiled brightly at Francesca. "Let's forget what happened last week. After all, it is past. The present and the future are what is important now." Her smile seemed lacquered into place.

Francesca could only stare. Surely Connie was not suggesting that they pretend that last week she had not left her husband, even if just for two nights? With her two daughters? Or that he had committed adultery—causing Connie to take her daughters and stay with a friend? "Have you and Neil had a chance to speak?" Francesca asked finally.

"Why, we speak every day!" Connie cried, too loudly. "Just last night we discussed Reinhold's new opera and the city's current fiscal condition. Everything is fine, Francesca, just fine." She smiled again—and she never called her sister Francesca. It was always Fran.

Francesca studied her with worry, but Connie turned quickly away. *If only Connie would express her feelings,* Francesca thought. She knew how she would feel if Neil had been her husband and she had found out that he had taken a lover. Neil Montrose was not just titled; he was a gorgeous, proud, and intelligent man, a doting father, and, until recently, an adoring husband. Had Neil been her husband—and when Francesca was younger she had wondered what it would be like to be the older sister and to be married to such a man—she would want to die. And then, probably, she would truly hate him.

But maybe not.

Francesca did not know what had happened between Neil and Connie, but up until the past few weeks she had admired him, thinking him an honorable man. Who was she to decide how Connie should act or feel? Especially as she did not know what had truly happened between them?

Perhaps she would call on Neil later and test the waters, trying to comprehend if all was as well as Connie claimed. Francesca did like that idea. She switched her thoughts. "You are here early. Are we having breakfast?" And as she spoke, she wondered why Connie was not sipping coffee and reading the *Tribune* at her own breakfast table, with Neil at its head, as was customary for her.

"We most certainly are, so get dressed," Connie said. "Oh, and by the by, Papa is quite annoyed. He cannot find today's *Sun,* and you know how devoted he is to all three morning papers."

Francesca smiled, and it was false. "Poor Papa. The

paperboy must have made a mistake. Or perhaps we have a new boy on our route."

"Yes, that must be the case," Connie said.

Francesca's fingers were crossed behind her back. What were the odds, she wondered, that Papa would not see a copy of that day's *Sun* at the office or on a newsstand?

Because if he did, it would be almost impossible for him to miss the headline glaring across the front page. In fact, the paper with its headline was under her own canopied bed. But Francesca felt no guilt.

For the headline read:

MILLIONAIRE'S DAUGHTER CAPTURES KILLER WITH FRY PAN

Above her head, the Ninth Avenue El thundered past, leaving a cloud of smoke and soot. Francesca winced until the elevated train had passed.

She stood on the corner of 23d Street, having just got off the train. The street was icy and the snow mostly black; wagons loaded with wares rumbled past her, while the pedestrians moving about the street were mostly immigrant workingmen. In this neighborhood, German was spoken as frequently as English. Two women in drab brown coats with scarves on their heads hurried into a brownstone, which Francesca knew was a factory. But those women had been speaking Russian. She glanced around for a cab.

It had been the worst morning. She had not been able to concentrate, worrying about the feature story in the *Sun*. On Thursdays, Francesca had two classes, Biology and French Literature. She was behind now in both courses, due to the past two cases she had helped Bragg solve. Her Biology teacher had actually given her a warning that her grades were dropping at a precarious rate. Francesca had not gone to all the trouble of secretly enrolling and scrap-

ing together the tuition, some of which she had borrowed
from Connie, in order to fail.

It was extremely hard being a student and a sleuth at
the exact same time, she thought grimly.

She stared into the sun, hoping for a cab. A horse-drawn
omnibus approached, and she considered taking it. She just
knew her father was going to see the *Sun*, and if that was
the case, Francesca did not think that she could cajole him
to keep her recent endeavors a secret. Not this time, and
never mind that she was the apple of his eye and he was
immensely proud of her. He would go directly to Julia,
and God only knew what would happen next. Francesca
was truly worried. Her mother would be furious, and Julia
Van Wyck Cahill was not a woman to cross. She was a
woman who moved mountains when she so chose; she was
renowned for bringing various parties together within society for social, financial, and political purposes, all to
everyone's gain. Had she ever failed in a cause or lost a
battle? Francesca did not think so.

But what could Julia now do? After all, Francesca was
a grown woman, and punishments were for children. And
even as a child, Francesca had been much as she now
was—determined, a champion of the underdog, and a bud-
ding bluestocking. At the age of six she had begun to read
anything she could get her hands on, and had begun her
lifelong love affair with the written word. At seven, she
had realized that there were children in Chicago, which is
where her family was from, who were hungry and without
families. She had sold lemonade for a year outside of her
church to raise money for those orphans.

She had only been punished once. Shortly after relo-
cating to New York, when she was eight, she had stolen
out of the house alone to explore her new city. There had
been hell to pay for that. Francesca had been made to stay
home from school for two days—and no punishment could

have been more effective, as she had loved school the way
most children hated it.

Francesca saw a black coach with a bay in the traces.
Her hand shot up and she dashed out into the street—only
to slip wildly on a patch of dirty gray ice and fall hard on
her backside. "Darn it," she breathed, shaking her head to
clear it. Perhaps she should have gone directly home from
the Barnard library. She had a feeling this day was only
going to become progressively worse.

"Are you OK, miss?" A hand closed on her elbow.

Francesca looked up, into the eyes of a middle-aged
man clad in a brown suit, coat, and bowler hat. "Yes, thank
you," she said, allowing the gentleman to help her up.

"You should be more careful," he said, but politely, and
he tipped his hat and walked off.

The cab had stopped beside her. Francesca opened the
door and settled inside, her left hip aching. "Three hundred
Mulberry Street, please," she said, her heart racing as she
spoke.

"Isn't that police headquarters?" her driver asked with
a distinct Irish brogue.

"It most certainly is," Francesca said, smiling widely.

The cabbie turned and glanced back at her. "You seem
terribly chipper for a lady going to the coppers," he said.

Francesca merely grinned at him. And as she settled
against the leather squabs, the mare's hooves softly clop-
ping on the snowy street, a trolley going by them from the
opposite direction, she smiled a little, her body tense with
anticipation. She had not seen Bragg in two days. In a way,
it seemed like two years. She had never called casually
before at police headquarters. In the past, she had always
come by with a new clue pertaining to a case, one that
could not wait, one that Bragg would be eager to see.

She did not think Bragg would mind a social call now.
Of course, it was terribly bold. But it wasn't even a social
call, now was it? He had to have seen the *Sun,* and he

would commiserate with her, perhaps even advise her on how to diffuse the situation with her parents. He would want to talk to her about the story, she knew.

And perhaps he was even worried about her.

She was somewhat breathless as she walked into the frenetic lobby of the police station, trying to appear brisk and businesslike. Police headquarters was housed in a squat brownstone building in a neighborhood filled with hooks and crooks, as well as pimps and prostitutes. It never ceased to amaze Francesca that the neighborhood's thieves, swindlers, and trollops carried on with their sordid and illegal affairs right beneath the police's noses. In fact, it amazed most of the city, and since his appointment, Bragg had doubled the roundsmen working Mulberry Bend.

Inside, the telegraph and telephones were pinging and ringing. Several sergeants stood behind the long desk, dealing with civilian inquiries and complaints. One shabby drunken man was being booked at the other end of the room, not far from the elevator cage. And two newsmen were standing behind the criminal, notepads posed in their hands, firing questions at the arresting officers.

Francesca recognized one of them as Arthur Kurland, who had come to be her nemesis in the past month. He was also the one who had put her story on the front page of the *Sun*.

She had been about to pause at the front desk to ask if she could go up, as one did not just prance into the police commissioner's office. But now she wanted to race for the stairs before Kurland saw her. For the man seemed to be present every time she called on Bragg, and he might very well begin to make something of it.

He might very well begin to suspect the truth.

Kurland's back remained to her, as he spoke with one of the arresting officers, hunting for a story. Francesca hurried forward, ignoring the chaos around her. Reaching the stairs, she walked calmly up to the first landing. As she turned the corner, she glanced down into the hall below.

Kurland had detached himself from the officers, the other reporters, and the criminal, and he now stood at the bottom of the stairs, staring thoughtfully up at her. He was a slim man in his thirties. Their gazes met; he smiled and waved at her.

Francesca felt herself flush and she quickened her steps. Kurland would, she knew, make more of her visit to the police commissioner than he had any right to. She would probably find a story in tomorrow's *Sun*: "Millionaire's Daughter Enamored of Married Police Commissioner."

Her heart lurched as she reached the second floor and she dismissed Kurland from her mind. Thus far he was an irritation, but no more. Perhaps in the future she should actively try to avoid him. And perhaps, now that she knew Bragg was married, she should not be such a frequent visitor at police headquarters.

That thought was sobering. Nor was it a happy one. She was determined not to lose his friendship now. How could she? He was a reformer as she was. He was one of the most noble and civic-minded men she had ever met. She admired him so.

And they made a great investigative team.

Before Francesca was a long hallway lined with doors. One of the very first was Bragg's office; across from it was a conference room. At the farthest end of the hall was an open area filled with desks where most of this precinct's detective force worked. Now it was fairly quiet, consisting of the hushed murmur of voices, a typewriter's staccato sound, and someone's brief and coarse laughter.

The door to his small office was open. It contained two desks, including the one where he now sat and worked. He lolled in his cane-backed chair behind it, on the telephone. The moment she paused in the doorway, he saw her and their eyes met.

Francesca smiled, not moving.

He smiled back, not looking away.

As he finished his conversation, Francesca studied him. His grandfather was part Apache. It was evident in Bragg's nearly olive coloring and his achingly high cheekbones. But his hair was a tawny, sun-streaked gold, and his eyes were amber: he had the most unusual coloring. She had seen the way other women eyed him. There was no question that his looks were striking. He was the kind of man who turned heads and made hearts flutter, yet he was also the kind of a man who walked into rooms with a quiet power and authority, the kind of a man who gave people pause and made conversation stop.

Bragg had removed both his jacket and vest, and his shirtsleeves were rolled up. His lack of attire revealed just how muscular and fit he was. For he was a broad-shouldered man with a very trim waist and small hips, and unlike most men, he had not an ounce of fat anywhere on his body. His body was, in fact, hard and powerful. She knew that for a fact.

She knew that from having been in his arms, not once, but twice. Of course, that must *never* happen again.

He put down the telephone and stood. His gaze did not waver, and a smile was there, in his eyes, one that was so warm it could surely melt ice.

Francesca felt her own answering smile. It crossed her mind that her feelings were so powerful that maybe this was just too dangerous, at least for her, if not for them both. But then she dismissed her thoughts, because she could see no alternative to the friendship they now had.

She closed the door behind her.

"Francesca," he said, moving out from behind his desk. "This is a very pleasant surprise."

She smiled back at him. "I hope you don't mind my calling this way. I do not have a case for us to discuss, Bragg."

"Thank God," he laughed.

She laughed a little, too.

"So this is a social call?" he asked, touching her arm lightly.

Francesca removed her mink-lined coat, which he hung upon a wall peg. "Yes, I suppose it is. I was on my way home from college, and I decided to say hello." She wondered if he would put his vest on, at least. He did not, and it was somewhat distracting.

"And how is my favorite bluestocking?" he asked with a teasing tone instead.

Her smile faded and she felt it. Bragg knew about her studies, too. "I am quite behind. I may soon fail Biology."

"You? Fail? I doubt that. You would never fail at anything," he said, his gaze upon her. "Not because of your intelligence, but because of your determination."

"You have so much faith in me," she returned, but she was flushing with pleasure at his words.

"Yes, I do," he said evenly.

She just looked at him and he simply looked back.

It was too much to bear. The innocence of friendship vanished, replaced by something that was so much more. How close they stood to each other now. Francesca wished, fervently, that he were free. If he were a single man, undoubtedly he would pull her into his arms for an extremely intimate kiss.

"I imagine you are behind," he said, somewhat unevenly. He cleared his throat. "When do you have time to study? You are either studying, raising money, or solving murders—that is hardly conducive to attaining a higher education."

"It is very hard, being a reformer, a sleuth, and a student," she said seriously.

"Yes, it is. Francesca, what is wrong? I can see that something is bothering you. I hope it is your schedule and nothing more." His golden gaze was penetrating.

She wondered if he was referring to the truth that now lay, acknowledged, between them. The truth of the fact that he had a wife. Or was he referring to the *Sun*? "How could I have given an interview Tuesday? How, Bragg?" she asked. "Have you seen the *Sun*?"

He seemed amused. "Yes, I have. You earned that interview, Francesca. Are you in trouble?"

"Not yet. I hid today's paper, and I have heard that Papa was very annoyed. I cannot even begin to explain to you what his morning papers mean to him. If he and Mama ever see that story, I am finished. I feel certain of that."

"Perhaps you should sit down," he said, appearing amused.

"Is this funny?" Francesca cried.

He guided her to an overstuffed and shabby chair; the tweed wool fabric was torn in places. "No, I am sorry, not really."

She sat and twisted to look up at him. He remained lighthearted and even amused. "Bragg, if I am punished like some small child, this will hardly be a subject for laughter."

"I am sorry. But you were in danger, Francesca." And he gave her a penetrating look, and he was no longer smiling.

Even though the subject they had turned upon was now a serious one, his golden gaze did odd things to her heartbeat. She gripped the arms of the chair. "I was *briefly* in danger," she said.

"So now you rebut? Francesca, you were tied up! To a bed—and by a killer and the killer's accomplice, I might add." His eyes flashed.

"I hardly knew what would happen when I went over to the house," Francesca said.

"You were in danger, Francesca, and you know that I do not approve of that. Perhaps you should rethink this new hobby of yours. Sleuthing, clearly, can be dangerous work, and you are a young woman."

"But we are partners. And I am a good sleuth. You said so yourself."

"You are an excellent detective," he admitted grimly.

"I cannot just quit, now. Are you working on a new case?" she asked suddenly, brightly.

He rested a lean hip on the edge of his desk. She felt herself blush and she looked away. He said, "My detective bureau woks on all investigations, Francesca. You know that. My personal involvement with Eliza Burton precipitated my interest in that case, and the fact that Randall was Calder's father assured my involvement there."

Calder Hart was Bragg's half brother. They shared the same mother, Lily Hart, who had died of cancer when Bragg was a boy of eleven, Hart two years younger. Bragg's father, Rathe Bragg, alerted to the existence of an illegitimate son, had taken both boys into his own rather large family. At the time, Rathe was a political appointee of President Grover Cleveland, and the family was residing in Washington, D.C. Later the Braggs returned to New York, but briefly, for their daughter Lucy's wedding brought them to Texas. Francesca had overheard that Rathe and Grace were soon returning to New York, with several of their five children. She assumed the oldest ones were living on their own.

Calder Hart had been a suspect in his father's murder, as he had grown up hating the man who had refused to ever acknowledge him or their relationship.

Bragg sighed a little. "Why don't you take a sabbatical from your new profession? That would be the best way to manage your parents, I think, should they learn of what happened in the Randall Murder, and it is also the best way to improve your grades."

"So there is no new case?" Francesca asked, somewhat glum.

Bragg sighed. "Francesca, my immediate agenda is to appoint a chief of police, which I have yet to do after being in office for an entire month."

She sat up straighter, her interest piqued. "And have you found an honest man for the job?"

His eyes twinkled. "There are a few honest men on the force, Francesca."

"Then I am glad," she returned with a smile. The city's police were notoriously corrupt. Bragg was a part of a reform administration, and police reform was on the top of the agenda. Graft and corruption ruled the day among the police, although last week Bragg had demoted 300 wardsmen while reassigning them to different wards, all in the hope of breaking the stranglehold of those officers in their precincts. "Do you have a genuine candidate in mind?"

"I am thinking of promoting Captain Shea."

"Shea?" She was surprised. He was often at the front desk downstairs, and he seemed a mild fellow indeed. "Doesn't an inspector usually get the job?"

"Until now," he said with a wink. "But Shea is honest, although not very forceful. I believe he might do well, with the right encouragement and incentive."

Her heart turned over with her admiration for Bragg and her smile failed and she looked at him and wished he were free.

And he felt it, too, for he did not look away, and in the long moment that ensued, the space between them closed, becoming small and tense. How she wished that things might be different between them. If only he had not been so foolish and impulsive when he had been younger, when he had become infatuated with Leigh Anne. He had married her without knowing her, but that could not be changed.

Bragg stood abruptly, as if to increase the distance between them. Francesca gripped her purse and did not move. Suddenly it was so terribly obvious—she wanted more than friendship. Instantly, Francesca was aghast at herself. She must *never* think in such a way again.

"Of course, you are right. Temporarily I should cease and desist with sleuthing." She sounded a bit frantic to her own ears, and he turned to face her now, his glance calm but searching. Bragg would never miss a trick, especially from her.

"I would be extremely pleased should you do that, Francesca," he said softly.

She knew he worried about her. She knew he did not like her putting herself in danger. She also stood up. His desk separated them. It was a huge, cluttered, and bulky obstacle between them. "But we do make a wonderful team," she said.

For one moment, he did not answer her. His hands were fisted on his hips. She now noticed his posture of tension. When had that happened? He had strong hands, powerful arms. She glanced from his whitened fists to his forearms. They were bare, dusted with dark hair, and all tendon and bone.

"We make a good team," he admitted, causing her to start, flush, and look up. "Francesca, may I advise you?"

"You may always advise me, Bragg. You need not even ask." She clutched her purse more tightly.

"Concentrate on your education now. So few women attain a university degree. I know you haven't had time to study with all the investigative work you have undertaken, and while justice has been served, perhaps, now, you might want to serve yourself *and* calm your parents down." He smiled at her. "And then I should not have to race about the city, chasing after you."

"But it is so nice when we chase about the city together," she said. And it was even nicer when he worried so, to chase about after *her*.

He no longer smiled. "Yes, it is. There, I have admitted

it. You are unique, and working with you has been a unique and exceedingly pleasant experience. But again, the danger that accompanies the job is just too much for any woman, even you, Francesca. And, fortunately, women do not work for the police, except occasionally as a secretary." Theodore Roosevelt had hired a woman for that post.

Francesca studied him. "I am going to concentrate on my education, as I am falling behind in my studies, so that leaves me with little choice. So you win, Bragg. For now, I shall behave in a most ladylike and decorous manner."

He grinned. "We shall see how long this intention of yours truly lasts. Shall we wager?"

"Bragg! You are corrupting me!" But she was laughing.

"I think so."

"A dollar? No, wait. I have a better wager."

His gaze narrowed. "It is . . . ?"

She swallowed, refusing to analyze her motivations now. "Escort me to that new musical. I believe it is playing at the Waldheim Theatre."

He seemed only slightly startled, and he quickly recovered. "Very well. I give you, oh, two weeks."

She blinked. Then, "Done. I am going to throw myself into my studies for the rest of the month," she said.

Now he laughed. "We shall see."

She didn't laugh. She had to win this wager now. He would escort her to the theater, and perhaps they would have a late supper afterward. He would be in a tuxedo, she in her new, bold red dress. It would be a glorious evening, even if they were only friends. Perhaps they would even dance afterward, in each other's arms. . . .

His smile had vanished. "Francesca?" His tone was somewhat rough. As if he knew what she was thinking.

She realized she had been smiling dreamily and bit her lip. Neither one moved, their gaze holding. Did he suspect the depth of her feelings? In the past few weeks, she had become a woman, one aware now of the meaning of desire and the difference between desire and need. She wanted him physically, as a lover, but even more, she needed him as a friend, but as a man.

Of course, they would *never* be lovers. And she would never be able to think of him merely as a friend, either.

He turned and gazed down at his desk, fiddling with a folder. The silence felt heavy now and fraught with tension and maybe danger. This was getting harder, she realized, not easier. Perhaps calling like this had been a terrible idea. But if she had not, they would not have this wager—which she intended to win. Would it ever become easy, seeing him, loving him, and being mere friends? Suddenly she was afraid; suddenly she had an inkling, one she hated and feared. For she did not think so.

"So," he said tersely, glancing sidelong at her. "As much as I enjoy your company, I must get back to work."

In a way, she was relieved by the change of topic. On the other hand, the glint in his eyes excited her no end. "And I must go home and continue studying," she agreed, her voice unusually hoarse.

He walked briskly over to her coat, removing it from the wall peg. Francesca let him help her on with it, aware of his hands upon her as he did so. Their eyes met and they moved apart. He walked her to the door and there they paused, without his opening it.

She could not help herself. She thought about their conversation on the steps of the Plaza Hotel, just before the newsmen had surrounded her. "Do you regret what you said the other day?" she asked softly.

He hesitated. "No."

Her reaction was instantaneous; she was inwardly thrilled. But she kept her expression as passive as possible. "Nor do I, Bragg," she said softly.

He nodded gruffly at her; she left.

*   *   *

"You have a caller, Francesca."

Francesca halted at the sound of her mother's voice, having just handed off her coat, hat, muff, and gloves to a servant. She slowly turned, with dread.

For her mother's voice had been sharp. Now disapproval covered Julia's attractive face. She was an older image of both of her daughters: blond, blue-eyed, with classic and fine features. Although over forty, she remained slim and glamorous; many men her own age often eyed her in a covert manner.

"Good day, Mama," Francesca said nervously. Julia had seen the *Sun*. Francesca would wager her life on it.

Julia Van Wyck Cahill was magnificently attired, clearly dressed for an early-evening affair. Her sapphire blue gown revealed a slim and pleasing figure, while two tiers of sapphires adorned her neck. Before she could answer, Andrew appeared on the stairs, in a white dinner jacket and satin-trimmed black trousers. He took one look at Francesca and his expression became pinched, with disbelief and accusations warring in his eyes.

"I can explain," Francesca whispered.

"What can you explain?" Andrew demanded, halting beside his wife. "That you have made the front page of the *Sun*? That you once again immersed yourself in a dangerous affair? One belonging, I believe, to the police?"

Francesca inhaled. How to begin? Before she could speak, her mother interrupted.

"I am aghast. I am aghast that my daughter would confront a killer and place herself in unspeakable danger. This shall not continue, Francesca. You have gone too far." Julia turned and nodded at a servant, who was holding her magnificent sable coat for her. She allowed him to slip it over her shoulders.

"I am beginning to wonder if my brilliant daughter has truly lost her mind," Andrew said.

Francesca cringed. Papa never spoke to her in such a

manner. "I helped the police enormously," Francesca murmured. The fact was, she had solved the case at the elev-
enth hour.

"You have been up to your ears in police affairs ever
since Bragg arrived in town," Julia said sharply. "Do you
think I am blind, Francesca? I can see what is happening."

"Nothing is happening," Francesca tried, stealing a
glance at her father. He knew about Bragg's married state,
she thought suddenly. This was the secret he had been
keeping. But why hadn't he told her?

"We are on our way out for the evening, but we shall
speak tomorrow morning, Francesca." Julia gave her a
look that was filled with warning. Julia did not look at her
again as Andrew donned his coat. But her father met her
gaze, shaking his head, looking so terribly grim that Francesca knew she was in the kind of trouble she had never
dreamed of. There was no relief when they stepped out of
the house. But what could they do? She was a grown
woman.

Francesca relaxed slightly. She would worry about her
parents tomorrow. She turned as Bette handed her a delicately engraved calling card on a small sterling tray. Francesca studied the card for a moment curiously. She did not
believe she had ever met a Mrs. Lincoln Stuart, and she
thanked Bette and entered the far salon.

It was beautifully appointed but small, and used for
more intimate gatherings, such as a meeting with a single
caller. It was painted a pale, dusky yellow, and most of
the furnishings were in various shades of yellow or gold,
with several red and navy blue accents. The moment Francesca entered the room, she saw Mrs. Lincoln Stuart. She
had been sitting on a sofa at the room's other end, but
upon espying Francesca, she instantly stood. Francesca
smiled and approached.

Mrs. Lincoln Stuart twisted her hands.

Francesca saw that Mrs. Stuart was a few years older

than her. She was rather plain in appearance, her features
usual and unsurprising. But her hair was a beautiful cas-
cade of chestnut curls, and it was what one noticed first.
She was very well dressed, in a green floral suit and skirt,
and she wore a rather large yellow diamond ring. Her husband was obviously wealthy. And she was nervous and
distressed.

"Miss Cahill. I do hope you do not mind me calling
like this," Mrs. Lincoln Stuart said in a husky voice, one
filled with tension. Worry was expressed in her eyes.

Francesca smiled warmly, pausing before her. "Of
course not," she said politely. "Have we met?"

"No, we have not, but I was given this by a boy the
other day." And Mrs. Stuart handed her a card.

Francesca recognized it instantly—how could she not?
Tiffany's had printed the cards at her request upon the
conclusion of the Burton Affair. It read:

> *Francesca Cahill*
> *Crime-Solver Extraordinaire*
> *No. 810 Fifth Avenue, New York City.*
> *All Cases Accepted, No Crime Too Small.*

"My assistant, Joel Kennedy, must have handed this to
you," Francesca mused, pleased. She had recently assigned
him the task of drumming up business for her. She glanced
up at Mrs. Stuart. Was she a prospective client? Francesca's heart thudded in anticipation.

"I don't know the boy's name; I only know that I am
frightened and I have no one to turn to!" Mrs. Stuart cried,
her eyes wide. Francesca saw that they were green and
lovely. Mrs. Stuart was the sort of woman who had a quiet
kind of beauty, one that was not instantly remarkable, she
decided.

Francesca also realized that she was on the verge of
tears. She took the woman's arm. "Do sit down, and I am

sure I can help you, Mrs. Stuart," she said. "No matter what your problem might be." There was no doubt now—Mrs. Stuart had come to her for help—this would be her second official case!

The woman dug a handkerchief out of her velvet purse. It was hunter green, like the trim on her elegant tea gown. "Please, call me Lydia," she said, dabbing at her eyes. "I saw today's article in the *Sun*, Miss Cahill. You are a heroine, a brave heroine, and when I realized that you were the same woman on this card, I knew it was you to whom I must turn."

"I am hardly a heroine, Lydia," Francesca said, barely containing her excitement. "Excuse me." She rushed to the salon door and closed it, so that no one might overhear the conversation. Her resolve to take a "sabbatical" from sleuthing had vanished. In fact, she forgot all about her studies now. She hurried back to her guest—her *client*—and sat down. What could this woman's problem be? And was she truly going to have, for the very first time, a paying client? In the past, she had offered her services for free. A paying client would truly make her a professional woman.

Lydia managed to smile at her and now handed her a small piece of paper, upon which were a name, Rebecca Hopper, and an address, 40 East 30th Street. "What is this?" Francesca asked.

Lydia Stuart's face changed, becoming filled with distaste. "Mrs. Hopper is a widow, and that is where she lives. I believe my husband is having an affair with her, but I want to know the truth."

Francesca stared.

"And I have no doubt that he will be there tonight, as he has said he is working late and he will not be home for supper," Lydia added.

*   *   *

Mrs. Hopper's residence was a corner one, and while all of the lights were on downstairs, only one bedroom upstairs was illuminated. It had been years since Francesca had climbed a tree, and now she was sorry that she had not gone farther downtown to locate Joel to do her evening's work for her. He would have been very useful indeed—especially as he did not have cumbersome skirts to deal with.

Huffing and puffing, her hands freezing, as she had stripped off her gloves, she sought another foothold in the huge tree she was climbing, clinging to the trunk.

She had decided to tackle Lydia's case head-on. It was 9:00 P.M., and a quick look at the house had shown Francesca that if she climbed the big tree in the yard, she might very well be able to locate and spy upon the lovers directly. In fact, if Lydia was right, this case might be solved before it was even begun.

Francesca made it to the large, higher branch. She clung to it, one leg atop it, both arms around it. Her skirts were in the way, but she had not had the foresight to wear men's clothing, for she had not had the psychic ability to know she would be climbing trees this night. With great effort, she somehow moved her other leg onto the thick branch, and then she hugged it with all of her might, afraid she was going to fall. She glanced down.

She was not sure she liked heights. When she had been upon the ground, in the yard, the tree had not seemed so tall. Now, as she looked down, her cheek upon the rough bark, her hands feeling rather scraped and raw, the ground seemed very far away.

She had not a doubt that if she fell, the snow would be rock-hard, as it was solidly frozen. It would not break her fall; she might wind up with a broken arm or, God forbid, a broken neck.

But she was determined to ignore her cowardice now. Very, very carefully, Francesca sat up. When she was astride the branch as if it were a horse, she began to breathe easier. This wasn't too bad. She believed she could manage.

Dismayed, she suddenly realized her eyes were still below the window and she could not see into the bedroom in order to learn what was going on. She would have to stand up.

But Francesca realized she was turned around the wrong way—the trunk of the tree was behind her. *Oh, dear. This might be far too dangerous a maneuver,* she thought.

She could not see into the bedroom and she was at a grave risk if she tried to turn around. Now what?

There was no choice. She had to turn herself around. She simply had to. *Because Lydia Stuart was her first paying client.*

Francesca lifted her right leg up slowly until she was able to move it up and over the branch. Now she sat with both legs dangling off of the same side of the tree, and her position was precarious at best. She failed to breathe now. She had to reverse herself, but she was afraid to move.

That was when she slipped.

Francesca cried out as she lost her balance and started to slide off the branch; instantly, desperately, she reached out, trying to grasp the branch with her hands, the bark scraping and abrading her palms, and for one moment she thought she had succeeded in stopping herself. She gripped the tree, but then her hands failed her and suddenly she was falling through space.

She saw the white snow below, racing toward her face, and she thought, *Oh, dear, this is it. It is all over now.*

Whomp.

Francesca landed hard on her shoulder and her side, not her face, her head smacking down last. And then she was spitting out snow.

God, she thought, dazed. Was she intact? Had she broken anything?

She began to move. The snow was not as frozen as she had thought it would be; it was not rock-hard, surprisingly. She wiggled her toes and fingers in the snow, moved her hands and legs.

She froze.

Had she just touched something? Something beneath the snow? Something *sticky*? And *solid*?

Francesca sat up shakily, and as she stood, she looked down at her own hands.

One was pale and white in the moonlight; the other was dark and splotched in places.

She had an inkling. She did not move. She recognized those splotches.

Her heart pounded.

She rubbed her fingers together. *Oh, no.*

Francesca was on her knees, tearing at the frozen snow. As she moved the top layer away, she found a piece of garment. She stared at a patch of brown wool, and the dark, still not thoroughly frozen, stain on it.

She touched the fresh blood; someone had been recently buried in the snow. Maybe the person was still alive!

Francesca pawed the snow frantically, shoving it away in clumps, until she saw the woman's face. The open, sightless blue eyes were glazed in terror. They were also strangely familiar. Then she saw the woman's throat.

Francesca stood, and, unable to help herself, screamed. For carved in the once pristine-white skin was a perfect, bloody cross. But Francesca screamed because she recognized the dead woman, dear God.

It was the woman who had almost approached her at the Plaza Hotel two days ago; it was the woman who had fled in terror instead.

TWO

Francesca tried to make herself invisible—no easy task. Two roundsmen stood guarding the woman's body, and two detectives were walking around the yard, looking for clues. A police wagon was coming down the block, apparently with more officers, and Bragg's sleek, shiny motorcar had just pulled up at the curb.

She almost cringed, but she was far too upset to do so. There was no mistake. The dead woman had been in the crowd behind the reporters on Tuesday as she had begun the interview. She had been staring at Francesca, clearly a woman in trouble and in fear. And when Francesca had tried to approach her, the woman had turned and fled, almost being run over by a coach in the process.

Oh, dear God. Francesca closed her eyes, finding it difficult to breathe. If only they had spoken, that woman might now be alive!

Francesca tried to regain her composure, hearing Bragg's car door slam. After finding the body, she had quickly looked around the grounds, but the killer had made sure to cover up all his tracks. The only footprints were hers. Spending no more than a few moments in a brief search of the scene, she had pounded on Mrs. Hopper's front door—only to realize she was at No. 42 East 30th Street, and that Mrs. Hopper lived next door. The couple who lived in the house she had been erroneously spying upon sent a servant to the police station, as they did not have a telephone. Instead of waiting inside with them, Francesca had gone back outside, walking along the street and looking for the murder weapon.

Bragg had told her once that it was usually found close to the victim. But she had not seen a knife anywhere.

Now, she watched him approach. Her breath stuck in her chest, but her emotions had little to do with eagerness to see him.

She did not know what he was doing there, but she could guess. One of the detectives, Murphy, knew her from the past two investigations. He had asked her to remain at the scene of the crime, only briefly questioning her. Somehow, he must have relayed to Bragg that she was present.

Their eyes connected in the dark, across the bloody expanse of turned-up snow. Hatless, his brown, wool overcoat open and swinging about him, he walked directly to the body. He knelt down, then began speaking with Murphy. Francesca wished she knew what they were saying.

How angry, she wondered, would he be at finding her at another murder scene? But this was no fault of hers, she thought defensively. And then she felt ill and guilty again.

He stood up, not brushing the snow from his knees. Then he approached her. She could not smile. "Fancy meeting you here," she said tightly.

"I am in shock," he said, not smiling. His eyes held a dangerous light.

"Bragg, this is not what you are thinking. This is not what it looks like."

"Did you, or did you not, find the corpse?" he demanded.

Her chin went up. "I did."

"So tell me not to think what I am thinking!" he cried. "Francesca, this is simply unacceptable. *One week ago,* I found you with another corpse. Or have you forgotten?"

"Bragg, please." She touched his bare hand. "That was different! Miss de Labouche hired me to help her dispose

of the body. This time I *fell* on the body, purely by
chance." She realized that she was trembling.

"You *fell* on the body?" He was disbelieving.

She nodded and looked up at the tree. "I was up there."

"In the tree?" He was even more incredulous.

She nodded grimly. "I am lucky I did not break my
neck," she added, strategically.

"Are you all right?" he asked instantly.

Her ploy had worked. She showed him her abraded and
raw hands. They looked much worse because she had the
victim's blood on her right one.

He turned her hands over, staring. Then he dropped
them and looked at her. "I can see I am going to chase
you all over the city, Francesca," he said tersely. "What
were you doing in the tree? No, let me guess. You are on
a case."

His anger had been diffused. But she had forgotten all
about their wager, which she had lost. She stared in dismay
at his striking features, imagining the evening of theater,
dancing, and dinner that they would not share.

"You have a new client," he said grimly.

She nodded slowly. "Yes, I do. Bragg—there is more."

His jaw seemed clenched. "I gave you two weeks." He
shook his head. "It was more like two hours, Francesca."

She inhaled. "Yes, it was. Bragg—"

"Who hired you and what were you doing in that tree?"

She opened her mouth to tell him and closed it. "Bragg,
that is confidential."

He smiled, not pleasantly. "Who hired you and what
were you doing in that tree?" he repeated, his tone very
hard.

She knew better than to press her luck. "Mrs. Lincoln
Stuart suspects her husband of having an affair. I was spying upon the man. Except—I was in the wrong tree. The
woman she suspects of being her husband's lover is at
No. 40, not No. 42."

"You are slipping, Francesca," he said.

"Yes, I am," she agreed. "Bragg, I know the murder victim."

His eyes widened. "What?"

She swallowed. "The woman who was almost run over in front of the Plaza Hotel. It's she, Bragg. I told you that she wanted to speak with me, that she was in trouble, but you did not believe me!" Tears came to her eyes.

Instantly, he slid his arm around her. She sagged against him. "This is all my fault," she said unsteadily. "Perhaps if—"

"Are you certain? This woman is the same woman who was in the crowd at the Plaza?"

She nodded, clinging to him, her gaze holding his. "I knocked her down to push her out of the way of the brougham, Bragg. I was on top of her in the street. I saw her face as clearly as if we were lovers. I am certain, Bragg, completely certain, and if only I had persisted, she might still be alive!"

"No! You are not to blame yourself. This is not your fault, Francesca." He tilted up her chin, speaking with urgency. "Do not do this to yourself."

She shook her head, briefly incapable of speech. "Bragg, did you see the cross carved in her throat?"

He was grim. "Yes, I did." He studied her for a moment, and Francesca fought for her composure. Then he turned and walked away from her, back to the body and the detectives standing around it. There were now four. Francesca also recognized the shorter man as Inspector Newman. She followed Bragg, still miserable.

"I want her moved to the morgue as carefully as possible. I do not even want her hands disturbed," he said. "But before she is moved, I want photographs."

"Photographs?" This from Murphy, a tall man with a big belly. He was disbelieving.

"That's right. Put two men on her until the sun comes

up. Find me a photographer tonight. First thing, I want photographs of the victim, exactly as she is now—exactly as she was found. I do not even want her eyelids closed."

The detectives all looked at one another. Clearly they thought Bragg mad.

Francesca was bewildered. She wanted to know why he was asking for such a thing—it was unheard of. But it did seem like a good idea.

"I want this entire yard cordoned off," Bragg added flatly. "I want a detail in here tonight. Find me the murder weapon, and barring that, anything else the killer might have left behind."

"Such as . . . ?" Murphy asked.

"A piece of his coat. A match. A nickel. Anything you find in this yard, I want it, whether you think it belongs to the killer or not."

Francesca stared at Bragg. Why was he taking this case on? He had enough on his plate with running—and re-forming—the entire police department.

She was suspicious, concerned. Something was afoot, something more significant than it seemed.

"Sir, I beg your pardon," a detective said. "But the yard's got a foot of snow. How—"

"Shovel it up and sift it like flour," Bragg said. He turned. "Miss Cahill? I shall give you a ride home."

Francesca hurried forward, and together they walked toward his handsome motorcar. Accidentally, her hip bumped his. He said, "How badly did you disturb the scene?"

"I dug up her body and I walked around a bit." She met his gaze and quickly looked away.

He paused and turned. "Murphy!"

Murphy hurried forward. "Yes, sir?"

"Send a roundsman to the Cahill residence. He shall collect the shoes she is now wearing. Before you shovel up the snow, check all the footprints. From Miss Cahill's shoes, you shall know which are hers."

"Yes, sir," he said, practically saluting.

"If you find other footprints—and I doubt you will—have an artist draw them. Perhaps we shall one day identify our killer by the size of his feet."

"Yes, sir," Murphy cried, clearly impressed.

"That is all," Bragg said. As Murphy left, he turned back to Francesca. "We have to borrow your shoes," he said.

"I hardly mind. That was quite impressive. Why the photographs, Bragg?" she asked, very curious. But she was also haunted by two competing images of the young woman, vitally alive and gruesomely dead.

He looked at her as he opened the passenger door, but he did not answer.

She did not slide in. "Bragg?"

He sighed. "You will learn of this sooner or later, I suppose. I am sure one of the newshounds at headquarters will pick up the story."

Her body tightened in anticipation—and dread. "What story?"

He faced her, resigned. "She is not the first. Another young woman was murdered the exact same way a month ago, shortly after I took office. Or at least, it looks like the same method."

She stared. "There was a cross carved into her throat?" Her stomach turned at the terrible recollection.

He nodded. "Yes. And her hands were clasped upon her breast as if in prayer, too."

Francesca had not noticed that. She trembled with fear. "Bragg? Is that why you have asked for photographs . . . in case it happens again?"

He nodded. "Yes, Francesca. In case our killer strikes a third time."

She stared. "We are dealing with a madman."

"It appears so," he said.

*   *   *

The long black motorcar was purring like a cat. Francesca shifted so she could face Bragg more fully, even though a delay now could be dangerous—her parents always returned from an evening out by eleven. She had to get inside before that event.

Bragg remained silent and thoughtful during the short drive to her house. She knew why he was so preoccupied.

She, too, could not get that ghastly image of the poor, terrified woman with her throat cut out of her mind, but recalling her alive at the Plaza was even worse. And now, she could remember her hands, clasped over her chest. Briefly, Francesca closed her eyes, but the images would not disappear.

Why hadn't she persevered? Why had she let that woman run away?

"Francesca, I do not want you involved in this case."

She tensed, meeting his very serious gaze. "Bragg," she began in protest. She was already involved, deeply so. Didn't he know that?

"We are dealing with a madman. This is far more dangerous than either the Burton Abduction or the Randall Murder."

She bit off her next words. "Very well." Who had that young woman been? Clearly, she had known that she was in danger. But why had she been singled out by this killer? Was there a connection between the two victims?

"You have a client now, don't you?" Bragg continued.

"Bragg, who was the first victim?" Determination filled her.

"Francesca!"

"I am merely curious, that is all." She crossed her fingers, hating lying to him. But a tiny lie in the cause of justice seemed acceptable.

"And curiosity killed the cat." He jumped out of the Daimler, seeming angry now as he strode around its hood.

He opened her door for her. "Do not let me find you in the midst of this investigation," he warned.

She realized he meant every word. Perhaps he was right. She did have a client now—and a reputation to build. "I promise," she said, smiling at him as she stepped out of the motorcar. She slipped on a patch of ice, and he caught her beneath both arms.

She forgot all about murders and madmen. She clung to him and they stood knee-to-knee and chest-to-chest. For one moment, he did not release her.

This is so hard, she thought, staring at his mouth.

He let her go. "Good night, Francesca."

Her breath seemed to catch painfully. "Good night."

Beside his door, he paused. "If you are free, I have tickets for Saturday. Perhaps we could even have dinner afterwards," he said.

"What?" she gasped.

"I happen to have tickets to *The Greatest World*," he said, and he finally smiled a little.

She smiled back. Briefly, the world of murder and death faded, and in its place was something else, a world of love and dreams. He had already gotten tickets to the musical she had spoken of. "Of course I am free, Bragg. And supper afterwards would be wonderful."

He started back toward the motorcar. "No sleuthing," he said.

She simply smiled at him.

FRIDAY, FEBRUARY 7, 1902 — NOON

Francesca was summoned to her mother's apartments at noon. This was hardly a surprise, as Julia never left her rooms before that hour. But as she entered the parlor, a large room with red-toned Oriental rugs, ochre walls, and several seating areas, she saw Andrew seated on a gold brocade sofa, his reading spectacles slipping down his nose. Francesca faltered.

Her father glanced up. Calmly he removed his spectacles, announcing, "She's here."

What was Papa doing at home? Why wasn't he at the office? Francesca had purposely avoided him that morning by skipping breakfast and rushing off to her single morning class.

Julia entered the parlor from her bedroom. She was dressed for a luncheon, resplendently, in an emerald-green gown. Her expression was severe. "Where were you this morning, Francesca?"

Francesca did not hesitate. She had almost thought her mother was going to ask her where she had been last night. "The library."

"Sit down," Andrew said.

As Francesca gingerly began to do so, taking a chair adjacent the sofa, Andrew tossed a newspaper down on an ivory-topped table. And Francesca saw a glaring headline on the *Sun*. She winced.

MILLIONAIRE'S DAUGHTER CAPTURES
RANDALL KILLER WITH FRY PAN

"I cannot even begin to tell you the shock I had when I read this article," he said.

"And I almost had a heart attack," Julia said, not sitting. She stared down coldly at her daughter.

"I can explain," Francesca said.

"According to this newsman," Andrew said, far too calmly, "you captured the murderer *yourself*, with a *fry pan*."

Francesca knew the article did not mention the fact that the event had happened after both Mary and her brother, Bill Randall, had tied her up. Fortunately, she had refrained from mentioning that fact to the reporters, perhaps as a matter of pride. "Papa, Mama, it is not at all as bad as it seems. After I met with this con man, I realized he

could not be the killer and that Bragg had arrested the
wrong man. So I went to the Randalls' because there were
loose ends that just could not be explained. Truly, I was
only trying to help Bragg and serve justice. I never meant
to confront a killer; indeed, until the last moment, I had
no clue as to who the killer was." She knew she must keep
her wits about her now.

Andrew was on his feet. "You met with a con man as
well? It is bad enough that you went alone to the Randalls'.
Francesca, what possessed you?"

"Papa, I did not intend, precisely, to confront a killer,
I merely wanted to help—"

He was the most courteous man she knew; now, he cut
her off. He was fully flushed. "I will not have it! I simply
will not have my daughter running about the city, consorting with con men and apprehending killers. That is
why we have a police force, Francesca. This behavior of
yours must stop. In fact, I forbid it."

Francesca said, "I am a grown woman. How can you
treat me as if I were a child? Especially as nothing happened, in the end." She looked at her mother.

"I have never been so angry," Julia said.

Her heart sank like a rock. "My entire life has been
devoted to the unfortunate. How could not I help in this
instance? I solved the case. I found the killer," she tried.

"To make matters even worse, I understand you better
than anyone," Julia continued. "Do you think I am a fool,
Francesca? I know you are a woman of extreme passion
and just as much determination. You have decided, I believe, that you are a detective of sorts. And you have sunk
your teeth into this new passion of yours the way you have
done with reform. Oh, I do understand."

Francesca could not look away from her mother's gaze.
Julia did understand, she thought with dismay, and no
good could come of it.

"What I understand is that you disposed of the newspapers before I or your mother saw them," Andrew cried, his voice raised. "So now you are dissembling—deceiving us? *Lying?*"

"Papa! You know I do not lie," she cried in return, but in a way, he was right. She had become adept at avoidance and dissembling in order to carry on with her new profession. Thank God they had not seen her calling cards. "Perhaps I have omitted facts here and there. But only because I knew you both would be upset. My intentions were good. I meant to help, not hurt anyone," Francesca tried.

Andrew stared. Julia's arms were crossed firmly over her chest. "Andrew, I told you this would be her reaction."

Andrew said, "Your mother is right. It is time to find you a husband."

Her heart felt as if it had dropped to the floor at her feet. She stared at him, suddenly ill. In this cause—her cause to remain single, a bluestocking and a reformer— her father had always been her ally. Until this actual moment in time, he had been in no rush to see her wed and out of the house. In fact, Francesca believed that Andrew did not want to see her go to a home of her own. "Papa, you don't mean it."

"He does mean it," Julia said. "We were up half the night, talking about you. I will not have my daughter running about the worst wards, consorting with crooks and con men, and chasing killers."

"Perhaps the right man will have a quieting effect on you, Francesca," Andrew added. "Ever since Bragg was appointed police commissioner, ever since he came to town, you have been carrying on like a detective."

She stood motionless now. There was only one man who was right for her, and he was Bragg. She was not marrying anyone else. "Surely you do not blame Bragg for this." She wet her lips and looked at Julia. "He had nothing to do with this, Mama. In fact, he has tried to dissuade me from investigative work, time and again."

"I am not blind, Francesca," Julia said, but with some kindness.

Desperation overcame her. And with it came fear. What did Julia mean? Had she guessed Francesca's feelings? "We are friends. That is all."

"And that is as it should be, of course. Andrew recently told me he has a wife. In any case, I shall begin a serious search for a proper husband for you."

Francesca was disbelieving. She turned her gaze upon her father. "Papa, surely you disagree! Besides, I cannot be forced to the altar. You could not force me to wed."

Andrew hesitated. Francesca saw an opening and seized it. "Papa, you know that one day I shall marry, but it must be the right man. And one cannot summon that man up as if one were a magician."

Julia cut in, also sensing that Andrew was wavering. "I shall do my best to find you the right man, Francesca. And until then, there shall be no more investigative work." She looked at Andrew. "You may speak with Bragg. I am certain he has not approved of Francesca's interference in police affairs. Tell him how concerned we are."

"I intend to do just that," Andrew said stoutly.

Her father and Bragg were both reformers, passionately so. They admired one another and were friends. Francesca turned to Andrew. "Papa? He did not know. I did not tell him where I was going, and if I had, he would not have let me go. Mama? That is the truth."

Julia shook her head. "I am going to lunch. I will be home tonight, and we shall have supper together," she said. She gave Francesca a look and she had a feeling her mother intended to stay in order to supervise her.

Francesca watched her leave the room. When she was alone, she faced her father. "So you did know, didn't you?"

He started. "I knew what, Francesca?"

"You knew that Bragg was married." It was hard to keep her feelings from showing.

"He told you?"

"Yes, he did." She remained calm, poised.

His gaze slipped over her features with some concern. "I met his wife once when they were first married, up in Boston. So I knew he was married, yes."

She closed her eyes, recalling the moment Bragg had told her about his wife, a woman he had not seen in over four years, a woman he despised. In that moment, all of her hopes and dreams had been shattered. It was a moment she would carry with her in her heart forever. She pulled herself together, and looked at her father, with a small smile. "Why didn't you tell me, Papa?" she asked lightly.

He stared, apparently surprised. "Should I have said something? The two of you have only just met. I do not know why his wife is not here in the city with him. I do not know why there has been no mention of her in all of the stories the press has written about him. A man is entitled to his privacy, and I never asked Rick what was amiss. I assumed he would treat you with respect, as you are my daughter. What has happened here?" he asked cautiously.

Francesca knew she must tread with extreme caution, now and in the future. "Over the course of the Burton Affair, we became friends. We have so much in common. I cannot recall exactly why, or when, he mentioned Leigh Anne to me, but it is a tragic story, and I, too, believe a man is entitled to his privacy, so I shall say no more." There, she thought on bated breath, she had done it.

"Yes, you do have a lot in common with him. And it is too bad he is not single himself. He would be a great match for you." Andrew looked at his pocketwatch. "I have a luncheon as well. Business. I must be off." He smiled now at her, and kissed her cheek. "Please behave sensibly, Francesca."

She knew he referred to her sleuthing. "I promise to try very hard to stay out of danger in the future. And I mean it, Papa." And that was the truth, pure and simple. "Papa, you aren't going to rush to marry me off, are you? Surely that was only your anger speaking?"

He hesitated. "I want you to be happy, Francesca. You know that. So, no, I will not rush you into marriage, but I agree with Julia, it is time to think seriously of marriage for you, and that means seeking a suitable man."

Francesca inhaled, hard. At least she had bought herself some time, at least Andrew was coming around to her point of view. "Thank you, Papa," she said.

"Have a good day," he returned.

Francesca watched him leave the room. Andrew would soon be on her side of the fence again, but Julia was another matter, indeed. Now that Evan was affianced, she would sink her teeth into finding Francesca a suitor—and a husband. Francesca sighed.

If ever the day came, she would have to be dragged kicking and screaming to the altar, she decided firmly.

With that unpleasant image in her head, Francesca left the room.

Francesca was in her bedroom at her desk, her biology notes in front of her, when Connie walked in. Fortunately, she was not able to concentrate, as she kept thinking about the young woman whom she had found dead in the snow. The guilt had lessened a bit, but her resolve to find the killer had grown. Her new client was also on her mind. Therefore, her sister's appearance was hardly an interruption. Francesca smiled and said, "Don't you ever knock?"

"The door was open," Connie returned, smiling widely. "How do I look?"

Francesca blinked, bewildered, for as always, her sister was sheer perfection. The pale pink dress she wore was more than lovely and more than elegant, and her blue eyes were sparkling. In fact, Connie looked quite happy, which pleased Francesca to no end. Maybe Connie had not been exaggerating when she had said the past must be dismissed; maybe she and Neil had truly mended their fences, and all was as it should be. Francesca was pleased. "You have never been more beautiful, and I must say, your spirits seem exceedingly good."

"They are," Connie said—and she grinned. She grinned and pirouetted a bit—and Francesca's smile vanished.

She shot to her feet. "Oh, God! I forgot! Today is Friday—you have a luncheon with Calder Hart!"

Connie smiled coyly. "I certainly do—at one. I only came to ask you if this dress is too prim and proper."

Francesca stared. "Too prim and proper?" she echoed.

"Well, it is a rather virginal shade of pink, don't you think?"

"Have you lost your mind? You cannot meet him for lunch!" Francesca cried, truly agitated. Calder Hart was a notorious ladies' man. He did not even try to elude his terrible reputation; indeed, he flaunted it. And Francesca knew beyond a doubt that he was preying upon her sister. For he was a man who found married ladies fascinating, and the whole world knew it. And this in spite of the fact that he had a mistress, and even consorted with a pair of beautiful sisters in a brothel.

"I can, and I shall, and we have already had this conversation. Do I look too prim?" Connie walked over to the Venetian mirror above an extraordinarily carved walnut bureau, and her reflection became anxious.

"How can you preen for him? What about your husband?" Francesca cried, moving to stand beside her.

Their gazes met in the mirror. "Hart is a friend and nothing more, and I am doing nothing wrong." Connie blushed. "I am well aware that he is a terrible flirt, but many married women enjoy an inconsequential flirtation now and then."

"But not you," Francesca pointed out.

Connie faced her. "I have changed. I am enjoying his attentions. Fran, you almost sound as if you do not trust me. It is *only* lunch."

"Oh, Con, I trust *you*," Francesca said. "It is Hart I do not trust. He thinks to seduce you!"

"At lunch?" Connie asked, rolling her eyes, but her color deepened.

"How much do you wish to wager that after lunch he will offer you a ride somewhere? And in his coach, I am certain he will make his move."

"But I am taking my own coach," Connie said.

"Then he will invite you to see his art collection!"

"I have already seen it," she said. Her gaze met Francesca's and now they both blushed. Hart's collection was infamous; one of the paintings he displayed openly in his entry hall was absolutely sacrilegious, and he had a very shocking nude woman hanging in his grand salon.

"I am sure he has a hundred paintings upstairs in his private apartments," Francesca muttered. She was going to have to have a serious conversation with Hart, oh yes.

"Oh please. Anyway, we are meeting at one, so I must be off."

"Please don't go," Francesca said, following her from the room. "Now I am worried, Con. What will happen when Neil finds out?"

"I am merely having lunch!" Connie said over her shoulder as they went downstairs. "Besides, I am not telling him—as there is nothing to tell."

Francesca had a terrible feeling—no good would come of this flirtation, oh no. "Where are you dining?"

"Sherry Netherland's," Connie said, and on the landing she whirled. "Why?"

"Perhaps I might chaperone," Francesca said bluntly.

"I don't think so," Connie returned evenly. "In fact, I seem to recall your suggesting just such a thing on Tuesday, and Hart quite clearly declined your offer."

Francesca folded her arms, annoyed now to no end, and
watched as Connie went downstairs. The two of them had
flirted madly on Tuesday in the dining room of the Plaza
Hotel. In fact, Francesca knew Hart was rather fond of her.
But on that afternoon, it had been as if she did not even
exist.

Why? She and Connie looked almost alike. Was it because she was the prim, bookish one? Of course, she
wasn't jealous, not a stitch. She was in love with Bragg.

Of course, Hart knew that, too. And Bragg was his half
brother, in spite of the rivalry and animosity they shared.

Francesca sighed, when she heard Connie call up to her.
"Fran! Mrs. Kennedy is here to see you."

Surprised, Francesca started down the last flight of
stairs, wondering what had brought Maggie Kennedy back
to see her so soon. She could not imagine it would be
something as innocuous as not being able to find one of
the ordered fabrics, and she could have sent Joel with such
a message. Since she also worked, shouldn't she be at the
Moe Levy factory?

Francesca entered the large entrance hall, which was
graced with pairs of huge Corinthian columns, marble pan-
els inset in the walls, and a magnificent pastoral scene
painted upon the high ceiling. Pleasure filled her when
she saw Joel's dark, shaggy-haired head, until she realized
he was standing protectively by his mother, and her smile
vanished.

Maggie turned. Her eyes were red from weeping, and
she held a handkerchief in her hand. It was crumpled.

Francesca met Connie's gaze briefly, and her sister left.
She hurried forward. "Mrs. Kennedy, what has happened!
Are you all right? Please, do come inside and sit down."

"Thank you," Maggie managed.

Francesca looked inquiringly at Joel as she ushered the
pair into the small salon. He gave her a long look, one she
could not decipher. What could be wrong?

Maggie sank into a chair. Clearly, she was fighting not to weep again.

Francesca did not sit. She took Maggie's hands in hers, kneeling in front of her. "Surely this is not about a few gowns. Has something happened?"

Maggie nodded, still not able to speak.

Joel, who was slim and short, his complexion extremely pale in a startling contrast to his dark eyes and black curly hair, stood by his mother. "Her friend been done in," he said bluntly. "Colder than a block o' ice."

"Oh, dear," Francesca said, gripping Maggie's hands more tightly.

Maggie inhaled hard. "I am sorry, Miss Cahill."

"Francesca. Please, do not worry."

"No." She attempted a smile and failed. "I . . . I am in shock. You see, I just heard . . . I was at work . . . Mary worked at Moe Levy for a few months last year, that was how we met." Her face seemed about to crumble again.

Francesca pulled up a tufted ottoman and sat down. "Please, start from the beginning."

"You have to find the killer," Joel cried. "She was a nice lady an' she got no man, just her two little girls."

Francesca looked at Joel. "You know I will do my best," she said.

He nodded fiercely. "I know."

"Joel," Maggie whispered, reaching out. He gave her his hand and she clung to it as if he were the stronger of the two.

Watching them, Francesca's heart turned over. Suddenly she wanted a son like Joel, someone smart and loyal and too adorable for words. In the next instant, she sat up straighter than a board, stunned by herself. She had never wanted a child before. Of course, she had always assumed that one day she would have several, but just then, the desire had been intense and tangible.

Of course, she would not have children now. Because

the man she loved was not available, and she would not marry anyone else.

Maggie was speaking, so softly Francesca had to lean forward to hear her. "The police came to the factory with a drawing of her. They asked if any of us knew her. I recognized the portrait instantly. They took me aside and began asking me questions—I realized something was terribly wrong. But I never dreamed she would be dead!"

"They told you she was dead?"

Maggie nodded. "Her body was found last night by a woman, buried in the snow. They wouldn't tell me how she had died, only that it had been murder."

Francesca stared. She could not speak. Dear God! Maggie's friend was the dead woman she had discovered last night!

Maggie looked at her. "Miss Cahill?"

Francesca swallowed, hard. "Who was she, Mrs. Kennedy?"

"Mary O'Shaunessy, a lovely girl, and as Joel said, she has two daughters, three and six. She never mentioned her husband, and my understanding was that he had left them years ago. She was a seamstress, until recently—a few months ago she began working in a private home as a lady's maid. She was so happy with the change," Maggie added sadly.

"Which home did she work in? Where did she live? Do you think her neighbors will speak with me?" Francesca asked quickly. "And did she mention that she knew she was in danger?"

Maggie seemed puzzled. "She never mentioned that she was in any danger, Miss Cahill. And I cannot recall where she was working, but I am sure one of the neighbors will know. And they are all good, hard-working people, they will speak to you, Miss Cahill."

"I can take you to her flat," Joel said eagerly. "We been out o' work too long," he added.

Impulsively, Francesca ruffled his thick hair. "Yes, we have." She was disappointed that Mary O'Shaunessy had not confided in her friend. "Mrs. Kennedy? I will do everything I can to solve your friend's murder," Francesca said resolutely. And she meant every word.

"Thank you." Maggie seemed relieved, and she had recovered her composure. "I knew you would help us. This is a terrible act of evil, Miss Cahill. Mary was a ray of sunshine. And those poor little girls."

Francesca patted her hand, when she heard her brother's voice in the foyer. Loudly, he was asking for Francesca. By the tone of his voice, she could see that his humor was quite good. But then, Evan was usually in a sunny mood; it was his disposition.

Maggie stood. "I must get back to the factory, or I will be let go, especially after calling in sick yesterday."

Francesca walked her into the hall. "If they think to dismiss you, let me know, as I will have a word with the manager."

Maggie smiled a bit at her.

Evan was approaching, his strides long and careless. He was dark-haired and handsome; now, his tie was askew, his suit jacket carelessly open as well, revealing his lean, muscular build. He was smiling at Francesca. "So there you are! I have had the oddest request." His gaze moved over Joel and Maggie with some curiosity. He paused beside her, flinging his arm around her. "And how is my daring, frying pan–wielding little sister?"

"Not funny," Francesca said, slipping free. "My, we are jolly today."

"I had a very interesting evening last night," he said, glancing at Maggie again. His brows furrowed a bit, as if puzzled. "Hello. Have we met?" he asked, his blue gaze sliding over her figure.

"No." Maggie looked at the floor.

"Evan, this is Mrs. Kennedy, and her son, Joel. My brother, Evan."

"So he's the one keepin' Grace Conway," Joel said flatly, his eyes bright with admiration.

Grace Conway was an actress. She was also Evan's mistress, never mind that he was unwillingly engaged to Sarah Channing. Francesca had never heard of her before she had discovered her relationship to her brother as, apparently, she did vaudeville theater in working neighborhoods. But clearly Joel knew the beautiful red-headed actress and singer, and as Maggie glanced up, blushing, it was clear that she did as well.

A silence fell.

Evan was also blushing, high up on his cheekbones. "Well," he said, looking from Joel to Fran. "I can see that your hoodlum friend is well-versed in my private affairs."

"I am sorry," Francesca managed, mortified.

"Wut's the ruckus? She's a beauty, an' we saw her in some play when I was ten. I ain't niver forgot her," Joel said, looking from Evan to Francesca and back again.

Evan took Joel by the arm. "Come with me a moment, young fellow," he said. He pulled him to the other end of the hall, and, as he was six foot tall, he leaned over to mutter in Joel's ear. There was nothing harsh or unkind in his manner, and Francesca smiled a bit, watching the pair. Joel turned red, looking abashed.

Francesca faced Maggie. "I am sorry about that," she said.

Maggie had been watching the exchange between Evan and Joel as well. "So am I. I didn't mean to cause your brother embarrassment. I will speak with Joel. He doesn't understand etiquette, Miss Cahill, but that is my fault," she said firmly.

Francesca felt a rush of warmth toward the other woman. "It's not your fault."

"No. I know the difference between your class and mine. But I haven't had time to teach Joel proper manners, and it didn't seem so very important—until now." She glanced toward Evan and Joel again as they returned, Joel still flushed, Evan apparently having recovered from the brief moment of embarrassment. Blushing, Maggie said, "Mr. Cahill, please forgive me and my son. We have been terribly rude."

Evan smiled at her, but he seemed a bit puzzled again. "There is nothing to forgive. If one dares to overstep oneself, why, I suppose one must face the consequences."

Maggie avoided his eyes. She nodded. "Joel? We have to go."

"Are you all right, Mrs. Kennedy?" Evan suddenly asked, reaching out to detain her.

She somehow sidestepped him. Very much like a skittish filly. "I am fine." She still refused to look at him. She smiled at Francesca, but it seemed strained. "Thank you again."

"I will not let you down," Francesca vowed. "But may I keep Joel for a while? I will see that he gets safely home by suppertime."

Maggie nodded. "Of course."

"Here, I will see you to the door," Evan said amiably.

Maggie barely looked at him. As she had never taken off her navy blue wool coat, she nodded and allowed him to walk with her to the front door, where a doorman opened it for her. Evan turned and hurried back to Francesca. "Has she been crying?" he asked with some concern.

Francesca hesitated, and gave Joel a look that meant, be quiet. "She has lost a dear friend."

"I am so sorry," Evan said, his expression turning grave. "If I had known, I would have been more gallant."

"You were very gallant," Francesca said.

Evan glanced back at the closed front door. "I would swear to it, though, that we have met before."

"Evan, I do not think so. She is a seamstress."

He shrugged. "Perhaps it was at one of Grace's performances."

"Perhaps. So why have you come looking for me? I am on my way out."

He faced her squarely. "Your friend the police commissioner called. He has asked me and my fiancée to join you and him at the theater this Saturday night."

Francesca stared.

"Am I missing something?" Evan asked.

"No, no, we thought to take in the new musical which had received such rave reviews. It would not be proper for us to go alone, so clearly Bragg thought you might wish to join us."

"I accepted, as I saw no graceful way not to," Evan said. "But let's make it a short evening, if you don't mind?" With that, he walked away.

Francesca did not know how to feel. Clearly, Evan had no wish to spend any time with his fiancée, Sarah Channing. And, as clearly, Bragg thought to keep the evening innocent by having another couple present.

Francesca realized she was disappointed when she had no right to be.

She turned to Joel, shrugging her disappointment aside. It was better this way. To yearn for a romantic evening had been terribly foolish—and wrong. Besides, she had more important matters on her mind. "How about a bit of lunch before we go speak with Mary O'Shaunessy's neighbors?" Her wish was to fatten him up.

He beamed. "Did you hear my stomach growlin'?" he asked.

Francesca smiled in return. "No, but I do believe we have lots of leftover roast turkey *and* a fresh apple pie waiting just for you."

THREE

It had been very tempting, as their cab had gone down
Fifth Avenue, to pause at Sherry Netherland's. In fact,
Francesca had recognized Hart's large, elegant brougham
standing not far from the famous hotel's entrance, in a line
of other, similar coaches, his carriage man chatting with
the hotel's doormen. However, she had more important
affairs to conduct now.

Joel had told her that Mary O'Shaunessy had lived on
Avenue C and 4th Street. This neighborhood was a sin-
gularly crowded and depressed one: the tenements seemed
older, more ramshackle, and more jam-packed. Francesca
felt uneasy even though it was broad daylight; she did not
like the various men loitering on the corner, and a pack of
boys hanging about one stone stoop made the hairs prickle
on her nape. They weren't playing jacks, cards, or dice;
they were merely standing about, staring at the passersby
with dark, sullen eyes.

"Forgive me if I am wrong," she said, after letting the
cabbie go. "But is that a gang of boys, Joel?"

He, too, looked uneasy. "Don't even look at 'em," he
warned, low. "Yep, they's the Mugheads, an' they're mean
an' ornery. I didn't think they'd be about at this hour, lady.
Wish you didn't stand out like a sore thumb."

An image of her parents flashed through her mind. If
she fell into jeopardy now, she did not know which party
would scare her more, the Mugheads or Andrew and Julia.

Joel had deliberately increased his pace, and Francesca did
so as well. She turned to look back at the stoop, but a huge
dray was blocking her view. There was hardly any vehic-
ular traffic in the neighborhood, she realized. That was
odd, too.

Then she realized that if the neighborhood was nothing
but tenements—and she saw but two saloons and one
small grocery store—there would be hardly any traffic,
other than that of its impoverished residents.

One of the boys had turned to stare openly at them. He
was a tall, lanky redhead, a wool cap pulled partly over
his shaggy hair. His gaze met Francesca's and he grinned.
He turned and nudged a companion.

"Don't look at 'em!" Joel hissed beneath his breath.

Francesca turned away as the entire pack of five boys
stared at them.

"This is it," Joel said, tugging hard on a rusted bolt.
The door fell slowly open, and a stench came from the
unlit hall inside.

"She lived here?" Francesca gasped.

"She and the girls shared a room with two other families. One of 'em is the Jadvics," he said.

"Poles?" she asked, finding a handkerchief in her purse.
She had to hold it to her nose. It was clear that someone
had become violently ill some time ago in the stairwell.

"Think so," Joel said. On the first landing he went to
the first door and pounded on it. "Mrs. Jadvic!" he called,
sounding very much like a ten-year-old boy. "You at
home? It's Joel Kennedy! Mrs. Jadvic?"

Francesca almost smiled, but the rotten building was
just too depressing.

The door was cracked open. An old woman with hanging jowls in a worn yellow housedress—the color now
more beige—eyed them suspiciously.

"It's me, Joel Kennedy, Grandma Jadvic. This is me
friend, a real lady, Miss Cahill. Can we come in? It stinks
out here," he protested.

The door was opened more widely and the woman's face softened. She nodded.

Francesca entered a room with a stove, a small table, two rickety chairs, and five mattresses. Four of the mattresses were inhabited by children of various ages, playing with paper dolls and one tin soldier. The youngest, a little girl of two or three, was sucking on a teat. Another door was partially ajar; inside, Francesca glimpsed a sleeping man, more mattresses, one chair, and a small bureau.

She had been inside tenements before. But never one as crowded and inhumane as this.

Somehow, she smiled at the old lady. "Hello, Mrs. Jadvic. I am Francesca Cahill." She extended her hand.

The old woman just looked at her. Then, "What you want?" She spoke with a heavy Polish accent.

Francesca pointed at the little blond girl with big blue eyes sucking on the teat. "Is that Mary O'Shaunessy's daughter?"

Before the old lady could answer, the front door opened and another woman entered, in a stained and faded brown coat. The hem was coming undone, but the woman's blond hair was pinned beneath a new red scarf. Her hazel eyes were bright. She looked from Joel to Francesca and her brows shot up. "Joel?"

"Hi, Mrs. Jadvic," Joel said. "This is Miz Cahill, from uptown."

"I see that," Mrs. Jadvic said. She had a slight accent, not as strong as her mother-in-law's. Francesca could not determine her age—she might be twenty, thirty, or forty; she was too worn-looking to tell.

"Miz Cahill's a sleuth," Joel continued. "She's here to solve Mary's murder. To find out who dun it."

Francesca had already taken one of her cards out of her purse. She handed it to Mrs. Jadvic, who put her bag of groceries down. The tired blonde said, "I don't read."

"I am a sleuth, Mrs. Jadvic. And Maggie Kennedy has

retained my services. She wants to know who murdered Mary O'Shaunessy, and why."

Mrs. Jadvic bit her lip and tears filled her eyes. "Them two are hers. We can't keep 'em. We just can't."

Francesca looked at the blond girl with the big blue eyes, who had thrown her teat aside. Then she looked at another skinny little girl, this one with dishwater brown hair and the exact same big blue eyes. She wondered if she could bring the girls home until they were placed with a real family; then she recalled that she was on a probation of sorts with her parents. The girls would have to go, temporarily, to a foster home or an orphanage, she realized. It hurt her thinking about it.

The older sister seemed to understand her thoughts, because her expression turned sullen and she took the little blonde's hand and gripped it tightly. The smaller child made a sound of protest.

"I will find them a home," Francesca said abruptly, turning back to Mrs. Jadvic. And the sisters would not be torn apart. "How long can you keep them here?" she asked.

"I cannot feed them. I can't feed my own," Mrs. Jadvic said tiredly. "When Mary was alive, it was different. She gave me five dollars every week for them, and she came home late Saturday night, returning to the Janson house on Monday morning."

Francesca took out a pen and notepad. She wrote down "Janson house." Do you have an address for the Jansons?" she asked.

"They're on Madison Square, twenty-fourth, I think," she said.

Francesca wrote "Mad Sq." on her pad. That was where Bragg lived. "Were you—" She stopped.

Bragg lived on Madison Square in a very nice town house with his servant, Peter. He had several bedrooms. Oh, dear, he might be furious at first, but couldn't he keep the two girls until she placed them? It broke her heart, sending them to an orphan asylum.

"Lady?" Joel asked curiously.

Francesca wet her lips. "Mrs. Jadvic? Have the police been by?"

She nodded. "But I wasn't home. They said they would come back. My mother-in-law told them about the girls. One of the detectives said he would take care of moving them, that he would alert the proper people."

Like a sack of potatoes, Francesca thought with heat. "We do not have much time," she murmured.

"Wut?" Joel asked.

"Mrs. Jadvic? Can you pack up the girls' things? I have a nice home for them to stay in until we find them new parents." Francesca walked over to the girl with dishwater brown hair. "Hello. And what is your name? I am Fran. My niece calls me Auntie Fran."

Big blue eyes stared suspiciously up at her. The six-year-old did not speak.

"That's Katie, an' her sister is Dot," Joel said.

Impulsively Francesca ran her hand over Katie's head. She pulled away, scowling. Her gaze remained wary and even hostile. Francesca smiled at Dot. The little blonde had been watching her, and now she grinned back. She had several new baby teeth and the grin was enough to melt anyone's heart.

Francesca faced Mrs. Jadvic. "Did Mary express any fears to you recently? Did she know her life was in danger?"

Mrs. Jadvic shook her head. "No. She was happy with her new job. She'd come here with food and trinkets for the girls, humming a ditty beneath her breath."

It was so unfair, Francesca thought, more determined than ever to bring Mary's killer to justice. "When did you last see her?"

"Sunday," she said, without hesitation.

So Francesca had seen her more recently, last Tuesday. Perhaps on Sunday, Mary hadn't known that her life was in danger.

"And her husband? Is he around?" Francesca asked.

"She never spoke of him to me." The blonde hesitated. "I don't think the girls have the same father."

Francesca nodded, hoping she was not blushing. "Where did Mary work before she was hired by the Jansons? And for how long? And when was that?"

"She worked in a small tailor shop with four other seamstresses; it's on Broadway, maybe on Eighteenth Street. She's been with the Jansons five or six weeks now, less than two months. They would know better than me," Mrs. Jadvic added.

Her mother-in-law had been unpacking the groceries, which consisted of several old potatoes, a loaf of stale bread, three eggs, and a slab of bacon. Francesca realized they were about to cook dinner. Mrs. Jadvic took two coats off of wall pegs and, along with them, several scarves. She handed Francesca a small burlap sack. "They each have a change in here, and a Sunday church dress. Mary was devout."

Francesca accepted the sack, then handed it to Joel. "Is there anyone else who was close to Mary? Someone that I might talk to?"

"Maggie Kennedy was her good friend. You might try some of the girls at the Broadway shop." She shrugged.

"And that is all?" Francesca asked.

"There's her brother," Mrs. Jadvic said. "Mike O'Donnell."

Francesca used the door knocker at No. 11 Madison Square. The door was opened almost instantly by a huge man. Peter was undoubtedly six inches over six feet, broad-shouldered, and large of frame. He was blond and blue-eyed; Francesca thought he was Swedish. He rarely spoke, although Bragg had said he was quite wise, and he was Bragg's man. That is, he did just about everything and anything for Bragg; when Francesca had first met Peter, she had thought him to be a police officer.

"Hello, Peter," she said brightly, clutching Katie's and Dot's hands. She had given both girls lollipops, and they were busy sucking on the candy sticks.

Peter nodded, glancing from her to the two children, then at the cab waiting in the street. He then espied the burlap sack that Joel held.

"Peter, this is a dire emergency," Francesca was brisk, and with courage she walked around him—no easy task— with the two girls and into the narrow entry of Bragg's town house. "These two little girls are homeless. I would bring them home with me, but I am rather in a predicament with my parents—I am not allowed to sleuth. However, I shall find these girls a new home—within the week, I assure you. But until then," and she did smile at him, "they must remain here. I shall send over a nanny."

Peter's expression did not change. If he was surprised or dismayed, he did not show it. He asked, "Does the commissioner know?"

"I am on my way to headquarters even as we speak," she said, very brightly. "You know Bragg. He will never turn these two little girls out on the street. I promise you, he shall welcome them with open arms."

Peter said, "Please call him. The telephone is in the study." He turned and started to walk down the hall, toward the small study that was just before the parlor. Francesca released the girls, closed the door firmly behind them and Joel so no one could leave, and ran after Peter. "Peter!"

He halted in the study, handing her the telephone.

Francesca took it. The study flooded her with memories, and briefly she did not move.

She looked around the small room, where a desk, its

chair, a huge and worn upholstered chair, and the fireplace were the only furnishings. Bragg still had three boxes of books to unpack, she noted. And the last time she had been in that room, he had kissed her, right there, pressing her up against the wall.

And the next day he had apologized, and told her about Leigh Anne.

"Miss Cahill?"

She jerked, and came out of the reverie that was at once painful and heated and sweet. She replaced the phone on its hook. In a low voice she said, "Bragg told you about the murdered woman we found last night?"

He nodded.

"Her name is Mary O'Shaunessy, and those are her two little girls."

If he was surprised, his blue eyes did not show it.

"I will convince Bragg to keep them here. It shall only be for a week or so. But I must speak with him in person."

Peter did not indicate what he was thinking, and he did not bat an eye.

"Please, Peter," Francesca whispered, and the plea was genuine.

He nodded, and he seemed to flush as he looked away. And then he was walking out of the study and into the front hall, where Dot was piddling on the floor, her sister watching and sucking her pop.

"We have one more stop to make before headquarters— and our visit to Mike O'Donnell," Francesca said breathlessly as the cab pulled away from the curb. She was still disbelieving. Dot had peed on Bragg's floor, not even asking to use the bathing room. Francesca had been horror-stricken. But Peter had not batted an eye, and he had helped her clean up the mess and change the little girl's drawers.

Francesca prayed that was not going to happen again.

She did not think Bragg would be so calm about another incident. "Driver! Sherry Netherland's, please!"

The horse began a brisk trot, behind an electric trolley. Joel faced her. "Why are we goin' there?"

Francesca patted his hand, which was wrapped in a rag to ward off the cold. She must buy him gloves, she decided, and the girls did need new clothes. Not to mention a nanny. There was so much to do now that it made her head spin, and then she recalled Biology.

She had promised to rewrite her essay, the one on mammalian digestive systems, the one she had failed. Oh, dear. Another task that she must add to her agenda.

She smiled at Joel. "My sister had a one o'clock luncheon there. I must stop by; it is urgent." She *had* to know what was happening between Hart and Connie.

"Lady, it's three or so, ain't it?"

"A two-hour luncheon is quite normal. I would even expect them to still be there at half past the hour."

Joel blinked, amazed. "How much do you rich folks eat?"

She laughed then. "Joel, it's far more social than it is anything else. We go out to dine to meet with a friend, to chat, to enjoy a few hours. The food is truly secondary."

He stared at her with disbelief. "Only the rich," he said, "would treat a good meal like that."

She sobered. For he was right. And which employment agency should she use to find a nanny for the girls, and could she hire one on credit? Sleuthing was quite expensive, as cab fares and bribes ate heavily into her allowance. Traveling back and forth to school did not help matters. And then there was the list of items she had promised herself while on the Randall Murder that she would purchase, items that she had quickly come to realize were crucial to investigative work. At the top of that list was a small gun. There were just too many killers in the city.

She sighed. Tomorrow she would visit a gun shop.

Fifteen minutes later, as it began to flurry, the cab halted at Sherry Netherland's. As Francesca had kept the cab waiting on Avenue C, the fare was outrageous—two and a half dollars. After she paid the driver, she and Joel alighted. The doormen smiled at her, then saw Joel and barred her way.

Francesca smiled her best smile. "Hullo. Might we enter?"

"No rowdies in here," one of the doormen said, a fat fellow with a handlebar mustache.

"I beg your pardon. I am Francesca Cahill, Andrew Cahill's daughter. And Joel Kennedy is my friend and assistant—he comes with me." She instantly dug a calling card out of her purse, slapping it against the man's chest. He caught it. "Or shall I speak with the manager of this fine establishment—where I dine frequently with my family?"

"Hey, are you the young lady who caught Randall's killer?" the second doorman asked.

Francesca nodded, surprised and proud all at once.

"Hey, Joe, she caught the killer all by herself, used a cast-iron pan or something. Been in the papers." The doormen exchanged looks. Then they moved aside.

"Please," the first doorman said. "And I beg your pardon, Miss Cahill."

Francesca felt like a famous person. She gave Joel an amazed look, and together they walked into the wide lobby of the hotel.

Pillars graced its perimeter and huge Oriental rugs covered its marble floors. Francesca knew the way to the restaurant, and she and Joel crossed the lobby quickly. A maître d' came forward, smiling apologetically. "I am afraid we are not serving lunch, miss."

Francesca did not answer. Only three parties remained in the large dining room, and in one corner, at a white, linen-clad table, sat her sister and Hart.

He was touching her hand. She was laughing and pulling her hand away. He leaned forward, speaking again. Connie seemed somewhat flustered and was definitely acting coy.

Francesca could only stare. Even from a distance, Hart was the kind of man to attract a woman's attention. He was dark, deadly so, with swarthy skin and thick black hair. He was tall, broad-shouldered, and had a small cleft in his chin. Today he was wearing a starkly black suit and a snowy white shirt. She realized every time she had seen him, he had been wearing black.

But it suited him.

As if sensing that he was being watched, he turned and looked her way.

And even from a distance, she sensed his surprise. And then, she sensed his pleasure.

He stood, still looking toward her.

Francesca turned to the maître d'. "My sister is dining with Mr. Hart. I have an urgent message for her."

"Oh, please, then do go in." He smiled and turned away, and she and Joel walked past his small desk and through the spacious dining room.

Hart remained standing, his gaze unwavering, upon her. Francesca briefly felt flustered, and she looked at Connie, who wasn't smiling. If looks could kill, why, Francesca surely would be dead.

There was also an empty bottle of wine on the table, she saw. Connie's glass contained a sip or two, while Hart's was empty.

"This is an exceedingly pleasant surprise," Hart murmured. He had a way of speaking that was purely sensual. It reminded Francesca of the fact that he enjoyed visiting two supposed sisters at the very same time. Daisy and Rose worked in a brothel and Francesca had met them on her last case. She could not stop her thoughts from turning to a very intimate image of Hart with both striking women.

"We were just passing by," Francesca said cheerfully. "My, a burgundy with lunch."

"I am sure you were," Connie said coolly.

"The wine was superb, as was the meal—and the company." He smiled warmly at Connie, who cast her eyes demurely down, and then Hart grinned at Joel. "Hey, kid," he said.

Joel eyed him with hostility. "Name's Kennedy."

"I see your little hoodlum has not changed his manners," Hart said, unruffled and amused. "Pray tell the both of you are not chasing ruffians these days."

"His manners are just fine," Francesca returned.

"Ever the defender of the underdog," Hart said. "It is ever so charming, Francesca."

She was pleased, because she knew he meant it. "Should I change overnight?" she bantered.

"I hope not!" He laughed, his hand going to his heart. "I would be stricken. What would I do without such a unique friend?"

She smiled, realizing he was flirting with her and she loved it. "You would be at a complete loss; I assure you of that." She glanced at Connie. "How was lunch?"

Hart looked at Connie, too. His eyes softened, then gleamed. "Lady Montrose?"

"Lunch was wonderful," Connie replied, but her gaze had locked with Hart's and something sizzled between them.

Testing her, Francesca asked, somewhat sourly, "And what did you have?"

"I am glad you so enjoyed yourself. I think a luncheon out, with myself, is exactly what the physician has ordered for you," Hart said softly.

"Yes, I do think so," Connie said. "I cannot recall when I have passed such a pleasant afternoon."

"And I was thinking the exact same thing," Hart told her.

In that moment, Francesca realized that Connie had changed her dress before meeting Hart. She was wearing a sapphire blue gown that was low-cut and extremely fitted, revealing her every curve and an expanse of cleavage; the prim and proper pink was gone. "What did you have for lunch?" Francesca insisted. She realized her tone was shrill.

Connie and Hart looked at her. "I do not remember," Connie said, and she blushed.

Hart laughed warmly, his gaze sliding over Connie and lingering on her small bosom, which hardly looked small now. Francesca felt like kicking her sister right in the butt. "Shall we? I hate to end a perfect afternoon, but I have a final meeting this afternoon at four-fifteen. Fortunately, it is uptown." He signaled to the waiter for the bill.

"And I must get home." As Connie began to stand, Hart rushed around the table to quickly move her chair and help her up. She leaned into him. "Thank you," she said, and her tone was husky.

"Oh, please," Francesca heard herself mutter.

Connie did not hear; Hart did. He glanced at Francesca and he grinned. Once again, he was clearly enjoying himself. He winked at her.

A waiter approached; Hart signed the bill. "Ladies?" As they all began to leave, he grabbed Joel's shoulder. "Ladies first, Kennedy," he said.

"As if you would know," Joel retorted, but he let Francesca and Connie walk out ahead of them.

Connie did not speak to her or even look at her; Francesca could tell that she was extremely annoyed at having her sister appear at her luncheon. As they walked out of the hotel, Connie's pace quickened. Francesca recognized her elegant brougham, parked one coach ahead of Hart's. Her driver, Clark, immediately opened the carriage door, having instantly remarked her approach.

Connie's strides lengthened, and as Francesca quick-

ened her step they outpaced Joel and Hart. Connie faced
her, and her eyes flashed. "Just what do you think you are
doing, Fran?" she demanded.

Francesca smiled pleasantly. "Rescuing you."

"Whoever said I needed rescuing?" Connie asked
coldly.

"All moral women need rescuing from Hart."

Connie's hands, encased in blue gloves a shade darker
than her dress and coat, fisted on her narrow hips. "If I
did not know about your feelings for Bragg, I would say
you are jealous."

"I am not jealous," Francesca said quickly, but with an
odd inkling that she lied—even to herself. "I do not want
to see you fall victim to Hart's considerable charms—not
to mention his expertise."

"I am not falling victim to anything or anyone," Connie
snapped. "And I suggest that you consider your own personal life before you make judgments about mine." Truly
angry, she turned to her coachman.

"May I?" Hart intoned from behind them.

Francesca started, truly hoping he had not eavesdropped
upon them. She backed away as Hart took Connie's arm.
Still, Francesca strained to hear them—and she watched
closely as her sister beamed at him.

"When will I have the opportunity to wine and dine
you again?" he asked softly. Oh, how seductive he was!

Connie did hesitate. "I must check my calendar. Perhaps
next week?"

"Next week!" He seemed dismayed. "An eternity shall
pass between now and then, Lady Montrose."

"I doubt it," she laughed.

He smiled and lifted her gloved hand, kissing it. "Your
husband is a very fortunate man," he said, staring into her
eyes.

Connie looked away. "I am the fortunate one," she murmured.

Hart smiled, but Francesca saw the speculative look in his gaze, and she felt like kicking his shin. He handed Connie up into her coach, slamming her door firmly closed. As Clark climbed up into the front box, releasing the brakes, Hart backed up one step, still smiling at Connie. She lifted one hand in return and did not look at Francesca, not even once.

Behind her, Joel breathed, "Blarney. Wut fools, all lovesick."

Francesca regarded him grimly as he shook his head in disgust.

The coach rolled off. Briefly Francesca hoped that Montrose would learn of Connie's luncheon and take her head off for it. Then she was sorry for her pettiness.

But someone had to protect her sister, and who better to do so than Neil?

Hart walked over to them. "May I offer you a lift? I am only going a few blocks, and then Raoul can take you where you wish."

Francesca hesitated.

"What? Is my company no longer alluring?" He seemed to be laughing at her.

"You are clearly an expert when it comes to being alluring, Hart," she said briskly.

He took her arm and glanced at Joel. "Let's go, kid. I am giving you both a ride."

Francesca did not protest as he guided her farther up the block, where his swarthy coachman was standing by the already-open door of his large, extremely turned out brougham. His team was four magnificent blacks with gilded nameplates on their harnesses. His driver wore royal blue livery, and the leather squabs inside of the coach were red; the lighting fixtures and railings were bronze. One would have judged his vehicle as belonging to royalty, except for the fact that Raoul appeared to be a hoodlum from downtown. He was of medium height, of Spanish,

Mexican, or Latin descent, and he looked too rough and too bulky for his impeccable uniform. He nodded at everyone, but had neither the manners nor the presence of a servant, for he seemed indifferent, surly, and perhaps bored.

Hart handed Francesca up the step, then allowed Joel to leap in. He settled eagerly against the rear-facing seats as Hart climbed in. The boy said with disgust, "Wut a fancy rig."

Hart settled down beside Francesca, and without a word, the coach started off. "So, Kennedy, why don't you like me?" he asked pleasantly.

Joel gave him a mulish look. " 'Cause you ain't no good," he said flatly.

That amused Hart, because he laughed and looked at Francesca. "Is your little cohort in crime-solving correct?"

"No," Francesca said tersely. "I am sure there is good somewhere in you, Hart."

"So today it is Hart. Not Calder. Hmm. You are still angry with me," he remarked, his gaze sliding over her features as if he found her beautiful and fascinating. "Perhaps your sister is right?"

Francesca felt herself begin to flush. "I beg your pardon?"

"I could not help overhearing." He grinned.

She crossed her arms. "I have no idea what you are speaking about."

He tried to take her hand, and as he was the stronger and more determined of them both, he succeeded. "Are you jealous, Francesca?" he asked softly.

"No!" she cried, far too quickly and far too loudly.

He was clearly pleased.

"Oh, do let go of my hand," she snapped.

He laughed and released it. "You have nothing to be jealous of," he said, still smiling, but he seemed thoughtful now. "The friendship we share is far better than any flirtation."

Francesca looked at him. "Do you think Connie and I look alike? Many consider us to be nearly identical."

"I believe we have discussed this before. And the answer is no, I do not."

Francesca felt hurt, but she smiled gamely. "Yes, Connie is far more beautiful. I have always thought so myself."

His eyes widened. "You are the more beautiful one, Francesca."

She was stunned. *"What?"*

He glanced briefly away. Was he now uncomfortable? And if so, why? "Why are we discussing beauty? And do you, of all women, wished to be judged on your appearance?"

"No," she managed, absolutely flustered. He thought her more beautiful than her glamorous and elegant sister?

"Remember, I am a connoisseur of art—and all fine things. I never judge a painting merely by its color, composition, or skilled execution. There is a subjective element to every judgment." He briefly met her gaze. "You and your sister share similar external qualities, but you are so vastly different, it would be like comparing the sun and the moon."

She stared at his handsome face. "You never cease to surprise me, Calder."

"Good." That apparently pleased him no end. "And now we are back to Calder?"

She flushed. "Apparently so." She hesitated. "My sister loves her husband very much."

He eyed her. "I am not in the mood for a lecture, Francesca."

"But you shall receive one anyway."

He sighed, as if an adolescent in no mood for a parental scolding.

"Calder! She loves Montrose. She has loved him from the moment she set eyes upon him five years ago."

"Perhaps," he murmured, gazing out of his window.

"Can you not chase someone else?"

He turned to meet her eyes. "She accepted my invitation to lunch, Francesca."

Francesca hesitated. It would not do to tell Calder too much about Connie's private affairs, and she had the unfortunate feeling that he would use that knowledge, should he have it, to his own perverse advantage. "As your friend, if I ask you to cease and desist, will you?"

"No."

She gaped, in shock.

"Your sister is an adult. I do believe she can manage her life very well without your interference."

Francesca folded her arms, trying not to become infuriated. "She has been through a difficult time recently!"

"Hmm. How difficult?"

"As if I shall tell you," she snapped.

"You are so protective of Lady Montrose. I wonder why."

"She is my sister!" she cried.

"Temper," he chided.

"So you will not do me this one favor? After all I have done for you?"

He stared. Then, dangerously, "Be careful of the marker you think to call in. You might wish to use it at another time. Once it is gone, why . . ." He shrugged and did not have to say any more.

"You are truly unscrupulous," she said, eyes wide.

"So it is said."

"I thought we were friends."

"We are. But that does not change my true nature. Remember? I am selfish, not selfless."

"Oh, please," Francesca said, annoyed. "I know you better than you think. You are not completely selfish, and that is that."

His mouth quirked as the coach rolled to a stop before

the grand entrance of the Waldorf Astoria Hotel. "I shall debate that point at another time." He waited patiently for Raoul to climb down from the driver's seat and open his door. He turned before alighting. "Where shall Raoul drop you and the rowdy?"

Joel scowled. Francesca touched his arm. "Police headquarters," she said sweetly.

Somehow she had known she would get a reaction. His eyes blackened. But his face remained impassive as he said to Raoul, "Three hundred Mulberry."

The olive-skinned driver nodded.

Hart glanced at her, still dispassionate. "So you are off to visit my esteemed and oh, so reputable brother. Are you back to your crime-solving ways? Or is this a social call?"

She lifted both brows. "Perhaps it is a bit of both."

His smile was somehow mocking and cool as he inclined his head, allowing Raoul to slam the door closed. Francesca watched Hart turn and stride up the street. She was still annoyed, and wondered at herself for it.

FOUR

Bragg was standing with his back to the door when Francesca paused on the threshold of his office. He was on the telephone, listening intently to whoever was on the other end of the line, and he did not seem to be aware of her. Francesca was about to knock when she saw the photograph on his desk. It was face up, but even from this distance, she knew who it was. She hesitated.

And before she could reprimand herself, she hurried across the small room as Bragg turned, seeing her. On his cluttered desk was one of the photographs he had requested; Mary O'Shaunessy lay in the snow face up, with her hands clasped in prayer on her chest, the ugly cross carved into her throat.

Francesca must have made a sound, because Bragg flipped the photograph over and the look he gave her was a dark one. But it was too late; in the light of day and his office Mary's expression in death of fear was all too vivid and all too clear. Francesca closed her eyes, instantly recalling a similar expression of fear when she had been alive. Why had she changed her mind and run away from Francesca?

Francesca sighed and opened her eyes. She was Katie and Dot's mother. It was such a terrible tragedy, for everyone—for the two little girls and for Mary, who on all accounts seemed to have been a wonderful person. Anger at the unknown killer suddenly swelled within Francesca, not for the first time. Why had he done this?

"Thank you," Bragg said, and he hung up the receiver. "Francesca?"

She tried to smile and failed. "Hello, Bragg." She felt like walking into his arms and laying her cheek upon his solid chest, but that would not do.

"I'm sorry you saw that." He seemed grim. "Please tell me you are not still blaming yourself for her death?"

"I am trying not to. Mary was young and pretty and she has two beautiful daughters who are now orphans. We have to find the madman who did this," Francesca said passionately. It was an outburst she could not contain.

He walked slowly out from behind his desk. "We? You are not on this investigation, Francesca. And how do you know that she has two daughters?" His golden regard was calm but intense, and infinitely patient as he waited for an answer.

She sighed. "Maggie Kennedy came calling this morning—and she was grief-stricken."

"Maggie Kennedy? Is she by chance related to the little hoodlum you are so fond of?"

"She is his mother, Bragg. And Mary O'Shaunessy was her dear friend," Francesca said bluntly. There was no point in telling him that she had been very involved in the case from the moment she had found Mary dead.

His eyes widened fractionally. "Please, do not tell me that Mrs. Kennedy has retained your services!"

"She has," Francesca said with an upward tilt of her chin. "Oh, Bragg. From what I have learned, Mary was a ray of sunshine, a wonderful mother, a devout Catholic! She did not deserve this, and now her two small girls are orphans." She knew she was angling for his consent in allowing the girls to remain in his home temporarily, but she also meant her every word.

He came closer and lifted up her chin with one fingertip. His fingers were long and strong and their eyes met and locked. "What have you been up to, Francesca?" His gaze was searching. She no longer feared him, not at all, and a tingle went from her head to her toes.

Somewhat breathlessly she said, "After I consoled Maggie, Joel showed me to the apartment Mary shared. I believe the police have already spoken with the Jadvics."

He dropped his hand and stared. "I will not have you involved, not in a case involving a deranged killer."

"Is that what you have concluded?" she asked—far too eagerly.

"No comment."

"Bragg!" she cried. "I am not the press."

"As I well know. By the by, are you not treading a thin line? You are supposed to be devoting yourself to your studies, and yet you have that new client, Mrs. Stuart. How is that case progressing, Francesca?" His gaze was narrowed.

"You think to divert me, and it will not work," she said sweetly.

"What shall I do with you?"

"Do you have any leads?" she returned swiftly.

"Yes, but I shall not share them with you." He was firm. Determination glimmered golden in his eyes.

She felt a thrill then and said slyly, "I was crucial to the conclusion of the Randall Murder."

He did not answer.

"Not to mention the Burton Abduction."

"No," he said. Then, "Have you come to badger me? If so, I have work to do."

"Bragg!" She was truly shocked. "Am I badgering you?"

Suddenly he seemed tired. He sat down on the edge of his desk. Softly he said, "You could never badger me. I am frustrated. That is all."

"Over this case?" she asked sympathetically, taking the seat in front of his desk.

"That and the appointment I have made. It was announced at City Hall an hour ago. At the last moment, I decided against Shea; I have appointed Inspector Farr instead. I do not think you have met him. His is a royal annoyance, too smart for his own good, and as crooked as Front Street. But he seems eager to please, now, in fact, he is eager to please *me,* and I think I shall be able to control him."

Francesca winced. "I do hope so."

"He is run by Tammany Hall through and through," Bragg added.

"Well, just be on guard. Make sure he is working for you—and not against you."

Bragg smiled at her, and it was filled with affection. "However did you come to be so intelligent?"

She flushed with pleasure. "My father encouraged my freethinking."

"I am glad."

She fell silent, smiling.

Then, "I invited your brother and Miss Channing for tomorrow night's musical. And supper afterward. I hope that is all right."

"Of course it is." Her gaze locked with his.

He seemed to flush. "I felt it was more appropriate."

She nodded. "I know." She had begun thinking about the two little girls when he said, "So what did you find out from the Jadvics?"

"Not much. Have your men been to the tailor shop where Mary worked before the Jansons'?"

"Newman is there now with a detail."

She nodded, smiling—he was discussing the case with her.

And suddenly he must have realized it, because he stood. "Francesca—"

"I'm sorry. I could not help myself." She wanted to ask him about the Jansons but did not dare. He did not fill in the brief, focused silence. Finally she said, meekly, "Do you have a suspect?"

"If I did, I would not tell you."

"Bragg!" She was truly frustrated.

"I apologize, but my mind is made up." He turned and picked up Mary's photograph, but in a way so Francesca could not see it. And Francesca thought about Katie and Dot.

"Bragg?" she asked, now nervous.

He glanced up.

She stood and shifted her weight. "I have a favor to ask of you."

His gaze widened and he put the photograph down. "I can tell already—this is not fair."

She wet her lips. "Please, just hear me out."

He folded his arms. "I am steeling myself to say no."

"Do you like children?" she asked quickly.

"What?!"

"You heard me. Do you like children?"

"Of course I do. What is this about?" he asked suspiciously.

She inhaled. "Katie and Dot have lost their mother. Mrs. Jadvic cannot keep them. The authorities may well separate them. I could not see that happening! I have brought them to your house," she finished in a rush.

It took him a moment to understand. "You *what*?!" he roared.

She backed up. "Please! You have room, they are so adorable, they have lost their mother—"

"Absolutely not!" he cried.

"But you said that you like children!" she cried in return.

"I do! But I am a very busy man, with one servant—and I cannot take care of two children!" He was shouting. His face was red.

"Please," she managed. "I will hire a nanny. You only have one servant?" She was shocked. She had assumed he also had a cook who doubled as a laundress.

"The only servant in my employ is Peter," he said rigidly.

She realized why. Because his moderate income was eaten up by his spoiled wife, who lived in Europe as if her husband were a prince, and he could not afford a second servant in his employ due to her outrageous expenses. "I am sorry," she whispered.

"What?" he shot.

"I mean, I will hire a nanny and it is only for a few weeks," Francesca pleaded.

"No."

"Bragg. You must meet them at least!"

"Says who?" he asked coldly.

She wondered if she had gone too far. And his coldness stunned her. "But they are two lost little girls," she whispered. "And it is only for a week or two, until I can find them a truly good foster home. I will help—"

"How? With all of your sleuthing, you are about to fail your studies at Barnard," he said, not giving an inch.

"I cannot believe this," Francesca whispered. "I thought you cared. This is so important to me. And we are fighting." She was aghast.

"I do care," he said, flushing. "But you do not seem to understand the pressure I am under. Mayor Low has told me in no uncertain terms I shall not close the saloons on Sundays. But I am morally committed to upholding the law, Francesca. I am about to battle my own mayor—a man I personally admire, respect, and believe in."

"I am sorry," she said, meaning it. "But two little girls have so little to do with the blue laws."

"When the press gets wind of Mary O'Shaunessy's murder, when they link it to Kathleen O'Donnell's, they will attempt to terrify this city with their words and fan the fires of hysteria."

She hugged herself. She had never really asked him for a favor before. She was hurt.

He sighed and moved to her and took her by her shoulders. "Don't make me feel guilty for refusing a burden I cannot now bear."

"I am sorry," she said, meaning it. "I wish to be the last person to add to your worries, and if I could, I would have taken the girls home with me. Of course, I cannot do so—not without lying to my parents—and that I refuse to do." She almost felt like crying.

He was staring, and she looked up. His gaze slipped over her features, slowly, one by one. His jaw tightened and he pulled her close and suddenly she was in his arms, her cheek upon his chest. Her heart thrummed with anticipation. And she sighed.

He felt so perfect, so strong and powerful, so right.

His hand slid into the hair coiled at her nape. "I am clay in your hands," he whispered.

She somehow glanced up. "No. It's all right. I will find someone else to take the girls—"

He feathered her mouth with a sudden kiss, clearly on impulse, and then his eyes widened in surprise and he stepped quickly away from her. She could not move. The brief sensation of his mouth on hers had done terrible things to her body. Her blood seemed to be racing wildly through her veins, but it was no longer blood; rather, it had become a roaring, rushing river, one filled with whirlpools.

He walked away from her, lifted his shades, which had been down, and gazed out at the brown town houses lining Mulberry Street. All were brothels and saloons except for one, which was a run-down brick building that was a tenement. His beautiful Daimler motorcar was parked below, Francesca knew, for she had seen it as she had come in, guarded by two leatherheads.

Suddenly she straightened as something he had said registered in her befuddled brain. "O'Donnell?"

He did not turn. "The first victim. Her name was Kathleen O'Donnell."

"Oh, God! Bragg!" she cried, dashing to him and whirling him about by his lapels.

"What is it?" he demanded.

"Didn't you know? Didn't you know that Mary O'Shaunessy has a brother and his name is Mike O'Donnell?"

As her brougham turned into the very short driveway of her home, which was on the corner of Madison Avenue and 61st Street, and moved through the vaulted archway into an interior courtyard that had been swept free of snow and salted, Connie did not move. Neil's carriage, slightly smaller and several years older than the one he liked her to use, was parked in front of their home, and a groom was leading two bays around the back to the stable. Panic filled her.

An image of her large, muscular, handsome husband competed with Calder Hart's darkly disturbing one. In her mind's eye, Hart was smiling, the look in his eyes so suggestive there could be no mistaking his meaning, while Neil's turquoise eyes were hard with anger. Her heart lurched with dread, with fear.

What was she doing?

Why had she had lunch with Calder Hart, a notorious seducer of women?

And why, oh why, was she there now, in front of this lovely house—which no longer felt like her own?

But it was her home, Connie reminded herself, the panic growing. What Neil had done could never change that.

"Lady Montrose?"

Connie realized that Clark had been standing at the carriage door, which he had opened, for a few minutes. She suddenly saw the look in his eyes and thought it was one of pity. She flushed, realizing he must know about the

discord that was unraveling her family. But wait—there
was no discord now! She had passed a most pleasant week.
She and Neil had attended a supper and a charity ball; they
had chatted most amicably; they had even danced at the
ball, as if nothing were wrong, as if nothing had ever happened. And her sources had told her that Eliza Burton, the
woman he had taken for a lover, was booked with her boys
for a winter passage to France. She was leaving next week.
Her home was up for sale.

She surely had no time to dally with another woman's
husband now, and Neil had promised her it would never
happen again. The one thing she knew about her husband
was that his word of honor was inviolable.

Something wrenched inside of her.

"Lady Montrose?"

Connie started. His voice had sounded far away. "Yes,
Clark? I have been daydreaming," she said too brightly,
and she smiled at the coachman she had hired shortly before her wedding, and as she was assisted from the coach,
he smiled back.

But the pity remained in his eyes. Now there was no
mistaking it.

Connie held her head high and sailed across the short
distance between the coach and her front doorstep. She did
not worry about the snow or any ice—as a child she had
been taught how to walk, as if on water, with grace and
poise, no matter what.

Suddenly a memory of Francesca stomping across the
ballroom in abject defiance of their instructor made her
smile. She, Connie, had mastered the art of a noble walk
within a day, while her sister still had a tendency to march
about like a man.

As Connie reached the front door, it opened. "Thank
you, Marsters," she began, and she faltered, her air catching in her throat and choking her.

Neil had opened the door for her, instead of the door-

man. His vivid turquoise gaze held hers, steady and unwavering. He did not smile.

He knows, she thought, panicked. *He knows I have been
flirting with Calder Hart!*

Then his lips turned into a slight smile. "I have just got
in," he said, taking her arm. "Did you have a pleasant
lunch?"

She could not move and she could not smile; for one
moment, she could only stare, incapable of speech.

"Connie?" His grip tightened. He was a big man, six-
foot-four and well over two hundred pounds, but there was
no flab on his large, muscular body. And in spite of his
size, there was no mistaking that he was an aristocrat—
other men this large would look like dockworkers. Perhaps
it was his perfectly chiseled features—the straight nose,
the stunning eyes, the wide jaw and high cheekbones that
pegged him for a nobleman. Perhaps it was his carriage—
he moved with innate pride and grace. Or maybe it was
the air of authority he never shed—other men looked to
him for answers and leadership.

He had been married once before. His wife had died in
the first year of their marriage in a carriage accident.

To this day, Connie did not know whether he had loved
his first wife or not. She had never asked. The question
would not have been seemly; it would have been intrusive,
an invasion of his privacy. But she wondered, often, if he
had loved his first wife.

"Are you ill?" he asked. "You are so pale."

She brightened and somehow slipped free. For his touch
did contradictory things to her—his touch thrilled her and
frightened her both.

"I am fine. How was your day?" She moved past him,
handing off her coat and hat, her back to him now. *Did
he know?*

"My day has been a good one. Our Midland Rails
stocks continue to climb, as they have just incorporated an

important way station, Basalt. And Fontana Ironworks is going right through the roof. Today I added to the children's trusts."

Connie did not turn back to him. "I am glad," she said breathlessly. Then she glanced across the entry hall. A large and formal salon, both double mahogany doors wide open, was on her right. The room was mostly shades of gold, with emerald accents. On one ebonized table was a bronze clock—it was almost five. "I must dress for the Waldorf affair. I do believe we are to arrive at seven."

Neil did not speak. Connie wanted to peek at him in order to judge his mood—and if he knew about her luncheon with Hart—but somehow, she did not dare. She had told Francesca that the past was finished and that only the present and the future mattered now. But it was hard not to recall the past—she did so every time Neil came near.

He had promised that he would never stray again. He had only done so because he had needs, and he claimed she did not enjoy that part of their relationship. He had gone to another woman because Connie had failed him and their marriage. She hadn't meant to, but she hadn't kept count of the times they shared a bed the way that, apparently, he had.

She moved too quickly across the hall. Then she heard him falling into step behind her and she started, turning to look back at him in surprise.

His smile was soft, but it did not reach his eyes. "You have two hours . . . more. I know it does not take you that long. Let's sit in the parlor and take a glass of sherry." His gaze was searching.

She wet her lips. It was on the tip of her tongue to accept, but of course, one never imbibed before an evening affair—otherwise one might become inebriated before the evening was done. "I have a migraine. I was thinking to lie down for a half hour, and I do want to check on the girls."

"The girls are fine. Charlotte is in the kitchen, making a mess of her dinner; there are peas and jelly all over the table. Lucy is sound asleep." His gaze did not waver.

"I . . ." she started and faltered.

"Let's have a glass of sherry," he said, more firmly— and she knew it was a husbandly command.

Connie had never refused him before. An image of him with another woman came to mind, and with it the knowledge that it was all her fault. A good wife saw to her husband's needs, all of them, circumventing any chance of betrayal, disappointment, and grief.

"I have a migraine," she whispered—a blatant lie. And she did not even know herself anymore, for she did not mean to lie and she did not mean to avoid him.

Disappointment flooded his face. "I am sorry," he said, too politely. "Is there anything I can do?"

She smiled as politely—it felt brittle, like plaster. "A nap should be enough, but thank you."

He stepped back and bowed.

Relieved—horrified—she hurried up a wide oak staircase with an Oriental runner and a bronze railing. Tears seemed to fill her eyes. What was she doing? Why was she behaving this way? She glanced down from the first landing and saw him in the foyer, staring up at her, looking grim. Her heart quickened with more worry and more fear. She meant to smile down at him; instead, she looked away.

"Connie?" he called up to her.

She faltered between steps and glanced down. He was so handsome and she loved him so much that her heart hurt her with a sudden and unbearable pang. "Yes?"

"So whom did you have lunch with?" he asked.

He had canceled his plans for the evening. Suddenly his interest in an affair to support the new public library on 40th Street seemed boring as all hell, when he was an active supporter of a few select charities, mostly those connected with the arts. He had also sent word to Alfred that he wished all of the servants dismissed; Cook was to leave him his supper cooked and warmed in the kitchen, and Alfred was to open the 1882 Château Figeac and decant it.

Hart knew they thought him eccentric; he knew that, behind his back, they gossiped about his habits, his wardrobe, his women, his wealth, and his art. The housemaids tiptoed around him wide-eyed, clearly expecting him to ravish them in their tracks. (He had never and would never seduce a woman in his employ. And housemaids did not run to his taste, anyway.) Once, he had returned unexpectedly and had found several servants in the master suite, ogling the nude there, shocked and scandalized, as the oil was quite graphic. Upon realizing he was present, they had fled as if he were a cyclone and they were afraid for their lives.

He had had the most pleasant luncheon with Lady Montrose, so there was only one explanation for his humor having become foul—and that was her sharp-tongued bluestocking sister. He refused to think about Francesca Cahill now, as doing so annoyed him—he could not think of her without also thinking of his oh, so noble half brother, the epitome of virtue, Rick Bragg. How they truly deserved each other, but unfortunately, Rick was shackled by his bitch-wife, Leigh Anne.

Hart realized that his coach had stopped in front of the fifteen-room house he had just purchased. It had been built thirty years ago in the Georgian style, and it took up the corner of Fifth Avenue and 18th Street. He began to relax as he let Raoul open the door for him. He nodded at his driver, who merely grunted in reply. As Raoul slammed the carriage door shut, Hart said, "I will be several hours." He glanced at his pocket watch. It was solid gold, and diamonds glittered around the bezel. "Be back at ten P.M.," he instructed.

Raoul's answer was another grunt, but his eyes gleamed. He knew what his employer was about.

Hart's pace increased and he began to smile. He was genuinely fond of Daisy, and she was, on the surface, the most beautiful woman he had ever beheld. She was also one of the most talented in bed, and her responses were genuine. He was very pleased to have reached an arrangement with her—she would be his mistress exclusively for a six-month period, after which she would be rewarded so handsomely she could leave her life of whoring behind. Of course, they had the option of renewing their agreement in six months, but Hart knew she would be eager to remain with him. He had the tendency to tire of women within several months, and he doubted he would wish for their arrangement to continue.

He walked up the pretty stone path leading to the front steps of the red brick mansion, noting that it was icy and had yet to be salted. Daisy had only moved in yesterday; still, even though she never discussed her past, he knew she had come from a good family and there was no reason for her not to have ordered a servant to sweep and salt the path. He knocked on the door.

It was opened after several minutes. "Yes?" a butler whom he did not recognize intoned.

Hart walked in and gave the man a cold stare. "I own this house and everything in it," he said softly. "Make sure there is a doorman at this door the next time I arrive."

The butler blanched. "I am sorry, sir," he said. "Mr. Hart." He bowed.

Hart did not even ask his name. "Where is Miss Jones?"

"In the salon, sir. She is—" He stopped as Hart shrugged off his coat, which the butler promptly took. Hart handed him his gold-tipped cane, which was for show only, and strode across the unpolished beige marble floors. He knocked once, something softening just a bit inside of him, and then he stepped inside, not waiting for Daisy's response.

His response to her was almost immediate. She was standing in the middle of the half-furnished salon, clad in a stunning dress that was the palest, softest shade of pink imaginable—it matched her lips, which she never rouged, as their natural tone was perfect. Daisy was ethereal. She was slender, her skin the palest ivory, her hair the color of moonlight. She appeared fragile and delicate, but so breathtaking in beauty that sometimes it hurt to look at her face. For ultimately, it was her face that was magnificent: it was triangular, her lips lush and full and dominant, her nose small and perfect, her eyes wide and childlike. Her cheekbones were very high, hinting at some Slavic ancestry. He had never seen a man glance at her and look away—it was simply impossible.

She was also good-hearted.

Now, he studied her, noting in a glance that her dress was perfectly respectable—and that pleased him no end. He hated mistresses who flaunted their station in life. In fact, Daisy had a natural elegance—even starkly naked, her mouth on him, there was something regal and graceful about her.

She turned as he entered. Her blue eyes widened and she cried in her soft, breathy voice, a voice that was childish and belied her extreme intelligence, "Calder!"

He had already remarked the interview in progress and its nature. A heavyset middle-aged woman was seated in a gold bergère, and she had been trying to keep her expression impassive—but he also saw the distaste and disapproval in her eyes.

Daisy glided to him, smiling with genuine pleasure. "What a surprise," she whispered.

He took one of her hands and kissed it gallantly—he refused to make an open display of either his affections or his desire in front of anyone, much less a servant.

Daisy smiled into his eyes.

He smiled back briefly and then walked in front of her and met the not quite blank gaze of the seated woman. Coolly he said, "Miss Jones will not be needing your services. Thank you. You may go."

The woman stood. Her jaw clenched, she said, "But I have good references, sir."

"You are dismissed." He did not move, reminding himself of patience.

Stunned, she stood. "But I don't understand," she began.

Daisy stepped forward, her smile kind and apologetic. "I am sorry, Mrs. Heller. Apparently Mr. Hart has already filled this post, and I do apologize for the waste of your time."

Mrs. Heller gripped her purse quite tightly. "If you change your mind, the agency will know where to reach me. Of course, by then I might be employed."

"I am sure you will be," Daisy said in her soft voice while Hart stood beside her, trying to be patient, acutely aware of the proximity of her slim, perfect body.

Mrs. Heller made a sound and hurried out of the salon. Hart knew it was an effort for her not to glare back at him, but to her credit, she did not.

Daisy walked after her and closed the salon doors behind her, so that she and Hart were entirely alone.

He watched her face him, wanting to take her in that moment, against the doors. He did not.

"Calder? Why?"

"She looks down on you as a whore, and thinks me the Devil," he said quietly.

Her eyes widened. "I trust your judgment, of course," she said, and she did not continue.

"I said I would take care of you, but perhaps you did not quite understand my meaning." He sauntered toward her. "I did not mean strictly monetarily, nor did I mean strictly in matters of the flesh. She would cause you grief in the end—she was not to be trusted."

Daisy relaxed against the door. He sensed the moment her interest changed, and his own interest flared. "Thank you." She regarded him with her steady blue cat eyes.

He leaned his shoulder against the door, near her but not touching her. "A glass of champagne? I sent over a case of Dom Perignon. Did you receive it?"

She nodded, smiling slightly, and she touched his cheek, cupping it with her soft, unblemished palm. "I even chilled a bottle." She moved her thumb over his lips. "This is such a nice surprise."

"I forgot to warn you—I am a man of impulse. I should have sent word I was coming—I apologize." On that last word, he kissed the heart of her palm.

"You never have to send word," she murmured.

"I want to kiss the heart of your sex," he said as she melted against him. "You know what, don't you?"

"Yes," she said on a tight and indrawn breath.

Their eyes locked. He slid his hands over her shoulders, smiling a little, feeling the last of his annoyance melting away. "I like the dress."

She smiled, pleased. "I hope so. If ever I do anything you do not like, you must tell me," she said.

He leaned close. "We shall argue and then make up." He smiled as he kissed her.

She did not answer, as she could not. His tongue was in her mouth, exploring every wet inch of her. "This is the prelude, Daisy," he said later. "My tongue here, this way, and there, later."

When she could speak, she asked, "What about now?"

He pulled his mouth from hers, sliding his hands down her satin-clad back and over her high, ripe buttocks. Even through several layers of fabric, he separated them. "First, champagne," he murmured. "And you shall tell me about your day and the progress you are making on the house."

FIVE

Bragg strode through the precinct, barking commands to
Inspector Murphy, who trailed him. Francesca raced beside
him excitedly, Joel on her heels. A roundsman assigned to
the station house that day rushed up to Murphy, waving a
piece of paper. The tall, burly inspector snatched it from
the young man's hands. "Is this the O'Donnell address?"

"Yes, sir," the young patrolman answered, his eyes
wide and excited behind owlish eyeglasses.

"Kathleen O'Donnell's place of residence," Murphy
said, handing it to Bragg. "Before she died," he added
unnecessarily.

Bragg glanced at the paper and handed it back to him.
"Take a police wagon. Bring two men, and follow me
downtown."

"Yes, sir," Murphy said. He turned to the bespectacled
young officer. "Harold, fetch Potter and let's go. Full
gear!"

Bragg was already donning the coat he had carried over
his arm. He suddenly looked at Francesca, his severe expression changing. It softened. "Once again, well done,
Miss Cahill."

She could not smile back; she was so breathless with
excitement. Was O'Donnell related to the first victim? Was
he her husband? A brother, a cousin? Surely there was a
connection, as the coincidence was too great, his being
Mary O'Shaunessy's brother and his having the same last

name as the first murder victim! "Thank you," she said
crisply. "I am coming, Bragg."

He had been about to launch himself through the precinct's wide front doors; now, he whirled. "Absolutely not.
It is time for you to go home while I conduct police affairs
alone."

His words were a stunning blow. "But I must come!"
she cried.

This time he did not answer her, racing through the
front door. She ran after him. He could not leave her behind now!

He had not put on his gloves, which were jammed in a
coat pocket. He began to crank up the roadster's engine,
turning the lever round and round.

Joel tugged on her sleeve.

"Not now," Francesca said. "Bragg," she began.

Joel stood up on his toes and whispered, "Lady! Did
you see the paper before he crushed it? Did you see her
address?"

She started and gazed at him. "Unfortunately, I did
not."

"Too bad," he said, giving her a significant look.

The engine coughed as if it would not start, and then it
roared to life.

By now, they had attracted a crowd of gawkers and
passersby—some prostitutes and several shady-looking
men, a ragged child or two. Bragg walked briskly around
to the driver's door, opened it, and slid in, reaching for the
goggles he kept at hand. A police wagon was now halting
behind the roadster; Murphy, Harold, and another officer
were rushing down headquarters' front steps.

Francesca did not hesitate. She pulled open the passenger's door, and as Joel scooted into the narrow space behind the front seats, she leaped into the Daimler. "It is
because of the girls, Bragg. I am not taking no for an
answer." She slammed her door closed.

He was disbelieving. "I cannot put you into this kind of danger," he said. "And I will not."

"What danger?" she cried. "We are merely going to question a man about his relationship to two women."

"Two *dead* women, who were brutally *murdered*," he said with anger.

She shivered, recalling the cross carved into Mary's throat. "The knife to the throat was not what killed her, was it?" The cut had not looked that deep. How Mary had actually died had been bothering her no end.

He stared, his jaw clenching. "Francesca, good night."

It was hard to believe, but she was going to lose this round—she was going to have to leave. "I will find out, eventually. I am sure the press will go into every ghastly detail."

"She was stabbed," he said bluntly. "In the back, repeatedly."

Francesca looked at him, and as his words sank in, she shivered. "What?"

"Now do you see why I do not want you involved? And after the brutal attack, her clothes were carefully rearranged. She died slowly, Francesca—but fortunately, she would have passed out first."

Francesca stared in horror.

"Please go home," he said, suddenly weary. "I have a responsibility to the families of these two young women, and I cannot be responsible for you, too."

Francesca got out of the car. She was grim. "I want to help you, Bragg. Can I help? Perhaps in some other way? I do not want to add to your worries."

"I know you wish to help. But you will have your chance, another time."

She managed to nod, crestfallen.

Suddenly he closed his eyes, but briefly. When he opened them he said, "I may not find O'Donnell today. You know that."

She nodded.

He added, "But I will meet you at my house in two hours or so."

She realized what he meant and she started. "You will meet the girls?" she asked, stunned.

"But they cannot stay," he warned. "Except for a single night."

She wanted to hug him. Of course, she did not dare; she beamed. "In two hours then, Bragg." And never mind that she might be late for her supper and that Julia would be waiting at home, demanding to know where she had been.

He smiled a little, and she watched him drive off. The police wagon followed, pulled by a large Clydesdale horse.

"Now wut?" Joel asked peevishly.

Francesca was thoughtful, watching the Daimler turn right at the end of the block. The crowd quickly dissipated and she turned. "It is five o'clock. I think I shall make a purchase I have postponed and then go check on the girls—before Bragg returns home." Suddenly that seemed like a very good idea, just in case Peter had had a rough time taking care of them.

Joel grinned at her slyly. "But don't you want Kathleen O'Donnell's address? Don't you want to go down there an' ask her folks all kind of questions?"

She studied him, somewhat amused. "You know I do! But I cannot go now, in any case, for Bragg and the police will be there. Besides, it might take some time to learn where she lived."

"I know how to get O'Donnell's address," Joel returned with a grin.

"You do?" she asked, startled. "How?"

"Got a fiver?"

Francesca was about to open her purse; she stopped. "Surely you do not expect me to bribe a police officer for the information?"

"Best way to get it," Joel said cheerfully.

"Joel! That happens to be a criminal offense!"

"Lady, everyone pays off the spots. An' you know it. He knows it." Joel said, nodding his head in the direction Bragg had disappeared.

She stared at Joel, for one moment debating walking inside the station house, handing Captain Shea the five-dollar bill, and asking for Kathleen O'Donnell's last known address. Then she shook her head, trying to clear her spinning mind. "I will not bribe a police officer," she said firmly.

Joel held out his hand.

"What?" But she knew what he wanted and, more important, what he intended to do.

He grinned at her.

She handed him the five dollars. "Oh, dear," she said.

"Be right back," he said, and he ran up the front steps of the squat brownstone building.

The gun shop was on Sixth Avenue and 45th Street, a block lined with stores, many of them apparel stores, with a music store next door. Joel had succeeded in gaining Kathleen O'Donnell's address, which was on Avenue C, but Francesca would wait until the morning to go there—as Bragg and his men might still be at the flat, looking for clues and evidence, and Julia was expecting her for supper. Sixth Avenue was busy now; suited men, huddled up in their overcoats, top hats pulled low, were either walking briskly up- or downtown on their way home from their place of employment or leaping onto one of the electric trolleys that ran uptown. Black cabs congested the traffic, and all were occupied. An occasional gentleman's carriage or coach was visible, and one block away a series of el trains roared downtown, one after another, clearly on a rush-hour schedule.

Francesca looked at the display window, which was

filled with every kind of gun imaginable, and then she faced Joel, her pulse accelerating. She did not like guns— she never had—nor had she ever fired one. "Wait out here, and under no circumstance are you to come inside. In fact, our relationship is a suspicious one, so pretend you do not know me."

"OK," Joel said happily.

She smiled at him and because his shaggy black hair was covered by his wool cap she tugged on his earlobe affectionately; then, inhaling, for courage, she walked into the small shop. After all, she was a citizen, and everyone had the right to bear arms, so how difficult could it be to purchase a gun?

Somehow, she expected it to be difficult indeed.

Inside, it was poorly lit, but perhaps that was due to the fact that it was almost closing time and outside it was already dark. The shop contained three glass counters in the shape of a U, all filled with merchandise, and a bulky bald man with a thick black mustache was behind one of the counters. He had his back to Francesca, and was shoving something into a cabinet drawer, but as the bell on the door tinkled, he turned.

"Hello," Francesca said with false cheer, gripping her purse tightly. She did not understand her own state of nerves. Perhaps it was because she did not believe in guns—they were tools of injury and death. Yet a gun was a necessity in her new line of work; she had learned that lesson the hard way.

Of course, she would only use it as a very last resort, when placed in the gravest imaginable danger.

Francesca smiled at the owner, a plump-cheeked man of forty or so. "Good evening, sir," she said, coming forward. As she did so, she saw that the counter to her right was filled with small weapons, some extremely dainty, and as a half a dozen had pearl handles, they were clearly for ladies.

"May I help you, miss?" he asked.

"I wish to purchase a gun," she said.

"Well, that is what we do here; we sell guns." He eyed her closely. "But I have very few young ladies asking to buy for themselves. If you do not mind my asking, how old are you?"

She hesitated, thinking quickly. "I am twenty-one, sir," she fabricated. "But the gun is not for myself. My sister wishes to learn to shoot, and as her birthday is dawning, I have decided to buy her a gun. She is Lady Montrose," she added.

Most Americans were in awe of nobility, and he was no exception. Connie's title gave him pause, and respectfully he said, "I have read about Lord and Lady Montrose in the social columns. So you are her sister?"

Francesca smiled. "I am Francesca Cahill."

It was a small town, in a way, and she knew he was familiar with her last name, as his eyes widened slightly. Her father was very wealthy, although it hadn't always been that way—as a boy, he had grown up on a farm, and he had worked in a butcher shop before he had acquired it himself. That had led him into meatpacking, and at the age of twenty-three Andrew Cahill had begun his first meatpacking plant.

"Well, let us look at some guns, then." The salesman smiled.

She walked to the counter filled with pearl-handled derringers and other small pistols. He followed. "Sir? What about that little one with the silvery pearl handle?"

He smiled at her and said, "The handle is opal. What kind of shooting does your sister wish to do?" He unlocked the case and removed the tiny gun.

Francesca accepted the gun from him. It was so small, it was the size of her hand. It weighed perhaps a half a pound, surely not an ounce more. She lifted it and pointed it at the mirror on the other side of the room. This gun would be easy to use.

"This will do nicely indeed," she breathed, suddenly fascinated. It was beautiful, actually, and it would fit inside her purse easily. "I think she merely wants to own a gun, in case she ever needs one for protection," Francesca added as he stared at her.

He softened. "Well, then perhaps that derringer will do. If your sister wished to become a marksman, I would not recommend it. But if she wants a pretty bauble, why, this is perfect for her. Shall I gift-wrap it?"

"That would be wonderful," Francesca said, thinking that no one would ever suspect she was carrying a gun if it was in the box and in a shopping bag. It crossed her mind that he had referred to a weapon of death as a pretty bauble, but then she dismissed the thought. After all, this salesman was used to handling weapons, and compared to the huge and threatening revolvers in the other cases, not to mention the hunting rifles mounted on the walls, he would consider such a pistol a bauble indeed.

It had been so easy!

A tiny warning voice told her it had been too easy, but she ignored it.

Outside, Joel was waiting for her, watching the passersby, his back against the storefront window, one foot up on the brick. Francesca smiled at him. "Mission accomplished," she said lightly.

"Let me see what you got!" he cried eagerly, coming off of the wall.

She held up the box, which was wrapped in a pretty red, white, and blue paper. She had asked not to use the store's wrap so that her sister would be genuinely surprised by the contents of the box; he had told her most of his customers preferred not to have AL'S GUN SHOP emblazoned on their box or bag. "I shall sneak it home this way," she said, feeling rather triumphant.

Joel was clearly disappointed that he would not have an opportunity to admire her new gun. "Can I see it tomorrow?"

"Of course." She took his arm. "I am off to Bragg's. Shall I put you in a cab and send you home? We can meet early tomorrow and continue our work then."

"Wut time?"

"How does nine o'clock sound? I can meet you directly at Kathleen O'Donnell's."

They agreed to meet at nine. "I'll take the crosstown," he said. "Why waste the dough?"

"Are you sure?" Francesca had begun when a voice said, "Miss Cahill! What are you doing down here, on Sixth and Forty-fifth?"

She recognized the male voice, although she had only met its owner twice. Reluctantly she turned to face Richard Wiley, a tall, thin man who had thought to court her and who was blushing furiously now. "Why, Mr. Wiley, what a pleasant surprise," she said.

Francesca knocked on the door to Bragg's house again— for the third time. Some anxiety filled her—in the past, the door had been opened by Peter almost the very moment she arrived on the stoop. Now she wondered what could be taking him so long. Then she told herself that no one answered the door so promptly all of the time.

Suddenly he was standing in front of her, his expression inscrutable.

"Peter!" she cried in relief. "Is everything all right? How are the girls?"

"Everything is fine," he said, glancing past her. Then he added, "You did not bring the nanny."

She blinked at him, as they had never had a conversation before. Did this mean he was eager to relinquish his temporary job as the girls' caretaker? "I haven't had time to hire one," she said. "I am meeting Bragg here shortly.

Where are they?" she asked, stepping inside.

"The kitchen." He closed the door behind her.

Francesca could guess where the kitchens were, and she walked through a small dining room that had been painted a soft moss green, a dark oak table and six chairs in the middle of it. She opened the kitchen door and faltered.

Both girls sat at the small pine table, which was a mess. Clearly Dot had been playing with her food, and applesauce, peas, and mashed potatoes were smeared everywhere. Katie sat beside her, potato clinging to her hair, a plate of food in front of her, which, while mushed and mashed, was so full it could not have been touched.

Katie sat like a soldier at attention, neither moving, smiling, nor speaking. In fact, she might have been a porcelain doll.

Dot saw them in the doorway and shrieked happily, then flung a drumstick at them.

Francesca ducked and the drumstick ricocheted off of Peter's broad chest.

She bit her lip and looked at him. "Oh, dear."

He said, "The brown-haired one won't eat."

"Her name is Katie," Francesca said, now realizing that milk had been spilled on the floor. It lay in a puddle by Katie's feet and Dot's chair.

Peter picked up the drumstick and walked past the girls and deposited it in a trash container by the large iron sink.

"Bragg is going to be home shortly, Peter," Francesca said with real fear. "If he sees this mess, he will never agree to let the girls stay here!" Then she realized that Peter might not want them, either, and stared at him as she hurried forward, but his attention seemed to be on the mop he was reaching for. "Peter? Are you certain you are all right?"

He gave her a brief look, one impossible to read as it was completely detached, and he approached the puddle.

As he began to mop, Francesca smiled at both girls. "Hello, Katie, Dot."

Dot clapped her hands and grinned, mostly toothlessly, and then she dug her fist into her sister's mashed potatoes.

Katie acted as if she had not heard Francesca's greeting. But her brow was knit, with either anger or determination.

"Dot, we do not play with food," Francesca said, removing both plates at once and depositing them in the sink. She found a rag and returned to the table as Dot laughed and threw food on the floor. "Katie, you did not eat."

Katie turned sullen eyes on her and said nothing.

"Miss Cahill, I will do that," Peter said.

"That is quite all right, as I am partly responsible for this mess and their behavior." She quickly wiped up all the food.

"Miss Cahill, I shall clean the kitchen. You take the girls," Peter said.

Francesca was about to argue when she realized that it would be faster this way—as the girls did need some cleaning up. "All right. Here we go, Dot," she said, lifting the small two-year-old up into her arms. Dot wrapped her skinny arms around Francesca's neck and said, "Nice. Mmm. Nice."

Francesca smiled against Dot's greasy cheek, suddenly hugging her a bit. "Yes, this is very nice, and you are a very sweet little girl."

Dot giggled.

"Except for the food throwing. We do not play with or throw food." She tried to sound stern.

"Sh . . . sh . . . sh . . . " Dot said.

"Sh?" Francesca returned.

"Sh!" Dot cried, and it was a demand.

"I do not know what 'sh' means, but I am certain I will find out. Katie? Let's go. Bragg will be back, and we must clean up."

Katie did not move. Her lower lip seemed to protrude even more.

"Katie? I am speaking to you," Francesca said, trying to be both stern and kind at once.

Suddenly Katie leaped to her feet and ran from the room.

Francesca stared after her in amazement.

"Kay-tie!" Dot shouted. "Kay-tie!" Clearly she was upset.

"Miss Cahill? The motorcar," Peter said, wiping the now-spotless table with a wet towel.

"He is back?" Francesca whispered, aghast. Their gazes met. Francesca did not wait for his reply; she dashed to the kitchen sink, reaching for a faucet. "Be a good girl, now," she tried.

"Kay-tie?"

Francesca shoved one hand after another into warm water, somehow lathering them with soap. She heard the faint sound of the roadster's door slamming.

Dot made a whistling sound, smearing Francesca's cheek with soap.

Francesca slid her to the floor and with a clean wet towel tried to remove food from the child's face and hair. Dot grinned at her and grabbed one end of the towel, tugging on it.

"Not now," Francesca managed, wetting another piece and scrubbing her mouth. Mistakenly, in her rush she was too harsh.

Tears filled Dot's big blue eyes.

"Don't cry," Francesca whispered, dismayed, as she heard footsteps in the dining room.

"Peter?" Bragg's voice drifted to her.

Peter gave her a look; then he hurried from the kitchen, clearly waylaying his employer to give Francesca more time.

"I am sorry; don't cry," Francesca whispered, her finger brushing the child's golden curls.

Dot slapped Francesca's hand away, her lower lip pouting.

Francesca glanced wildly around, and to her amazement, the kitchen seemed fresh and clean—except for the gooey dishes in the sink.

Bragg stepped onto the kitchen's threshold. "So you are here."

She whirled, pulling Dot to stand in front of her, smiling. And then, as their eyes met, her tension vanished. Suddenly acutely aware of the child she held by the shoulders, the man facing her, and the kitchen they stood in, she was struck by the domesticity of the scene. "Hello, Bragg."

But this scenario would never belong to them.

He was smiling at her, and then his gaze went to Dot. His eyes softened even more. "What a pretty child," he said.

"She is very . . . sweet," Francesca returned, praying Dot would return to her normal, ebullient self.

"Why is she crying?"

"I was washing her face," Francesca said.

"I see."

"Kay-tie!" Dot suddenly screamed. And her voice was so loud it was as if a siren had gone off in the room.

Bragg winced. "What the hell was that?"

Francesca lifted Dot into her arms. "She wants her sister. Let's go find Katie, Dot," she said brightly.

Dot grinned brightly, the mood change instantaneous. "Find," she ordered. "Find!"

"Yes, we will find Katie now," Francesca said. She approached Bragg with the child clinging to her neck. As he fell into step beside her, she saw Dot's expression change. Suspicion covered her features as she stared at him.

"This is my friend, and his name is Rick," Francesca

said quickly, afraid that Dot was about to become upset. "He is a good friend, Dot. Katie?" she called.

There was no answer. They were crossing the dining room, Dot continuing to regard Bragg darkly.

"I do not think she likes me," he said.

"She likes everyone," Francesca said quickly. "She is an adorable little girl. Katie?" They paused in the entry hall as she tried again.

"It is odd, seeing you with a child this way," Bragg said.

She started and their eyes connected. "Why?" she managed. Had he felt as she had?

"It makes me think of you as a mother," he said, and he seemed rather grim.

Her heart turned over, hard and uncomfortably. "Do you want children, Bragg?"

"I did. Not anymore," he said.

His answer was hardly a surprise. But he would be a wonderful role model for a son and a wonderful father to a little girl; Francesca just knew it. Still, she was too selfish to advise him to have children, although surely one day he would. Perhaps by then she would be accustomed to the fact that he had a wife.

"I wish she would stop glaring at me," Bragg remarked.

Francesca realized that Dot *was* glaring at him, and she stroked her hair. "Dot? Bragg is my friend. He is your friend. Friend. Do you know what that means?"

"Find," Dot cried angrily. "Find find find!"

"We had better find her sister. Katie?" Bragg called.

They walked down the hall, toward the parlor. Two wall sconces illuminated the way. "On that subject, what did you find out at Kathleen O'Donnell's?" Francesca asked.

"That she worked hard, that she was a good mother to her child, that she attended church every Sunday," Bragg said. He shoved open the parlor door. "Katie?" But the salon was empty. "She was also a seamstress by trade."

Francesca halted and stared at him. "Two murder victims, both seamstresses? Is this a coincidence?"

"I don't know."

"Did you learn who Mike O'Donnell is?" Francesca asked.

"He is her husband," Bragg said.

Francesca felt her eyes widen. "Well, that is getting us somewhere."

"But apparently, they have not lived together as man and wife in several years," Bragg added.

Her mind sped. "So she was a seamstress raising a child alone? But that is just like Mary!"

"Yes, it is quite similar," Bragg said.

"Do you know where her husband is?" she asked after a moment.

"He is a longshoreman, but no, no one knows his place of residence or employment. I have put men on it already. We will find him eventually if he is anywhere in the vicinity of the docks."

His study door faced them. It was solidly closed. "She would not be in there," Francesca began. "Katie?" she called toward the upstairs, now becoming worried.

"Kay-tie, Kay-tie, Kay-tie," Dot chanted. She started to sniffle, as if about to sob.

"We will find Katie," Francesca said quickly, stroking Dot's back, as Bragg pushed open the study door.

"No one," he began, and stopped.

Francesca knew he had found Katie, and peered past him.

The study was cast entirely in shadow, as not a single light was on. A small human form was hunched over in the far corner by the fireplace, and it was Katie, sitting absolutely still, hugging her knees to her chest.

"Katie," Francesca said, saddened by the sight. She entered the room, Bragg following her and turning on a lamp.

"Katie? Are you all right?" Francesca asked softly.

"Kay-tie!" Dot screamed.

Katie might not have heard them, she was so still and motionless.

Francesca felt Bragg regarding the tableau from behind her. She slid Dot to her feet, praying Katie would act like a normal child—at least for now. "Hello, Katie. My, it is dark in here. What are you doing by yourself? Would you like some company?"

Katie lifted her head and stared coldly at her. She did not speak.

"Kay-tie!" Dot whooped. She swooped in on her sister.

"I can see this shall not be an easy night," Bragg said flatly.

Francesca glanced at him. "They are no trouble, really, Bragg."

He just looked at her, not angry, but clearly not pleased. "I am hardly a fool, Francesca."

"They just need some time to adjust," she tried.

"One night," he warned. Suddenly his expression changed. He paled. "What is she doing?" he cried.

Francesca turned.

Dot was squatting, and as she peed on the Oriental carpet, she beamed at them both.

"I am so sorry about that," Francesca said, a good half an hour later. Both girls were tucked together into blankets and sheets on the floor in a small, unfurnished spare bedroom. Peter was reading them a story—unfortunately, it was from the *Iliad*. However, Dot seemed rapt even if she did not understand a word, while Katie had yet to speak.

"So am I. I liked that rug," Bragg said as they entered the foyer.

"The rug is hardly ruined," Francesca returned.

"Well, it was an accident. I am sure it will not happen again." He carried her coat in his hands.

Francesca smiled at him. How to tell him that Dot

clearly was not used to a toilet? To prevent future accidents, behind Bragg's back she had found a napkin, intending to use it as a diaper, but Dot had taken one look at the white fabric and she had screamed, giving in to a two-year-old temper tantrum. She had won; Francesca had not pinned the napkin on her. "They have just lost their mother. Katie is grief-stricken, I think. But Dot is adorable, in spite of her little accident. Isn't she?"

Bragg sighed. "Please try to place them tomorrow," he said, helping her on with her coat.

Tomorrow was Saturday. Francesca knew she needed a good week to find them a proper home—at least. "I will do my best," she said staunchly, shrugging into the sleeves. She was standing beside a small table that contained a lamp, a mirror above. As she found her sleeves, something fell to the floor. "Oh, I am sorry," Francesca said, glancing down.

Bragg was already retrieving what was clearly the day's mail. He stood, a handful of envelopes in hand. "Peter is not himself today," he remarked. "He always puts my mail on my desk."

Francesca merely smiled about him, thankful no end that he had not seen the kitchen before it had been cleaned up. Then she realized one more envelope lay on the floor, and she quickly scooped it up. As she did so, the stamp on the front caught her eye; the letter had been posted from Le Havre, France.

Was it from Leigh Anne? It was addressed to Bragg, obviously, and the cursive was so elegant it could only be from a woman. Francesca turned over the envelope and the words on its back swam in her eyes:

Mrs. Rick Bragg

It was from his wife. Francesca could only gawk at the envelope. In fact, she could not even seem to think.

She felt as if someone had landed a rude blow between her eyes.

She was stunned.

"Francesca?"

"Oh!" She smiled and handed him the envelope; suddenly her hand was shaking.

"What's wrong?" he asked sharply.

"Nothing," she said, the smile plastered on her face. Now her mind raced. It hardly mattered if he had received word from his wife. For all Francesca knew, Leigh Anne wrote to him on a regular basis. Or perhaps the envelope contained her bills. Or a request for more funds. It did not mean anything at all!

They despised each other, and they had not seen each other in four years, Francesca reminded herself.

"Come, let me get you a cab." He took her arm and they left the house. "Are you certain you are all right?"

"I am fine," she lied, because a sick and terrible feeling consumed her now.

She knew, she just knew, that the letter was significant—and that no good would come of it.

In fact, quite the opposite.

SIX

Julia was waiting for her.

Her mother always dressed for supper, and she walked out of the yellow salon as Francesca left the hall. Tonight Julia's gown was a watered-beige silk, so simple that it was marvelously elegant. Francesca smiled, acutely aware of the gun inside her purse. But she was not about to relinquish it to a maid; she was afraid the purse might fall or somehow come open, revealing its contents.

Julia studied her and said, "You are just in time. I am afraid to ask where you have been all day."

"I have been making plans for the Ladies Society for the Eradication of Tenements," Francesca said. The excuse just popped into her mind. She had founded the society a month ago, and thus far there were only two members, herself and Calder Hart.

Julia's expression softened. "I heard that Calder Hart gave you a very generous donation, Francesca."

For one moment, Francesca could not believe her mother had somehow learned of his check, but then, Julia knew everything of importance in the city's uppermost circles. Then Francesca realized that Connie had been with her when he had handed her his stunning gift. "Connie told you?"

"Yes, she did." Julia smiled. "You know, Hart is an avid supporter of the arts—he donates generously to several of the city's museums, and he has given to the public library twice, I think. He also gave a scholarship to Columbia University for their Beaux-Arts program last fall. But he does not give political contributions, and it is a fact. He adamantly refuses to join any party or support any political candidate—much to everyone's frustration. He also does not support reform. Many have sought aid from him for their various causes. I even approached him for a contribution to the Lenox Hill Hospital, and he politely refused."

Francesca flushed. "Well, he has decided to support this cause."

"He must be taken with you, Francesca," Julia said, pleased.

"Oh, balderdash."

"He gave you five thousand dollars. That is a tremendous sum."

"Mama, please! Hart is not taken with any one woman; his reputation is based on fact, not fiction. He is a ladies' man, Mama," Francesca said. She plopped down on the closest sofa, still clutching her purse too tightly, still too aware of her new gun. She felt like telling her mother that Connie was his next prey, but of course she would never do such a thing.

"Well, I for one am pleased that you have met him and somehow captured his attention," Julia said. "But you have been gone all day. Surely you were not making plans for your newest society the entire time?"

Francesca blinked at her. Was her mother now tracking her movements? If she was, Francesca was in trouble indeed. She hesitated. "The commissioner has taken in two orphans. He asked me if I would look in on them as he could not get home to do so, and I did."

"Two orphans!" Julia exclaimed. "Rick Bragg has taken in two orphans?"

"He also asked me to hire a nanny. Mama, might you recommend an agency?"

"Of course I shall. There is only one that you should go to, as they have the finest help in the city. It is called Mansfield's Butlers and Maids. Most of the servants they represent are British, and they are impeccably trained."

"Thank you, Mama," Francesca said. She would go to the agency first thing in the morning, before she met Joel.

"Well, let's call your father and go in to supper. I hear you are going to the theater tomorrow night with your brother, Miss Channing, her cousin, and Rick Bragg. That should be an amusing evening. It is a nice group."

Francesca stood. "Evan mentioned our plans?"

"He did."

Francesca hadn't known that Sarah had a cousin who was joining them, but she hardly cared. "I have wanted to see this musical ever since it first opened," she said, praying her mother would not remark on Bragg's being in their group.

"Too bad you did not invite Hart," she commented as they left the salon. Then, before Francesca could reply, she said, "You are clutching your bag as if it contains gold."

Francesca inhaled sharply. "Mama, I must go upstairs, but I shall be down in a moment."

"Why don't you invite Hart?" she said.

Francesca met her gaze. "You know, that is a good idea," she lied.

Julia beamed.

Francesca turned and hurried out of the hall, her bag—with its gun—in her hand. Of course, she was not about to invite Hart to join them. It would ruin the evening. He and Bragg would probably murder each other—or at least come to blows.

SATURDAY, FEBRUARY 8, 1902 — 11:00 A.M.

Francesca and Joel slowly walked toward Water Street. Ahead, three large cargo ships, all under steam, were visible at several busy piers. A tugboat was chugging past, guiding an old-fashioned schooner that had seen far better days. The air was salty-sweet and crisp, and blocks of ice floated on the East River.

The narrow side street they were on was dirt; now it was rutted and frozen. The sidewalks were board, and as they made their way down them they passed saloon after saloon. There was no other kind of commercial establishment present, at least not on the street.

Two drunken sailors stumbled out of the closest bar, lurching precariously close to them. Francesca grabbed Joel's hand and she halted, watching as the sailors made their way to and then across the street. A lone rider almost ran them down.

"Is this it?" Francesca asked. "Kathleen's cousin said the saloon Mike O'Donnell frequents has no name."

"Can't see any sign," Joel said, squinting up at the building that was made of rough wood siding. It looked cheap, disreputable, and as if it might come down at any moment. They had thus far learned that Mike did work on the docks, but that he picked up whatever labor he could, by the piece. Kathleen's cousin, an older man named Doug Barrett, had said the only thing he knew for sure about Mike O'Donnell was that he loved to drink and that there were a dozen bars just past Water Street favored by him and his kind.

Doug also hadn't had any idea if Kathleen remained in touch with her husband.

"Shall we go in?" Francesca asked, pretending to herself that she was not apprehensive.

"I'll go in," Joel said. "An' I'll bring him out."

They had done this before when faced with other disreputable and possibly dangerous establishments. Francesca nodded, and as Joel walked in she slid her hand into her coat pocket, where she had put her gun.

Gripping the dainty handle made her feel a bit better, but not much.

The lone rider, a man who was clearly not a gentleman, although his horse was quite nice, had reached the end of the street. He turned abruptly and started riding directly toward Francesca.

Her breath caught in her throat. She was vaguely aware of a group of men entering an adjacent saloon. Did that rider wish to speak to her? And for God's sake, why?

His bay horse skittered as he came up beside her. Francesca's eyes felt wide; she stared.

He grinned at her, broke into a canter, and went on past.

Thank God! For one moment, she had thought him about to accost her.

Francesca moved quickly closer to the side of the building, as if that might hide her presence in this unsavory neighborhood. As she did so, a man turned the corner by Water Street and started up the block where she was standing.

His bulk seemed familiar, but she was nervous and clearly not of sound mind. Francesca studied the ground, wishing Joel would come out of the saloon.

"Well, well, fancy meetin' you here, Miss Cahill."

She would recognize that voice anywhere—because she would never forget his accosting her and kissing her. Francesca started, meeting Gordino's gaze. Real fear seized her.

He grinned, and it was leering. "All by yorself? Hey, you must be. The spot you're so fond of would never leave you alone on the street like this."

She heard herself say, "Hello, Mr. Gordino. How are you?"

He burst into rough laughter. "So now it's Mr. Gordino? When before it was like, Mr. Murderer, Mr. Rough, Mr. Get Away From Me?"

She had nowhere to back up to. "I am sorry for any past misunderstanding," she whispered. "You were a go-between and we mistook you for the Burton boy's abductor."

He shoved his face close to hers, with his foul breath and pockmarked skin. " 'Cause of you an' your lover, I spent too many nights to count in the Tombs. I owe you one, Miss Cahill." His eyes were black and dangerous.

"I am sorry," she said. "A little boy's life was at stake—"

He cut her off. "An' I owe Bragg. He'll get his. Oh ho, I look forward to givin' it to him." With a savage smile, he whirled and shoved past her, knocking her hard into the wall as he did.

She did not cry out. She could only stand there, breathless with fear, until he disappeared into another saloon, and even then, there was no relief.

Oh, dear. Clearly she had made an enemy while solving the Burton Abduction. It was almost impossible to believe. Francesca had never had an enemy before, and especially not one who was a dangerous thug.

"Lady?"

Francesca turned in abject relief at the sound of Joel's voice. Then she stiffened, face-to-face with a man who was perhaps thirty, with a shock of pale blond hair, bleached by the sun and the sea, and sun-bronzed skin that was weathered and rough-looking. "Mr. O'Donnell?"

"That's me," he said, and he did not seem drunk, never mind that he had been located in a saloon before noon.

"I am so sorry about your wife," she said, watching him closely.

He folded his arms. "Yeah? Why?" he challenged bitterly.

"Why? Because she did not deserve her fate, and she left behind a young girl." Her child had already been sent to an orphan asylum. Francesca had learned that Kathleen's murder had taken place on January 10.

She hadn't even known Bragg then. They had met on the eighteenth.

Mike O'Donnell shrugged. "Fate's fate."

Francesca inhaled. "Can we ask you a few questions?"

"Why?"

She felt like telling him, "Because your sister and your wife were murdered in the exact same way!" Instead, she said, "Maggie Kennedy is a good friend of mine."

There was no reaction to Maggie's name from Mike.

"She was very close with your sister, Mr. O'Donnell."

"Yeah? So what's it to me?" He shrugged and started toward the saloon entrance.

"Your sister and your wife are dead—both murdered—within the span of a month. I must ask you some questions!" Francesca cried, rushing after him.

"Only if you buy me a drink. I got one hour and I'm back to work." He did not look back at her.

Francesca started, looking at Joel, who seemed uncertain what to do. "Don't worry," she said. "It's quite all right." She patted his shoulder and hurried inside after O'Donnell, with Joel behind her.

The saloon was crude. A rough oak bar was on one side of the large room, some stairs directly beside it. A woman's laughter came from upstairs. Inside, Francesca saw five rickety tables, all square, all occupied. A very large man was tending the bar. Clearly he could toss out any patron that he wished, in spite of his age—he was in his fifties, she thought.

O'Donnell was at the bar. Francesca went to stand beside him. The white-haired bartender stared, but not quite curiously. O'Donnell said, "The lady's buying."

The bartender put glasses down in front of them both. He poured what appeared to be whiskey into them.

O'Donnell lifted his, smiled sourly at Francesca, and belted down his shot. The bartender poured instantly.

"When did you last see your wife, Mr. O'Donnell?" Francesca asked, removing a notepad and lead pencil from her purse.

He eyed her accoutrements, then said, "Dunno. A year.

Two." He shrugged. "Why? You think I done it?"

She blinked, taken by surprise. "I never said that."

He grinned and sipped his second shot.

"You did not visit your daughter on a regular basis?" She had already noted that both murder victims had daughters, not sons.

"Nope." He eyed her over the rim of his glass. "Kathleen didn't want me around. Said I was a bad influence."

Francesca tried to determine if he had cared at all about his wife or what she had said, but he seemed absolutely indifferent. "When was the last time you saw your daughter? I believe her name was Margaret."

"Dunno." He finished the shot.

"Can you try to remember?" she asked.

"It was a long time ago!" he exploded. "But it was the winter, maybe just before Christmas, or was it before Thanksgiving? Last year, the year before, I don't know!" He was angry now. He shoved his glass toward the bartender, who promptly filled it up.

Francesca said, "I am not trying to upset you. What about Mary? How often did you see her?"

Not looking at her, he said, "From time to time. Maybe every week or so."

She could not tell if he was lying. "So you were close."

He looked at her. "I didn't say that."

She hesitated—if he didn't care about his own daughter, would he care about his nieces? "Dot and Katie need a new home now that their mother is dead."

He eyed her. "An' I hope they find it."

She met his blue gaze. Did this man have any compassion inside him at all?

He returned her gaze, sighing loudly. "I don't know why they're both dead. But don't pin the rap on me! I didn't have nuthin' to do with either of 'em. An' I'm a busy man. I got no time for the girls." He was defensive.

"I never said you had anything to do with either your

wife's or your sister's murder. I hadn't even thought such a thing," Francesca said, a vast lie.

His face became anguished. "I'm sorry. I'm sorry for 'em both!" Suddenly he cradled his head with both hands. "I wouldn't kill Kathleen. I . . . loved her. She's the one who hated me. I never wanted to go. She wanted me out." He did not look up.

"I am sorry," Francesca said, meaning it. "Have the police spoken to you?"

His eyes widened fractionally, and then he recovered his poise. "No."

Francesca bit her lip. She was going to have to tell Bragg that she had found O'Donnell. He would not be very happy that she had been the one to locate him.

"I ain't talkin' to the fuckin' leatherheads," he said harshly. "They're all scum, every last sotted one of 'em."

"Don't you want to find Kathleen's killer?" Francesca asked. "Mary's?"

"People die here every day. Every day, every hour. Most of 'em meet a rude end. No one's goin' to find out who killed Kathleen or Mary. Why bother? They wasn't like you." He gave her a hard look. "They were just poor Micks. The leatherheads ain't gonna care to find out who done it." He glared now at the bartender.

The bartender refilled his half-empty shot.

But Mike O'Donnell did not reach for it. His gaze held Francesca's, and he seemed angry.

"I have one more question," she managed after a short pause.

He made a disparaging sound.

She took it to mean "yes." "Do you have any idea who might have wanted Kathleen or Mary dead?"

He pushed off the bar. "You mean, do I know who killed them? The answer is no. But I know who hated my wife. Oh, yeah."

"Who?"

He grinned. "Her boyfriend, Sam Carter."

Joel had insisted upon waiting outside, never mind the cold. Francesca knew him well enough, as she left him hanging about the front steps of police headquarters, to know that he hated the police and had no desire to go into the station. She waved at Captain Shea as she crossed the reception room. He was speaking to a citizen, another officer in blue serge beside him. Shea saw her, smiled, and waved her on through.

Francesca looked away and *whomp!* She collided with another person.

"I am so sorry," she began, disengaging herself from the man.

"Hello, Miss Cahill," Arthur Kurland said.

Her smile vanished.

"What? You are not thrilled to see me?" the reporter from the *Sun* asked with a grin. He was of medium build and height, dark-haired, about thirty. He was a man she should never underestimate.

"How pleased I am to see you," Francesca recovered.

"So, you are visiting your 'friend' the police commissioner?"

"Is that a crime? Or a newsworthy tidbit?" She was far colder than she meant to be. She did not want him to know how she disliked him—and even feared him.

"It is not a crime, and right now, I doubt it is newsworthy." He was as relaxed as she was not. "You know, Miss Cahill, I do admire you. For your fortitude, intelligence, and all the good works you are involved in."

Francesca stiffened. "Have you been investigating *me*?"

He smiled. "How could I write the story I did without doing a bit of background on you? You are a *most* interesting woman. I can well understand why a man like Bragg would find your friendship so essential."

He did not inflect on the word "friendship," but his meaning was clear. She started past him. "I must go."

"In a hurry?" He followed her.

"Yes, I am." She did not look at him now.

"Well, the biggest news to hit this city is the O'Shaunessy and O'Donnell murders."

She whirled, facing him. Of course he would have linked the two murders.

His smile widened. "Are you aiding the police yet again? Perhaps you have missed your true calling in life, Miss Cahill. Perhaps you should become an investigator, instead of a reform activist?"

"This is a social call, nothing more."

"Bragg has taken in O'Shaunessy's girls. How odd."

"You are despicable!" she cried. "Can you not leave anyone's life alone?"

His gaze locked with hers. "But what do you have to hide?"

She inhaled sharply and loudly.

He did not move.

She whirled, and even though the elevator was available, she fled past its cage, having no desire to leap in and become trapped there with Kurland. She gripped the banister and ran up the stairs and down the hall to Bragg's office. Today the door was solidly closed.

The top half was a thick frosted glass that she could not see through. She leaned on the wall beside it, panting and breathless. If Kurland did not guess her feelings for Bragg already, he soon would. He was too determined and too astute and, worse, far too unscrupulous to not use that information one day, somehow.

She wanted to cry. She must guard her secret at all costs. No, she must guard *their* secret!

An image of the envelope addressed to Bragg with his wife's title on the back assailed her mind's eye. She faced his door grimly and knocked.

"Come in."

His voice warmed her thoroughly. She pushed open the door and saw him standing near his desk, speaking to a big, brawny man with a head of thick gray hair. The badge on his blue uniform was inescapable—so this was the new chief of police, Brendan Farr.

He did not look like a corrupt officer now. He had an air of authority and power, and he seemed more than respectful toward Bragg.

"Francesca." Bragg seemed surprised to see her. Then his surprise vanished and his amber eyes warmed. His look was enough to melt her bones. "Farr, Miss Cahill. As I am certain you know, she was indispensable to the solutions of both the Burton Abduction and the Randall Killing."

Farr extended his hand. "I have read all about you. You are a brave little lady, Miss Cahill. Imagine that. Capturing a killer with a fry pan. Who would have thought?" He smiled. Francesca had opened her long wool overcoat, and his gaze slid over her chest, in spite of the fact that her fitted jacket was buttoned to the throat, with a touch of white silk peeping past the lapels.

While his words were pleasant enough—except for the "little lady" part—Francesca sensed that condescension hung behind them. She smiled sweetly. "Thank you."

"Sir," Farr said. "The moment we resolve this matter, I will be the first to let you know. And I shall do so personally," he added.

"Thank you," Bragg said.

Farr left. Bragg and Francesca remained silent until he had closed the door behind him. She turned. "I found O'Donnell," she said abruptly.

"What?" His eyes widened. Then, "I thought we had agreed that you were not to become involved in this case."

"Actually, I never agreed to any such thing. Have you forgotten that Mary tried to come to me for help before she was murdered? Not to mention that I promised Maggie

Kennedy I would solve the murder of her friend." She folded her arms firmly across her chest.

"What am I going to do with you?" he asked darkly.

"You admire me because I am intelligent and determined. You have said so yourself."

He was silent, but only for a moment. His golden gaze slipped over her. "That is true. But what do my feelings have to do with anything now? This murderer is extremely dangerous, Francesca. And you know that. I do not want you hurt," he added.

She was always pleased when he worried about her, but now she was unsettled, Kurland's presence downstairs disturbing her, as did the letter he had received from his wife and the fact that two women had been gruesomely murdered and they still did not know why. She sighed. "Do you want to know what O'Donnell said?"

He studied her for another moment. "Yes."

She smiled. "We found him in a saloon by Water Street. I do not know whether he is a killer or not, but he claims to have loved Kathleen—and he claims not to recall when he last saw her. He said her boyfriend, Sam Carter, hated her. He gave me the name of the warehouse where he works."

"I have had twelve men scouring the docks, attempting to locate O'Donnell. They have been at it since yesterday afternoon, but you have succeeded where the professionals have not. I wish to be exasperated. Instead, I find myself resigned."

She plucked his sleeve. "I am a young woman. People like O'Donnell don't mind talking to me, or if they do not wish to speak to me, they are eager to speak to Joel, as he is one of them."

Their eyes locked. Francesca did not drop her hand from his arm. A long moment ensued in which neither of them moved. Finally, she let her palm fall to her side.

"What am I going to do with you?" he finally murmered.

She was a heartbeat away from walking into his arms and saying, "Just kiss me." She remained utterly still—and it was a terrible battle that she waged. Finally she murmured as softly, "We make a wonderful team."

"We do."

"I like working with you."

"So do I." He was grim.

"No one has to know."

"Francesca . . ."

"Bragg! You love me because I am this way. You would not want me to become a wallflower."

He began to smile. "We have enough wallflowers—and debutantes—in this city as it is. I wish more of the women in town were as original and concerned about our issues and affairs as you."

She also smiled. Victory was at hand.

He brushed a tendril of golden hair away from her eyes. "I suppose no harm has been done . . . yet."

"I will stay out of danger," she promised fervently. She debated telling him about her gun and decided against it. He might not be as enthused as she.

"Is that a promise?"

"Yes."

He nodded and suddenly he took her hand and pressed it, knuckle side up, to his lips.

It was stunning, what such a simple and chaste kiss could do. Francesca felt its heat all the way through the core of her body and to her toes. She realized, in that moment, that not having him was unacceptable. She loved him—he loved her. It was a tragedy that he had an awful wife. But should that fact bar them from finding happiness?

"What is it?" he asked.

She slipped her hand free of his, stepping back, stunned by her treacherous thoughts—and by the new rationale that had stolen unwanted into her mind. "Nothing."

Surely she was not thinking in such a manner now.

He clearly did not believe her. His dark brown brows were raised skeptically.

She wet her lips and smiled. "How are the girls?"

"I don't know. I left the house at six-thirty this morning; they were still asleep." His eyes sparkled. "As was Peter. He is *always* up at five."

Francesca had a feeling that all had not gone well last night at 11 Madison Square. Bragg walked past her now, taking his brown overcoat from a wall peg, ignoring the hat hanging beside it. "Shall we?"

"Where are we going?" she asked, with growing excitement.

"To find Sam Carter," he said.

SEVEN

The warehouse where Sam Carter worked was on the West Side of the city on 21st Street. They took a cab, which was far less conspicuous than Bragg's motorcar. Inspector Murphy had been asked to join them, and Francesca learned that he was the detective in charge of the case.

The warehouse had a huge sign on its sloping roof that was hanging askew, and it read: PAULEY AND SONS. A large wagon was being loaded with barrels in the yard in front as they left their cab.

Francesca and Bragg walked over to the wide open door of the warehouse, Murphy and Joel behind them. They paused by the two men loading the wagon. Bragg looked at Murphy.

He stepped forward and said, "I am Inspector Murphy. Do you know where Sam Carter can be found?"

Both men dropped the barrel they had been lifting back down to the ground. One put his hands on his hips. "Inspector? You mean police?"

Murphy nodded. "I have to locate Sam Carter and I was told that he works here," he said.

The two men exchanged a glance. "Never heard of him," they said.

Francesca felt a floodtide of impatience rise up in her. She glanced at Bragg; he shook his head.

"Who is the supervisor here?" Murphy asked.

"Office in back," said the first man, spitting out a wad

of tobacco not far from Murphy's shiny polished Oxford shoes. Then he looked at Francesca. "Sorry, ma'am."

Francesca glanced at Bragg, pleading with him silently. He nodded slightly.

"Sir? I am Sam's cousin. He is the only family I have in the entire city, and I am newly arrived here. I was hoping desperately that we might find him today."

The man looked at her. He was short and heavyset, with a barrel-like chest and huge, thick arms. His brown hair was thinning, and in spite of the cold, he only wore a flannel shirt over the shirt beneath. "Guess you're out of luck. Carter don't work here anymore. No one's seen him in months."

"Really?" Francesca asked.

"Yeah, really. But if he comes around, or if I see him, I can tell him his cousin was looking for him."

"That would be wonderful," Francesca said, realizing they were at a dead end. And she could not give the man her card, as then he would realize she had lied about being Sam's cousin—she doubted anyone would believe that Carter had a cousin living on Fifth Avenue. "My name is Francesca Cahill, and the police will know where to find me."

Inspector Murphy said, "I'm at police headquarters. Three hundred Mulberry."

The man ignored him, and he and his fellow worker reached for the barrel, heaving it up and toward the back of the wagon.

Bragg touched her arm, and they went inside the large, dimly illuminated warehouse. It was a huge expanse of boxes and bales. They stood for a moment and then, down a center aisle and off to the side, saw a small cubicle serving as a room, with a man seated there, bent over his ledgers. They all started forward.

Joel said, "He was lying."

Francesca looked curiously at him; Bragg gave him a

dismissive glance. "What makes you say that?"

"I can tell; that's all," Joel said, speaking only to Francesca.

They reached the office space. The man had become aware of their approach, and he had stood up to face them. In his shirtsleeves, a bill cap on his head, he said, "Can I help you folks?"

"Are you the manager?" Bragg asked.

"Actually, I am the owner. John Pauley," he said, extending his hand.

Bragg shook it. "I am the police commissioner," he said. Pauley's eyes widened. "Inspector Murphy, Miss Cahill, and Joel."

"How can I help you, Commissioner?" Pauley asked.

"I am looking for a man in your employ, or at least, he was in your employ until recently. His name is Sam Carter. Do you know where he is?"

For one moment, Pauley looked confused, and Francesca thought that there had been a huge mistake and he did not even know the man. But then he said, "Commissioner, he's right outside, loading up a wagon."

They all looked at one another; then they turned and ran.

But when they reached the street, Sam Carter was gone.

Francesca stared thoughtfully out the window of a cab, Joel beside her, as the cab moved uptown on Madison Avenue, patiently plodding behind two other black cabs, a trolley on their right. Bragg had gone back to headquarters with Murphy, and she had a client to visit and appease. She was only slightly worried about Lydia Stuart.

Carter had been clever, oh yes. How he must be laughing at her now. She felt herself flush.

Joel patted her knee. "Don't fret, lady. We'll find the ruffian again."

"I hope so, but he has the advantage now—as he knows

we are looking for him." Unease assailed her. If Carter
was innocent, why would he run away from them as he
had? She knew that most of the city did not like the police,
neither the poor nor the well-to-do. Still, he had given
quite the performance, for never in a thousand years would
she have guessed that she was talking to the man they were
looking for.

She hoped that he was not the killer. Because he had
an advantage now, and he also had nerve.

But then, the madman who had viciously stabbed both
Kathleen and Mary to death had had nerve, too. He had
crossed their hands in prayer and then left his signature on
their throats.

Francesca had learned that Kathleen had also been
found covered with snow, but in an alley not far from
where she had lived.

She sighed, her gaze on the pedestrians on the street—
when she thought she saw a woman she knew and she
blinked, looked again, and sat up straight.

Rose Jones was walking down the street. She was alone
and carrying a shopping bag. She was beautifully dressed—
her coat and hat were matching burgundy wool, and she
had a fur stole the same color wrapped about her throat.
She had just walked past two gentlemen, and they had both
turned around to look back at her.

Francesca and Joel were only two blocks from 37th
Street, where the cab would turn right in order to drop
them off in front of the Stuart home. She knocked on the
partition between her and the driver. "Sir! Pull over—we
must get out!"

A moment later Francesca was racing up the block, Joel
on her heels. "Rose! Miss Jones! Do wait!"

Rose turned, and her eyes widened when she recognized
Francesca. Then her gaze narrowed with suspicion.

Francesca slowed her steps. The last time she had seen
Rose, she and her "sister" Daisy were barely dressed and

being hauled off in a police wagon to spend the night in the Tombs, Bragg having raided the establishment where they worked. Francesca guessed now that Rose was not pleased to see her, considering her relationship with Bragg and the police. She smiled. "I saw you from my cab. Hello, Miss Jones. Francesca Cahill." She extended her hand.

Rose put her shopping bag down but did not shake hands. She put her gloved fists on her hips. "So?" Her tone was challenging. "What do you want?" She spoke with the intonation of a woman who had been brought up in a genteel manner, with an education.

She seemed angry. But even angry, she was a stunning woman—tall, dark-skinned, with startling green eyes. Francesca said, "I am so sorry about the night you and Daisy spent in jail. I truly begged Bragg to reconsider, but he would not."

"Why would you want to help us?" Rose asked, but less harshly.

"Why? Because I do not like seeing anyone treated abusively, that is why."

Rose stared. Then, with less hostility, "I read about you in the *Sun*. Why did you hunt down that killer?"

Francesca shrugged. "An innocent man was murdered. There was justice to be had."

She stared. "When you're rich, justice is a grand thing. Most people do not have time for it."

"No, they do not. But I do," Francesca said.

Rose did not reply.

"How is Daisy?" Francesca asked. "Perhaps you could say hello to her for me." Daisy was, without a doubt, the most beautiful woman Francesca had ever seen. Like Rose, she spoke in cultured tones, and Francesca had not been able to figure out why they chose to use their bodies to make their living. Also, it had been very clear that they were not sisters, and far more than friends.

Rose stiffened. Her eyes seemed to turn black. "Why don't you ask your *friend* how she is?"

For one moment, Francesca was utterly confused. "I beg your pardon? I should ask Bragg how Daisy is?"

"Not the commissioner. Hart. Calder *Hart*." She spit his last name.

Francesca blinked. "Oh, no. I can see that you are upset." She clasped Rose's shoulder, meaning to comfort the other, much taller woman, but Rose pulled away. "What has happened? Is Daisy all right?" Francesca could hardly imagine what Hart had done to so anger Rose.

Rose stared, and Francesca realized that she was so distraught she could not speak. "Rose?" she prodded.

"Hart has made her his mistress," Rose said.

"What?" Francesca gasped, an image of Hart, Daisy, and Rose in bed together coming instantly to mind.

"He made her an offer she could not refuse. She has moved into the house he has bought her," Rose said. "He bought her a house!"

Francesca was stunned. The last she had heard, Hart was fond of both women. And he also kept a mistress. "But . . . he has a mistress." How many women could one man keep?

"He got rid of her. Now he has Daisy!"

Francesca did not know what to think, much less what to say. "I am sorry," she whispered.

Rose said, "Their agreement is for six months. I could kill him for this!"

"Well, it is only six months," Francesca tried, remaining stunned. Of course, she knew why Hart had asked Daisy to become his mistress. She was beautiful, sensual, and kind. Francesca could understand his being smitten with her.

Still, Rose was more than upset, and she was a very volatile woman. Francesca had comprehended that the moment she had first met her. It worried her a little, that Rose was so angry with Hart. But what could she do?

Then she thought about Hart's recent pursuit of Connie.

"A lot can happen in six months," Rose returned. "And he is such a bastard, he has made *rules*."

Francesca heard her but did not instantly answer. She was appalled now, that he should be setting up Daisy as his mistress while chasing so blatantly after Connie. Of course, she must tell Connie this latest bit of news right away. Then she thought of Connie's reaction to Hart's latest love affair. Connie would be upset—very upset, in fact—and Francesca knew she would give Hart the cold shoulder the next time he approached. She began to smile—their little flirtation would be over the moment Connie learned about Daisy.

This was a blessing in disguise, she realized, and she thanked God for it.

Francesca had heard Rose's words, however. She turned her attention upon her. Was she somehow feeling threatened by Hart? "Surely you and Rose have had a chance to discuss this."

"Not really. It has happened so quickly, I still feel as if my head is spinning!" She looked away. Francesca thought she had seen a tear sparkling on Rose's long black lashes.

Francesca took her hand. Rose removed it. "The two of you are good friends, and no matter what happens in the next six months, your friendship will survive. I am sure of it."

Rose stared. Her rigid face softened. "Thank you, Miss Cahill. You are kind. Daisy was right. She likes you," she added.

Francesca smiled. "Please call me Francesca." An idea swept into her mind. "You know, I would love to call on Daisy. Would you care to join me?"

Rose blinked, and brightened.

*   *   *

Francesca quickly decided that Mrs. Stuart could wait, especially as Francesca had no news to relate to her regarding her husband's affair. Daisy's house was only a few blocks downtown, and they quickly hailed a cab. As they paused at the curb before an older home that had been impeccably maintained, Francesca heard Rose inhale sharply.

Francesca glanced at her and saw how nervous she seemed to be. She could only wonder why as she reached into her purse for the fare. Finding the small gun there still surprised her.

Rose touched her hand. "I have the fare," she said, handing the driver a half-dollar and some change.

"Thank you," Francesca said.

They alighted and walked through a wrought-iron gate and up the stone path leading to the stately brick house. Francesca decided not to share her enthusiasm—the home was lovely, and she could imagine the grounds in summer abloom. Their knock was answered instantly by a manservant.

But Daisy had appeared at the far end of the hall, a spacious entry with highly polished wood floors, a wide staircase at its end. "Rose!" she cried, hurrying forward, an angelic vision in pale blue silk.

The two women hugged for a long and emotional moment. Francesca watched, smiling a little, and then, when they separated, she saw that Rose had tears in her eyes. "I miss you," Rose said.

"I miss you, too," Daisy responded, smiling and taking her hand. But she was not crying. She seemed breathless with her happiness and had never been more beautiful. Her eyes were shining, and even her magnificent skin seemed to glow from a light within.

Francesca suddenly wondered if she was in love—with Hart. Surprise and something else she did not care to identify stiffened her spine.

Daisy turned to Francesca. "This is a wonderful surprise, Miss Cahill," she said in her soft, breathy voice.

Francesca recovered. Daisy loved Rose—she was certain of that. "I just happened to meet Rose on the street. She told me your news, and quite impulsively, we decided to call on you."

"You are my first caller," Daisy said, and then she blushed. It was obvious she was thinking about Hart, who undoubtedly had been her first real caller—if he could be termed that.

Rose pulled her hand free. She looked around. Francesca followed her gaze.

The hall was lovely. The mauve ceiling had beautiful moldings, which were painted a soft shade of pink. The walls were a different pastel pink, and three paintings had been placed on them. One was a stunning landscape that Francesca guessed to be from the Romantic period, another was a portrait of a medieval nobleman, clearly executed centuries earlier, and the last was an oil that Francesca thought was a seascape but could not be sure, as it was so impressionistic. A beautiful mahogany table with an inlaid ivory top was centered on the largest wall, a gilded tray for calling cards upon it. There was also a huge arrangement of fresh flowers there.

Francesca was impressed. Calder must have given Daisy the art—or at least insisted she hang his paintings—and the flowers alone had been extremely costly. Clearly Hart wished for Daisy to live in the most elegant manner.

Daisy followed her gaze. "Hart told me I should keep fresh flowers there. They are so expensive—I would prefer dry ones. But I would never refuse him." She smiled. "Shall we go sit down?"

"The flowers are beautiful; your new home is beautiful. Are you enjoying it?" Francesca asked as Daisy led the way into a salon with rich yellow walls. Heavy gold velvet drapes hung on the windows, and the furnishings were all rich, warm hues of gold and red and orange, in wools, satins, and damask.

"I feel as if I am in a dream," Daisy said, smiling softly.

Francesca saw that she was happy. She glanced at Rose, who was clearly as unhappy. Rose was brusque. She said, "I feel as if I am in a nightmare."

Daisy rushed to her. "Rose, please. This is for the best. We have discussed it. I . . . I am so happy you decided to visit me."

"Well, at least he has not outlawed that," Rose said, her hands on her hips.

"And he shall not," Daisy said softly but firmly. "You know I would never agree to that."

Rose softened. She slipped her arm around Daisy's waist, and they leaned into each other's bodies. Francesca could not help but be both fascinated and disturbed; she looked away.

"Perhaps the time will fly," Rose said, her gaze searching.

"Perhaps," Daisy returned, and then she looked away.

Rose dropped her arm. She gave Francesca an anguished look and strode over to the window, staring out of it, her back to everyone in the room. Francesca felt sorry for her. She did not think Daisy wished for her six-month arrangement to end anytime soon.

And Francesca had seen the "house" where they had both been living and working, previous to Bragg's raid on the establishment and Daisy's relocation. Daisy had moved up in the world—Francesca was happy for her. She wondered where Rose was living. She hoped she was not back in Mrs. Pinke's employ.

Daisy had ordered refreshments, and the manservant entered, wheeling a cart containing pastries and tea. Strolling behind him was Hart.

Francesca stiffened. Hart, as usual, was very dashing in his black suit, dark tie, and snowy white shirt. The shirt made a stunning contrast to his swarthy skin. His strides were long and loose, his jacket carelessly open. Hart smiled at her, Francesca, first.

She was oddly pleased.

He then glanced at his mistress, walking over to Daisy. She seemed startled to see him. "Hello," he said. He did not kiss her or reach for her. He was a perfect gentleman. Francesca was impressed, but what had she expected? For him to embrace Daisy and kiss her in front of everyone?

He faced Francesca. "This is a welcome surprise." He glanced at Joel, who seemed bored. "Hey there, Kennedy."

Joel gave him a grudging look. He had been ogling both women with a boy's fascinated admiration.

And then there was silence.

Francesca looked from Rose, who had turned to the room, to Hart, who stared at her. Rose looked as if she wanted to claw his eyes out, while Hart seemed amused. "Hello, Rose," he said softly.

"Hart."

"I thought you vowed to never set foot in my new home?" His brows lifted and he seemed on the verge of laughing at her.

"Miss Cahill persuaded me to call."

"I see. Well, your resolve lasted all of three days." Now he was laughing.

"Calder," Daisy protested.

He ignored her. Rose erupted, "You are such a bastard. I don't know what she sees in you."

"I think you do. Rather, I think you have. Seen what she sees in me."

Francesca felt herself turn red.

"How can you put up with his arrogance?" Rose demanded. "Six months is a lifetime! Daisy . . . " she trailed off, but it was a plea.

Daisy looked worriedly from the one to the other. She started toward Rose, but Hart seized her hand and stopped her in her tracks. "Do not think to make a scene, Rose. Not in my house," he said, and his words were soft and filled with warning.

Rose smiled tightly at him. "You know what? I don't care how filthy rich you are! And you don't scare me, either, Hart." She was practically bristling.

"Do you think to scare me?" Hart asked, mocking her.

Rose looked as if she were about to leap on him. Daisy stepped forward. "Enough! We have guests, and I cannot abide the two of you fighting like this."

Hart said, "Don't even think of trying to push me, Rose. I suggest you come to grips with the reality I have made. Otherwise I shall change the rules—and you will not be allowed in this house."

Rose stared. Daisy looked at Hart with wide, disbelieving eyes.

Francesca said briskly, "Joel and I must go. Daisy, I am so pleased to have seen you again." She could not believe Hart was being so coldhearted with Rose. She glanced at Rose. "Do you need a lift?" Not that she had a vehicle. But she knew it would be best if Rose left now. Besides, Hart had undoubtedly come to see his mistress for a reason. Francesca tried not to think too much about it, but it was impossible.

"No," Rose said tersely. "But I have clearly overstayed my welcome."

"Yes, you have," Hart agreed. He walked over to Francesca. "I shall walk you out." He smiled at her as if the hostile, tension-ridden exchange had not just occurred.

Francesca walked over to Daisy. They clasped hands. Daisy tried to brighten, but her eyes were filled with anxiety and her smile fell flat. "Thank you so for calling," she said. "Please, call anytime."

"I shall. Chin up," Francesca added softly. "I know everything will work out—I feel certain of it."

"Do you think so?" Daisy spoke so softly now it was

almost impossible to hear her. She seemed a bit relieved. "I hate seeing them argue this way."

"I know. Rose needs time to adjust. Hart need a smack on the hand." She glanced at him.

He grinned at her.

Impulsively Francesca gave Daisy a brief hug. She did not want to add that she thought Daisy deserved the life Hart had suddenly given her—for now. But it was probably too much to hope that one day Daisy and Rose would become honest and genteel women. Francesca wished she knew the story behind them both.

Hart took her arm, and with Joel in tow, they left the two women in the salon. "So, what are you and your little partner in crime-solving up to these days?" His eyes were warm as they slid over her features slowly, lingering a bit on her eyes.

Francesca could not help but return his smile, warming. "We are on a case, actually. Not one, but two." Her smile increased.

His eyes widened. "I was actually hoping you were merely in this neighborhood for a social call. What kind of case?"

She hesitated. "One is routine. One is quite . . . shocking."

He halted, facing her. "I hope you are not involved in something dangerous."

Francesca smiled sweetly. "It is dangerous, but I am equipped."

He eyed her. "What does 'equipped' mean? I do not like the sound of that!"

Francesca hesitated, then opened her purse and showed him the gun.

"What the hell is that!" he exclaimed.

She snapped the clutch closed. "It is a gun."

He grabbed the purse and opened it, ignoring her sound of protest. He pulled out the gun. "This is a gun!"

"It is for self-protection." She tried to take the gun from him, but he did not let her do so.

He stared at her as if she were some creature come down from the moon or Mars. "Francesca, this is too much. I must insist that you get rid of the gun."

"Absolutely not. May I have my purse—and gun—back please?"

"Having a gun will only get you in trouble." His gaze narrowed. "Does Bragg know about this?"

"He does not. And do not think to tell him," she huffed, becoming angry. "My purse, Hart. My gun."

He handed her the purse and snapped open the gun. Relief filled his features. "It's not loaded," he said. He smiled and handed the gun to her.

Francesca blinked. In her excitement, she had forgotten to load the gun. Not only that; she had forgotten to buy bullets. How could she have been so foolish?

"Still," Hart said, "even unloaded, you should not carry this about. Guns are dangerous—provocative and lethal. I insist you get rid of it."

She closed the purse and snapped, "Excuse me; you cannot insist upon anything."

His eyes glinted. "Oh, no?"

She grew uneasy. "Would you betray our friendship by going to Bragg?"

"Yes."

"You are unscrupulous!"

"I am."

There was absolutely nothing to say to that. She could only stare.

He softened and chucked her chin. "Dear, don't you understand? If you ever really needed a weapon, that toy would not serve you."

"I am not asking your advice." She turned her back on him. "Joel? We are running late. Let's go."

Hart chuckled and grasped her arm and pulled her back

around. "Francesca, someone has to curb your appetites. That is quite obvious."

She had no choice but to face him, so she eyed him warily. "That one shall not be you. Besides, your hands are full now—aren't they?"

His own dark eyes sparkled. "Oh ho. So someone wishes to comment on my personal life?"

She fisted her hands on her hips. "Yes, I do. You have the charm of a mad bull! I *insist* that you treat Rose with compassion. Do you have to be so unkind to her?"

He smiled at her. It was feral. But he did not speak.

She grew uneasy. "I do not like the way you are looking at me."

"Rose is having a temper tantrum, or rather a series of them, because I do not share what is mine."

Comprehension began. She flushed.

"And if Daisy is living in my house, and provided for lavishly by me, it is my right to *insist* upon a certain amount of loyalty."

Was he saying what she thought he was? "Surely Rose is not angry because you have . . ." She faltered. "Because you have . . ." She could not complete her thought.

"Yes. Daisy is now exclusively mine, and if Rose lays even a finger on her, I shall toss Daisy out."

Francesca stared. "You are so cold!"

"Am I? I don't think so. Daisy and I have made an arrangement. She is costing me dearly; in return, I expect her undivided attentions."

Francesca flushed again. "This is not about . . . love-making. I think it is about love."

"How naive you are," he laughed.

"No, how jaded *you* are. It *is* about love," Francesca said firmly.

He cupped her cheek. "My dear, it is about sex."

She pulled away. No one uttered such a word in any kind of circle! "Hart, love exists. Rose loves Daisy. She is afraid that Daisy will fall in love with you, and that she will lose her."

He laughed again. "Rose is horny. She is horny for my mistress, and it is as simple as that."

Francesca knew their conversation was not seemly, but she was in shock at his cynical attitude. "Is that what you really think?"

"Yes."

"I feel sorry for you, Hart."

His smile vanished. He became thoughtful. "You know, I envy you your romanticism, but I fear for the day your sweet naïveté comes crumbling down, all around you."

"There is good in the world, Hart, good and love," she tried. She touched him lightly.

He shook his head. "There is lust, my dear. Lust is all. Lust for wealth, power, position, prestige . . . for sex, drink, food, possessions. And for vengeance. Lust, Francesca. That is what this world is about. Lust is what mankind is about."

She shook her head. "No. No. You are a terrible cynic."

He shrugged. "And you are a romantic. A delightful one, but I do fear for you." He smiled again. "So, is there anything else you wish to *insist* upon?"

She smiled back, even though she remained shaken— because he was wrong, she was certain. "I insist you do not tell Bragg about my gun."

He guided her toward the door. "Francesca, I will tell him as soon as I have the chance. There is no doubt in my mind that a young lady with your penchant for trouble should *not* be carrying a weapon."

She was dismayed. At the door she faced him. "Fine. Betray our friendship."

He hesitated. "Is that what you think my telling Bragg about the gun would be? A betrayal?"

"Yes, Calder, it would be a betrayal."

His jaw flexed and he sighed, looking up over her head, toward the ceiling.

She was surprised. Would he be so easy to maneuver? She started to smile in delight, then quickly rearranged her expression.

He looked at her unhappily. "Very well. Promise me you will hide the gun at home. I will keep this to myself. It shall be our secret."

She really did not want to lie to him, but he was being so unreasonable now. "Fine." She extended her hand. "Do we have an agreement?"

He took her hand and kissed the back, and as it was not an air kiss, she actually felt the pressure of his lips on her skin. She shivered, taken by surprise.

"Agreed," he said.

EIGHT

"Do you want a drink?" Bragg asked.

The lobby was becoming crowded. Francesca stepped closer to Bragg. It was hard not to stare. He was devastating in his white dinner jacket, as it contrasted so boldly with his golden skin and hair. There was satin piping along the seams of his black trousers, and he wore a dark signet ring. "A sherry would be wonderful," she said. She was hoping that she appeared far more calm than she actually was.

There were butterflies in her belly. She had felt like a schoolgirl waiting for a date to the Saturday night church dance earlier, while waiting for him to arrive to take her to the theater. Fortunately, Andrew and Julia had left for the evening earlier, so there had been no one about but servants to see Francesca check her appearance repeatedly in the hall mirrors.

She and Bragg had agreed to wait in the lobby for the others before taking their seats. Evan had gone to pick up Sarah and her cousin, dutifully and not very happily. Francesca had not made him promise to be a gentleman, as she knew his manners would be impeccable no matter how disinterested he was in the evening and his fiancée.

She watched Bragg lean across the long gleaming oak bar, where several theatergoers were sipping glasses of wine or cocktails. She could not help comparing him to his half brother. In some ways, they were so similar: the swarthy skin, the air of authority and power, the blatant masculinity. But in other ways, they were as different as night and day, with Hart most definitely the night, with his dark hair and even darker world view. She was relieved that Bragg was an optimist. She would feel quite differently about him if he were not.

He glanced over his shoulder at her and caught her staring. She flushed.

He did not smile. His gaze was dark and intense.

She could not help thinking about the end of the evening, when he would bring her home. Francesca turned away, imagining herself in his arms as he kissed her. She knew she should try not to think of it, because she was probably going to be sorely disappointed—he would cling to virtue and leave her untouched. She was certain.

She sighed.

He handed her a glass of sherry. "What is wrong?"

She managed a smile. "Nothing. I am glad you are an optimist, Bragg."

He was amused. "What has brought this on?"

"I don't know. But without hope, there is not much left to live for."

"You are wise beyond your years, Francesca," he said. "And you are right."

She was pleased.

He hesitated, then said, "I cannot get used to seeing you like this—even though we first met at a ball."

Francesca smiled, as his gaze skimmed from her face to her décolletage. She had dressed with real care for the occasion—she had never dressed to attract a man before. Her pale pink gown had tiny, useless straps, a fitted bodice that left a large expanse of her chest bare, an empire waist, and it flowed in gentle pleats about her beaded pink shoes. The color did amazing things to her complexion, and she had lightly rouged her lips.

She could not even recall what she had been wearing

the night they had met—then, as usual, she had been oblivious to her appearance. "Do you like my dress?" she could not help asking, far too boldly—as she looked him right in the eye as she spoke.

"Very much," he said.

She smiled, leaning closer, her back touching the rim of the bar. "Thank you, Bragg," she said very softly.

He hesitated, his gaze so intent that her pulse quickened, but he only said lightly, "So how goes it with your parents?"

It was hard to think clearly. The lobby was becoming full now, as patrons continued to enter. This gave her the perfect excuse to sidle closer to him, and their hips brushed. Francesca knew she should chastise herself, but the evening already felt magical and almost perfect. The only thing that would be better was if she had not seen that blasted envelope from his wife on his floor.

She wondered if she should ask him about it.

She was afraid to.

"Francesca?"

She started. "I am sorry. What?"

"I asked about your parents. You seem preoccupied. Is something wrong?"

"No. They are fine. I am on my best behavior."

His mouth quirked. "I find that hard to believe."

"It is no easy task," she said. Then, recalling Julia's latest scheme, and interested in his reaction, she said, "Mama is thinking to match me up with Hart."

He choked on his scotch. "I hope that is a joke!" His eyes were wide with astonishment.

She met his golden gaze. She knew she had just done a terrible thing. She should not encourage any rivalry between the two brothers. What had possessed her to say such a thing—even if it was somewhat true? "Unfortunately, it is not. Never mind that she is fully aware of his

reputation with women. If worse comes to worst, I might
tell her that he is chasing after my sister."

Bragg set his glass aside on the bar, taking a napkin to
wipe his hands. "Should I have a long talk with Andrew?"
he asked grimly. "I can think of no worse match for you.
I should not be able to allow it."

Their gazes locked. A long moment passed. Of course,
Hart was never going to approach her with marriage in
mind, so the point was terribly moot. Still, Bragg would
not allow it, she knew. "Would you do that for me?" she
asked, aware of being a bit coy.

"Of course I would. Even though I should not worry,
as Hart has no intention of marrying anyone." Suddenly
he stopped, staring at her closely. "Are you trying to provoke me?"

She felt her eyes widen with false innocence. "Of
course not!"

He leaned against the bar, folding his arms across his
chest. "You need only ask, Francesca," he said softly, and
somehow the words felt dangerous, "if I should be jealous.
And my answer would be yes."

A thrill swept over her. She looked quickly away, before he might see how pleased she was. "I hardly thought
you would be jealous of Hart, Bragg," she fibbed.

He did not comment.

She took a deep, calming breath. "In any case, he has
taken Daisy Jones for his mistress, so he is quite occupied
now. We do not have to worry about Mama's hopes and
dreams." She suddenly smiled. Hart would laugh uproari-
ously, she knew, if ever told of Julia's interest. "I called
on her. He happened by while we were there. He bought
a huge house for her, Bragg."

Bragg seemed to relax, and he shook his head. "So now
it is Daisy. I wonder if he will ever find happiness. He flits
from woman to woman, buys more art than a museum,

consumes himself with work, but clearly, he is not content."

"No. He is not. I feel sorry for him." She meant it, too, or at least, she wanted to. But it was hard to pity someone who was so arrogant.

He smiled a little at her. "Just don't feel too sorry for him."

"You don't have to worry. He is so annoying; I should never become a victim of his charms. Besides, he wants my sister, and the more I think about him and Daisy, the more angry I get that he thinks to win Connie, too." It was actually insufferable.

"He is very selfish," Bragg said. "But I intend to set him straight about your sister. I like Lady Montrose, and I would hate to see her do something she will later regret."

Francesca could imagine the kind of reception Bragg would get if he told Hart to stay away from Connie. They would come to blows; of that she had no doubt. "Let me speak to Hart about Connie. I think he will be more amenable to my pleas." She winced. "I have meant to call on Neil and gently pry into their situation. Connie claims things are now fine."

"Francesca, do *not* pry," he said. "Let them sort their private affairs out in privacy, please."

"But I am worried, Bragg. And I *hate* Hart chasing after Connie." The passion in her tone surprised her.

He stared. "Maybe *you* are the jealous one?" he said after a moment.

"Jealous? Of what? Of . . . Connie and . . . Hart?" She could hardly get the words out, they were so absurd.

He took another sip of scotch, rather grimly.

"I am not jealous, Bragg," she said, more softly but insistently.

He smiled a little at her.

Someone bumped into her. Francesca slipped against Bragg, and instantly he slid his arm around her; she forgot

what they were discussing. His frame felt so hard and masculine and she thought about the end of the night and
wished, desperately, that it would be the kind of ending
she kept envisioning in her treacherous mind.

Yet she knew it would not.

And for one moment he held her that way, and then,
reluctantly, he removed his arm and put a small space between them. They exchanged a very long glance. There
was no doubt in Francesca's mind that he was feeling the
same stirrings as she was.

Bragg said, "There has been no luck finding Carter."

This was a much safer topic indeed. She felt relief.
"And have you spoken with Mike O'Donnell?"

"Yes. He would not give me anything, Francesca. He
hates all policemen. As I am one of them, he refused to
speak with me in anything other than monosyllables." He
shook his head.

She had to smile. "I suspected your interview would be
a difficult one."

"You have been extremely helpful, once again." His
gaze was warm, but then it slipped to her mouth. He
seemed to tear his gaze away with an effort. "I am highly
suspicious of him." He cleared his throat again.

"Because he is the link between the two women?" she
asked, her heart thundering now. How would they get
through the evening when all she could think about was
being in his arms? Would she even hear the musical num-
bers?

"That and because I learned from several dockworkers
that he did not think kindly of his wife. He has had nothing
but disparaging things to say about her, apparently, and he
did not even go to her funeral." His gaze held hers, the
look highly significant.

Francesca started, finally diverted from her shameless
thoughts. "He did not go to Kathleen's funeral? Bragg,
what if he is our man!"

He took her arm. "We do not know that. Tomorrow I am returning to the Jadvics'. I am wondering now how he really felt about Mary."

"He said he loved her. But now I am wondering, too!" Excitement filled her.

"Words are very cheap," Bragg remarked.

Francesca absorbed that. "Can I join you tomorrow?" she asked, almost holding her breath until he replied.

"Yes."

Her eyes widened; she was thrilled. "I cannot believe you have changed your mind about allowing me on this case!" she exclaimed.

"It is so much easier when you ask the questions. I want this case solved, Francesca. Which means I need real answers, now."

She put her sherry down. "Are you afraid there might be a third victim?"

"I pray not. I have no reason to believe so. But I want the killer nabbed, so he does not have the chance to kill again. I also wish to speak with O'Donnell's confessor."

Francesca's eyes widened. "But . . . anything said in the confessional is—"

"I know. But this is different. His priest may well know if O'Donnell is sane or not."

"Are you thinking of bringing him in?"

"It is too early to charge him with either murder, but if I get an inkling that he might be involved, I shall drag him downtown on drunk and disorderly charges."

"And keep him off the streets."

"Yes." He smiled at her. "And how is your case going?" He brushed a strand of hair away from her cheek.

The gesture was so intimate that Francesca just looked at him. He dropped his hand, and his color seemed to heighten. "Well." She recovered. "I am about to lose a client." She took a breath. "I have totally neglected Lydia Stuart's complaint. But tomorrow night I intend to discover whether or not her husband is seeing Rebecca Hopper."

"Please, do not climb any trees." He was laughing a little now.

Francesca flushed, and in a very unladylike way she poked him in the ribs. "Bragg! Do not remind me of that fiasco. I shall enlist Joel to do such dirty work. Although he is too young to see that sort of thing." She felt her color increase.

His amusement vanished. "You are the one who should not view a pair of lovers in an intimate moment."

"Do you think to guard my innocence?"

"I am trying."

"I saw Montrose with Eliza, Bragg. You know that."

His color *was* high, there was no mistaking his flush. "You should have never been sneaking about her house, no matter the circumstance. Surely that taught you a lesson!"

It most certainly had. She had seen the two lovers in acts she had never dreamed existed. Worse, she had seen Montrose in all of his virile glory. She blushed at the memory.

"Francesca?"

"I have certainly learned my lesson," she said demurely, looking at the floor.

"Somehow, I do not think so," Bragg muttered.

She had to smile at him.

"You are the most enchanting woman," he suddenly said. "I know of no woman with the zest for life that you have. Your eyes sparkle, Francesca, like gems, when you are laughing or excited."

She could only blink at him in amazement. "Bragg, that is the nicest—"

"I am not trying to be nice, and I am not trying to flatter you."

She did not know what to say or do. She plucked his sleeve. "But you are—"

"I am thirsty," he said, cutting her off before she could tell him how she admired him, too. He faced the bar, asking for a glass of water, and breathlessly Francesca stood behind him, gazing at his back.

He received his glass of water and turned back to her, now composed. "Perhaps we should go to our seats?" he asked. "They are running late, and the curtain goes up in a few minutes."

"That would be fine," Francesca said.

Bragg set his glass down and she smiled at him, allowing him to loop her arm tightly in his. They turned, their hips brushing, and came face-to-face with Julia's close friend Cecilia Thornton of the Boston Thorntons. She was a small but heavy woman wearing far too many jewels, and she smiled widely at them both.

"Francesca!" she cried. "How wonderful to run into you like this. And you are with the police commissioner. How splendid," she said.

But her gaze went back and forth between them both, and it lingered on their linked arms.

"We have made it just in time," Evan announced.

Francesca sat beside Bragg, three seats vacant on her left. She turned as Bragg stood up. Evan smiled at her, and she was surprised, because he seemed in quite the good mood. He allowed the ladies to go past Bragg and Francesca first. As always, Evan was so handsome with his curly black hair and vivid blue eyes, his complexion rather fair. He was just shy of six feet tall, and as he enjoyed tennis, golfing, and football, not to mention skiing and his yacht, he was a well-built young man.

And every time Francesca saw him, she prayed that he would fall in love with his fiancée, or that Andrew would change his mind about forcing Evan to wed her. The amount of his gaming debt was staggering. Andrew had refused to pay the bills unless Evan married Miss Channing.

Sarah Channing was a small, slender woman with big brown eyes and chocolate brown hair. Her face was small, her features rather ordinary, except when she smiled. She nodded at Bragg, but as she stepped past Francesca she smiled and it filled her eyes with warmth. "Francesca, hello." She spoke somewhat shyly.

Francesca smiled in return, although inwardly she winced. She knew Sarah gave not one whit about fashion and that her mother pushed her into her clothes. It was hardly surprising to find her in a dark red gown, one that was entirely wrong for her. Every detail of it was too large for Sarah's petite frame, and the color was overwhelming. It was too bold for a demure and soft-spoken young woman like Sarah. "I'm sorry I haven't had time to call," Francesca said, taking the other woman's hands and squeezing them.

Sarah gave her a significant look. "But you have been very busy, Francesca. I read all about your latest crime-solving efforts. How wonderful for you, to have apprehended Randall's killer all by yourself." Her eyes shone with admiration.

"Thank you. But I had little choice, as the situation was a bit risky."

"I should imagine." They exchanged conspiratorial glances. Sarah was very much like Francesca, although one would never think so upon first meeting her. But Francesca had learned Sarah's secret—she was an artist and passionate about her work. Francesca thought her portraits especially brilliant. Evan had yet to visit her studio; he had no clue as to the talent his fiancée possessed.

"May I introduce my cousin, Contessa Benevente?" Sarah asked.

Francesca looked past Sarah and saw a stunning woman

she instantly recognized in a quiet but animated conversation with Evan. He was grinning at her as she gestured and spoke; Francesca narrowed her eyes and watched Evan laugh at something the countess said. Oh ho! He clearly found Bartolla Benevente beautiful, which she was.

Francesca recognized the auburn-haired widow because she had seen her portrait in Sarah's studio. Apparently the countess was something of a black sheep in the Channing family.

"Bartolla? I do want you to meet our city's police commissioner and my dear new friend, Francesca Cahill."

Bartolla turned away from Evan, already smiling. Her long dark red hair spilled in a wild manner about her bare shoulders, and she wore a low-cut red dress that, on her, was perfect—at once elegant and alluring. She was tall, her figure gorgeous. Francesca guessed her age to be about twenty-five. A necklace of diamonds that had to be worth a small ransom covered an expanse of her bare chest, and black gloves ended above her elbows.

Francesca noticed that she wore a chunky diamond-and-ruby bracelet on top of one gloved wrist. The effect was rather exciting—Francesca had never seen anyone wear a bracelet over her glove before.

Bartolla extended her hand, and Bragg took it. Francesca saw his gaze skim over her figure, and although his expression remained impassive, she was instantly jealous—she felt like kicking him . . . hard. He murmured a polite greeting. Bartolla said, "I am so excited to meet you, Commissioner. I have been in the city only three days, but already I have read so much about you!" Her smile was unusually wide and very infectious. "You are as handsome as the sketches in the *New York Magazine*."

"It is my pleasure to meet you," Bragg said with a slight smile. "I hope that thus far your stay has been an enjoyable one?"

She gripped his wrist. "Very much so." She leaned

close. The cleavage between her breasts became more obvious. "So tell me, is it difficult to run such a department? What is it like to be in charge of so many police officers? I would love to go round with you one day and see all that you do. How interesting it seems to me!"

Francesca bristled. Was this woman thinking to seduce Bragg? She felt like ripping her magnificent hair right off of her head!

Bragg smiled. "I should be delighted to give you a tour of headquarters, at your convenience, Countess."

She beamed and clapped her gloved hands together. Then she sidled past him. Although Bragg stepped back against his seat as far as he could, she didn't make much of an effort to get by him, and her body brushed his rather thoroughly.

Francesca despised her.

"Miss Cahill! You are the one I have been waiting to meet! Sarah speaks so highly of you. She admires you no end, and I have found myself doing the same," Bartolla cried, with her wide, engaging smile. She had green eyes, and they sparkled.

Francesca did not want to believe her to be genuine. She refused to succumb to her charms. "I am pleased to meet you," she said tersely.

"A woman who dares to aid the police in their work." Bartolla's eyes snapped with excitement. "That is fabulous. There should be more women like you and my cousin, more women who dare to do as they choose!" She spoke with extreme passion.

Francesca refused to be enticed; still, she felt herself softening. "Yes, I am in complete agreement with that." *And keep away from Rick Bragg,* she added silently.

"Although I have lived in Firenze for almost eight years, I refused to follow the European traditions. There, women must never take the initiative; they must remain at home; they cannot follow their passions." Bartolla shook her head. Then she burst into a grin. "Unless, of course, it is their passion for love, as everyone engages in affairs there."

Francesca could only blink in amazement—for what did one say to that?

Bartolla took her hand briefly. "It is true. It is a different way of life! My husband, may he rest his soul, adored my boldness, but most of his family did not." She gave Francesca a sly look. "As if I cared."

"I am sorry about your loss," Francesca said, trying not to wonder if this woman was a kindred spirit.

"Oh, do not feel badly." She shrugged elaborately. "He was sixty-five when he died; that was two years ago. He lived a long and happy life; he had five children from his first marriage. What more could any man ask?" And she rolled her eyes and Francesca had to smile. Then she leaned close and whispered, "And he had me for his last six years." She grinned.

That was it. Francesca liked her, but if she flirted with Bragg one more time, she would step on her toes—or pull her aside and stake her claim. "How long will you stay in the city?" she asked.

"I do not know. For I do love Italy, and I have been in Paris since last summer. I feel Firenze calling to me! But this return home is long overdue. However," and she laughed with a very European shrug, "my family has decided to ignore my return, except for Sarah and her mother."

Francesca did not know what to say. "I am sorry."

"Don't be. They are stuck-up bores. And more important, they want me to dole out my husband's wealth, which I shall not do."

"Oh," Francesca said, and now she was intrigued.

Bartolla Benevente grinned at her again. "At least my life is never dull. Dullness should be a crime, don't you think?"

Francesca had to laugh. "Yes, it most certainly should."

Bartolla joined her in her laughter and moved past, to take a seat between Francesca and Sarah. As Evan moved past, he whispered to Francesca, "Have you ever seen such an enchanting creature?"

Francesca sighed. She refused to answer him, at least not now, but later she would set him straight. The countess was full of life and quite enchanting, but clearly she was a flirt—and Sarah Channing's cousin.

Sarah leaned past Bartolla and smiled a little at Francesca. "I knew the two of you would instantly become friends," she said.

They had a late supper reservation at Delmonico's, one of the city's best restaurants. The table they were seated at could seat six, and it was a rectangular one; somehow, Bartolla wound up at its head, with Evan and Sarah on either side. Francesca faced Bragg, seated beside her brother. While Evan and Bragg discussed the wine list, the three women discussed the musical, which had been thoroughly enjoyable, and then the party the Channings were giving for Bartolla on Tuesday.

"I am simply stunned by your family's kindness to me," Bartolla told Sarah, reaching for her hand and clasping it on top of the table. "Of course, my family will not come."

Sarah smiled at her. "We love you. We always have. And even though people mistake Mother for being a bit of a goose, she is actually quite clever. And she thinks only as she chooses, not as others expect her to."

"Yes, I know."

"I have ordered a new dress for the affair," Francesca said. "I never order new gowns."

"My, whatever has gotten into you?" Sarah asked teasingly, and then she looked at Bragg with significance.

Unfortunately, Bartolla followed her gaze and then

quickly looked back at Francesca. "Have you known Rick for long?" she asked.

Francesca felt that the other woman was far too astute, and carefully, she replied, "Only since he has come to the city to take up his appointment. But we have worked together on two cases, and in the course of our investigative work, we have become friends."

Bartolla was smiling, but her eyes had inexplicably changed. "I know his wife."

Francesca almost fell off her chair. She was so stunned that she could only stare.

Sarah said, eyes wide, "Oh! I did not know he was married." And she looked at Francesca with mortification.

Francesca forced a smile to her face. "Really?"

"She lived in Firenze for some time, and last summer we became friends while she was in Paris." Bartolla spoke lightly, with a Gallic shrug. "She, too, enjoys life to the fullest. She is an unusual woman."

"I am sure," Francesca managed.

"We have agreed upon a wine, a burgundy," Evan announced, but he was looking at Francesca oddly and she knew he had heard the exchange. Evan had not known that Bragg was married, either, and had already figured out that there were feelings between Francesca and him. He seemed incredulous.

"I am sure it shall be wonderful," Bartolla said, clasping his hand.

He looked at her, clearly forgetting all about Francesca and her ill-begotten feelings. "If it is not to your liking, we shall send it back."

"I should never expect such a thing," Bartolla returned, her voice somehow changing in pitch and becoming a bit seductive.

Francesca turned to Bragg and realized he had heard Bartolla's comment about her friendship with Leigh Anne, too. His face was composed, but she knew him so well now, and she could see that his eyes were not.

She wanted to take his hand and squeeze it reassuringly, but she did not.

Sarah said, "Lord and Lady Montrose have just walked in. Should we invite them to join us?" Her tone reflected the worry Francesca had just glimpsed in her eyes.

Francesca turned in her seat and realized that Connie and Neil had spotted them as well. She waved; they smiled and, after speaking to the maître d', began to come over. Francesca turned to Bartolla. "My sister and her husband."

"Oh, I should so love to meet them," Bartolla said with a smile that lit up her sea green eyes.

Francesca wondered how Bartolla would feel about sharing the limelight with Connie, who was breathtaking in her beige-and-gold evening gown, the outermost layer of which was gold lace. Montrose, following behind her, was handsome and elegant in his evening clothes. Several of the female patrons in the restaurant had already turned to glimpse him as he passed. She noticed that he did not have his hand on the small of Connie's back. It was un-usual—she had seen him guide Connie through a crowd hundreds of times, and his hand would always be resting there.

Francesca saw that Connie was smiling, but then, her sister was the perfect social butterfly—as Julia had taught her well. Her smile seemed a bit relieved—was she eager, then, to escape her husband? Francesca prayed that was not the case.

The two men stood up. Francesca also stood and hugged her sister. "How lovely you look!" she exclaimed.

Connie looked her right in the eye, and the glance said, *What are you doing?*

Francesca understood. Connie was not happy to see Francesca dining out with Bragg as her dinner partner. "How are you? Neil. Hello." She kissed his cheek and when she pulled back she looked into his eyes.

And she knew instantly that nothing was right and too much was wrong; his turquoise eyes were lackluster, grim, resigned. "Hello, Francesca," he said.

Greetings were exchanged all around.

"Would you care to join us?" Bragg asked.

Francesca hoped they would. And then she saw Calder Hart walking into the room. She almost fainted. They did not need this now!

He was with a stunning brunette who was about thirty, clearly a woman of means. Another couple was with them. In his white dinner jacket, Hart was, perhaps, the most outstanding man in the room. Francesca wondered who his dinner partner was; she wondered if she would ever see him with the same woman twice.

"We are meeting another party," Montrose said.

Francesca hesitated and knew the moment Calder had seen them. He grinned across the room at her, spoke to his group, then detached himself from them. *Oh no,* Francesca thought as he began to approach them with long, careless strides.

Francesca said, "Hart is here." If he caused trouble, she would murder him, she thought.

His gaze was lazily scanning their group. But Montrose had turned, and Francesca thought he looked tense and angry. Or was it her imagination? She glanced at Connie, who seemed more than anxious; she seemed afraid.

Francesca felt like saying, "Well, what did you expect?"

Sarah cried in an excited whisper, "Is that Calder Hart?"

Francesca glanced at her. She knew that Sarah was simply dying to view his art collection. "Yes."

"Please, introduce me—but do not tell him I am an artist!"

Francesca softened and nodded. "I promise."

"Rick," Hart said, pausing at their table.

"Calder," Bragg returned, and neither man seemed particularly amiable.

Hart turned to her, Francesca, first. His eyes warmed and as he reached for her hand his gaze moved over her beautiful pink dress. "Well, well," he murmured, lifting her hand and kissing it. "You *never* cease to surprise me, Francesca."

She gripped his hand hard and gave him a look that was almost frantic. It meant, *Please! Do not let Montrose know that you are hunting his wife!*

She was too apprehensive to care about Hart's admiration now.

He grinned at her and turned to Connie and Neil. "Lady Montrose. You are lovelier every time I lay eyes upon you."

Connie said breathlessly, "Mr. Hart."

Francesca stared from her and Hart to Neil. He was flushed. He knew. He had to.

Hart nodded at him. "Montrose. How goes it?"

Neil's jaw rippled with tension. His smile was a baring of the teeth. "My *wife* is the loveliest woman in this room, is she not?" he asked. And his stance was wide, as if he were bracing for a physical fight.

"Ah, you put me on the spot. There are so many lovely women here tonight, I am afraid to insult anyone." Hart did not look away from Montrose. His smile did not reach his eyes. The two men reminded Francesca of two bulls in the same pen.

Neil stepped in front of Connie. "Do you think to insult my *wife*?" he asked dangerously.

Connie looked faint now with fear. "Neil," she whispered.

Francesca realized that Neil wished to provoke a fight. "Neil," she tried.

But Bragg stepped between the two of them, moving past her to do so. He took Hart's arm and said, "I believe you know Evan Cahill and Sarah Channing, his fiancée." Hart gave Montrose another moment, staring at him with

mockery in his eyes, and then turned. "I have not met Miss
Channing." He nodded at her.

Sarah flushed. "Mr. Hart, I have heard so much about
you, and I so admire your efforts in support of the arts."

He started and then smiled, and it was genuine. "Are
you also a collector?" he asked, studying her now.

She hesitated. "I hope to be."

He inclined his head. "And I wish you success."

"This is my cousin, Countess Benevente," Sarah said
shyly.

It had taken a while to get round to Bartolla, the most
flamboyantly beautiful woman in the room. Francesca was
surprised that Hart had not beelined for her, but perhaps
that was because he was currently pursuing Connie.

Hart looked at Bartolla for the first time since he had
arrived at their table. She remained seated, which was a
bit odd, as she was the only one to do so. He bowed in
her direction. Francesca was rather surprised by his non-
predatory behavior, but perhaps he sensed Montrose standing rigidly behind him and was afraid of a knife in the
back. Then he said, with a mocking smile, "I do believe
that we have met."

"Yes, I think in London." She was cool. The flirtatious
woman had disappeared.

He did grin. "Actually, it was Lisbon. I never forget a
night that includes a full moon, the sea, and candlelight."

"Oh, really? Your memory is better than mine." She
arched her brows imperiously.

"Or perhaps I am thinking of a different supper companion?" he said.

Bartolla smiled, and if smiles could kill, he would now
be dead. "Yes, that must be it. You are thinking of a different woman entirely. How *nice* to meet you, Mr., ah,
Hyde?"

Francesca sighed—loudly. Everyone turned. She did

not care. Clearly Hart and Bartolla had once been intimate. She should have known.

Hart was laughing, and he did not bother to correct Bartolla's mistake concerning his name. "Well, it was a pleasure," Hart said. "And I am off to my party." He smiled, his gaze moving to Francesca.

Francesca could not be more relieved. Thank God, he was not going to cause trouble tonight. "Good night," she said to him in a rush, meaning, *Please go, now!*

He suddenly turned to Bragg. "Oh, have you heard the news?"

"What news?" Bragg said flatly, clearly wishing for Hart to go as well.

"Leigh Anne is in Boston," he said.

NINE

The evening had been unbearable. She did not know what to do.

Connie moved about her dressing room, already in her pale cream-colored silk-and-lace peignoir. She had yet to let her hair down, and when she faced herself in the mirror over the Tensu chest she used as a bureau, she saw a pale and frightened woman gazing back at her, a woman she did not know or recognize.

But the week had been such an amicable one, she thought in sudden despair. How had it all unraveled in a single evening?

She shivered. Neil had not spoken directly to her all night. The tension between them had been so thick one could slice it with a steak knife. The couple they had been dining with had noticed. The waiters had noticed—everyone had noticed. And of course, it was all her fault.

But she hadn't done anything wrong. Having lunch with another man, a male friend, was hardly a crime. Nothing had come of that luncheon.

Except for several rather disturbing fantasies, which shamed her no end, increasing the guilt already afflicting her. But in her fantasies, Hart's face always changed, immediately becoming Neil's.

What was she doing? And more important, why?

She was flushed now; she could feel the heat in her cheeks. She must not recall those very illicit acts of her imagination now. What would Neil think if he knew that she had dreamed of him touching her in terribly shocking ways?

She knew *exactly* what he would think. He would think her a whore.

The heat in her cheeks increased. Even when she had been having lunch with Hart, even when they had been flirting grandly, Neil had remained firmly on her mind. There was no escaping him—there was no escaping the betrayal of their marriage. She did not know what to do.

And Neil knew.

He had not said a word, but his behavior that evening, and the way he had acted with Hart, told her that.

Of course, there was no crime in flirtation. Even though Connie knew exactly what Hart wanted from her, it was only a flirtation. Hart had a mesmerizing charm, and it was pleasant and amusing, but nothing more. How could she not enjoy flirting with him? But God, flirting with her own husband before his treachery had been a million times more exciting.

Connie realized that a tear was slipping down her face.

It was hard to breathe. Was this what it was like to be trapped in a small, airless space? Connie suddenly had the gruesome image of being contained in a coffin—of being buried alive in her own coffin.

She shuddered, ill.

She had thought that he and Hart were going to come to blows, right there in Delmonico's.

What was she doing?

I am punishing him, she heard a little voice inside her answer, and its tone was cold with satisfaction.

Horrified by that voice in her head, Connie gripped the wrought-iron edge of the Tensu chest, staring at her wide-eyed reflection in the mirror. She did not recognize the woman she was looking at. The woman smiling back at her was cold and ugly. Of course she was not punishing him!

The past was *over*. She had told that to Francesca and had meant it. Mama had even lectured her on letting it go as well. And Mama was always right.

Besides, the past would never be repeated. Neil had promised her that, and she believed him. The one thing he was, was a man of his word.

Then why was there this horrible tension between them?

And if he knew about her lunch, why hadn't he said anything?

What if he did not know?

What if she was imagining everything?

But she hadn't imagined his affair with Eliza Burton!

Connie did not know what to think. Her mind felt as if it had become useless, stupid, spinning round and round helplessly, incapable of forming a coherent conclusion from the many parts. She could not even organize her thoughts, so of course she could not organize her life! And if she could not organize her thoughts, or herself, then how could she organize and manage her marriage? Fool! Failure! Oh, what would Mama do?

Mama would do whatever she had to do to make her husband happy. Because Mama always did what was right.

What Mama would *not* do was flirt with another man.

Never speak back to your husband. Never refute his opinions. Never debate. Always bring him his paper and slippers. Never deny him his rights. Laugh when he tries to be amusing. Frown when he is upset. You are his help-meet, not just his wife . . . Never betray him. . . .

Connie clapped her hands over her ears.

"Connie?"

Tears were blurring her vision, and the woman standing in the mirror, while beautiful, looked so fragile now that she appeared to be made of porcelain, a lovely painted porcelain doll, which surely must soon break.

"Connie? Are you all right?"

She realized with horror that Neil was standing on the threshold of her dressing room, and she whirled, dropping her hands to her sides. Instantly she pushed her mouth into a smile. "Neil?" What did he want? Why was he there? It was late; they had said good night; he had gone to bed! she thought frantically.

"What's wrong?" he asked quietly, and there was real concern in his vivid turquoise eyes. He started to her, but she backed up, and he halted in his tracks.

"Nothing." She beamed brightly, but did not move. The last time he had come to her rooms at such an hour, he had wanted to take her to bed. But that had been a long time ago.

But surely that was not why he was now present. Surely not. They had not made love in months and months, and just recently he had been in Eliza Burton's bed. Wasn't that enough for him? She was suddenly dizzy.

"Are you ill? Is it another migraine?" he asked, his expression almost agonized. He had removed his dinner jacket and replaced it with a paisley smoking coat in shades of red, black, and gold. He still wore his black evening trousers, but black velvet slippers, monogrammed in gold with his initials, NMC, the C standing for the baronetcy of Caameron, replaced his shoes. He had removed his white dress shirt, and she could glimpse a swath of hard, bare chest, dusted with dark hair, where the robe gaped slightly open.

She looked away, flushing. She had seen Neil without his shirt several times, and her husband might have been a logger, as he was all huge, thick muscle. "Yes," she said quickly. Then, "No. I don't know." If only he would go! She could not manage this encounter now!

"Come into the sitting room," he said.

She did not move. What could he possibly want? The answer, unfortunately, was obvious.

She thought about his touch and his kisses. He was not an inhibited or gentle lover; he liked to touch her everywhere, no matter how she might protest, no matter her surprise. Why was she recalling his style of lovemaking now? And her recent fantasies? A tingle began inside of her, but she hated it, and she shoved it away. "I am tired," she said, and to her surprise, she heard how her tone had changed, becoming odd, flat and hard.

"Come into the sitting room," he repeated.

Connie stiffened, because it was an order and they both knew it.

Just as they both knew she would never refuse him when he spoke in such a manner. Still, her feet did not move, even though her brain told her to obey. She stood stock-still.

"Connie?" he asked, startled.

Never refute. Never debate. Never disobey . . .

Something was wrong with her, Connie thought, feeling frantic. She nodded and this time, somehow, she started forward. He did not move, watching her. She had to go past him, and she felt his eyes on her back once she did so. Inside of her, she felt angry that he would stare at her so. Was he disapproving of her now? Perhaps he did not like her peignoir!

She was even angrier that she had obeyed him.

He followed her into the next room, which was situated between her lovely pink-and-white bedroom and her dressing room.

A maid had stoked the fire, and all the lights had been turned on when Connie had first come in. Neil had clearly turned off all of the lights except for one. She went to stand in front of the fire, clasping her hands firmly. How could he be thinking of passion now, after the night they had just endured?

Connie's confusion increased. Anger was not in her nature. And it was her duty to please him. She knew that. In the past, she had enjoyed pleasing him. As a wife, it was her priority to make him happy and comfortable.

The reason he had gone to Eliza—*the whore*—was because she had failed in her duties entirely.

She was so imperfect.

He paused behind her and she tensed even more. "When are you going to tell me about the lunch you had today?"

She stiffened so much that a real headache began. She did not dare face him. Yesterday, when he had asked her about lunch, she had been entirely evasive, mumbling that she had been with a friend.

"Connie?" His tone was hard. And his hand clamped down on her shoulder.

She shook as he turned her around. She managed to think, *This isn't about sharing a bed. He will be furious now.*

"Look at me," he ground out.

She obeyed, and realized he was so angry, but trying as hard to control himself.

"Whom did you have lunch with?" he asked.

He knew, so why was he asking? Of course, she would answer him now. She smiled, feeling as if she might snap in two. "If you know the answer, then why ask?" she heard herself say, and it was a different woman speaking—a woman she simply did not know.

His eyes widened and his hand tightened on her shoulder. "What?!"

She inhaled. "You're hurting me."

He dropped his hand. "You have lied to me." He was incredulous.

"No, I haven't lied." Why didn't she beg his forgiveness and be done with it? Connie grew frightened—why couldn't she control her responses now?

"I asked you who you had lunch with, and you lied."

"Hart is a friend." She was more aghast—there could be no denials now.

His smile was menacing. "No, he is not."

She lifted her chin. "You cannot choose my friends, Neil." What was she doing?

He trembled. "I know you. I know you better than you know yourself, and I know you would never do to me what I have done to you. So I am at a loss. Is this your way of hurting me? Because if it is, it has worked. I am insanely jealous, and I will not allow you to see him again."

He was insanely jealous. Connie stared at him, feeling as if she were outside her own body, objectively observing the marital argument below. Shouldn't she be pleased that he was jealous? She felt so odd now, as if she were floating. "I am a grown woman," she said calmly, stunned by her detached tone. "I surely can choose my own friends."

He gripped her by her shoulders. "I will kill Hart if he has touched you."

"Release me, Neil."

He stared, and slowly, he dropped his hands. "What are you doing? Wait; I know what you are doing—you are thinking to hurt me, to punish me, for what I have done. But I have never regretted anything more! My guilt and my regrets are punishment enough. I love you, Connie. Did you hear me? I love you and I want our marriage back."

It was so odd, for she did hear him; but once, when he had said those words before, on their wedding night, she had been thrilled. Now, she felt nothing except confusion. "I love you, too, Neil," she heard herself say, and it was automatic and said coolly, by rote.

Something was happening here, Connie thought with a fluttering of new panic. And she did not know what it was.

He stared. It was a moment before he spoke. "I don't think you do," he said, and he turned abruptly and walked out.

The woman drifting above the room suddenly rushed back inside her body; Connie could almost feel her return, and as Connie saw him disappearing through her doorway, real fear seized her. But she did love Neil! She loved him with all of her heart and all of her soul; she did not want to lose him, and she did not even know what had just happened now! She desperately wanted to call him back, but now, when she had to speak, her mouth would not move; her tongue would not form the words.

Panic consumed her.

It was as if there were another woman inside her, one determined to destroy them all.

His wife was in the country.

She was a mere half-day away by rail.

Francesca could think of little else now that Bragg was driving her home.

"Francesca? You have not said a word since we left the restaurant."

She slowly turned to face him, somehow smiling. "It is late and I am tired. It was a nice night." Her smile was carved in stone upon her face. The evening hadn't been nice at all; it had been fraught with tension, most of it thanks to Hart. But Bartolla's flirtatious presence hadn't helped, either. Evan had been too charming around her.

"Why are you dissembling now?" he asked softly. They sat in the two front seats of the Daimler, which purred softly as it idled in front of her house.

Francesca did not know what to say. She tried to smile again. "Bragg, thank you so much for the evening. I lost our little wager, but you took me to the theater anyway. It means so much to me." She pulled her hand away from his, and the refrain continued in her mind: Leigh Anne was in Boston. Would he see her now?

She was more upset now than ever. And she was frightened. Nor did she understand her own feelings. "I had better go in," she managed harshly.

"Francesca? Please. You are so upset. I suspect this is about my wife."

She whirled. "Yes, it is." Then, "You didn't tell me!"

"I didn't tell you what?" He seemed bewildered.

"That she is here—a half a day away!"

His eyes widened. "Her father is ailing. Her mother is a cold, shallow woman, her sister a serious problem, and apparently she has returned to Boston to be with her father. I only learned yesterday that she was nearby, in a letter she sent when disembarking from France." He kept his tone calm. "Francesca?" He tried to touch her, but she pulled away.

And she felt like crying. In a way, his wife had seemed unreal—or surreal. She was certainly a woman Francesca never wished to meet. Now, she had a horrid feeling that their paths would indeed cross. How could they not? She was a mere few hours away, and Bragg was her lawful husband.

A small voice suddenly piped up inside her head: *This is the price one pays for loving a man who is married.*

"Francesca?"

She met his amber gaze. Even now, when she was upset, with his unusually high cheekbones, his straight nose, his swarthy skin and golden hair, he stole her breath. Even now, upset and frightened as she was, she only had to glance at his mouth to recall his kiss, and the urge to move closer flared.

"Were you ever going to tell me that Leigh Anne was in Boston?" she asked stiffly.

"It hadn't even crossed my mind. Frankly, between Katie and Dot and the two Cross Murders, I haven't spared my wife a thought." He was genuinely surprised. "What difference does it make where she is?"

"She is a half a day away from here by rail," Francesca

said. "A half a day separates you and her—not an entire ocean!"

He sat up straighter, for she had been shouting.

"I am sorry," she whispered, feeling frightened and miserable and finding her own behavior inexcusable. "I am truly sorry. Bragg, my feelings haven't changed. They seem to grow stronger every day. Now, I am miserable."

He stared. She looked away. Wasn't he going to say anything?

She glanced at him. "I had better go."

"Wait. No." As she reached for her door, he restrained her.

She really didn't want to go, because they had to somehow resolve this, even though there was, in a way, nothing to resolve but her inexplicable fear. For it felt as if she had just found Bragg, only to lose him now, so soon.

His gaze moved over her face. "Our friendship is a struggle, isn't it?"

She stiffened. "What?"

"You are being hurt because of it, and frankly, so am I. Every day becomes harder, not easier; I know I am a man of honor, but around you, my thoughts are not honorable or honest at all."

"No," she said gripping his arm. "What are you saying?"

"We have begun to spend a lot of time together. And it is testing both of us in our resolve to remain mere friends. I, for one, see my resolve faltering."

She could hardly breathe. Was he also thinking, as she had so recently done, that a miserable, cruel, and calculating woman stood in the way of their happiness? That Leigh Anne did not need to stand in their way? That they might find happiness in spite of her existence? How quickly her fear vanished; how quickly excitement fluttered in her breast. "But we are friends. And nothing more." Her tone was strangled with her excitement.

He shook his head, then gripped the wheel with both gloved hands, staring straight ahead. "We are far more than friends and you know it. The tension between us, the tension that never dissipates, is that of a man and a woman, Francesca. It is a struggle being around you when we are alone. It is painful not being able to court you. Worse, it is more than painful knowing that one day you shall blithely move on, to marriage with a man who is worthy of you. Marriage and more. Love." He turned his head and stared unblinkingly at her.

It was hard to breathe now. "Don't even begin to say that we must not be friends now! I have treasured our friendship the way I have never treasured anything or anyone before! And I shall not *blithely* move on! I have never given my love to any man before, Bragg. I am the kind of woman who gives her love only once in a lifetime." A tear fell down her cheek. But it did not surprise her.

"Now you are frightening me, because you should not love me this way. It is wrong. And our friendship has encouraged it."

"No!" She grabbed his wrist hard. He was not going to declare that their friendship must end—for that was impossibility. "I am strong enough to manage this; I swear I am, Bragg."

"I am already hurting you!" he exclaimed. "And it hurts me, being with you like this, with my hands manacled behind my back. Preventing me from acting the way I really want to."

"You are *not* the one hurting me. We are friends—and we will always be friends. I know you know that, Bragg. I know this may sound terribly romantic, but it sometimes feels as if we are destined to be together. It is so right. We understand each other so completely. Our souls are in unity, I think."

For a long moment he simply stared at her, his eyes agonized, but moving over her face. Her heart raced. "Yes,

I have felt that, too," he said after a pause. "You don't have to be afraid, Francesca. Not of Leigh Anne. She will not come to New York. In fact, because I am here, she will avoid the city at all costs."

Some of her tension drained away. "See? You knew the reason I am afraid, without my even telling you," she whispered.

He smiled a little, but the sadness did not leave his eyes. "Even if she came to New York, you need never be frightened of her. You know how I feel about her—and you know how I feel about you."

She could not look away. She wondered if he could hear her heart now, as it was drumming wildly in her chest. "Bragg?" It was a soft-spoken plea.

But he shook his head, ignoring the dangerous desire that seemed to sizzle between them. Still, as he spoke, his eyes were on her mouth. "Damn Calder. He always finds a way to overturn every single boat in his path. He hasn't changed—he was a dangerous boy, and now he is a dangerous man."

For once, Francesca did not feel like defending him. "You wait until I get a chance to tell him what I think of his behavior," she said.

"Do not bother, as it will go in one ear and out the other," he replied. He wore gloves, but they were made specifically for drivers, and through the cut-out portion she saw his knuckles were white with tension as he gripped the leather-braided steering wheel.

She could not think about Hart now. Her heart jumped. The very dangerous thoughts she had had yesterday returned in full force. Why should Leigh Anne be able to stand there as a barrier between them, denying them love and happiness?

Was she, Francesca, brave enough to ignore societal mores and find the love and happiness she knew she could have with Bragg, in spite of his wife?

Did she dare?

She shivered uncontrollably.

"What is it?" he asked harshly. Then, because he had to know, he said, "You should go."

She couldn't smile, but she managed to swallow. These thoughts could not even be discussed with Bragg. But she would spend hours making what could be the most life-transforming decision of her life.

"Something is going on in that clever mind of yours. But you look frightened—and determined—all at once," he whispered.

She smiled a little and summoned up her courage and resolve. "Don't move," she heard herself say, and when he started, it was too late.

She was leaning toward him, until her mouth was on his.

His response was immediate. Francesca had expected him to pull away; he did not. For one moment, he pulled slightly back and their eyes met and she felt triumph soar in her breast, for the look in his eyes was unmistakable. Then he threw his arms around her, crushing her against his chest, and as she lay back against the seat, their open mouths fused. As he kissed her—as she kissed him back—they explored each other with their hands, and she was exultant.

She knew the passion they felt for one another was extraordinary.

His hands moved to her face, cupping it. She opened her eyes and saw him gazing at her, his breathing harsh and uneven. "You are so beautiful," he whispered. "And the best part is that your beauty comes from within, Francesca. The most beautiful thing about you is your mind."

Tears almost came to her eyes. "Kiss me again, Bragg," she said unevenly.

This time he hesitated. It was at that moment he began to war with himself, the man of honor versus the man of desire. Francesca felt it, knew it, and to forestall his ending the encounter, she kissed him again.

He took control immediately, his tongue deep within her, his hands beneath her coat. Francesca lost her ability to think; there was only sensation, rioting through her veins, pooling in her loins. She did not know how long they kissed, but the heat was blinding. And when he finally moved away from her, she half-lay on her seat.

And her first coherent thought was, of course they must become lovers. There was not even a choice.

He sat up fully, breathing with exertion, and it was a moment before he could speak. "I must be mad. What if Andrew or Julia is upstairs, awake, at a window?"

Fear filled her instantly, and with it came panic.

He helped her to sit up. Their gazes locked. Denying what had just happened would be sheer folly, especially now, after the conversation they had just had.

Francesca did not know what to say. So she said, "Even if they were upstairs, they could not see into the car."

"But they would demand to know what we were doing, sitting in here for so long." He was grim now, and he ran his hand through his thick hair, which in the night appeared far darker than it was. "Damn it." He looked at her. "I lost my head. What am I doing? The last thing I want to do is to encourage our feelings for each other."

She reached for his hand. "But I don't mind."

Startled, he looked at her with wide eyes, and he pulled his hand away. "You had better mind. You had better mind being treated with a complete lack of respect!"

He rarely raised his voice. She was hardly disturbed by what had happened, but she saw how upset he was. "Bragg, I know you respect me."

"No, Francesca. If the day ever came—and it shall not—when I took you to bed, that would mean one thing: I am a selfish man incapable of respecting and deserving a woman like yourself."

Dismay began. It slowly filled her. "Don't say that. We l—"

He shook his head. "We are friends. Nothing more." Then he smiled, but it was grim. "And tomorrow we have a bit of sleuthing to do. Remember?"

She could not smile now. "Yes."

"Good." He stepped out of his side of the car, and, not bothering to adjust her clothes or her hair, she watched him walk around the hood to her door. If she decided to go forward with Bragg—if she decided to become his lover, secretly, in defiance of her parents and all of society and the ways he had been raised—it might not be easily done. He might resist her.

The dilemma was almost a laughable one.

Except that loving him so much now was so hurtful, and there was no way she might laugh when thinking of her and Bragg.

He opened her door.

Francesca smiled bravely and he escorted her to the house. At her front door they paused. He pushed some hair out of her face, blown there by an evening breeze. "I will see you tomorrow, then. Is ten too early?"

"No, it is perfect," she said.

He nodded, then his smile faded, and he looked sharply around.

Instantly she tensed. "What is it?"

"I had an odd feeling—that we were being watched."

Instantly she thought of her parents. "I am sure they are asleep, Bragg."

"No, I felt as if we were being watched . . . in a rather unpleasant way."

"You are almost frightening me."

"I did not mean to do that." He smiled and touched her cheek. "Good night. And, Francesca? Do not forget about the girls."

Her heart sank. "But haven't they adjusted? You did

not mention them all night!" She had been afraid to bring up the subject.

"Peter's hands are full. But I am sure you have a foster home lined up for Monday."

"Of course," she said quickly, dismayed. She must check on the girls tomorrow, she thought as she opened the door.

He said, behind her, "It's not locked?"

"There is a houseful of servants, Bragg. And it is not locked as the last one to come in locks it, and tonight that is me."

He glanced around, toward the lawns on either side of the house, then said, "Very well. But next time, take a key."

He was making her nervous. She slipped inside, but kept the door cracked open. "Sweet dreams," she whispered.

He gave her a sharp look.

She watched him stride back to the roadster, which he had let run, and she continued to stand in the door as he began driving around the circular drive until he was heading out of the driveway. She sighed and closed the door, recalling his lovemaking in the automobile, the memory making her dreamily happy—until Leigh Anne dared to intrude upon her thoughts.

But she did not feel guilty, as Leigh Anne had abandoned him—as she hated him, and flaunted her lovers to prove it.

What should she do?

She was about to lock the door when a hand clamped down hard over her mouth, cutting off her cry of fear.

Almost simultaneously she was pulled away from the door, and the body behind hers was hard and masculine.

Terror began.

"You ain't my cousin," a male voice hissed in her ear. "An' I want to know why you lied."

TEN

Terror seized her, and she knew she was in the hands of the man who had gruesomely murdered both Mary and Kathleen.

"Don't move an' don't make a sound," he warned in her ear.

She couldn't move, as he held her far too tightly. Francesca tried to nod, but that, too, was almost impossible.

He dragged her outside, not bothering to close the door, and then he released her.

Francesca did not scream. She staggered backward, wiping her mouth with the back of her hand, somehow having tasted his flesh, the taste horridly bitter. She glanced desperately across the circular driveway; it was starkly empty and Bragg was long gone. There would be no help from him—she was alone with a madman.

As she could not speak, he spoke. "What do you want, Miz Cahill?"

It was dark out, so it was very hard to see his expression, but there was no mistaking the menace in his voice.

She cleared her throat, but her words came out in a whisper. "I am trying to find the man who killed Kathleen O'Donnell and Mary O'Shaunessy," she finally gasped.

"Oh! An' you think it's me?"

She backed up and hit the wall of the house. "No! I merely was hoping that you might provide a clue."

He stepped so close to her that she could smell his

breath. He hadn't been drinking, but it was foul with decay and tobacco. "I liked fucking Kathleen, and that's what I been doing, fucking her—not killing her an' carving her up."

Francesca froze. *He was their man.* How else would he know about the cross carved into Kathleen's throat?

"You got any more questions for me?" he asked angrily. " 'Cause this is your one chance, lady."

She somehow shook her head.

"Good! Got no time for a bitch like you." He whirled and then turned back. "Next time you might think to lock your fancy door." He laughed and began stomping up the drive.

Francesca fled into the house, through it, and to the study. Her hands were shaking wildly, uncontrollably, as she dialed Bragg's home number. As it began to ring, she realized that there was simply no way he could be home yet. She hung up.

She should follow Sam Carter, so they would not lose him now.

Francesca ran back through the house, and as she did so, she cursed herself for leaving her gun behind when she had gone out for the evening. But how on earth would she have ever guessed that something like this would happen? She had been at the theater with the police commissioner, for God's sake!

She raced to the closest window looking out over the frozen grounds and toward the avenue. It was in one of the salons. As she did, she saw Sam Carter about to walk through the open front gates at the end of the driveway. Her fear warred with the few remaining shreds of courage left to her.

She could not go after him alone. God only knew what he would do if he discovered her tailing him. She inhaled and raced up the stairs and into the side of the house that belonged to her brother. He might not be in at this hour, but she prayed he had dropped Sarah and Bartolla off and come directly home. She began to shout his name. "Evan!"

He appeared almost instantly, stepping out of his ground-floor study, still clad in his evening clothes, a glass of whiskey in hand. His eyes widened at the sight of her skidding to a stop before him.

"There is a killer outside; we must follow him—before we lose him and he kills again!" she cried, grabbing Evan's hand.

Whiskey sloshed over them both. "What in God's name are you talking about?" he demanded.

"I am—" Francesca stopped. She stared over her brother's shoulder and into the library where he had, apparently, been sipping a drink before bed.

Bartolla sat on the sofa in her stockings, her red satin slippers on the floor. She also held a scotch, and she smiled at Francesca benignly.

Francesca could only stare.

"It is only an after-dinner drink," Evan said stiffly.

Francesca was appalled. She glanced briefly at him, feeling how wide her eyes were.

Bartolla stood, smiling in the infectious way she had. "Francesca! Please, do not leap to conclusions, I would never betray my sweet cousin in any way. She knows we are here—she declined to join us. Would you care for a brandy?"

Francesca was slightly relieved—and still thoroughly taken aback. "This is not done," she managed.

"I cannot believe you, of all women, would ever say such a thing," Evan growled.

Bartolla shrugged. "I am a widow, my dear. A wealthy one. I can do whatever I choose, as long as I don't care what they say about me." She shrugged. "And I really couldn't care less what the gossips say. Truly, they are all envious of my freedom." She sipped her drink and sighed. "Dear Evan, this scotch whiskey is marvelous."

"I brought it back from McLaren after my last hunting trip," he said, smiling at her.

Francesca decided that now was not the time to analyze Bartolla's liberal spirit or her relationship with her brother. "Evan, by now he is gone!"

"Who?" Evan asked.

Bartolla sat up straighter, allowing her legs to fall over the couch, her feet to the floor, where they belonged. "Yes, what is this about a killer?"

"Damn it!" Francesca cried. She began to shake all over again. Tears of frustration came to her eyes.

"Are you all right?" Evan asked, setting his scotch down and putting his arm around her.

"No, I am not! As the man responsible for killing two innocent young women just accosted me in the house and is even now getting away!" she shouted.

His eyes went wide. "Good God." Then he darkened. "I cannot believe you, Fran. Enough is enough. I suggest you call your *friend*. That is, I suggest you call the police."

SUNDAY, FEBRUARY 9, 1902 — 10:00 A.M.

Francesca arrived on Bragg's doorstep at a quarter to ten— before he might think to pick her up. She was not surprised to find him answering the door, his coat already on.

He was surprised, however, to see her. "Francesca! I was on my way to pick you up."

"I thought to see the girls before we go." She stepped inside, removing her gloves. "Any luck last night?" She had called him after leaving Evan and Bartolla to their drinks—and then had decided to join the pair so as to chaperone them. Her evening had ended after two, and she was quite tired as a result.

"No. We scoured the Upper East Side, but he disappeared after leaving you." His eyes were dark, resting upon her.

"I am so sorry. There was a time lapse—he had quite the head start."

"I am the one who is sorry. I should have known something was amiss—I sensed it, for God's sake! And to leave your front door unlocked . . . " he trailed off, shaking his head.

Francesca touched his arm. "He didn't hurt me, Bragg."

"No, he did not, and I thank the heavens above for that."

"Me, too," Francesca had to agree. Before she could ask him what he thought of the morning newspapers—both the *Sun* and the *Tribune* had run headlines about the murders and the case was now fodder for the public—Peter jogged into the hall.

Francesca could only blink, as his shirt was coming out from beneath his black jacket and Dot was on his back, giggling with delight. He saw them and halted, turning red.

Dot shouted, "Pee, Pee!"

Francesca was alarmed. "I believe we must use the facilities," she said, rushing toward them. "Hello, Dot."

Bragg followed as Peter slid Dot to the floor. "I do believe she has decided to call my man Pee. Considering she has a rather nasty habit, it is probably appropriate."

Francesca didn't dare look at him now. Had Dot made another mess on the floor? It sounded like it. "How are the girls, Peter?" she asked.

"Where is the nanny?" was his impassive reply.

She wet her lips, but Bragg spoke. "Never fear. The girls leave tomorrow." He gave Francesca a stern look.

Dot pointed at Bragg, her face accusatory. "Bad," she said. "Bad!" she shrieked.

"And neither one likes me," Bragg added.

"Well, have you even bothered to play with them?" Francesca asked curtly, taking Dot's hand. The child gave her a beatific smile.

"Play? When do I have time to play?" he asked incredulously.

He was right. She sighed. "Bragg, it might take more than a single day to find them a home," she said, leading Dot to the bathing room.

"Good luck," Bragg said.

Francesca did not know whether he referred to the event that she hoped was about to happen or to her finding a family for the girls tomorrow. She led Dot inside and seated her on the lavatory. Dot grinned at her and began to play with the doors on the adjacent vanity, not evincing much interest in any biological function.

"Dot, now is the perfect time—and place—to make a pee. Please, Dot, pee," Francesca urged, squatting beside her.

Dot said, "Pee! Pee!"

From outside the door, Bragg said, "Peter has undergone a distasteful personality change. I have not had fresh shirts—or sheets—since Friday."

Francesca winced. "What if I hire a nanny tomorrow?" She looked at Dot, who grinned back at her, and nodded encouragingly.

"The girls leave tomorrow," Bragg said firmly. "It has been an entire weekend, Francesca."

Dot did not seem to like the sound of his voice, because she glared at the door and stood up.

"Dot, you must do your business," Francesca said, sitting her back on the toilet seat.

Dot shook her head, trying to punch Francesca. "Pee!" she shouted. *"Pee!"*

Francesca decided Dot did not have to go, and it crossed her mind that Connie and Mrs. Partridge might be helpful here. She said, "Very well. Off you go to Peter."

Dot left the bathroom at a run, beelining for the big man who had tucked in his shirt and combed his wispy blond hair. She leaped at him.

He caught her and put her on his shoulders and she laughed in delight, grabbing his ears.

Francesca watched them leaving the hall, smiling a bit. She thought Peter was enjoying himself—although, of course, it was hard to tell.

Then she felt the eyes.

She turned, no longer smiling.

Katie sat on the stairs, staring at Francesca and Bragg. Her expression was as closed as a book, as hard as a rock. When she realized Francesca was regarding her, she leaped to her feet and fled back upstairs.

Francesca looked at Bragg.

He said grimly, "She is very sullen. She doesn't speak. She might need the help of an expert, Francesca."

Francesca nodded. "I wonder if she was like this before her mother died."

Bragg shrugged. "She is more than you, I, or Peter can handle. That is clear." He smiled at her then. "Shall we? We have work to do."

She smiled back and had started toward him when she slipped. "Oh!"

Bragg reacted, catching her before she fell. "Are you all right?"

"I am fine," she said breathlessly, having almost wound up on her head. "The floor is wet—" She stopped.

They both looked down.

"I have had it!" Bragg said.

"He was a very devout man," Father O'Connor said. "He came to mass every Sunday, and sometimes during the week as well."

Francesca stood beside Bragg as the interview with Mike O'Donnell's priest began. It hadn't been hard to locate him—they had found the small church where Father O'Connor preached to his parishioners just a few blocks north of Water Street. The mass had just ended and the last of his parishioners were leaving the church. She was surprised to learn that Mike O'Donnell had been a church-going man. He hadn't seemed very religious when she had met him.

"When did you last see him?" Bragg asked.

"Just last Sunday," O'Connor replied. He was a tall white-haired man in his later years. "It was a terrible thing, his wife murdered like that—and now his sister, too."

"Yes, it was. So you knew both women?"

"Not really. I knew Kathleen. In the old days, before they separated, she would come here with him to worship. Then, they shared an apartment in a tenement a few blocks from here with two other families. But I have not seen her in two or three years," the priest replied. They were all seated in his small office just behind the church. It was a simple room, square, with oak floors and stone walls, a bookcase, and the priest's desk. "She was such a gentle woman, Commissioner. Quiet and retiring, and also devout. I was disappointed that they went their separate ways. I counseled them not to."

"So you never met Mary?"

"No, I didn't say that. I met her once, briefly, at Kathleen's funeral."

"The funeral Mike did not go to," Bragg said.

The priest hesitated. "I am sure he had his reasons."

"What reasons could there be?" Francesca murmured.

O'Connor looked at her. "He loved Kathleen. He did not want to leave her. I believe her death devastated him. He has not been the same since."

Francesca looked at Bragg. Mike O'Donnell hadn't seemed very devastated the other day. "Did you ever meet her boyfriend, Sam Carter?"

O'Connor blinked. He had pale gray eyes that were almost colorless. With his white hair and fair complexion, he almost appeared to be an albino. "I did not even know that she had taken a lover. I am truly disappointed in her."

He had spoken as if she were still alive, Francesca thought. How odd.

"Did Mike ever show or evince any anger toward Kathleen for the failure of their marriage? Did you ever hear him speak of her in any kind of threatening way?" Bragg asked. "Did he ever threaten her?"

"I wouldn't know if he ever threatened her; I assume they had their share of arguments. But no, I did not ever hear him speak unkindly toward Kathleen."

"So he is a saint," Francesca murmured.

O'Connor looked sharply at her. "I hardly said he was a saint. Intemperance is a sin."

"He never threatened her, or spoke angrily about her, not even in the confessional?" Bragg asked.

"Commissioner! You know I cannot reveal anything I have heard in confession."

Francesca tried to tamp down her impatience.

"Two women have been brutally murdered, Father," Bragg said coldly. "And if you have heard anything that might help me find the killer, even if during confession, I suggest you share it with me."

"I would never violate my holy oath," Father O'Connor said rather abruptly. "Now, is that all?"

"Mary is being buried tomorrow. Has O'Donnell said anything about her death? Has he shared his grief—or other feelings—with you?"

O'Connor was standing, a signal that the interview was over. "No, he has not. Not really."

"What does that mean?" Bragg asked, not moving, although Francesca had also risen to her feet.

O'Connor sighed. "He and Mary were not close. In fact, they were not close at all."

"What does that mean?" Bragg asked.

"It means exactly that."

"You know more than you are telling me," Bragg remarked.

"I cannot say anything else." He looked away from them both, upward, as if toward God, for heavenly advice.

"Not even to prevent a third murder?" Bragg remained cold.

O'Connor's eyes went wide. "Surely you don't think this madman will strike again?"

"I do," Bragg said.

Francesca tried not to give him too sharp a glance. What did he know that she did not?

"Very well," O'Connor said. "O'Donnell lusted after his own sister."

Outside, Francesca confronted Bragg. "I still think it is Carter, but dear God, the man confessed to wanting to bed his sister!" She felt herself flush. "That is the urging of a madman."

"So O'Connnor says," Bragg remarked.

"What does that mean?"

"It means that he gave up his confidential information far too easily for my taste. It means I do not trust him. There is one fact. O'Donnell did not go to his wife's funeral. Let's see if he shows up tomorrow at Mary's." He walked over to the carriage that they had taken downtown. His motorcar had, oddly, refused to start up. Today a police officer was driving them about the city.

"But why would O'Connor say something if it was not true?"

"I do not know. But he about-faced. He went from telling us how devout O'Donnel is, and the next thing, we learn he is coveting his own sister, which is hardly the thinking of a godly man." He opened the carriage door for Francesca. "A cross was carved onto both women's throats, Francesca."

Francesca almost tripped while entering the carriage. She faced him with horror. "You don't think—you don't suspect O'Connor!"

"I wonder," was all that he said.

"But what about Carter? He knew about the crosses!" she cried.

"It is in all the newspapers," he said calmly, climbing in beside her. "Where am I dropping you?"

"Lydia Stuart's," she said, giving him the address. "I saw the headlines in the *Sun* and the *Trib*. They have dubbed the killings 'The Cross Murders.' But those papers went on sale early this morning. Do not tell me they came off the press before five or six! I saw Carter last night, perhaps at one or so, and he said specifically that he didn't kill or *carve* anyone."

"He might have heard about the details of both murders on the streets," Bragg said. "Or maybe not. In any case, I did not say that O'Connor is a suspect. But he gave in to me far too easily. My intuition tells me he is not honest— or rather, that he is not being honest with us."

Francesca shivered. "So we now have three possible suspects?"

"We certainly have two," Bragg said as their carriage merged onto the Bowery.

"There is Carter, who is very hostile and who knows both women were carved. But did he know both women?"

"That is a good question, and I shall ask him directly when we find him."

"O'Donnell did know both women, being the husband of one and the brother of the other. He is 'devout'—and a cross was carved into each victim's throat, indicating some kind of religious fanaticism. He did not attend his wife's funeral, yet he told me he loved her and did not want to leave her." Francesca met Bragg's gaze. "Hmm. He also spoke angrily of Carter. And according to O'Connor, he lusted after his sister. Bragg, he has the makings of our man."

Bragg smiled fondly at her. "A moment ago your vote was in favor of Carter."

"He scared me last night."

His smile faded. "I know."

She shook off her memory of being seized by him. "O'Connor is a man of God, a check for the religious connection, and he also knew both women." She was thinking about the cross carved onto both women's throats.

"He claims to have met Mary once," Bragg said.

"You don't believe him?"

"I don't believe or disbelieve him. Let's see if he shows up at Mary's funeral. It is at noon tomorrow. It shall be an interesting day."

Francesca hesitated. "Shall we go together?"

He glanced at her. "Why not?"

Relief filled her. "I thought that after last night, you might not wish to do so."

"I have done a good deal of thinking since then," Bragg said. He lowered his voice, although the carriage partition separated them from the driver. "I also treasure our friendship. I refuse to give it up. It is very important to me— even if it means that my man has turned himself into a nanny."

She felt her heart turn over with joy and exultation. "Good," she said. "Then we remain friends and partners, and I can think of little that might be better."

He gave her a look.

Her choice of words had been poor; she knew it the moment she spoke and the moment he met her gaze. She flushed. "Given the circumstances," she amended.

"I do hope this is not a bad time to call," Francesca said, upon greeting Lydia Stuart. It was early that afternoon now, and they were in a small and cheerful salon.

"Of course it is not," Lydia said, with a smile that seemed strained. She turned to the manservant at the door. "That will be all, Thomas. Please close the door as you go." As they waited for him to leave, Francesca felt guilty for not dealing with her client's problem. The moment Thomas was gone, the door solidly closed behind him, Lydia faced her. "Mr. Stuart is not at home," she said nervously. "I can imagine where he is, and with whom."

"Mrs. Stuart," Francesca began, feeling terrible for not having news to deliver.

"Please, you must call me Lydia!" she cried. "Did you find out if he is doing what I think he is?" she asked.

"No, I did not," Francesca began.

"What?" Her expression changed; she seemed stunned.

"I am so sorry, but two innocent young women have been brutally murdered, and I have been working with the police on solving the murders."

Lydia blinked at her. "Oh. I see."

"But I will not let you down," Francesca said firmly. "It is just that everything has happened so quickly."

Lydia nodded, seeming terribly upset. Suddenly she stiffened, her eyes widening. "Oh, dear!" she cried.

"What is it?" Francesca asked—as the door to the salon opened.

Lydia pasted an artificial smile on her face and turned. "Darling, I did not expect you back," she said brightly. But her tone was strained.

A gentleman of medium height with graying hair, a beard, and a mustache entered the room. His gaze moved from his wife to Francesca; he was smiling. "Hello, dear." He kissed her warmly and turned to Francesca.

"This is Miss Francesca Cahill," Lydia said. "She is a new friend; we met the other night at that music reception! I am so pleased she has called." She took Francesca's hands. "It has been difficult, you know, as I am sure I have told you, moving here just a few months ago from Philadelphia. My husband seems to know everybody, but I know no one."

Francesca hadn't realized they were newly arrived in the city.

Lincoln Stuart faced her. He was a pleasant-looking man of medium height and build. "I am pleased to find that my wife has made a friend here." Then he squinted at her. "Why is your name so familiar?"

"Perhaps you know my father," Francesca asked quickly, "Andrew Cahill?"

"No, I do not think that I do."

Francesca could imagine why he knew her name—he might have read Kurland's article in the *Sun* on Thursday. She smiled at him. "Perhaps we met at the reception? Although I confess I am good with faces and I do not quite recollect yours."

"The Haverford affair?" he asked.

Francesca hesitated, darting a glance at Lydia.

"No, darling, the Bledding music reception; remember that stunning trio from Saint Petersburg? That young man on the violin was so superb!" She was perspiring and it was obvious.

But Lincoln did not seem to realize how tense and uncomfortable his own wife was. He studied Francesca very closely. "How odd, that I cannot place you," he said.

"Well, I am sure we will both recall where it is that we have met," Francesca said lightly.

"Yes, I am sure." He smiled. Then he said to his wife, "Darling, I forgot my cigars. I am off now, but I shall be back for supper. Say, at seven or so?"

"That is perfect," Lydia said swiftly.

Lincoln bowed to Francesca and they exchanged goodbyes, and then he left the room.

A short silence reigned. "He knows," Lydia whispered. "He knows I have hired you to spy upon him."

She was frightened. Francesca gripped her hand. "Balderdash," she said. "But this is the perfect opportunity. You think he is off to Mrs. Hopper's?"

Lydia nodded fearfully.

Francesca squeezed her hand. "Then I am following him!" Francesca cried.

"Now?" Lydia gasped.

"Now," Francesca said.

It became obvious almost instantly that Lincoln Stuart was not going to Rebecca Hopper's. His coach traveled north, bewildering Francesca, especially once he had traveled past Central Park. She could not imagine where he was going; this far north of the city, the land was undeveloped, consisting mostly of pasture and cows. On 103d Street, his carriage turned onto an even more desolate stretch of avenue with an occasional farmhouse in evidence. Her cabbie dutifully followed, keeping a city block between Francesca and her quarry. And finally, well over an hour after leaving the Stuart home downtown, Lincoln Stuart's carriage cruised to a halt.

On the west side was a huge meadow that was unenclosed and dotted with oak trees. On the east side of the road, where his carriage had stopped, was a cemetery.

Her first reaction was disbelief, and as Lincoln alighted from the coach, her second was to wonder if Kathleen O'Donnell was buried there.

Francesca watched him walking slowly through a pair of wide iron gates. They had been closed but not locked, and he pushed them open. Her mind raced. There was simply no connection between Stuart and the murders, but arriving at a cemetery was so completely unexpected. Then she realized that her cab was slowing.

She pounded on the partition. "Do not stop," she ordered her cabbie. "Keep going. Go right past the coach, please!"

"Whatever you want, miss," the driver said, and the black cab and bay horse cruised past the Stuart carriage.

As it did so, Francesca ducked back against the seat where she sat so Stuart might not glimpse her inside the

hansom, in case he turned to look at them, as they were
the only other vehicle on the road. A moment later, she
dared to peek out of her window, back toward the cemetery. He did not seem to be looking; he was slowly walking
up a dirt path among a dozen headstones.

Francesca was thoroughly perplexed. But she had seen
enough for now. "Driver! We are going back to the city,
please."

The letter was waiting for her on her desk inside of her
bedroom when she returned.

Francesca was actually very organized, although one
would not think so to look at her desk, which was usually
an indecipherable mass of books and papers. Now, however, it was very neatly organized; a maid had clearly
cleaned it earlier that day. In fact, Francesca's books and
notebooks were arranged in such a manner that the pristine
white envelope was the first thing she saw upon entering
her bedroom, as it sat propped up in the desk's center.

Her mind remained filled with questions about Lincoln
Stuart; now she moved swiftly to her desk, curious, and
realized the envelope was not marked. It had not been
posted—someone had delivered it to her. In fact, it might
not even be meant for her, as her name was not anywhere
on the envelope.

She opened it and pulled out a sheet of paper.

A poem had been typed there in block letters. It read:

> A SIGH
> ONE WHISPER
> A LIE
> THREE LASSES
> MUST DIE

ELEVEN

Peter answered the door—with Dot.

Francesca could hardly concentrate on the child, who shrieked with pleasure upon seeing her. "Frack, Frack, Frack!" she cried.

Somehow, she lifted the two-year-old into her arms, and of course instantly Dot began to struggle to get down. ll"Where is he?" Francesca asked breathlessly. She had phoned police headquarters and had been told that Bragg was on his way home; upon telephoning his house, she found the line busy. Jennings had driven to Madison Square at a breakneck speed. Francesca thought they had managed the trip in ten or twelve minutes; fortunately, this hour on a Sunday did not have a lot of street traffic.

"He is in the study," Peter said.

Francesca shoved Dot into his arms and ran down the hall. She did not knock. He started when she raced into the small room, where a fire glowed in the hearth. Bragg was standing at his desk. "Francesca?"

She handed him the poem.

He looked at the page and paled. "Where did you find this?"

She was already closing his door. She leaned against it. "On my desk."

"On your desk?" His eyes widened.

"In my bedroom. I had just returned from following my

client's husband—to a cemetery!" she cried. "Bragg, there is going to be another victim."

Bragg stared. It was a moment before he spoke. "The killer delivered his warning to you—not to me or to the police. I want you off of this case."

She cried out. "But that's impossible!"

"Is it? Do you have any more doubts that we are dealing with a madman?" He lifted the telephone. Francesca listened as he asked Inspector Murphy to meet him in his office. He then said, "Have we located Sam Carter yet? . . . All right. Pick up Mike O'Donnell. Bring him to headquarters. Charge him with anything you can think of. I imagine a drunk and disorderly will do. I'll be down shortly." He hung up.

Francesca had folded her arms across her chest. "Did they find Sam Carter?"

"No."

"Now we must hope that Mike O'Donnell is our man. Bragg? I know this is unlikely, but is Kathleen buried at the Greenlawn Cemetery on One Hundred and Third Street?"

"No. She's buried downtown. Surely you do not have some reason to believe that Stuart is involved in these murders?"

"No." Relief did fill her. It crossed her mind that she must ask Lydia what her husband had been doing at that cemetery, but she would do so at another time. "How can I help?" she asked quietly. "Please, do not tell me I cannot!"

"Francesca." He put on his jacket. "Someone delivered this death threat to you. Carter, O'Donnell, and O'Connor all know you are working on this case. Who else knows?"

She hesitated. "My brother."

"Who else?"

"No one," she said. "Except for your officers." Sud-

denly she recalled Bartolla's presence last night at the
house. "And Bartolla Benevente."

He clearly dismissed that. "Perhaps Maggie Kennedy
has told a friend or friends about asking you for help?"

"I can ask her," she said thoughtfully.

"That is what you can do then," he said. "But not tonight. I imagine she will be at the funeral tomorrow.
Which servant put the poem on your desk?" He took her
arm and guided her to the door.

"I haven't had time to ask." Suddenly she froze, balking
at leaving the room. "Bragg, my parents are at home. You
cannot come round now and start asking questions."

"Unfortunately, I will have to do just that, unless you
can learn which servant put the note on your desk. I must
interview him or her, the sooner the better."

She was relieved. "I will inquire tonight. Shall I call
you the moment I learn anything?"

"Leave Peter a message. I may not be home for some
time," he said.

She followed him down the hall. "Do you expect
O'Donnell to confess?"

"No. But I shall pressure him and watch him squirm."
He eyed her but called, "Peter! I am off. Where is Katie?"
He sounded suspicious and irritable now.

Peter had appeared in the doorway of the dining room,
with Dot in hand. The little girl grinned at them. Francesca
could not smile back. "She is in the kitchen, refusing to
eat," he said.

To Francesca's amazement, Bragg stalked past Peter.
Francesca followed him into the kitchen. He paused before
the little girl, who glanced at him with a sullen expression.
"Do you think to starve?" he demanded.

She didn't respond.

"Frankly, I could hardly care whether you eat or not,"
he said. "I am not a rich man, and that leaves more for
myself."

She glowered at him.

"I did not ask to have you and your sister brought here. In fact, tomorrow you shall both be sent to another home."

The stare was unwavering. Or did she quickly blink?

"I look forward to the day. Why would I want to keep such a sullen child in my home, one who thinks to starve herself to death? Not to mention the fact that your sister is annoyingly messy. So do not eat. Go to your new foster parents tomorrow hungry. Perhaps they will be even poorer than myself." He looked at Peter. "Have them ready to leave this house at nine A.M."

"Bragg?" Francesca was disbelieving.

"I have had enough," he said, stalking out.

Francesca did not move, stunned and incredulous.

Tears filled Katie's eyes.

"It's all right," Francesca began soothingly.

Katie picked up her fork and stabbed at a piece of meat, then glared at the doorway where Bragg had disappeared.

Francesca started.

Katie glared at her and jammed the piece of beef into her mouth. Another glare followed with little or no apparent chewing action.

Peter caught Francesca's eye. She understood that he wanted her to leave. Francesca did so, but at the last moment she glanced over her shoulder and caught Katie swallowing. She grimaced as if she were ingesting medicine.

"That was a bit harsh, don't you think?" Francesca said to Bragg in the hallway.

"My mood is not a pleasant one," he responded. "Dot still dislikes me—now I suspect she is following her sister's lead. I have simply had enough. Is she eating?" They stepped outside. The temperature was dropping precipitously, and Francesca shivered.

"Yes, she is, or at least, she did take one bite."

His hand shot up to hail a cab, and she saw him hide a smile. Then, appearing stern and grim again, he said,

"She hasn't eaten for two days. I had Dr. Byrnes over."

"Oh, dear," Francesca said. "I didn't realize it was so serious."

"It is." The cab was approaching, the bay in its traces trotting down the icy cobbled street. "There was another poem, Francesca," he said.

"What?" she gasped, his abrupt statement so surprising her that she stumbled on a patch of blue ice, but righted herself by grabbing onto him.

He steadied her as the hansom halted at the curb. "There was a poem found in Mary O'Shaunessy's room—the room she slept in at the Jansons'."

For a heartbeat she could only stare. "Oh, dear God. What did it say?"

He smiled grimly at her. He said, " 'A sigh, one whisper, a lie. Two lasses, good-bye.' "

MONDAY, FEBRUARY 10, 1902—NOON

In order to attend Mary O'Shaunessy's funeral, which had been arranged by her priest and Maggie Kennedy, Francesca would have to miss her afternoon class. There was no possible way she could return from St. Mary's downtown where the service was being held and make her class or even a part of it. The realization, as she traveled across town in a quickly hired cab, was sobering: she was so far behind now in all of her classes that she might have to take a leave of absence for the semester. It was either that, give up sleuthing, or fail.

But the semester had only just begun, and while Francesca was new to criminal investigations, her previous experience with both the Burton Abduction and the Randall Killing had shown her that cases could be solved swiftly. It took but one big lead. There was a chance that they might find the madman behind the Cross Murders at any time, and then she would be able to recover her grades.

As long as another case did not come her way.

As Francesca's cab pulled up at the curb in front of the gray stone church on East 16th Street, she pondered the fact that her own maid, Bessie, had found the envelope with the poem in it on the calling card tray in the front hall. Whoever had left it there—and Francesca assumed it was the killer—had simply walked into the house to do so. His audacity was frightening.

Two men were entering St. Mary's Chapel. She paid her cabbie and alighted; unlike the funeral she had been to only a week ago, these men were in rough wool coats and black wool caps, not dark suits and bowler hats.

Francesca entered the church. Inside, the mass had begun, and she quickly took a seat in the back on the aisle. She quickly scanned the crowd, which was thin. She did not see Mike O'Donnell, but perhaps he had been picked up last night and was already in custody. Bragg sat in the front pew, with Peter and the two girls. Francesca did not know why she was surprised to see them all there, but she was. Yet the girls had to attend their mother's funeral. So much had happened so quickly that somehow Francesca hadn't thought of it. And even from this distance, Francesca could see that Katie's tiny shoulders were ramrod straight. Was she crying? Had she cried at all since her mother had died? Francesca's heart went out to them both, lurching hard, with incredible sadness.

The Jadvics were present as well. Mrs. Jadvic and her elderly mother sat in the second aisle, with a man Francesca assumed was Mrs. Jadvic's husband.

Francesca saw a number of young working women in the center aisles, and she assumed they were Mary's friends and co-workers. Then she squinted with suspicion at a man in black with a head of white hair. Was that Father O'Connor? She felt almost certain that it was. But why would he be present?

He claimed to have met Mary once.

Suddenly the woman in the black hat and veil in front

of her turned. She smiled a little at Francesca. "Hello," she whispered.

It was Maggie Kennedy. Her eyes were red, as was the tip of her nose, and Francesca realized she had been crying. They briefly squeezed palms. "I need to speak with you before you leave, after the mass," Francesca said softly.

Maggie nodded and turned back to the front of the church.

Suddenly Francesca felt that she had attracted attention, possibly for whispering during the service. She looked around and saw a woman in a well-made navy blue coat, a matching hat pulled low over her face, its half-veil shielding her features, looking her way. The woman seemed familiar. Francesca stiffened. But the woman in navy blue instantly turned away.

Who was that? Francesca thought, disturbed and racking her brain. And whoever it was, she did not belong there, at the funeral, as her clothes were those of a gentlewoman.

Francesca and Maggie paused outside the church. It had begun to flurry; the news was calling for heavy snow later that night. "How are you?" Francesca asked as the fat white flakes drifted slowly about them.

"I am fine, thank you," Maggie said evenly, but she did not appear composed and her tone was hoarse. "Thank you for taking care of the girls," she added. "I was so worried about them."

"It was the least I could do. I only wish that I could have brought them home with me." She smiled a bit, but could not tell Maggie why that hadn't been possible. "Maggie, I do have a few questions for you, but I am a bit worried about Katie. Has she always been sullen and even hostile?"

Maggie shook her head no. "She has always been a bit

difficult, a bit defiant, but she became very angry when Mary took the job at the Jansons'. Mary and I spoke about it—Mary was so worried about her. Apparently Katie wasn't able to understand that Mary simply had to sleep out. She started ignoring her mother and her sister—or lashing out at them, and others, in anger. She lost her appetite. She lost weight. Mary was so worried. She would bring her treats on Sundays when she came home, hoping to get her to eat! We discussed this time and again, Mary and I. Mary thought that Katie felt that Mary was abandoning them. Mary tried to explain to her again and again that she wasn't going anywhere, that she would be home every Sunday, but Katie could not or would not accept it." Maggie's eyes filled with tears. "Now she isn't coming home, not on this Sunday or any other one," she said huskily.

Francesca could not speak for a moment. "What should we do? Last night Bragg got her to eat . . . I think." Actually, for all she knew, Katie had taken one bite and that had been the end of her meal. And she was so thin to begin with.

"Perhaps I can speak with her now, briefly? And perhaps I can visit the girls next Sunday? I could take them out with my own children; we could go the zoo or some such thing." Maggie brightened with hope.

"That is a wonderful idea," Francesca said, recalling that Maggie's son Paddy was about Katie's age. The mourners were filing past them as they spoke, while leaving the church. "Maybe I could join you as well."

"Of course you could, Miss Cahill," Maggie said.

"Maggie, have you mentioned to anyone that you have enlisted my aid in solving Mary's murder?"

Maggie seemed surprised by the question, and she took a moment to think about it. "No, I don't think that I have," she said slowly.

Francesca paused as the woman in navy blue hurried

past them, her head down, making it impossible to try to see who she was. Francesca turned to stare after her. She was certain she knew that woman.

The woman was heading toward the curb, where three private carriages were lined up, alongside Bragg's motor-car.

Maggie murmured, "Is that Lizzie O'Brien?"

"Who?" Francesca shot. "Do you know that woman?"

Maggie suddenly shook her head. "No, it can't be. If it were Lizzie, she would say hello to me." Tears filled her eyes again. "Besides, she is getting into that carriage."

Francesca turned in time to see the woman being ushered into a carriage that seemed new by a dark-haired servant in tan trousers and a long black coat. The servant climbed into the driver's seat, picking up the reins and unlocking the brake.

Francesca turned back to Maggie, taking her hand. "You are taking this so hard. Do you wish to sit down?"

She shook her head, and it was a moment before she could speak. "I have not been able to get over what I read in the papers yesterday," she said.

"What is that?"

Maggie looked up at her, her blue eyes filled with grief. "When I came to you for help, Miss Cahill, I had no idea that the same man had murdered Kathleen."

It took Francesca a moment to absorb the implications of Maggie's statement. "Wait a moment. You also knew Kathleen O'Donnell?"

Maggie nodded. "We were best friends, Mary, Kathleen, and myself." She smiled then, as if a good memory had come to mind. Then she said, "And Lizzie, too. But Lizzie moved away two years ago. No one has heard from her in at least six months."

Francesca stared at her, wide-eyed. Maggie had been a best friend of *both* murder victims? And all three were poor, single, hard-working women of Irish descent? The possibility struck her then with brutal and terrifying force.

Maggie Kennedy could be the madman's next target.

"I don't have to tell her the truth," Francesca said stubbornly.

Bragg folded his arms across his chest. "If your theory is correct, then Miss Kennedy may well be the murderer's next target. In which case, your parents have every right to know what is happening under their very own roof."

They were arguing quietly outside of her father's study. As it was Monday, Andrew was long since gone to his office on the southern tip of Manhattan. Julia had just left the house for a luncheon, and Maggie was inside Andrew's study. Francesca had insisted Maggie come home with her. "Mama will have a conniption fit if she learns of my involvement in this investigation. Why can't I tell them that Maggie is staying here in order to complete the wardrobe I have ordered?"

"Francesca, I have stationed two roundsmen in front of your house!" Bragg exclaimed with exasperation.

"Miss Cahill? Commissioner?" Maggie had come to the doorway. "You said you wished to speak to me. It is late. I must go to work." Her cornflower blue eyes were worried.

Francesca and Bragg locked gazes. They had yet to explain to Maggie that her life might be in danger—and that she simply could not go about her business as if it were not.

Bragg sighed and took Maggie's arm, guiding her back into the study. "Mrs. Kennedy, it is best if you stay with Miss Cahill for a while. We believe your acquaintance with Kathleen O'Donnell and Mary O'Shaunessy may put your own life in danger."

It took Maggie a moment to grasp what he had said. "What? But how could my life be in danger? I have no idea who would do this!" she cried.

Francesca wondered what Bragg would say next. She edged closer.

"Could Mike O'Donnell have done this? Did he hate his wife for her abandonment?" Bragg asked.

She blinked. "I think he did hate Kathleen, but that he could murder her in such a way, I find it hard to believe!"

"What was his relationship with Mary like?"

If possible, Maggie blanched even more, no easy feat. "You think Mike is the killer?" she gasped.

"Please," Bragg said gently. "I am asking you what *you* think."

She sank down on the sofa. "I . . . I don't know. Mary was a warm and wonderful person. She never had anything unkind to say about anyone. Except . . ."

"Except for her brother?"

She flushed. "She did not speak of him, period. And that, in itself, said volumes."

"What did that say?"

She wet her lips. "It said that she did not care for him at all, Mr. Bragg. And . . ." She stopped abruptly again, flushing.

"Please. Spare no detail," Bragg said softly.

Maggie seemed upset. Francesca sat down beside her, taking her hand. "We have every reason to believe that the killer will strike again," she whispered.

Maggie met her eyes, and tearfully she nodded. "I didn't like him. But . . . one night, when he was drunk, when he and Kathleen were still together, he made improper advances toward me."

Francesca met Bragg's golden gaze. He seemed to nod at her. "And . . . ?" he said.

She looked at her knees. "He was rather insistent, but I eluded him. I have avoided him ever since. And to this day," she choked, "Kathleen does not know. It is a terrible secret that I have kept."

Francesca put her arm around her.

"I *must* go to work," Maggie said. "I shall be fired if I miss any more time! I have four children to feed." She started to stand, glanced past Bragg toward the doorway, and she abruptly sat back down.

Francesca glanced at the door as well, realizing that someone had paused there. Her heart sinking, she felt sure it was Julia. But it was not. Evan stood there looking as if he had just gotten up, which perhaps he had. But even sleepy-eyed, he appeared rather rakish in a brown suit, his red tie askew.

"What is going on here? I have come to use the telephone," he said. His gaze went from Bragg, to Francesca, to Maggie.

Francesca stood. "Good morning. Or should I say, 'Good afternoon'?" Her tone was cool. She hadn't seen him since she had endured an hour of brandies with him and Bartolla Saturday night. She was not about to approve of his admiration for Sarah Channing's cousin.

"My, someone is snippy today." He smiled, but at Maggie. "Hullo, Mrs. Kennedy. This is a rather pleasant surprise."

Maggie lowered her gaze. "Mr. Cahill."

Evan gave Bragg a cool look. "Surely this is not police business?"

"It is," Bragg said. "But we are almost through."

Evan stared at him, unsmiling. Then he said, "My sister is surely not involved in another case."

"Your sister has a mind and a will of her own," Bragg said calmly.

Evan looked at her. "Let's have a word, Fran."

"Can't it wait?" She was incredulous. But she knew what was really bothering Evan. It wasn't her involvement in another investigation; now that he knew Bragg was married, Evan wished to keep them apart.

"It cannot," Evan said flatly.

"I can't leave now," Francesca returned.

Bragg made a sound of exasperation. "Mrs. Kennedy. I shall speak personally with your supervisor, but for the time being, you are not to go to work."

She faced him, wide-eyed and earnest and imploring. "Even if you speak with him, they will have to replace me, as we have quotas to fill every day!"

He took her hands, sitting beside her. "You will not be able to feed your children if you meet the same fate as your friends," he said quietly.

She cried out.

"What the hell is this?" Evan demanded.

He was ignored. Maggie started to cry.

Francesca came forward. "I shall go down to your flat and bring the children here. We certainly have enough rooms."

Maggie looked at her. "But your parents?"

Bragg also regarded her. "Yes, Francesca. Your parents shall have to be told."

A headache began. "Very well," she said rather testily. "In fact"—she turned to Evan—"you may help me present my case."

"And what case is that?" he asked with sheer suspicion.

"Mrs. Kennedy may be the next target of the madman behind the Cross Murders. She must stay here, and she has four children."

Evan's eyes were wide. He faced Maggie. "Of course you must stay with us. No murderer could possibly get in here."

She met his gaze for a fleeting second. "Thank you. You are kind." Her tone was so low it was almost inaudible.

"Fran? I can help you pick up her children if you want," Evan said.

Francesca softened. "You would do that?"

"Of course I would. Even if you are entirely wrong about me and the contessa," he said.

She flushed. "If I am wrong, then I do apologize."

"Thank you," he said.

Bragg gave them both a look. "May I finish, please? With some privacy?"

"I shall go have my carriage readied," Evan said. He smiled at Maggie. "Have no fear, Mrs. Kennedy. Between us all, you are in good hands."

She nodded, not looking at him.

He appeared a bit bewildered, but then he shrugged. "Meet me out front in ten minutes," he told Francesca. He strode out.

Bragg turned back to Maggie while Francesca sat down beside her. "What about your other friend, Lizzie O'Brien? You said the four of you were best friends?"

Maggie nodded. "Very much so, for a good ten years. But Lizzie moved away about a year and a half ago. I think she lives in Philadelphia now, but she originally moved to Pittsburgh. Or maybe it is the other way around. I can't remember. In any case, Mary was the last one to hear from her, and that was six months ago, or even longer."

Bragg absorbed that. Finally he asked, "Did Mike O'Donnell know her as well?"

Maggie looked up, surprised. "Before he met Kathleen, they were childhood sweethearts," she said.

TWELVE

Francesca was afraid that Lydia Stuart would be out to
lunch as well, but fortunately she was home, and she received Francesca immediately in the same small salon as
the day before. Francesca and Evan had already brought
all the Kennedy children to the Cahill mansion, where
Maggie had been given two adjoining rooms. She had been
overwhelmed by the hospitality, and Francesca had left her
instructing her children on how to behave, with Evan being
poked and prodded by her youngest, her little dark-haired
daughter, Lizzie.

As they greeted each other now, Francesca noticed that
fatigue had etched shadows beneath Lydia's eyes. As she
had yesterday, she seemed worried and anxious.

"This is unexpected, Miss Cahill," Lydia said, gesturing
for Francesca to take a chair. She managed a tight smile.

"I hope I am not disturbing you, but I do need to speak
to you again," Francesca said. "Is Mr. Stuart home?"

Lydia appeared to consider her question. "No. He has
a small lighting business, and I do not expect him until
this evening." She hesitated. "Although his hours have
been odd of late. Miss Cahill, perhaps this is not a good
idea!"

Francesca started. "Do you mean you have no wish for
me to continue this investigation?"

Lydia seemed on the verge of tears. "Yes, that is what
I mean. I must be wrong about Lincoln."

Francesca was so surprised, for a moment she could not speak. Then, "Perhaps you are wrong about him. Lydia, yesterday I followed your husband to a cemetery," she said softly. "Not to Mrs. Hopper's."

Lydia's eyes widened. "What?"

"The Greenlawn Cemetery, which is quite a bit north of the city. I was as surprised as you are. In any case, he did not visit Mrs. Hopper."

Lydia seemed overcome with relief, and she sank into the big yellow chair. "I am very pleased," she finally said. "I just haven't known what to think."

Francesca finally took an ottoman in red and white. On the day Lydia had first approached her, and that had been Thursday, she had been adamant in her belief that her husband was unfaithful. "Lydia? Whom did he pay his respects to?"

"His mother. She died recently, four months ago. Just a month after our wedding."

"I am so sorry." It crossed Francesca's mind that something was off-kilter here, but she was tired and worried about Maggie and could not grasp what her mind was trying to tell her. "I hadn't realized you were newlyweds."

"We were married in September." Her smile was faint. "I know; it is rather old to be married for the first time at twenty-five. I am very lucky." Her tone dropped as she finished her words.

Clearly, Francesca thought, she was unhappy and disturbed. "Are you certain you wish for me to drop the case?" she asked.

Again Lydia hesitated. "He will be upset if he ever learns of this," she said quickly. "He caught you here yesterday. I think he is suspicious!"

"But we have every right to be friends," Francesca said.

"Miss Cahill, we are well-to-do, but rather simple gentlefolk. You are a millionaire's daughter; your sister is a baroness, your brother the heir to a huge fortune. Our paths will probably cross here and there in society, but not often. I am sure your friends are all more prominently placed than I."

"But I have never given a hoot about wealth or position or blue blood," Francesca said with a smile. "And I do expect for us to become real friends."

Lydia started, and her eyes filled with tears. "That is so nice of you," she whispered.

"So why are you concerned about your husband's affections?"

She sighed. "He has become so distant from me—so quickly. And I have done nothing to change his feelings for me!" she added with anguish.

"Perhaps he is mourning his mother's passing. Perhaps it is nothing more than that."

Lydia finally nodded. "Perhaps that is the case. Lincoln adored his mother. I found her a rather difficult woman, but his feelings for her were appropriate." She sighed again. "And Rebecca Hopper is very beautiful, and she is also very obvious. Clearly she wishes to entice my husband away from me. Of her intentions I have no doubt." Lydia stood, suddenly angry as well as anxious. Her fists were clenched.

Francesca also stood. "Give me another day or two," she said gently, "before we drop the case."

"Of course," Lydia said automatically. And the salon door opened, causing her to stiffen with surprise and then fear.

For Lincoln poked his head inside, smiling. "Good afternoon, ladies," he said.

Francesca smiled, but she was looking from husband to wife. Lincoln seemed amused, and Lydia was frozen, and had they not just been discussing her husband, her expression might have been comical, but it was not.

"Am I intruding?" he asked, opening the door fully and stepping into the room. He was carrying a gift-wrapped parcel. He kissed his wife's cheek. If he had overheard them, he was hiding it, and well. "I see you are entertaining Miss Cahill once again. How wonderful, dear."

Lydia nodded. "Yes. Lincoln, are you not well? It is so early for you to come home." Her lips barely moved as she spoke.

"I just could not stay away, my dear," he said. "Have you been out?"

"No, no, I have a bit of a migraine, and I have been at home all day," Lydia said in a rush. She was eerily white.

"Miss Cahill, I am pleased to see my beautiful young wife making friends." He smiled at Francesca.

For the first time, Francesca noticed that his blue gaze was very sharp and incisive. In fact, it was a bit unsettling as it slid over her from head to toe. "Well, ladies do love to chat and gossip. I was hoping that Lydia might join me for a walk on the Ladies Mile."

"It is snowing," he said lightly.

Inwardly Francesca winced. In fact, he was right, and already an inch of new snow had accumulated on the streets. "Or perhaps a drive in the park? Central Park is always so magical after a snowstorm."

"I shall go another time," Lydia said hoarsely. "Perhaps tomorrow? I have heard we shall have several inches overnight."

Francesca wondered how Lincoln Stuart could not notice that his wife was stricken with anxiety and discomfort now.

"Dear? This is for you," Lincoln said, handing his wife the wrapped parcel. The paper was a bright red, tied with a darker red ribbon. Francesca found the choice of colors somber and even grim.

"Oh, Lincoln, this is so thoughtful of you."

"Open it, and then I shall leave you ladies to your gossip."

Francesca was intending to leave, but she was curious

as to what his gift contained, as the nature of it might very well indicate his feelings for his bride. So she did not remark that her departure was imminent. She watched Lydia remove the ribbon and wrapper, her hands trembling slightly. A leather-bound volume with a title engraved in gold was revealed.

Her husband had bought her a book? Francesca sensed that Lydia was the kind of woman who would prefer jewels from Tiffany's or French lingerie.

She wondered what kind of book it was.

"This volume was edited by a friend of mine who works at *Harper's Weekly*. Lydia loves poetry. Don't you, dear?" Lincoln looked from Francesca to his wife.

Francesca stiffened with surprise. *Lincoln was giving his wife a collection of poems?* Of course, it meant nothing. It was a coincidence, and not at all related to the threatening poem she had received last night.

Lydia clasped the book, appearing pale now, but with what emotion? Francesca could have sworn it was fright. "You have taught me so much," she whispered.

Lincoln seemed very pleased, and he turned to Francesca, his gaze sliding over her frankly. But he did not speak.

Francesca found her voice. "What a wonderful gift," she said. But she was filled with tension now, for nothing felt right in that room, nothing at all. Or was she imagining the hint of danger in the air? "I think I shall go, actually. As you are here to spend the afternoon with your wife." She smiled at Lincoln. She realized that his pale blue eyes had been unwavering upon her for some time.

"Am I chasing you away?" he asked, walking with her to the door. "That was not my intention."

"Oh, no," she tried to reassure him. She smiled at Lydia. "Shall we lunch tomorrow? Or drive in the park?"

Lydia nodded, but she was clearly speechless now, and she said not a word.

"Henry, please escort Miss Cahill out!" Lincoln called. He smiled at Francesca one last time as a manservant appeared, and then he returned to the salon where his wife stood motionless in the center of the room, closing the door behind him.

For one moment Francesca did not move, her mind spinning wildly. She tried to stop her nearly hysterical thoughts. It was a coincidence that Lincoln Stuart was giving his wife a book of poems.

But now she wished to read some of those poems.

Francesca was escorted across the hall and handed her coat. She wondered if she should have asked Lydia if she had ever met Lizzie O'Brien while in Philadelphia. But the odds of that were astronomically low.

Jennings was waiting for her outside. Previously, when Francesca had arrived, the curb had been empty. Now a handsome carriage with a chestnut mare was parked beside the Cahill brougham. It was terribly familiar.

Francesca stared.

And a servant in tan trousers and a long black jacket appeared from the other side of the coach. Francesca did not move. It seared her mind that this coach and driver was the same vehicle and man she had seen outside St. Mary's just a few hours ago.

An image of the mysterious woman in navy blue, hurrying past her and Maggie Kennedy, her head down, filled Francesca's astonished mind.

An image of Lydia, standing frozen in the parlor in a pale yellow-and-white dress, followed.

Lydia had been at Mary O'Shaunessy's funeral.

Francesca was almost certain. She ran over to the driver. "Wait! Young man! I must speak with you!"

He was standing with his hands in his coat pockets, clearly waiting for his master or mistress to appear. He seemed startled. "Yes, ma'am?"

"Who do you work for?"

His confusion increased. "Mr. Stuart. Do you mind me asking why?"

She wet her lips, feeling frantic. "Did you take Mrs. Stuart to the funeral at St. Mary's earlier today?"

He seemed to square his shoulders. His complexion was already impossibly fair, so it was hard to tell if he blanched or not. "I beg your pardon?" he said.

"I must know if Mrs. Stuart was at that funeral!" Francesca cried.

He hesitated. His gaze went to a point past Francesca— to a point that was behind her.

She turned.

Lincoln Stuart stood on the front steps of the house. "Tom!" he called. "You can put the coach away. We won't be needing it until tonight."

"Yes, sir," the driver said, instantly taking the mare by the bridle to lead her away.

And across the distance separating them, a distance of twenty feet, no more, as the house had no grounds and no yard, Francesca locked gazes with Lincoln Stuart.

"May I help you?" he asked, his stare unwavering.

She shook her head and hurried to her own carriage.

It simply made no sense. Why would Lydia have gone to Mary O'Shaunessy's funeral?

Her husband had given her a book of poems.

What if her husband had been the one to go to the funeral?

But a woman in navy blue had gotten into the coach. Could it have been someone else? Could someone have borrowed the Stuart coach? Could Rebecca Hopper have borrowed the coach? Had Stuart been in the coach when the woman had gotten into it?

Lydia had said she had been home all day with a migraine. Still, she was small and slim, just like the woman in navy blue.

And Francesca finally realized what so bothered her about Lincoln Stuart. His eyes were so thoroughly dispassionate.

"What are you doing now, Francesca?"

Francesca started at the sound of her mother's voice. She had been so preoccupied that she couldn't even recall leaving the carriage and entering the house. But she still had her coat, hat, and gloves on.

"You are standing there like a statue," Julia said with some concern. She peered closely at her daughter.

Francesca forced herself to think about her current predicament. "Has Evan spoken to you?"

Julia smiled, not particularly pleasantly, and she put her hands on her trim hips. She was wearing a moss green silk jacket and a matching skirt. "Do you mean has he mentioned that you have a guest—a seamstress with four children? He gave me an absurd story, Francesca, that you have ordered a vast wardrobe and she will be staying here until it is completed." Her expression indicated that she did not believe a word and that she was waiting for the truth.

Francesca sighed. She was simply too stunned to lie. She handed a servant her coat and gloves. "Mama, Maggie Kennedy's two best friends were brutally murdered. We are afraid for her life."

Julia paled. "I thought you had promised to give up sleuthing!"

"And I meant it. And then Maggie came to me begging me to help her find the madman who killed Mary and, as it turned out, her other dear friend, Kathleen."

Julia looked around and Francesca realized she wished to sit. She was definitely pale. "Mama? Are you all right?"

"No, I do believe my heart has stopped."

Francesca reached for her arm, but Julia shook it off. She entered the closest room, the largest of the three salons on the hall, and sat down in the nearest chair. She picked up a delicate silver ashtray and used it to fan herself.

"We believe Maggie may be the madman's next target," Francesca said. "I offered her our hospitality."

"I think I preferred it when you were consoling prisoners on Blackman's Island. This is too much, Francesca."

Francesca sat down beside her. "She is a good woman, Mama. One who is grief-stricken. With four small children who depend upon her—"

"One of whom stole all of our silver," Julia snapped, referring to an incident a few weeks ago when the Cahill silver had gone missing. "They cannot stay here. What if the killer steals into our house? What if he harms someone in this family?"

"Mama, please," Francesca said. She decided she would kill her brother for not representing their case in a more efficacious manner. "And Joel did not steal anything from us. Someone who works for us is a crook, Mama. I haven't had a chance to think about it, but shortly I shall set a trap for the thief."

Julia cast her eyes to heaven and shook both her hands in the very same direction.

"Mama, if you send Maggie and her children back to their flat, she might wind up dead!" Francesca pleaded.

"Do not make me seem heartless," Julia snapped. "I am more concerned about your welfare, Francesca. It is you I do not want in danger."

Francesca hesitated. "What if I promise to at least entertain whomever you choose as a suitor?"

Julia sat up. "What?"

God, she was playing her trump card. And her heart was pounding, hard. "Mama, if you let Maggie and her children stay with us until the Cross Murderer is found, I will politely receive the suitor of your choice." And inwardly she winced. But she could deal with the likes of Richard Wiley, at least for a while. He would be easy to

manipulate and forestall. "I do believe you ran into Mr.
Wiley the other day?" She smiled brightly.

Julia's blue gaze was narrowed. She stared.

"Mama?"

"You are very motivated, Francesca," Julia remarked.

Francesca was instantly uneasy. Was she making a mistake? She had never won any battle, surreptitious or otherwise, against her mother. Julia was far cleverer than she
was. She swallowed. "Yes, I am."

"Very well. Then Mrs. Kennedy and the children may
stay. And you shall receive the suitor of my choice."

"Yes," Francesca said, more uneasy now than before.
"So, will you be inviting Mr. Wiley for supper?"

Julia stood. "Actually, I shall not." She was smiling.

Francesca did not care for her expression.

Julia said, "I forgot to mention that you have a caller
in the next room. And I do believe I shall invite him to
supper, Francesca. Say, on Sunday?"

She stared into her mother's eyes and Julia did not look
away. She had a very bad feeling, oh yes. "Who is it?"
she asked with fear.

"Calder Hart," Julia said.

He was making no effort to hide his impatience; when
Francesca paused on the threshold of the small gold salon
where he was waiting, he was pacing the room restlessly
and glancing at his watch. The moment she halted in the
doorway, he either heard or sensed her, for he turned. He
smiled, but she did not.

As always, Hart wore a pitch-black suit and snowy
white shirt, his vest and tie almost black. As always, his
presence was stunning—Francesca was even aware of feeling jolted by it. They stared at each other and his smile
disappeared.

He strode forward. "Hello, Francesca." He paused before her, not taking her hand.

"Calder," she managed stiffly. She could murder her mother for this. Hart would not be easy to manipulate; however, he was not interested in being a suitor, so maybe she was off the hook.

"I see you have been pining away for my company," he remarked with a flash of white teeth that was not a smile. Francesca did not smile in return. "What is wrong?" he asked.

"Nothing." Now she forced her lips into a smile. "This is unexpected. Do sit down. Can I offer you refreshments?" Too late, she saw a coffee cup and pot on a small table, but clearly nothing had been touched.

"No, you may not," he said, his jaw tensing. "Where have you been? I saw your carriage drive up fifteen minutes ago."

"I have been battling Mama," Francesca said tartly, walking away from him. Her back was to him now. She could feel his gaze upon it.

"Need you take this out on me?" he asked.

She half-turned. "Hart, Mama wants to make a match. That is, you and me." Now she smiled. "Is that not absurd?"

For one moment he did not smile. "I hate to tell you this, Francesca, but most mothers in this city have set their caps on me for their daughters at one time or another. I happen to be considered an ultimate catch."

"Hart! I am not the usual debutante and you know it." She looked at him with sudden unease. "Why aren't you laughing?"

"I am trying to fathom that myself. I suppose you find me a ridiculous prospect because I do not have the virtue that my half brother has?" One brow slashed upward.

She stared, incredulous. "What are we discussing? You are not here to court me!"

"I do not court, period," he said, relaxing visibly. "I am

not interested in marriage, and I am happy to set your mother straight."

Francesca blinked at him and realized that she was, most definitely, off the hook.

"Why does that make you so happy?" he asked suspiciously.

"Do not tell Mama this! And please, come to supper when she invites you!" Francesca flew to him and grabbed both his hands. "I beg you, as I have agreed to let her choose a suitor for me and she has chosen you. But being as you are not interested in matrimony, this shall work out perfectly, oh yes!" She was now exultant.

He held her hands and his dark gaze moved slowly over her face. "I suppose I could play along with this. What is in it for me?"

She stiffened, but he did not release her hands, so she failed to pull away. "I do not understand."

He smiled. It was crooked, dangerous, and unsettling. "Come, Francesca. Surely there is something in this for me?"

"We are friends," she said, disbelieving. "Friends do favors for each other without adding a price."

"But I am not like other men. I like price tags." He grinned. "I shall have to consider this carefully. I am sure there is something I might wish to have from you." His smile widened.

She yanked her hands away. "If we were not friends, I would almost think you to be preying upon me the way you prey upon all women!"

His smile slowly faded.

"Hart?"

Finally he said, with no trace of amusement, "Francesca, I never prey upon innocents, so, unfortunately, as intriguing as you are, you are not in the game."

She blinked. It took her a moment to comprehend him.

"I see. So that is why married women—and prostitutes— are your specialty?"

His mouth quirked. She was annoyed now but had failed to annoy him. "Yes."

"You don't even deny it."

"I enjoy life, Francesca. I enjoy wealth, art, and women, in that order."

"Your wealth comes first?" she gasped, repulsed yet fascinated.

"Were I still a poor man, if I resided in a tenement, loading sacks onto a freighter for a living, I would not have beauty in my life, now would I? Of any kind?"

He was right. He would not have a world-renowned art collection, and the women he slept with would hardly be in the category of Daisy Jones or Bartolla Benevente. Or Connie. "On that note, I want you to leave my sister alone."

"Oh, really?" He was amused. His eyes were dancing.

"Yes, really. I find it intolerable—disgusting—that you pursue her for one reason and one reason only: to get her into your bed." She felt the fury then.

He stared at her without speaking.

Francesca became uncomfortable.

He said, "I shall think about ceasing and desisting."

She had not expected that answer from him. "What is there to think about? I love Connie. She is very troubled right now—and very vulnerable. I am asking you not to destroy her marriage, her happiness, or her! If we are really friends, then you will leave her alone."

"Done," he said.

She could only stare, and after a long moment, she said, "Done? Like that?"

He cupped her cheek. "Yes, done, like that. Our friend-ship is more important to me than a few nights in your sister's bed. Besides, I suspect it would be difficult to entice her there in the first place. I don't like to work too hard," he added with a cheeky grin.

Francesca was flooded with relief. She clasped his hand, then realized what she was doing and released it, but his palm lingered another moment on her cheek. She moved back, saying hoarsely, "Thank you, Calder. Thank you."

He shook his head, studying her, his gaze unwavering, the smile and mirth gone.

Now she was uncomfortable. "Calder? So what brings you here?"

"You."

She felt herself flush. "Please."

"It is true." He raked his hand through his thick dark hair, which was fashionably cut but not center-parted. In a way, with that dark curly hair, the straight, strong nose, the achingly high cheekbones, the firm mouth and cleft chin, he resembled a Greek or Roman god, straight out of classical mythology. Of course, there was nothing godlike, or immortal, about him. She watched him wander about the room, pausing before a rather boring portrait of three children and a spaniel. She could see he was not interested in it. There was just no escaping the fact that he was an extremely interesting man—perhaps because he was so complicated, perhaps because he was not all bad.

He faced her. "I was surprised to find Rick squiring you about town on Saturday night."

She started. "It was a wager," she said. "I lost, and he still took me to the theater and dinner." She smiled now as she spoke.

"You are still in love, aren't you?"

She tensed. During the investigation of his father's murder, Hart had quickly realized the feelings Francesca and his half brother shared.

"Calder, I am not a woman who loves one day and then not the next."

It was a long moment before he spoke, during which

his intense regard caused her to flush. "Francesca, he is married. It was one thing for you to become infatuated before he told you he had a wife. It is another to remain so now. I must disapprove."

"I beg your pardon, but it is not your place to approve or disapprove."

"Oh, so the two of you, the two most impossibly virtuous people in this city, think it is all right to lust for one another while his wife comforts her family in Boston?"

The anger was instantaneous. "You are the last person to judge us!" she cried, pacing to him.

"I agree, but it is a free country, and my opinions are my own. What the hell is the matter with him? My brother is always on the highest moral ground." He seemed angry. "You I understand. You are young, you have never looked at a man before, so you think this is true love or some such thing. It is not, by the way."

She was furious. "How would you know? You do not even believe in love at all!"

He laughed at her. "That is why I know. It is lust, not love, that you are feeling. Tell me, how many times has he kissed and touched you?"

She wanted to slap him. She began to lift her hand and it was instinctive, but then she realized what she was doing and was horrified. He caught her wrist anyway, forestalling her.

"That is uncalled for."

She jerked her arm free of his grip. "Yes, it is, but so are your unsolicited comments."

"If you will not stay away from him, he should stay away from you." His eyes were dark and cool.

"Are you now my champion?"

"Perhaps."

"Oh, please."

"Francesca, no good can possibly come of your telling yourself that you are in love with my brother. He will never leave or divorce his wife. And while he might take a mistress here and there, he will never ruin you. Of that I have no doubt."

She stepped back. His words were a blow, no, the stabbing of a knife in her most vital organs. *"What?"*

"He will never ruin you, but your—"

"No! He has a *mistress*?" Calder's face seemed to be blurring now. Was she going to faint?

"I don't think so. Are you all right?" he asked, coming back into focus.

She realized that he was gripping her arm and she was leaning upon him. "What do you mean?" she cried. "Is there another woman?"

"For God's sake, I feel certain there is not, not now. But do you think my brother, who is a man, would be celibate for four years? Obviously he has had women since his wife abandoned him, Francesca."

Francesca had not thought about it. She tore free of Hart and fell onto the sofa, only to realize that she was shaking. She held her face in her hands.

Of course Hart had to be right.

Of course there had been women—or a woman—since Leigh Anne.

Had there also been love?

Francesca could not imagine Bragg being with a woman whom she did not love.

"Jesus Christ," Hart said, and she felt him staring at her.

"I must ask him about this!" she cried defiantly, looking up.

"I did not mean to upset you." He sat down beside her; she moved to the other end of the sofa. He sighed. "The man you *think* you love is a man, Francesca, and all men need a woman from time to time. That is a fact of life."

She faced him. "But he doesn't have a mistress now?"

"How could he? He is in the public eye."

"Have you ever met anyone he was with . . . that way?"

Hart folded his arms across his broad chest, his face closing. "You had better ask him these questions, Francesca."

"You have!" she cried. She stood. "Why reluctant to talk now? You were happy to tell me on Saturday that his wife is just two states away!"

He stood slowly. "You seemed so happy. I thought a reminder of the facts was in order."

"No, you are exactly as Bragg has described! You were a troublesome boy, and now you are a troublesome—and dangerous—man!"

He stared, and he flushed.

Francesca felt that she had gone too far—she saw the withdrawal in his eyes. "Hart, I am sorry."

"Clearly it is time for me to go."

"No." She caught his elbow. "I shouldn't have said that."

"Why not? It is a free country. You clearly find me troublesome. And I thought you enjoyed our friendship," he added coldly.

"I do." She meant her every word. Panic seemed to fill her now.

"I do not think so. You are obsessed with Rick. Good luck, Francesca. Perhaps you will get what you are wishing for. Perhaps I am wrong to think of protecting you from ruin and what can only become shame. A night or two in his bed will surely cool you off."

This time she slapped him.

Directly across the face.

It was pure instinct.

Hart walked out.

It was almost ten. Francesca had left the supper table a half an hour ago, pleading fatigue. But she was so distressed that she knew that everyone at the table had been

222   BRENDA JOYCE

aware of her state of mind; somehow Evan and her father
had held up the conversation, with Julia regarding her
thoughtfully and Francesca staring at her plate. Francesca,
upon leaving the table with her family sitting there taking
dessert, had simply walked into the foyer, asked for her
coat, and walked out of the house.

The cab she had hired left her standing on the curb in
front of Bragg's house. No lights illuminated the upper
windows, but a light was on in the window facing the
street and Madison Park. That window belonged to the
dining room.

She reminded herself now that he did not have a mistress, that he loved her, and that Hart enjoyed causing trouble.

She was sorry Hart had bothered to call; even now, she
was far more disturbed and dismayed than she had any
right to be.

Francesca walked up the short concrete path to Bragg's
front steps, two or more inches of new soft snow underfoot. She used the doorbell.

Peter answered the door, but not immediately. In fact,
several minutes passed while she waited, and when he did
open the door, the big man was in his shirtsleeves, his shirt
stained with what looked like tomato sauce. Francesca
wondered what had happened.

"Miss Cahill." He let her in, evincing no surprise at
seeing her at such an hour.

"Surely Bragg is about?" she asked, slipping off her
coat.

"He is in the study." Peter draped her mink-lined cash-
mere coat over his arm, leading the way to the study. He
rapped softly upon the door before opening it. "Miss Cahill, sir."

Francesca entered and Peter left. Bragg was standing in
front of the fireplace, where a fire crackled brightly. He'd
had one hand on the wood mantel above it, which was

now covered with a dozen family photographs. Francesca wondered if he had a picture of his wife somewhere, tucked away, one that would raise bittersweet memories. As he turned, his hand dropped to his side. "Francesca?"

It was hard not to run into his arms. "I had to come over," she said.

He moved swiftly to her, taking her by her shoulders. "Has something else happened?" he demanded.

"No, not really. I do have some information that is odd, though, and I thought you should know." She avoided his gaze. The truth was, it made sense that he had involved himself with someone when his wife left him. He was too passionate and too virile a man to be alone for very long. Still, she wished Hart had not stirred up this particular hornets' nest for her.

"What information?" he asked, his eyes moving slowly over her face.

Her heart skipped in response. The study was in shadow, except for where they stood, bathed in the fire's glow and heat. "I had an odd encounter with my client, Lydia Stuart." Francesca realized her tone was husky. She could not shake off her distress, and perhaps it *was* jealousy. She felt oddly confused. "Bragg, her coach was at Mary O'Shaunessy's funeral. And perhaps she or her husband was there as well."

"What?" he exclaimed.

Francesca told him about the woman in navy blue and then told him about Stuart's gift of poems, watching him closely.

He was very surprised. "Well. This would be a most unusual turn, if your client, or her husband, was somehow involved. Tomorrow I shall pay them both a casual call."

"I think you should. They moved here from Philadelphia, Bragg. Perhaps they know Lizzie O'Brien?"

"That would be a long shot. And I think the gift of poems is a coincidence," Bragg added thoughtfully. "But

it is certainly worth checking out. But why did she—or
he, or a friend—attend Mary's funeral? That is the crucial
question."

"I agree." She grimaced as she studied his face, her
heart aching now. "And I am not mistaken, for their driver
is a young man that I recognized from the funeral immediately."

"Well, we finally found Mike O'Donnell and Sam Carter. They are both in the hold. I spent an hour with each
of them earlier," he told her.

"And . . . ?" she asked eagerly, instantly diverted from
all that had happened and been said with Hart a few hours
ago. This was good news!

"Well, if O'Donnell hated his wife and sister, he is very
good at hiding it. Carter is the one filled with anger—and
he is open about it. But he did not know Mary, as it turns
out, and he does not know Maggie Kennedy. Or so he
claims. I believe him."

"Did you ask Mike about Maggie?" Francesca had to
ask.

"He spoke very highly of her. The man is coming across
as a God-fearing saint."

She touched his sleeve. "Perhaps *God-fearing* is the op-
erative word here. But we have both met him—he is no
saint."

"He is definitely no saint. Francesca? You are trying to
hide your feelings from me. What has happened?"

She hesitated and looked away. "I am very worried
about Maggie. I want this case solved." And that was the
truth, but only a part of it.

"So do I." He slid his hand over her shoulder. "There
is more." It was not a question.

She glanced up. "It's just . . ." She was too proud to ask
him about his personal life. It was so highly inappropriate.
Besides, whatever it was, it was in the past. Of that she
had no doubt.

"It's just what?"

She shook her head, then muttered, "Your blasted brother came calling, and he annoyed me no end."

He dropped his hand abruptly. "He cannot stay away from you, it seems."

"I doubt that," she said.

"What did he want?"

She hesitated. "He wanted to know why we were dining together Saturday night."

Bragg looked at her and then turned away to face the fire.

She touched his back. It was a rock-hard slab of muscle beneath her fingertips. He, like Peter, was casually dressed. His shirtsleeves were rolled up. Francesca imagined that she could feel his skin through the soft cotton dress shirt.

"And you said . . . ?"

"I told him about our wager," she murmured, removing her hand. Accidentally, it slid down his back.

Bragg turned and their eyes locked. Neither one of them moved.

Her heart was behaving most erratically now. "Anyway, it is not important," she whispered.

"Isn't it? Damn my bothersome brother," Bragg said harshly. He did not move. "I find myself jealous. I shall beat him soundly if he doesn't keep his distance from you."

His response was so passionate that she was briefly stunned. "There is no rivalry here, Bragg," she said, her pulse pounding. "He is only a friend—as I have pointed out before. I cannot believe you would be jealous of him! God, he is not half the man that you are!" she cried.

"You came here tonight because you were upset, not to share information with me about the Stuarts," he said flatly. "You came here tonight because he upset you."

She nodded, feeling oddly tearful. "You are right," she whispered.

He cupped her face. "Don't cry."

"I don't know what's wrong with me," she said. But she did know. He was the first man she had ever loved, but he had loved several other women, and somehow it was hard to fathom. And as she spoke she closed her eyes and turned her face, not intending to, but somehow her lips pressed a kiss into the center of his hand.

Stunned by herself, her eyes flew open, and their gazes met, his also wide.

It was a tangible moment of decision and choice. Of desire and need.

Suddenly she stepped forward—into his arms.

They closed about her in a powerful embrace, crushing her entire body against his larger, stronger one. His mouth covered hers.

Her heart seemed to drop to the floor and then shoot into the sky as their lips locked, then opened; Bragg kept her wrapped in his powerful arms and she felt every inch of muscle that he had. His tongue found hers. She cried out, thrilled and frantic, frantic and thrilled.

Her back found a wall. One of his hands braced her head against it, his fingers underneath her chin and jaw, while his body kept her immobilized as well. The kiss deepened.

A long time later, he tore his mouth from hers and their eyes met. Neither one of them could breathe properly, and neither one of them smiled, as the situation was far too urgent. Somehow his eyes had turned black. Desire strained his expression. Suddenly he popped two buttons open at her throat and he bent and kissed the hollow there, touching it with the tip of his tongue.

Francesca felt as if she might die if they did not finish this tonight.

And soon.

Suddenly he wrapped his arms around her again, burying his face against her neck, pressing his loins, which were clearly aroused, against her. They rocked together for a long, terrible moment.

Francesca did not know what to do; she could not think. Her body was demanding that she consummate with this man, and that was the only fact that she was aware of. She ran her hand over his taut waist and then over his hard buttock again. "Take me upstairs," she said harshly.

"Christ!" He moved away from her as if he had been shot.

"Bragg!"

He stared at her, breathless, his chest heaving. Somehow, his own shirt had become partially opened, revealing a swath of hard, sculpted chest muscle and dark brown hairs. "Don't even think it!" he cried.

She did not move from where she leaned against the wall, feeling as if her entire body had been reduced to a mass of quivering jelly. "But I *am* thinking it. And so are you. We are adults. Take me upstairs," she said again.

He closed his eyes and ran a shaking hand through his hair. "No." He looked at her.

Behind him, the telephone rang.

Francesca began to cry. She closed her eyes and fought tears of frustrated desire—a feeling she had never before had. Then she wondered if Hart was right. For this might be love, but it was certainly lust.

She hated Hart for appearing in her mind now.

The telephone continued to ring.

"You have to go," Bragg said harshly.

She opened her eyes in time to see him turning to the phone. She wanted to move, but her body continued to fail her. Instead, she tried to calm her breathing down. This urgency, this frustrated desire, was a terrible thing.

She watched him lift the receiver. He said, "Yes?" and stiffened. A moment later he slammed down the phone, turning to her—and his eyes were wide and clear.

Something had happened.

"What is it?" Francesca cried.

"Maggie has just opened a letter from Mary O'Shaunessy, a letter written on the day of her death."

THIRTEEN

When Francesca and Bragg arrived at the house, a servant told them that Mr. Cahill was waiting for them in Mrs. Kennedy's room. Francesca had already been hoping that her parents had retired to their rooms, as it was late, and as neither Andrew nor Julia was waiting for her—and an explanation—at the door, she assumed her brief prayer had been answered.

Maggie's door was wide open. She sat on a moss green velvet sofa in front of the hearth, where a fire burned. Evan was seated beside her, but Maggie was hugging herself and sitting very stiffly, staring unseeingly at the flames. Joel was dwarfed by a huge forest green and blue striped wing chair. No other children were in sight, and Francesca assumed they were all asleep in the adjoining bedroom.

As Francesca and Bragg entered, Evan and Joel leaped to their feet. Evan regarded Francesca grimly, and she knew he was very displeased because he had found her at Bragg's at such a late hour. Francesca ignored him. She went swiftly to Maggie, sitting down beside her and taking her hands. "Are you all right?"

Maggie met her gaze. "It is like hearing from the dead."

"I know."

Bragg had approached. "May I see the letter?"

Maggie nodded at the low table in front of the sofa, where the letter lay.

As Bragg read it, Francesca said, "Did she mention that she was afraid for her life?"

Maggie shook her head. "The letter is innocent enough. We hadn't seen each other in a few months, not since she had begun to work at the Jansons'. She described her job, her mistress, the house. She sounded so happy," Maggie added huskily.

Evan lifted a glass of scotch from the table by Maggie's knees. "Do take a sip. It will help. Truly. I promise."

Maggie bit her lower lip and flushed, not looking at him. "I do not imbibe, Mr. Cahill."

He sighed. "This is rather a bit of a crisis."

She stared at her knees.

"Mama?" Joel said, hovering behind the sofa. "Mr. Cahill'z tryin' to be nice."

Maggie turned and looked at her earnest son. "I know." She sighed and glanced at Evan briefly. "Thank you." She looked away.

"I feel as if I have done something terribly wrong," Evan said sourly, "when I am only trying to be helpful."

"You are very kind . . . sir," Maggie murmured.

"Evan? Why don't you take Joel down to the kitchen for a cookie?"

Joel brightened. He gave Evan a sideways glance that seemed partly shy and partly admiring.

Evan slapped his shoulder. "Good idea. I could use one myself. We'll even bring your mother one. How's that, son?"

Joel grinned. "I didn't want to hog it all at supper," he said.

The two walked out, Evan still clasping the boy's shoulder. Francesca regarded them until they had disappeared, pleased to see them getting along. She realized Maggie had been watching them, too. Suddenly Bragg said, "Well, it looks as if we have found Lizzie O'Brien."

"We have?" Excitement filled her.

"Mary mentions that she has heard from Lizzie, who is living in Philadelphia. Apparently she received a letter from her. My men have already searched her flat, but they were not looking for that letter."

Francesca stood. "Most people do not throw their letters out, especially not from close friends who have moved away."

"I intend to find that letter tonight." He met Francesca's gaze. "The sooner as I have an address on Lizzie, the better. Newman can go to Philadelphia to question her, and perhaps bring her up to New York." He softened, looking at Maggie. "I am so sorry you had to receive this now. How did you receive it, by the way?"

"When Francesca, I mean Miss Cahill, and her brother went to get the children, Joel brought my mail. I don't receive mail, usually, and a letter is rather an occasion. But in the excitement of moving into the house here, he forgot to give it to me until a half hour ago." She paled. "I went into shock when I realized who it was from."

Bragg looked at Francesca. "The letter is innocent enough. Mary was very happy with her new employment—in fact, with her life. Her one concern was for Katie, whom she mentions remained sullen and unforgiving. There is, however, one loose end."

Francesca raised both brows. "And that is . . . ?"

Maggie said, "I know. I was rather surprised myself."

Bragg regarded her closely. "She says, and I quote, 'To make matters even better, I have met a man. Wish me luck.' And that is how she ends her letter. Do you have any idea of who this man was?"

Maggie shook her head. "I had no idea she had met anyone."

Francesca said, "We must find this man. What if he is the killer? We must find him, and the place to start might be the list I had Newman make of everyone in attendance at Mary's funeral."

"My thoughts exactly," he said.

TUESDAY, FEBRUARY 11, 1902 — 10:00 A.M.

Her dreams were so odd. She was in Bragg's arms, his bed. Their clothes had disappeared and their passion knew no bounds. Francesca could actually feel his skin, his muscles, his manhood. It was so right.

But when she awoke, shocked because the dream was so vivid and real, something inside of her was sick and afraid.

As if it were all wrong.

Which made no sense. Francesca wondered if her conscience was warring with her determination not to let Leigh Anne destroy their happiness. Perhaps her morals were far too ingrained for her to go forward as she wished.

Or was it something else?

Francesca had overslept. She'd been up far too late recently, and as she went downstairs she was thankful she did not have a class until noon. Her resolve to take a leave of absence had lessened. It would be far better to find the Cross Murderer soon and return to her studies and some semblance of normal life.

Feminine chatter sounded from the breakfast room.

Francesca halted in surprise. If she did not miss her guess, she could hear Sarah Channing's voice.

Recovering, she hurried forward, to find Sarah and Bartolla at the table with her brother. Evan grinned at her. "Good morning, lazybones."

She scowled fondly at him. Then she turned to Sarah, who was almost pretty in a plain blue dress, and Bartolla, who was breathtaking in a vivid pink ensemble. "What a surprise! It's just past ten."

"We were hoping you might wish to join us for a day

of adventure," Bartolla said easily with her wide, infectious grin. "That is, a bit of shopping, a decadent lunch, with perhaps a good wine, and then, who knows? I would love to ski Cherry Hill in the park."

Francesca had to smile. "I do dislike shopping," she said. "In fact, I rather abhor it."

Evan stood. "And this from the woman who has ordered ten new gowns from our resident seamstress?" He was laughing at her. Then he turned to Bartolla. "I have an odd feeling I am not invited," he remarked with a twinkle in his eyes.

"It is a day strictly for the ladies," she responded, her green eyes also sparkling.

"I did not know you skied. I don't know any woman who does ski," he said.

"I adore it," she grinned.

"So do I. I am an avid skier. Perhaps we should plan to go up to Vermont for a few days? The skiing there is superb."

"I would love to do so," Bartolla replied, smiling at him. "Do you ski fast?"

"Not in mixed company."

"I am very fast," she warned. "In fact, I prefer skiing at high speeds."

Evan seemed stunned and pleased. "Do not tell me you like to race?"

"Of course I do!"

He laughed. Then Evan turned to his fiancée. "Would you like to learn to ski, Sarah?"

Sarah hesitated. Francesca knew she had not the slightest wish to engage in the sport and she felt sorry for her. In fact, there was no question now that Bartolla and Evan were drawn to each other. Couldn't Sarah see that, too?

And clearly Evan knew that Sarah had no desire to learn

to ski, too. He said, "You could sip hot cocoa in the lodge. It is very quaint up in the mountains."

Sarah wet her lips. "Maybe you could both go without me? I have been neglecting my studio, Evan. It would be wonderful to lock myself inside for a few days."

His benign expression did not change. "I should be sorry if you do not join us," he said, and Francesca knew he was merely being polite.

"I think you and Bartolla will have a much better time if I do not come," Sarah said softly. "You are both so similar in your interests and tastes. I am sure I would merely dampen the occasion, waiting for you both to finish skiing. No, I should prefer to work in my studio while you are gone." Her tone had changed, becoming quite firm.

"If you prefer to paint . . ." Evan shrugged.

Eagerness flared in Sarah's eyes. "I truly do. But I should be so happy if you both went together. I am sure you will have a wonderful time!"

Francesca felt like yanking on Sarah's long brown hair. Did she wish to encourage the pair? Because even though Bartolla seemed very fond of Sarah, Francesca was afraid that the countess and her brother, both of whom were high-spirited, passionate, and experienced, would inevitably wind up in each other's arms. "I will go," Sarah announced suddenly. "I have been yearning to learn to ski."

Evan looked at her. "Since when?"

"Since a moment ago," she said sweetly. "In fact, the two of you make it seem impossibly marvelous!"

Evan gave her an annoyed look. Then he bowed briefly at them all. "I am off. Let's continue to plan our trip, then." His last words seemed to be directed at Bartolla.

When he was gone, Bartolla said thoughtfully, "You might like skiing, Francesca. It is quite thrilling, actually."

Francesca said, "I might. But we cannot go until the Cross Murders are solved."

Bartolla eyed her with speculation and interest, while

Sarah seemed impressed and dismayed all at once. "Bartolla told me you are looking for a killer—that he was here, at the house!" she cried softly. "Francesca, I would be so upset if anything should happen to you."

Francesca smiled at her. "Thank you, Sarah. But I am clever enough to catch a killer without getting hurt." Or so she hoped.

"I do hope so," Sarah said with real worry.

"Hmm," Bartolla said reflectively.

Francesca had walked over to the sideboard, where she was about to help herself to a pastry. She looked at Bartolla, suddenly uneasy.

"So where are you in your investigation?" Bartolla asked.

"I hope we are close to its conclusion," Francesca said. "In fact, I cannot go shopping or have lunch because I must do some work regarding the case." Actually, she had a class to attend, but of course she could not tell Sarah and Bartolla that. And once that was over, she intended to confront Lydia Stuart and ask her point-blank if she had been at Mary O'Shaunessy's funeral.

Sarah's eyes widened. Bartolla grinned. "Guess what?" she said. "You have a pair of helpers. We shall come with you," and she smiled at Sarah, "and do all that we can to solve the case. Now this shall truly be an adventure."

Francesca stared in dismay.

As they got out of the Channing carriage, Francesca said quietly, "So Mrs. Stuart is a client of mine, but that is strictly confidential. I cannot tell you anything more. This will be a social call—I am sure she will be thrilled to meet you both, as she is new to town. But when the opportunity arises, I must ask her a question or two, privately."

"It is a bit boring not to know what one is investigating," Bartolla said flatly, her hands on her hips. Her coat was a magnificent sable, and she did not wear gloves. A very large diamond bracelet covered her wrist, and several large rings were upon her fingers. "And I had hoped we would be attempting to solve those gruesome Cross Murders."

Francesca sighed. "It is very important that I build a clientele and a reputation," she said.

"I think it is simply wonderful that you have the courage and will to become a professional sleuth," Sarah remarked.

Francesca smiled. "But are we not the same? Your passion has led you to art," she said.

Sarah sighed. "I am hardly like you, Francesca. Except, perhaps, when it comes to my passion for my work—which only you and my cousin seem to understand." Sarah was wearing a navy blue coat and she shivered, apparently chilled.

"I do understand it," Francesca said. "We should go inside."

"You are brilliant," Bartolla added as they started toward the house.

"Well, I am skilled, but hardly brilliant," Sarah demurred. Then she brightened. "I am so excited. Calder Hart has RSVPed that he will be attending the party tomorrow." She looked at Bartolla. "I hope it will not be uncomfortable for you?"

Bartolla laughed and halted. "Hart hardly bothers me! But God, he is so full of himself." She shook her head.

Francesca imagined Hart and Bartolla in bed together. The thought was both disturbing and intriguing. "How well did you know him?" she had to ask.

"I think you already know," Bartolla laughed. "We were lovers, and he was simply superb."

Francesca had not expected her to be so blunt, and she flushed. "Really?"

"Oh, come, Francesca, you might be a virgin, but you are an intelligent and worldly woman nonetheless. It's rather obvious that the man is extremely virile, is it not? My only complaint is that he is so sure of himself. But"— she smiled with a gleam in her eyes—"every dog has its day. That man will be brought to heel sooner or later, and I do hope I am around to witness the event."

Francesca did not know what to say, but she hardly thought a woman existed on the planet who might bring Hart to heel.

Sarah was blushing. "You are so open about it. I wish I were brave enough to never marry, and take a lover if I ever wanted to."

Francesca gaped at Sarah.

"You should do exactly what you wish to do. Society is a bunch of nonsense. Rules are made to be flouted and broken. Especially by you, Sarah, as clearly you are a bohemian at heart," Bartolla said.

"I am no bohemian," Sarah murmured.

Francesca could hardly believe her ears, and she did like Bartolla. She might wind up in Evan's bed, in which case Francesca would never speak to her again, but she liked her—how could she not? "Sarah? Is that what you really want? To remain unwed?'

Sarah was alarmed. "Francesca! I do hope you don't think I am insulting your brother! I do like Evan; truly I do!"

"But you are not in love with him," Francesca said flatly, as it had become quite obvious, even though it was rather incredible. A young, shy, and plain woman like Sarah should now be ecstatic with her luck in finding a man such as Francesca's brother. But there was so much more to Sarah than met the eye.

Sarah flushed. "I am not in love with him. But I am sure I will come to love him, in time, when we are married." There was a hint of despair to her words.

Bartolla snorted, the sound unladylike and inelegant.

"The two of you do not suit, not at all. It is the worst match I have ever seen."

Francesca blinked.

"Well?" Bartolla demanded. "Do you not agree?"

"Yes," Francesca managed. "I do. I have thought that myself, all along."

Sarah said, "Our parents are determined, and I am not strong enough to go up against Mother."

"Of course you are. You must simply let your bohemian soul tell you what to do," Bartolla said.

"Sarah? Did you really mean it when you said you would prefer to never marry?" Francesca had to ask. Because even though she had uttered those exact sentiments, she did not really mean it. One day she wanted to marry. One day she wanted to marry the other half of her heart. Bragg.

They would solve crimes together, fight for reform together, and grow old together. It would be perfect.

Sarah said, "I am not romantic, Francesca. I love one thing—my work. I am afraid to marry."

"Afraid?"

"I am afraid my husband will deny me my true passion. I am free now to paint all day if I choose. Or at least I was free to do so until this engagement came up." Her face had fallen.

Francesca looked at Bartolla. They exchanged a long glance. "This isn't right," Francesca finally said.

"No, it isn't. Sarah is different from us, isn't she? She has a genius we do not have. God gave it to her for a reason. And Evan, as much as I do like him, doesn't have a clue."

"No, he doesn't," Francesca said. "Can we talk Mrs. Channing into breaking off the agreement?"

"We can try," Bartolla said, and suddenly she was grinning in a conspiratorial manner. "It is worth it, don't you think?"

Francesca did not hesitate. "Yes," she said.

And Sarah looked wide-eyed from the one to the other. She finally said, "I should be very happy if I did not have to marry."

This time there was no interruption from Lincoln Stuart. Lydia was surprised and then pleased to receive them, and in no time tea and breakfast cakes were served. Conversation meandered about from Bartolla's arrival in the country just a week ago to her life in Europe and then the party being held at the Channings' that night. Lydia and her husband were promptly invited to attend, by both Sarah and her cousin. Lydia declined, but Francesca could see from the shining light in her eyes that she desperately wished to come.

When Lydia excused herself from the room to ask for more lemon for their tea, Francesca got up and followed her into the hall. "Lydia?"

Lydia turned, apparently surprised to find Francesca there. "Yes?"

"Might we speak privately for a moment?"

Lydia's expression changed. She had been enjoying herself all morning; now, anxiety flitted through her eyes. She lowered her voice. "Francesca, I do appreciate all that you have done on my behalf. But I have decided that you are right. Lincoln is not seeing Rebecca Hopper, and his distraction of late has other causes. I have decided that I do not need your services after all, but I am more than happy to pay your bill for all that you have done thus far."

It was odd, but Francesca had the feeling that Lydia truly wished to be rid of her in her investigative capacity. It did not seem, or feel, innocent. "Did you enjoy the book your husband gave you?" she heard herself ask.

Lydia started. "I haven't had time to read it," she said.

"Do you collect poetry?"

Lydia seemed puzzled by the question. "No, I do not.

In fact, I am not fond of poetry at all. It is my husband who reads avidly, in all genres, and he has been insistent that I do so, too."

Francesca stared. Many, many questions flitted through her mind. "While you were living in Philadelphia, did you ever meet a young woman named Lizzie O'Brien? She was a working girl—a seamstress, I believe."

Lydia's confusion increased. She was flushed now. "What a strange question," she said. "I have no idea. I shall think about it, but the seamstress I used while there was Matilde Lacroix," she said.

It had been a shot in the dark, Francesca thought. "Were you at Mary O'Shaunessy's funeral?" she asked abruptly.

Lydia blinked. So quickly that Francesca felt certain she was hiding something. "What? Did you ask me if I have been to a funeral?" Her color *had* increased, Francesca noted.

"Have you read about the Cross Murders?" Francesca asked softly.

Lydia stiffened. "What is this about?" she demanded.

"I am working on them with Commissioner Bragg," Francesca said.

"But what does that have to do with me?" Lydia cried.

"Your carriage and driver were at one of the victims' funerals. Mary O'Shaunessy was buried Monday afternoon. The service was at St. Mary's that day at noon. I saw a woman about your height, in navy blue, leaving the service. She climbed into your carriage."

Lydia stared coldly. "It was not me."

Francesca thought that she lied. "Are you certain?"

Her smile was brittle. "I am very certain that I was not there, and I do believe you were mistaken about my carriage. Lincoln had the coach. We have but one, and Monday he took it with him to his store."

"I see," Francesca said, second-guessing her own conviction now. Perhaps Lydia was telling the truth. She could no longer be sure. But she had to find out who the lady in blue had been. That much was clear.

"Are you accusing me of something?" Lydia finally asked, her expression strained.

"It is not a crime to go to a funeral," Francesca returned.

"The only funeral I have recently been to was that of my mother-in-law."

"I am sorry," Francesca said.

"Yes, so am I. The murder was a senseless one."

Francesca blinked. "Your mother-in-law was *murdered*?"

Lydia seemed taken aback. "Yes. I thought you knew."

"I had no idea," Francesca said. And her calm was only surface deep.

FOURTEEN

Francesca could not believe her ears. "How was she killed?" she asked. "And more important, why?"

Lydia glanced toward the room they had just left. "As I said, it was senseless. She was an elderly woman, and a bedchamber sneak was at his work. The police decided she had caught him trying to lift one or two of her jewels. Unfortunately, the crook, who was never caught, stabbed her in the back before fleeing."

Francesca stared. "How unusual. Most sneaks simply steal. Most are not even armed. Why kill an old lady when you could simply outrun her?"

"I do not know," Lydia said. "Poor Lincoln. He was so distraught. We never went to Niagara Falls for our honeymoon as we had planned."

"I am sorry," Francesca said, her blood thrumming within her. She had to search the house. She did not know what she might be looking for, but all was off-kilter here. "And you must have been distraught as well."

"I have yet to recover," Lydia said. "She was such a kind lady. I lost my own mother when I was a child; it was so nice having Dorothea about. Now, is that all? I do believe we need more lemons for our tea."

Francesca smiled, but it was superficial. Previously, Lydia had not seemed fond of her mother-in-law. "I am sorry to be so nosey," she said. And as Lydia turned away, Francesca thought of how eager she was to tell Bragg!

"Well?" Maggie Kennedy asked breathlessly. "What do you think?"

Francesca could only gape at her reflection in the full-length mirror in her dressing room.

"Miss Cahill? You do like it?" Maggie asked with worry.

Francesca stared. "This is not me," she managed. The woman she regarded was a vision, a bold and daring vision in dark red. She was a temptress, a seductress—there was nothing intellectual about her. The woman she stared at now was not a reformer or a bluestocking. She was a woman who had but one thought: to turn male heads.

"You are so beautiful like this," Maggie whispered. "But perhaps it is a bit much."

The gown was bare and fitted. Francesca felt extremely naked, as the bodice was low, the vee very deep, and, more important, both the body and the short sleeves attached to it were a very sheer layer of fabric, the bodice lined with lace. But more significantly, the red silk, which had a snakelike pattern upon it, slithered over her hips and backside and thighs before flaring out gracefully at the hem. Most evening gowns had much fuller skirts. "I look like my sister."

"Not really." Maggie met her regard in the mirror. "Connie is so . . . polished . . . and . . . cool. There is nothing cold about this."

Francesca trembled. "Everyone will stare."

"Yes, they will."

Bragg would faint when he saw her, she thought. Then she felt a small thrill begin deep within her. No, he would not faint, but he would never be able to say "no" to her again when she was in his arms.

Hart would be admiring as well.

She tensed. She had not seen him since she had slapped his face. Was he still angry? She had the unfortunate feeling that he was the kind of man to harbor a grudge. She did not look forward to crossing his path that night.

"Can I loosen your hair? It is too tightly pulled back."

Francesca hesitated, then thought, *Why not?* Unlike most women, she hated having her hair done, and her solution was to pull her long hair into a tight chignon. Fashion dictated a much softer style, with the hair rolled and waved and swept softly back into a chignon or a roll.

"I can curl it," Maggie said. She came to stand directly behind Francesca. "We have time. It's five-thirty."

Francesca was due at the Channings' at seven; they most certainly did have time. Maggie had wanted her to try on the dress early in case it needed another dart or two. But it fit perfectly. No last-minute alterations were necessary. "All right. I shall go all out for this one single night."

Maggie smiled at her.

There was a knock on her door and at the very same time Evan poked his head inside. "Fran, have you seen—" He stopped. He straightened, blinking at her.

"Please, if you say anything at all, be kind!" Francesca cried, facing him. "I feel a bit like a little girl dressed up to play grown-up!"

Evan's eyes remained wide, but admiration filled them. He whistled. "I never imagined that you could look like this. You will break a hundred hearts tonight."

She had to smile. "Do you think so?" There was only one heart she was interested in, and breaking it was not on her agenda.

"I know so," he said. He smiled at Maggie. "This is your handiwork?"

Maggie nodded, flushed with pleasure. "Yes, sir, it is."

"Will you please call me Evan?" he cried with exasperation and a smile. "Mrs. Kennedy?"

She smiled a little but ducked her head. "I shall try," she said.

"Mrs. Kennedy, I was actually wondering if I might take the boys for a sleigh ride again tomorrow. They did enjoy themselves today." He smiled at her.

"You are very kind to them. I have no objections," she said.

"Perhaps you might wish to join us? Say, around noon?"

"Oh!" Maggie looked at him, startled. "I simply cannot. I have Miss Cahill's wardrobe to finish and—"

If Francesca did not know better, she would think an odd romantic chemistry existed between her brother and Maggie. But Francesca knew it did not, as he was a man who enjoyed the attention of the most beautiful and elegant women—women like Bartolla Benevente and his mistress, the actress Grace Conway. Maggie was pretty, but she was a seamstress, and Evan would never look twice at such a woman romantically.

Francesca interrupted them. "Maggie, I should love it if you went sledding with my brother and your children. It would be a perfect escape from all that has happened. In fact, it would be so much fun that if I were invited, I should also join you."

Evan grinned at her, promptly embracing her in a huge bear hug, one that crushed her ribs and swept her off her feet.

"Evan!" she protested. "My dress!"

"Oh ho!" He laughed at her. "So now it is your dress?" He winked at Maggie. "Well done, we shall reform *her* yet. At noon, then." Smiling, he strode out, forgetting to close the door behind him.

Francesca had to laugh, but nervously. However, Evan would never lie to her, and if he approved of her gown, why, then so be it.

"Your hair," Maggie said, sounding breathless.

Francesca whirled and stared, but Maggie was looking away.

Francesca entered the ballroom on Evan's arm, behind her parents. He was grinning proudly as he led her in, and Francesca had never felt quite so good, especially not at a fete like this one. Julia was also extremely pleased; at the sight of Francesca in her Chinese red ball gown, a slender chain with a pearl-and-diamond pendant about her neck, and her hair done so correctly and sweetly, she had stared as if gazing upon a stranger. She had even whispered, in stunned surprise, "Francesca? Is that *you*?"

For once, Francesca had been happy to have her mother's approval. It was an odd feeling to have.

They were a few minutes late, and as they greeted Sarah, her mother, and Bartolla, the guest of honor, Francesca saw that the ballroom was quickly filling up. Not far from where they stood, she saw Connie and Montrose. They were not alone; Connie was smiling and chatting with several of their friends, but Neil seemed stiff and unhappy.

Guilt assailed Francesca. She had forgotten all about calling on him. Clearly all of their troubles were not solved, and a sudden determination to help them through this patch filled her.

"My, Francesca. That is a stunning gown."

Francesca met Bartolla's gaze. She was looking her over from head to foot, and she wasn't smiling. Francesca was jolted, for she had an odd feeling that her new friend did not like seeing her in such a dress. "Thank you."

"I must have the name of your seamstress," Bartolla said, and then she smiled in her usual infectious manner. She was wearing a daring gold gown, a combination of satin and lace, with more diamonds than even Julia had on. The gold was not the most flattering color for her, but she remained a beautiful woman, and men were glancing their way.

Suddenly Francesca caught a gentleman staring—and it almost seemed as if he was staring at *her*.

But Francesca knew that was not the case and that she was mistaken.

"Is that my sister-in-law?" Montrose asked in her ear.

Francesca jumped, not having been aware of his approach. She noticed that Connie remained across the room with their group of friends, although she met Francesca's eye, and she waved. Her expression was also incredulous. "Hello, Neil." She took his hands impulsively and kissed his cheek firmly.

He drew back, surprised. But then, why should he not be? For years she had stammered and stuttered in his presence, and it was only a few weeks ago that she had walked in on him and his lover, catching them in the most intimate and unforgettable of acts. "What is this?" he asked. "Is this my little sister?"

"I have not changed. Do not let a dress fool you. How are you?"

His brief moment of amusement faded. "Why, I am fine," he said.

She took his arm and they started to stroll around the room. White-coated waiters were serving flutes of champagne and glasses of punch; other white-jacketed waiters were passing hors d'oeuvres. Dinner would be served at eight—in the adjacent room, fifty tables were set with white linens, flowers, silver, and crystal. Several guests called out to Neil as they passed, and Francesca became aware of stares being directed at her. "You don't look fine," Francesca said frankly. "Neil, am I being stared at?"

They paused. His smile was brief and tired. "Of course you are being stared at. Tonight you are the most beautiful woman in this room. Bar none."

Francesca met his warm turquoise gaze and realized

how much she had changed. Once, and it felt so long ago, she had been infatuated with this man. In her own way, as the younger sister, she had fallen hopelessly in love with him the moment she had met him, which was within minutes of his introduction to Connie. For years, Francesca had adored him. Until last month, in fact, when she had discovered his dastardly and unconscionable secret.

"You know, a month or so ago, I would have died to hear such genuine admiration from you."

"You have changed," he agreed. "The little girl has become a mature—and confident—woman."

She did blush. "Thank you, Neil. But it is you I wish to discuss."

His eyes darkened. "And you have *not* changed. Francesca, I do not wish to discuss myself—or my personal affairs—with you. Please, this once, do not meddle."

"I want to help, Neil."

He just looked at her. He could have said, "You have done enough," but he did not. After all, she had been the one to tell Connie about his affair, but of course Connie had suspected, and she had demanded that Francesca reveal what she knew.

"Is there anything I can do?" she asked.

"Not really," he said, looking grim. And suddenly he stiffened.

Francesca turned so she might see why he had become so tense, and she saw Hart pausing before Connie and her group. Her heart jumped.

And that did annoy her.

Connie was allowing him to kiss her hand. Hart did so, and whatever it was that he said, Connie smiled. Instantly Neil started forward.

Francesca grabbed his arm, halting him. "Neil, you do not have to worry about Hart."

"Oh, no? Tonight we shall have this out; I am certain of it."

"Neil! Listen to me," Francesca pleaded, low. "I spoke to Hart. He will not pursue Connie. I am certain of it."

Neil actually looked at her, when he had been staring at his wife and Hart. "What?"

Francesca repeated what she had said.

"And you believe him? The man has not one moral bone in his body. He is a liar through and through. He senses Connie is vulnerable now to his efforts, and he is ruthlessly pursuing her." His smile was dangerous.

She still held his arm. Francesca felt a tremor go through him. "You really love her, don't you?"

He met her gaze. "Yes, I do. And God help me, because I have lost her."

His words, and worse, his tone, thoroughly alarmed her. "She loves you, Neil. But she needs some time to find her feelings again. She has been hurt."

"Do you think I do not know that? God! I wish I could undo what I did; I do!" he cried.

Francesca could not help herself as she studied his anguished face. "Why? Why did you go to another woman?"

The anguish disappeared; his face closed. "That is not your affair," he said, and he pulled free of her grasp and stalked away—toward his wife, Hart, and the others in their midst.

Francesca hesitated when she realized that Hart was staring at her. The moment their gazes met, he turned his back to her. Her pulse rioted.

She tried to compose herself. He was the last person she wished to see. Truly. But she would have to get her apology over with and, more important, forestall any battle between him and Montrose. Francesca hurried after her brother-in-law, feeling a bit as if she were approaching an executioner.

As she approached Connie and Hart's group, she felt every eye turn to her, except of course for those of Hart, who kept his back to her. She watched Montrose walk over to Connie, and he put his arm around her, a bit roughly, because Connie gasped. "Hart," he said coldly.

Hart sighed—as if resigned and bored. "Montrose." His back was partly to Francesca.

Francesca reached them. "Connie!" she cried, stepping directly between the two men, both of whom were large men, and it felt like she had just stepped into the path of two oncoming trains. "You are ravishing tonight!" In truth, Connie was always stunning, and Francesca had not even bothered to note the color of her gown. It was turquoise— it matched Neil's eyes exactly.

Connie's eyes were filled with worry, but she smiled. "Francesca, is that *you?*"

She had used Julia's exact words. "Yes, it is." She was acutely aware of Hart standing behind her as she faced her sister; in fact, his eyes were boring holes in her back. She had become used to the daring gown; now, however, she felt naked once again. Taking a deep breath, she turned. "Hello, Calder."

He gave her a cool look, and then he gave her a rude and disinterested once-over.

Francesca was shocked.

Not as much by his coldness but by the rudest glance she had ever seen—it was the glance of a man interested in sex and then deciding that she was not worth the effort. It was as if he had been choosing and dismissing a side of beef.

"Miss Cahill." His nod was abrupt, he did not smile, and he turned and walked away.

Francesca gaped.

One of the ladies in their group tittered nervously. And she or someone else said, "Oh, dear."

"Fran? What was that about?" Connie gasped.

Amazingly, Francesca felt tears rush into her eyes. She hardly heard her sister, but she was already lifting her skirts and racing after Hart. "Wait!"

He hesitated without turning, then continued on.

"Hart! Blast it!" she cried.

He halted, then turned. His jaw was so hard that he might be trying to grind down his own teeth.

She was panting when she reached him. "I am sorry."

He stared. "Really?"

"Yes, I am sorry," Francesca repeated, realizing that she was perspiring. *So much for being beautiful,* she thought. "But you were out of line."

He turned away.

She seized his arm. "But you were—"

"I have been defending your virtue," Hart said harshly. "Foolishly, I might add."

"My virtue does not need defending," she said, both defiant and nervous.

"Not by me it doesn't," he said. "But oddly, I was compelled to protect you from making a drastic mistake—to protect you from a broken heart."

Francesca bit her lip. "I am a grown woman."

"No, you are not."

She stared, about to protest.

"A red dress does not make you a grown woman, Francesca," he said.

His words hurt.

And he seemed to realize it, because he softened. "You are very beautiful tonight, but you are not a grown woman."

"I am twenty," she said.

"With your nose in a book and your head in the clouds."

"You are a skeptic!"

"Yes, I am."

They stared at each other.

"Calder, I appreciate your wanting to protect me. I overreacted. Can we simply forget about what happened?" She stopped.

His gaze had slipped over the bodice of her gown.

Francesca stood still. He had never looked at her this way before, and she knew it. There was nothing disparaging in his manner, and she doubted he even knew that his eyes had been drawn to her breasts. She wanted to fold her arms over her chest, but that would be immature and childish, and after what he had just said, she did not.

She did not move. "Calder, please." It was hard to speak. His gaze jerked up to her eyes. "We are friends. And your friendship is important to me. I don't know what possessed me. I have never struck *anyone* before. Can't we forget what happened?"

His gaze held hers. A long moment passed. Francesca was no longer perspiring—she was sweating. It felt as if the world had stopped turning—nothing had ever felt so important. And she wished to smile at him winningly or take his hand or do something to encourage him to really forgive her, but she simply could not move.

He finally said, "I do not want to lose our friendship, but *never* strike me again, Francesca, or you will be very sorry indeed."

Francesca shivered because the threat he was making was so clearly real. She could only stare. What would he do if she hit him again? Not that she would, of course. Then she shook her head, trying to clear away her confusion. It was vast. "Calder, I would never strike you again," she said.

"No. I think not."

"And . . ." She hesitated, then gave in to impulse. She touched his sleeve. "I know you meant well. I—" She stopped.

Hart wasn't listening to a word she said. He was looking at her legs. It was as if he could see through her gown. But then, the dress was very revealing; the fabric was thin, the skirts fluidly flowing over her form, leaving nothing to the imagination.

Or nothing to his imagination. What *had* she been thinking to wear such a gown?

"Hart?"

His gaze shot to her face and Francesca could have sworn he flushed. "Yes?"

"So we are friends?" she asked hoarsely.

"Yes, we are friends."

Their gazes had locked. Something absolutely unfathomable came to mind, and Francesca had the urge to twirl about and ask him if he liked her dress, she had the urge to be coy and tease him, to swing her hips and play the temptress, but her other self, her usual self, the bluestocking and the reformer, knew that she did not dare. For she would have to be a fool not to know that something had changed between them, somehow, sometime, for it was there now, dark and deep and frightening.

And Hart was simply not a man one toyed with.

As she had said to Connie, play with fire and one gets burned.

Hart's eyes changed. Any feelings he might be having vanished. It was as if a cloak had gone over his very soul. His smile was tight. "Well. This might be your lucky night."

She did not like his tone. Francesca, already rigid, tensed even more as she turned.

Bragg stood behind them, staring at her. And she wondered how long he had been there.

FIFTEEN

Francesca forgot all about Hart, who walked swiftly past them. She smiled, but Bragg did not smile back. "I have been trying to reach you all day," she said nervously. She reminded herself that she had done nothing wrong—then why did she feel as if she were a thief caught with one hand in a bank safe?

His gaze went from her face to her dress and then back to her eyes. "What is going on with you and Hart?"

She became rigid. "Nothing. How long were you standing there?"

"Long enough to see that he is looking at you the way he looks at all women." Bragg was angry. His eyes were so dark they were almost black. "If you think he is another friend, then you are sorely underestimating him."

She stared, both dismayed and angry, and oddly defensive as well. "Bragg, we *are* friends." To make matters even worse, she felt like a liar now. "In fact, he told me a red dress does not make me a grown woman." She flushed at the recollection. But of course, she was not the kind of woman who would ever impress a man with Hart's past.

"And he is also rude and insulting," Bragg said, softening somewhat. "You are obviously a grown woman, Francesca." In fact, he seemed to flush. "The moment I entered this room, my eyes were drawn to you. For one moment, I did not even know it was you." He smiled a little, but grimly.

She stepped closer to him. She had chosen the dress with him in mind—thinking about his reaction when he first glimpsed her. "You don't care for me this way," she spoke as the realization struck her.

"No, that's not it," he said quickly.

"I can see it in your eyes." She was stunned, dismayed—shaken.

He hesitated. "How could I not like you when you are wearing such a dress? Every man in this room has been looking at you—admiring you."

She understood her mistake now—too well. "You're not jealous." It was not a question.

"No."

She began to shake. "You admire the reformer, the bluestocking, even the sleuth."

He smiled a little. "Francesca, do not misunderstand."

"I understand you completely," she whispered, shaken to her core because she did. "This is not who I am—and only you and I know it."

Their gazes locked. "Yes," he finally said, very low. "You are not the lady in red."

She could only stare. He was so right—she would never be the lady in red, either. And he did not care; he loved her for who she really was. How was it that he knew her so well? How was it that, at times like just then, she could feel his very thoughts, as if she were a mind reader? "It's funny," she finally said slowly. "I accepted this dress pattern, the fabric, the color, everything, while imagining the look in your eyes when you first saw me in it. Yet I never felt comfortable, not when I saw the pattern, not when I put on the dress."

He said quietly, "The look in my eyes is always the same when it comes to you. You could be in rags, and it would not change."

Once again, the response he had was not what she had hoped for—not at all. Yet it was so much better, so much more. And she was ashamed, then, terribly so, for even briefly finding Hart alluring. "How has this happened? My world changed overnight, Bragg. I was a reformer and a student, and now, nothing is as it was."

He smiled. "Life has a way of twisting and turning with very little notice. But Francesca, there is nothing to prevent you from being a reformer and a student—solely—again."

Her hands found her hips. "On that note, shall we take a walk? I have been trying to reach you all day with a matter I have discovered, one that may or may not be meaningless to our investigation." And this was a safer topic.

He sighed and rolled his eyes, but he was smiling—and relieved to discuss a less personal matter as well. "Ah, even in red, the woman I am so fond of has returned."

"She has never left."

He took her arm, and as they began to cross the room, Francesca was aware of heads turning their way—her way. She ignored the glances and said, "Bragg, this may be nothing at all. But my client Lydia Stuart is a newlywed. And a month after her marriage, her mother-in-law was murdered. As she is buried here, I can only assume she was murdered here, but they were living in Philadelphia, I believe, so on that point I may be wrong."

He halted and regarded her with wide eyes. "How was she murdered?"

"It was a simple burglary. She surprised a sneak in the midst of his work, and he stabbed her with a knife. He apparently stole some jewels. No one was ever apprehended."

"Interesting. I doubt the murder is related; still, most bedchamber sneaks flee without the goods, rather than murder and continue on with their burglary. And the Stuart coach was at the funeral. Lincoln Stuart was in meetings

all day, and I have not had the opportunity to speak with
him. I did call on Mrs. Stuart, however. She insists she
was at home with a migraine and that her husband had the
coach." He paused and added, "I saw them arriving a moment ago."

"They are here?" Francesca asked in surprise.

"Yes, they are, and Mrs. Stuart is bubbling over with
happiness at having been invited. I overheard her."

"Yes, she was invited this afternoon by Sarah and Bartolla. I did not think she would come. And that is what
she told me as well, Bragg." Francesca glanced past him,
catching the regard of a good-looking blond gentleman.
He smiled at her. She looked away, not smiling in return.

As she did so, she saw Bartolla surrounded by a group
of six men, all of whom were laughing and admiring her.
That kind of event, however, was no surprise, and Evan
was in the group. Then, however, Francesca saw two of
the men smile at her, Francesca, across a goodly distance.
She was absolutely stunned.

Bartolla turned and looked her way, as if to see what
was distracting her admirers. She smiled at Francesca too.

Francesca smiled back and looked at Bragg. "You
know," she said thoughtfully, "perhaps that is why everyone is staring. Perhaps everyone knows the real Francesca
Cahill would rather have her nose in a book than be at an
evening affair." *Or have her head in the clouds*, she
thought, dismayed with that recollection. "Perhaps they are
laughing at me for dressing up like a temptress. I am not
making a fool of myself, am I?"

"No." He took her arm and looped it securely in his.
"Francesca, how could you ever make a fool of yourself?
In fact, the commotion you are causing is twofold. The
eligible men here want to know who you are and why they
have not discovered you before; the other women are jealous." They left the ballroom and most of the crowd. "Your
new friend Bartolla Benevente has her claws out, for one."

Francesca blinked. She had to glance back. Bartolla remained surrounded by her cadre of admiring men, flirting
and carrying on. Francesca could even hear her infectious
laughter from across the room. But even as she spoke, the
countess was glancing toward Francesca and Bragg. "I
hope you are wrong," Francesca said. "I really do. I have
come to like her. In some ways, we are very alike. And
we are allies now—we both want Sarah and my brother
freed from the chains of their engagement to each other."

"The chains of their engagement? Aren't you exaggerating a bit? Sarah might prove the best thing that ever
happened to your brother."

Feeling more eyes upon her, Francesca glanced over her
shoulder one last time before stepping into the library,
where a pair of gentlemen were in a quiet and earnest
conversation. As she did so, she caught Hart staring at her
and Bragg. He was expressionless, and he turned and
walked away the moment Francesca realized it was his
gaze she had felt so strongly on her back.

"If Hart ever makes an improper advance toward you,
I will break his neck with my own two hands," Bragg said
harshly, having seen his brother as well.

Francesca, who had become rigid, whirled. "Please,
don't speak that way! He's your brother."

"He's my half brother, and he has been nothing but
trouble since . . ." He stopped very angrily.

"Since when, Bragg? Since the day he was born?".

"Don't."

"I want the two of you to become friends."

"It will never happen."

"You did not want to see him tried and convicted for
Randall's murder!" she cried.

He sighed as the gentlemen walked out, smiling briefly
at them. "If he had been guilty . . ." he began.

She cut him off. "He wasn't."

Inside the library, a very large room with several seating

areas and one book-lined wall, he faced her. "Why do you always defend him?"

He had taken her by surprise. She hesitated and then asked, "Are you jealous of him?"

He also hesitated. "Yes, I am. Because he is free and I am not—where you are concerned."

She smiled then.

"And this pleases you?" His tawny brows lifted, but she could see that his inherent good humor was getting the best of him now.

"Yes, it does." She was tart. "So where were you all day?"

"I had several official meetings, Francesca. Sleuthing is not a normal part of my day. We did find the letter Lizzie O'Brien wrote to Mary before her death, early this morning. I dispatched Newman to Philadelphia, and if she is still at the address, we may very well hear from him as early as tonight."

Excitement filled her. "Will he bring her back with him?"

"Only if there is an urgent reason to do so. He has been instructed to question her thoroughly when he does find her, and he knows where I am."

Francesca accepted that. As she thought about what Lizzie might or might not say, Bragg did a double take as someone walked past the door, in the hall. It had been a woman, and he left Francesca standing there by herself, striding to the hall and staring down it.

Surprise was her very first response, followed by unease. She quickly hurried over to him, as he was turning back to her. The person disappearing down the hall was a very petite woman with hair so dark it was almost blue.

With the unease came dread. "Bragg? Do you know that woman?"

He shook his head, but two bright spots of color were apparent, high up on his cheekbones.

"You seem upset," she whispered, filled with worry. Who was that woman?

"I am sorry." He smiled at her, but it was strained. "For one moment, I thought it was Leigh Anne. At a glance, they are very similar in appearance."

She stared at him and said, almost ill, "You only saw her from behind, and for one moment. Are you certain it's not her?"

He shook his head. "Leigh Anne is even smaller, her skin fairer. And I did see her from a profile. No, it is not her, and besides, she will not come to New York."

Francesca just stared at him, utterly shaken. In fact, she almost felt devastated. *His wife was a single train ride away.*

She was in love with a married man.

Why did she keep forgetting that? She wet her lips. "What would you have done if it had been her?"

"I beg your pardon?" He did not seem calm, although he had spoken quite calmly. He seemed distraught—and Francesca could not recall ever seeing him that way.

"What would you have done if it had been her?" she repeated.

"I don't understand the point of the question." He was terse.

His tone of voice was a blow. Stunned and hurt, she froze. He had never spoken to her in such a manner.

He turned away, running one hand through his thick, sun-streaked hair.

"Is she still in Boston?"

He turned back, gave her a long look—one that was not particularly happy—and then walked behind her and closed the door. Francesca did not move.

He returned and took her hands. "I am sorry. I did not mean to speak to you in such a way. Francesca, forgive me."

She pulled her hands away. "One would almost think

that you still love her." Her tone sounded choked to her own ears.

"I have never loved her!" he exclaimed.

"You told me so yourself—you fell madly in love with her the moment you saw her," she said, and to her dismay, she had the worst urge to cry.

"That was lust," he said tersely. "Nothing more."

It felt like another blow. "You were not consumed with lust when you first met me," she said bitterly.

He stared. "How would you know?"

She stiffened. "You hardly batted an eye—"

"The moment I saw you, you turned my entire world upside down. I saw you from across the room, before we were ever introduced. You looked absolutely beautiful and even more miserable—clearly, you hated the affair. And when Andrew made the introductions, you started a political debate with me, Francesca." He suddenly smiled. It vanished. "I remember every word. I remember everything. You were wearing the most plain and prim blue dress. It matched your eyes exactly."

She trembled. "Is that lust?" She knew it was not.

His jaw clamped down. "No, that's not lust."

She turned away.

He seized her arm and whirled her back around. "This is lust, Francesca, God damn it."

To her shock, his arms went around her in the most uncompromising manner. Before she could even begin to understand what he was doing, his mouth was on hers, forcing her lips open. One of his hands slid up to and held the back of her neck, anchoring her head so she could not move. The kiss somehow, impossibly, deepened. Francesca felt a surge of desire, very much like a bolt of lightning, and it went through her body, inflaming her completely, as he bent her over backward. The back of her thighs came up against an object of furniture. An instant later, she fell back onto a sofa, and Bragg did not release her. He came down on top of her.

She felt every inch of his arousal against her hip, and somehow the shock and excitement of it caused her to cry out. And she managed to think, *Dear God, this is what he is like.*

He wrapped both of his arms around her and leaned his full weight on her and lifted his head. Their gazes locked.

She inhaled, shaking—his eyes were all heat. *Heat and desire.*

"Never tell me what I am feeling," he said roughly. "It is only the vast respect which I have for you which holds me back."

She nodded, incapable of speech.

He shifted. There was no mistaking what he was doing and what the movement meant; he was hugely aroused and letting her know it, and somehow it was dangerous. He stared.

She stared back, incapable of thought, of movement. There was only feeling—there was only wild excitement.

"There was lust the first moment I looked at you, Francesca, but I am a gentleman and I did not show it."

She nodded and realized he was going to get up. It was just too soon . . . Impulsively she managed to get an arm free from between their bodies and she gripped his head. His eyes widened. Francesca strained forward, and this time she was the one to kiss him. Her tongue tasted his lips.

His breath escaped slowly as she touched his mouth with hers, gently at first, and she tested the seam of his lips and felt him throb with a surge of fresh blood and she moaned and moved her legs, and for one moment, as he settled there, the amount of excitement was simply impossible to resist. She cried out, needing him then and there, absolutely. He gripped the hair by her nape and kissed her, openmouthed, with his tongue thrusting deep.

Vaguely Francesca heard the door.

Bragg had his tongue in her throat, his palm cupping her breast through red silk and darker lace, his manhood surging against her hip. She wanted to reach down and find him. She heard a footstep. Alarm began.

"Bragg." She pushed at him.

He froze, and leaped off of her as if shot from a cannon.

Francesca turned her head and saw Bartolla staring at them. The auburn-haired countess smiled and walked out.

Francesca sat up, her hair falling down over her shoulders like a cape.

Bragg looked from the door, which Bartolla had kindly closed, to Francesca, his eyes wide, as if astonished at her, at him, at them. Then his eyes widened impossibly as her state of dishevelment registered—or was it what they had just done?

"Shit," he said.

It was the worst language she had ever heard him use, and certainly the worst language he could use given the circumstance. Francesca laughed hysterically.

She did not make it undetected into the powder room. A gentleman and a lady whom Francesca did not know saw her and gaped as she made the mad dash down the hall. Repairs were almost impossible. Her hair had been ruined, she hadn't thought to bring extra hairpins, and worse, her skin was blotchy, perhaps from Bragg's beard. Francesca had had the good sense to find several hairpins before fleeing the library, and with her fingers she managed to comb her hair before twisting it tightly into a chignon. Perhaps, she thought breathlessly, Connie could fix the mess she had made.

She stopped and stared at herself in the mirror, dropping her arms to her sides. She was unrecognizable now.

She was no longer in Bragg's arms, but being there was all that she could think about now. She was no longer in his arms, but her heart raced at an impossible speed, and she could not seem to breathe normally. Her skin tingled; her body throbbed. And the woman she stared at in the mirror was clearly and stunningly aroused.

Francesca thought she looked very much like a harlot now. How ironic it was.

What were they going to do?

She had never seen this side of him before. She shivered, but the thrill was a delicious one.

Francesca adjusted her bodice, but it wasn't quite correct and she could not discern where it was pulling. She gave up. She smoothed down the skirts, and with a deep breath for courage, she left the powder room. She had to find Bartolla and beg her for her discretion.

She was afraid.

The ballroom was filled to capacity now; in about a half an hour, the guests would be asked to find their seats in the next room, for the supper that would follow. As it was still the cocktail hour, the ladies and gentlemen sipped champagne, nibbled on treats, and conversed in small and large groups with one another. Still, it was easy to find Bartolla. She had surrounded herself with another group of men.

As Francesca approached, she began to flush. Evan stood beside Bartolla, so closely that surely her hip touched his. He saw her, began to smile; then his eyes popped and disbelief filled them. Francesca steeled herself for a good set-down.

He left the group. "What the hell happened to you?" he demanded. "You look like you've been tossed in the hay!"

"Nothing happened," Francesca lied nervously. "Please, Evan, not now!"

"I am going to kill whoever took liberties with you," he began.

She seized his hand. "No. You are going to mind your

own business, Evan, while accepting that your little sister has grown up."

He stiffened.

Francesca added, "Please."

He hesitated. "Just tell me who it was."

She ignored him and walked over to Bartolla. "Can we have a word?"

Bartolla smiled at her, as if she had not seen Francesca in a most compromising position. "Of course." She excused herself and walked away with Francesca from the group of gentlemen.

"Bartolla, I am begging you not to say anything about what you saw!" Francesca cried anxiously.

Bartolla smiled. "I am happy you are enjoying yourself, Francesca; truly I am."

"But are your lips sealed?" Francesca asked.

"Of course they are. My dear, we are friends now, and I never betray my friends."

Relief washed over her in huge, engulfing waves. "Thank you."

Bartolla took her hand and squeezed it. "But I do hope you are ready for what you are doing. A married man is a very dangerous proposition for a young, unwed, and inexperienced woman like you."

Francesca felt herself turn crimson. "I am not doing anything."

"Really? That is not what I have seen." She was amused.

Francesca's unease escalated dramatically. She prayed that she could trust this woman, whom she hardly knew. "I mean, I intend to remain friends, period."

"You are in love, infatuated. And so is he. You will never remain friends."

Francesca shivered and hugged herself. But she did not want to remain friends, so why was she worried and frightened?

Bartolla patted her back. "My dear, don't think too much. But you might be better off if you had an infatuation for an eligible man—one not quite as experienced as Bragg."

She pulled away, rigid with more tension. "What do you mean by 'experienced'? What does that mean?"

"It means he is older than you, he has had his affairs, and he is married. You are a virgin, which makes you a bit of a schoolgirl."

"What affairs?" Francesca cried.

"I wouldn't know exactly," Bartolla said with some exasperation. "A sexy man in his late twenties has had experience, Francesca; that is all I am saying."

She blinked at Bartolla. "Sexy?" she whispered, having never heard such a word in her life.

Bartolla grinned widely. "Well, he *is* sexy; I wouldn't mind a shot at him when you are through."

Francesca was disbelieving.

"Except, of course, I could not—as I am friends with Leigh Anne."

Francesca stared.

Bartolla continued to smile.

"Tell me about her," Francesca heard herself say. And her every instinct shouted at her now that she could *not* trust this woman.

"What do you want to know?" Bartolla was clearly amused.

"What is she like?"

"She is extremely beautiful. A hundred times more so than I . . . or you. Perhaps it is because she is so amazingly small and fragile. Men flock to her like bees to honey."

In a way, Francesca knew Bartolla wished to distress her. And she was succeeding. "Go on."

"But I think it is her face that is the coup de grâce. She has such an innocent face. Very full cheeks, a heart shape, and huge blue eyes. Her mouth is always in a pout. Men love swollen lips." Bartolla shrugged. "It can be annoying, actually, because she has not one whit of innocence, but to look at her, you would think she is a little angel."

Wonderful, Francesca thought, *just wonderful*. "How could she have left Bragg?"

"I don't know. She refuses to discuss him. *Ever*. But that refusal says everything, doesn't it?"

Francesca hugged herself. "What do you mean, Bartolla?"

"It means there is still passion there. If she is still angry with him, after all of these years, wouldn't you agree?"

Francesca heard her and thought about Bragg's reaction to the small dark-haired woman who had walked down the hall. She felt ill and afraid. "Yes," she heard herself whisper. "There is still passion there." And she could only pray that it was hatred.

Bartolla patted her back. "They haven't seen each other in four years. I wouldn't worry about it now."

Francesca forced a smile. Then, behind Bartolla, she saw Sarah approaching swiftly, a delighted smile on her face—and with her was Calder Hart. Dismay filled her. She was upset—he would see. She had been making love—he would see that, too, in a heartbeat.

"Francesca! Bartolla! Mr. Hart has invited us to see his collection of art. At any time!" Sarah cried, smiling widely.

Francesca could not summon up even the tightest of smiles in return. With dread, she finally looked past Sarah.

Hart's face was impossible to read. But his eyes moved over her features slowly, and clearly he was taking inventory. Then he looked at her shoulders, her chest, her bosom, her hips. His gaze ended at her toes.

Francesca couldn't be more dismayed. She said, "Why, that is wonderful, Sarah." She had to cry. She did not know why. But where could she go to do so?

"Your shoes are black," Hart said calmly.

Francesca had never had the chance to order shoes to match her dress. Her black slippers were far too heavy for her gown, but she had hoped no one would notice, and she had forgotten about it. She found herself meeting Hart's eyes. "Yes," she said, and her tone sounded husky with unshed tears. "Sarah is as passionate about art as you are," she managed.

His implacable, unreadable expression remained. "So she has told me."

Bartolla sighed with impatience. "Sarah? Isn't there something else you wish to say to Mr. Hart?"

Sarah flushed. She gazed up at Hart with admiration. "I actually paint a bit."

His gaze had remained on Francesca. In fact, their stares were locked. If she cried now, she would surely die. She must not let Hart see that she was upset. But he turned to Sarah and he did smile. "I know."

Sarah was surprised. "But . . . how do you know?"

His expression finally softened. "An interesting portrait of three children playing beneath the el caught my eye at the Gallery Hague. I inquired about it, and was told that the artist was a Miss Sarah Channing."

Sarah stared in amazement.

"You have talent, Miss Channing," Hart said. "In a few years I would expect to see a certain maturity in your work which you cannot possibly now possess, given your age and experience."

Sarah flushed with pleasure. "I would love to give you the painting, Mr. Hart. That is, if you should decide you would want it."

"Hague thinks he shall sell it. Although I appreciate the offer and I did like it, I suggest you let him make a first sale for you."

Sarah nodded, but she seemed a bit dismayed that he did not want the painting.

Francesca wanted to tell Hart to take the painting. But

instead, she kept thinking about Leigh Anne now, who was but a half a day away. If she came to town, no good would come of it—of that she had no doubt. Still, Bragg was in love with *her*. Not his wife.

And to make matters worse, she was acutely conscious of the dark, powerful man standing with her now. She did not have to look at him to feel his presence, his aura.

"Sarah is brilliant, I think," Bartolla said. "Her portraits are simply marvelous."

"Yes, they are," Francesca said, but she had not drawn Hart's gaze by speaking, she realized, looking his way again. For he continued to stare at her. "Her portrait of Bartolla is more than lovely. She managed to capture her soul, I think, there on canvas." How tremulous her tone was.

"Really," Hart said, his gaze unwavering upon her.

"Yes," Francesca returned unevenly, lifting her chin.

"Portraits of women are my favorite subject," Sarah said eagerly. "I do not know why, but I am always determined to capture the real essence of the person I am painting, and not just the exterior. It can be quite the challenge."

Hart turned to her. "Perhaps I shall commission a portrait," he said thoughtfully.

Sarah froze, her eyes wide and stunned.

"You should do so, Hart," Bartolla said frankly. "You would not be disappointed."

Francesca forgot about herself. Sarah was immobilized with shock, hope, and excitement. Francesca realized what it would mean to her career if Hart did commission a portrait. He was a premier collector in the world. His single stamp of approval might well escalate her overnight into stardom and success.

"Would you do a portrait for me?" Hart asked, his gaze only on Sarah now.

"Of course!" she gasped.

"We could discuss the price at another time."

"I would do it for nothing!" Sarah cried, and she was trembling visibly.

His smile was shockingly gentle. "Miss Channing, I shall purchase the portrait."

Sarah simply could not speak.

Francesca was happy for her. She hugged her. "This is wonderful." She looked at Hart. "You are kind after all."

His gaze was cool. "No, I'm not."

Francesca did not like his words, his tone, or his expression. An instinct warned her that a deadly blow was coming.

Bartolla laughed. "Oh ho. I sense an explosion." She was gleeful. "So who is the subject of the portrait, Hart?"

Hart smiled tightly at her, and then he directed his black stare at Francesca. "Miss Cahill."

Francesca froze.

"Like that. In that red dress, with her hair hastily put up, with her bodice askew. Exactly like that."

Francesca was so stunned that she could only stare.

Hart stalked away.

SIXTEEN

Francesca was seated at a table with Bartolla, Sarah, and her brother. A young, recently affianced couple was at the table, John and Lisa Blackwell. It was a bit distracting, as they seemed terribly in love. Two gentlemen rounded out the seating arrangements, and one of them was Hart. Francesca knew that her mother was behind this.

They had been ushered in to sit about a half an hour ago, and a first course of caviar and blinis had been served with more crisp and icy champagne. Hart hadn't looked at her or spoken to her once, and he and John Blackwell were discussing various dangerous political situations in the regions where their companies shipped and had offices.

Francesca had a splitting headache. Still, it was interesting to learn Hart frequented places like Hong Kong and Constantinople. If she were not so aggravated, she would ask about the current ruling kingdom in Arabia, as his caravans passed through that desert land as well. But she was not about to participate in their conversation, oh no. She knew Hart had no intention of commissioning her portrait. That had been his ugly way of telling her that he knew what had happened to her gown and hair and that he disapproved. As if she cared what he thought of her behavior! But it was extremely cold of him—for poor Sarah remained flushed with her expectation now. Francesca imagined that Sarah was already planning how to pose Francesca for the portrait. Not that she would sit for a portrait for him anyway—not under any circumstances.

Bartolla caught her eye and smiled at her; Francesca could not manage to smile back.

She wondered if she should make an excuse and simply go home for the rest of the evening. What had happened between her and Bragg had shaken her to the core—a part of her was clinging to the memory of being in his arms as if it were the most important event of her life, which was odd. And she also remained shaken by his reaction to the woman who resembled his wife. Francesca wished that had not happened tonight of all nights.

"Fran, you are very quiet tonight," Evan remarked when John Blackwell and Hart fell silent, each taking a sip of his respective flute of champagne. They had been discussing the possibility of several tribes going to war in Arabia and how it would affect their business there.

"I have had a long day," Francesca said. "It is catching up with me."

Hart finally looked at her.

Francesca looked back, keeping her expression as impassive as his—or so she hoped.

It was impossible to know what he was thinking, but the tension between them was unbearable, truly. It was like having a mass of highly powered black energy on her right side. She was afraid to move for fear of touching him. And with Sarah on his other side, there was simply no way for her to take him to task for his behavior or to ask him why they were still at odds.

They should not be at odds. They had settled the issue of her having struck him yesterday.

Bartolla said, "So when shall you sit for Hart's portrait, Francesca?"

Hart seemed to smile at her. He sat back and folded his arms across his chest.

Francesca felt like throttling the other woman. "I have no idea."

"We could begin tomorrow," Sarah said eagerly.

"You are an artist?" Lisa Blackwell asked with wide brown eyes. She was a pretty woman with honey-colored hair, and Francesca had never seen two people more in love than Lisa and John. More important, there was something frank about her, for she had no pretensions, as most women did. Every few seconds Blackwell would smile softly at her and she would smile back.

Sarah said softly, "Yes."

"She is brilliant," Bartolla said firmly. "And Mr. Hart has commissioned a portrait of Francesca."

"How wonderful," Lisa said, looking from Hart to Francesca with suddenly wide eyes. And Francesca could almost hear the wedding bells ringing in her head.

"Well, well," John Blackwell said. He was a bigger man than Hart, with dark black hair, although his skin was medium in coloring and his eyes were green. "Are we finally seeing the city's most eligible bachelor take a fall?" He chuckled.

"You may call it what you will. I have merely had a sudden yearning for a portrait of Miss Cahill," Hart said easily, his shoulder to Francesca, which was the same thing as giving her his back.

Francesca gave him a look that said, *Not in a million years.*

Hart met her gaze and did not look away. While she was flustered and angry, he seemed cool and in control. She felt like kicking him until something bothered him, even if it were only her foot.

"I am so excited that I cannot breathe properly," Sarah said. "Mr. Hart wishes to own a work of *mine*."

Evan was staring at her. "I guess that is amazing good luck."

She turned to him, her eyes shining. "Oh, it is! And you have no idea just what it means to me."

He stared and then smiled a little. "I am happy for you, Sarah."

She did not look away. "Thank you, Evan."

Suddenly Francesca saw Bragg making his way through the tables and toward one of the doorways leading out of the room. She stiffened; he had been seated some distance from her, at a table with the city's most powerful leaders. Then her eyes widened when she saw Inspector Newman standing at the door, waiting for Bragg, his expression one of urgency.

He was back from Philadelphia.

Francesca jumped to her feet. "Excuse me. I shall be right back." She smiled but at no one in particular, and trying not to run, she hurried after the two men, who had disappeared from view.

Bragg was listening with a grim expression and Newman was speaking urgently. Francesca reached Bragg's side. "What is it?"

Bragg looked at her. "Well," he said, his expression odd.

"Well what?" Francesca cried with real impatience. "Did you find Lizzie O'Brien?"

Bragg patted Newman's shoulder and said to Francesca, "The address Lizzie gave Mary in order that they might correspond is a vacant home. A very well-to-do vacant home that is up for sale. It is up for sale because its owner recently married and moved to New York."

It took Francesca a moment to comprehend him. "You mean that the house is owned by Lincoln Stuart?"

Bragg smiled. "Yes."

Francesca was on pins and needles as she waited with Newman for Bragg to return to the library—with Lincoln and Lydia. An endless moment passed, and finally he entered with the couple. Lydia Stuart seemed wide-eyed and anxious in her pale peach satin evening gown. Lincoln was demanding to know what this was about.

"Please, do sit down," Bragg said quietly, gesturing at the couch.

"I have no desire to sit," Lincoln said stiffly. "I wish to know why my wife and I have been hauled away from our table!"

"You have been asked to meet with me in order that I may ask you some questions, Mr. Stuart," Bragg said calmly. "I am working round-the-clock on a police investigation, one on which you or your wife may shed some light."

Lincoln glared. "I know nothing about any investigation," he said.

"Nor do I," Lydia whispered, now ashen.

Bragg said, "Mr. Stuart, do you have a house up for sale at Number Two-thirty-six Harold Square in Philadelphia?"

Lincoln blinked. "What does this have to do with anything?"

"Please, answer the question."

"Yes, I do."

"You are the owner of that house?"

"Yes. Haven't I just said so?"

"How long did you live there, Mr. Stuart?" Bragg ignored his rather nasty tone.

"Two years. What is this about?"

"Did you have a woman named Lizzie O'Brien in your employ?"

"No," he snapped.

Bragg waited a beat, then said softly, "Are you quite certain?"

"Very. We keep a staff of three. Our driver, Tom, our cook, Giselle, and one housemaid. Her name is not Lizzie. It is Jane." He folded his arms across his chest.

Bragg looked at Lydia. "Mrs. Stuart? There has never

been, not even temporarily, a woman named Lizzie O'Brien in your employ?"

Lydia shook her head. "I must sit down," she said, looking faint. She sank onto the gold sofa. "Have we done something wrong?" she whispered.

"No." Bragg smiled reassuringly at her.

Francesca went to her, sat down beside her, and took her hand. They exchanged a glance and Francesca saw that Lydia was stiff with fear.

"Have you ever used Lizzie O'Brien as a seamstress? I believe that was her trade," Bragg said.

"I don't think so." Lydia shook her head. "I don't know."

"The name does not sound familiar?"

"No," Lydia murmured.

Francesca squeezed her hand.

"I demand to know what this is about!" Lincoln nearly shouted. "We are missing one of the finest suppers I have ever had."

"Two young women have been brutally murdered, Mr. Stuart. You have surely read about the Cross Murders?"

Lincoln stared. He shifted uncomfortably. "But what does that have to do with me?"

"Lizzie O'Brien might be next, if she is still alive."

"I still don't understand." But he was as pale as his wife now.

Bragg smiled and it was grim. "She gave a friend Number Two-thirty-six Harold Square as her home address," he said.

Lincoln seemed stunned. He looked at Lydia, who also seemed astonished. It was Lincoln who turned back to Bragg first and spoke. "That is simply impossible," he said.

"Is it?" Bragg asked with a smile that did not reach his eyes. "I have one more question, and I would appreciate a direct answer."

Francesca looked at him with real expectation. So did the Stuarts.

"Which one of you attended Mary O'Shaunessy's funeral, and why?"

"What? We do not know any Mary O'Shaunessy," Lincoln said firmly.

Lydia said nothing.

"Where were you on Monday, Mr. Stuart?"

"On Monday? What is this about?" He was flushed now. "On Monday I was at my store, from nine in the morning until five, which is when we close."

"You did not go out for lunch?" Bragg asked.

Lincoln shook his head in a negation, and then he sighed. "Of course I did. As if I can remember now—when I am being treated like a criminal! I went out at twelve as I do every day. There is a good and inexpensive restaurant a few blocks away."

Bragg said, "So a waiter there will be able to corroborate your story? That you were at lunch Monday at noon?"

Lincoln stared. "Yes, I do not see why not."

"Mrs. Stuart?" Bragg prodded.

She inhaled. "I was at home with a migraine."

"Are you satisfied now?" Lincoln asked.

"Did you go to lunch on foot?" Bragg asked.

Lincoln appeared bewildered. "Of course I did. It is only four blocks away. Besides, I leave the carriage at home for my wife."

The Stuarts had returned to supper. Newman had left, in order to go home for the evening. Francesca and Bragg stared at each other. Finally she said, "Who is lying?"

"I don't know. But today their driver had a sudden memory loss—he simply could not recall where he had been on Monday afternoon." Bragg gave her a significant look. "I suspect that he has been told to keep his mouth shut or risk his job. I did not pressure him. . . . I hate to see him lose his employment, especially if the Stuarts are not involved."

"They have to be involved! Their coach was at the funeral. One of them—or a friend—knew Mary O'Shaunessy!" Francesca cried.

Bragg patted her shoulder. "Stay calm. It does look that way. But all the evidence is not in."

"Whoever is lying, the other one is protecting her or him," Francesca said.

"Yes."

"Lizzie must have worked for them, Bragg. Why else give their home address?"

"You may be right. Or perhaps another servant was a friend of Lizzie's and she was using her to retrieve her mail? We shall have to question the entire household," he said. "And now I am wondering if she is still alive," Bragg added grimly. "In any case, I shall have to make a trip to Number Two-thirty-six Harold Square. But tonight I shall alert the Philadelphia police about the investigation here and have them begin a thorough search of the premises."

"To search the house . . . for her body?" Francesca asked.

"Yes." He gave her a long and thoughtful look. "And for any possible clues. It's not as if we have a lot of leads here."

"Well, if she is found there, then we shall know that the killer is Lincoln."

His brows arched. "Perhaps. Or perhaps it is Lydia, or a servant."

Francesca blinked. "You suspect Lydia?"

"I have ruled no one out. Mike O'Donnell remains the most obvious choice, and he remains in custody on drunk and disorderly charges. I shall have to release him shortly, Francesca. It is against the law to detain anyone without pressing charges."

"I know."

"And the most obvious choice is not necessarily the right choice of suspect," Bragg added.

She took his sleeve. "Bragg? You do know that you just said 'we' must question the entire household." She did grin.

He blinked. "That was a slip of the tongue."

"Bragg!" She took his arm. "You know I am indispensable to this case. Admit it."

He sighed and smiled at her. "All right. But I am not sure it is the case you are indispensable to."

She tensed with expectation.

He held her gaze. "You are indispensable to me, Francesca, and it has happened so quickly that sometimes it makes my head spin."

She was thrilled. All the anguish and irritation of the entire evening vanished in that moment. "You know I feel the same way," she said softly.

"I know."

A moment passed. Francesca knew he wished to take her in his arms, but she also knew that they would both exercise extreme caution now. "I have an idea."

"I am hardly surprised." He smiled at her.

"The Stuarts are dining. The ball will go on well past midnight. I think we should go over to their house right now and see if we can turn up anything interesting."

"It's funny that you should say that. That is my intention precisely."

Excitement flooded her. "We can walk right out without anyone but servants seeing us go."

"Do you not have to make your excuses?"

"I will have a servant tell Evan that I have gone home with a terrible migraine." She grinned at him.

The front door was locked, of course. But the back door was not.

No staff seemed present as they stepped into the kitchen pantry. Francesca glanced at Bragg, and she smiled. There was a half-moon out and several street lamps were on, so she knew he could just make out her expression. "You will be impressed," she whispered.

He waited and she opened her small evening bag, removing a candle.

"I beg your pardon?" he said.

"I made a list of items I should always carry with me after the Burton Affair. But it was not until we solved the Randall Killing that I actually got round to keeping the items at hand. I also have a match." She was somewhat gleeful.

"*No*. What the hell is this?" He pulled her tiny pistol out of the bag.

She blinked. "Why, it is a gun."

"I do not like this, Francesca." He had not kept his voice down.

"Bragg, it is for self-protection."

"Self-protection!" He was incredulous. "The next time you met up with a real thug, someone like Gordino or Carter, he could rip this out of your hand! A bullet from this will hardly stop them—unless your aim is to kill."

She winced. Now was not the time to tell him that she had recently encountered Gordino and that the midnight encounter with Carter had spurred her to carry her weapon at all times. "I hope to never have to use it," she said.

"Balderdash," he snapped.

He deposited the gun in her purse and took the matches from her. "Is it loaded?" he asked.

She nodded. She had figured out how to load it while en route to school yesterday. On her way home, she had purchased the necessary bullets.

"We shall discuss this later," he said, lighting the candle. "But you are not carrying a gun, Francesca, and that is that."

She led the way out of the pantry. "That is hardly a discussion."

He ignored her as they quickly crossed the small kitchen. The Stuarts' home was an older one, built perhaps fifty years ago. While it was not half of a larger residence, the rooms were small and the layout typical of Victorian homes. They went through a small dining room, also unlit. "The staff probably sleeps out. Which means no one is here, as their driver will be at the Channing affair."

Francesca thought so, too. "That must be the library. I would like to go upstairs and through their personal rooms."

"Those are my sentiments exactly," Bragg said, but he paused at the library door, which was closed. "However, I shall do a brief search here. One never knows."

Francesca met his gaze and nodded. As he slipped into the room, she turned, suddenly acutely aware of being alone in a house of shadows, guided by the small taper in her hand. Suddenly uneasy, she started up the stairs. She reminded herself that Bragg was but a shout away and would never let anything happen to her. She also reminded herself that Mike O'Donnell knew both victims, as well as Maggie and Lizzie, and he would probably prove to be their man. Still, Lizzie having used the Stuarts' Philadelphia home as an address for her mail simply had to be explained.

The steps creaked underfoot. Francesca worried with each groan of wood, but reminded herself that the Stuarts would not be home for hours and hours. Still, she would not relish confronting Lincoln while alone in his home— not that that would ever occur.

There were two rooms upstairs. As Francesca stepped into one, she saw that it was a spare bedroom that was not used at all—sheets covered the furniture there. She quickly opened the adjacent door, and upon seeing the large four-

poster bed she knew this was the master bedroom. She
hesitated, glancing around.

There was a Chinese lacquer screen in one corner, and
a large tufted chair and ottoman were in front of a small
hearth, which was dark. An upholstered bench was at the
foot of the bed, and two end tables were on its either side.
There was a secretary in the room's farthest corner. It was
a dainty piece—Lydia would be the one to use it.

Francesca walked over to the mantel but saw nothing
but two photos atop it, one a wedding photo, the other a
picture of an older woman, who she guessed was Lincoln's
deceased mother. She moved to one end table by the bed.

A cross was there. Francesca hesitated, as it was a small
and dainty pendant hanging on a delicate gold chain. It
obviously belonged to Lydia, but a cross did not make her
a murderess.

Francesca opened the bureau's single drawer. There was
a folded piece of paper there, and she quickly opened it.
The letter was from Mary. Her stunned mind tried to comprehend why Lydia would be receiving a short note from
Mary when she held up the candle and realized that the
letter had been penned to her husband, Lincoln. It said:

> Dear Sir,
>   I am writing to tell you that, as much as I have enjoyed
> meeting you, I simply cannot accept your invitation to dine.
> The reason speaks for itself. Were you an eligible man, I would
> be more than happy to further our acquaintance. In fact, my
> regrets are deep.
>
>   Sincerely,
>   Mary O'Shaunessy

Francesca sat down on the bed, stunned.

Lincoln and Mary?

*Lincoln Stuart had been romantically pursuing Mary
O'Shaunessy?*

Which would explain why he had been at the funeral, if he had been, or maybe Lydia had gone to catch her husband grieving for another woman. She did not move. But did this mean that Lincoln had killed Mary?

No, it most certainly did not—although it could, as Mary had rejected him. Still, Francesca sensed that Mary had liked Lincoln—and only her strong sense of virtue had kept her away from him.

A killer was out there who had viciously murdered two young women who had been close friends, and two other friends of theirs remained as potential victims—if Lizzie was still alive. But this did explain the funeral. Surely Lincoln had been there in disguise and Lydia had gone to catch him mourning.

Francesca had smiled grimly, then heard a door closing downstairs.

She jumped to her feet. Then she tried to become calm, as the door surely had been closed by Bragg.

But it had sounded like the front door.

She folded the letter and tucked it into her bodice. She hesitated, then ran to the other side of the bed, quickly opening the table drawer there. She saw some loose change, some receipts, and a small Bible.

Was Lincoln a religious man? She had no doubt that this was his side of the bed.

She froze, straining to hear. She thought she had heard footsteps on the stairs. What if it was not Bragg?

Suddenly a man entered the room. She almost cried out, but he approached her too swiftly for her to do so, snuffing out the candle with his fingertips. It was Bragg. He grabbed her arm. "They have just returned." He spoke in a whisper. "I found a poem downstairs. Innocent enough, although it mentions God's master plan, and it is written in a man's hand. Lincoln Stuart fancies himself a poet."

"He was pursuing Mary, Bragg," Francesca whispered. "And Lydia knew, as she had a note written by Mary to him. Is it at all possible that the two murders were not related? Perhaps she killed Mary out of jealousy."

"No. We have a mad killer, Francesca, one who has threatened to strike again, or have you forgotten? But Lincoln lied. He claimed he did not know Mary." He was grim. "The plot thickens. Let's get out of here before we are discovered. Searching his home without a warrant is illegal. I shall have him brought downtown tonight for a thorough interrogation."

Francesca had not known that their night's police work was illegal, and she was somewhat surprised. He took her arm when they heard footsteps on the stairs. She stiffened, her gaze going to his.

It quickly crossed her mind that if Lincoln was the killer, he had murdered two innocent women already, brutally, and he was about to murder a third. That is, he was a dangerous man, and they could be in jeopardy if he had a weapon.

She reminded herself that she had a gun. Was Bragg carrying one?

In their interlude in the study at the Channings', she had not noticed any weapon. She doubted she would not have felt a gun if he had it tucked in his belt or elsewhere.

Francesca realized that a closet was behind them. She tugged his hand, moving her gaze significantly to it.

Bragg pulled himself free of her grasp, and he walked confidently to the door. "Hello, Stuart," he said. "We have been hoping you would return."

SEVENTEEN

TUESDAY, FEBRUARY 11, 1902—10:30 P.M.
Lincoln stood there with a grim and surprised expression,
his wife behind him. She said, "What is this!"

"I am sorry to have intruded," Bragg said swiftly.
"Please, come inside."

Lincoln did not move. "You can't simply walk into my
house as if you own it! How did you get in? The door was
locked."

"I am here on official police business," Bragg said.
"Unfortunately, the back door was unlocked."

Lincoln gave Lydia an angry glance. She said, "I will
speak to Giselle about this."

He said, "I am not answering any more questions. It is
late, and you have upset us both terribly—and enough for
one night. This is hardly gentlemanly behavior, Commissioner."

"Why didn't you tell me that you knew Mary
O'Shaunessy?" Bragg asked.

"What?" Lincoln turned white.

Lydia was also extremely pale. "What is this about?"
she whispered.

Bragg looked at Francesca. "Why don't you take Mrs.
Stuart downstairs?"

Francesca started to reach for her, but Lydia shook her
head. "I am not going anywhere!" she cried with some
degree of hysteria. "What are you accusing my husband
of?"

"Accusations have yet to be made." Bragg faced Lincoln. "I should like for you to join me downtown for some questions."

"Downtown?" he gasped.

"At police headquarters," Bragg added.

Lincoln shook his head and then he gave a pleading look to his wife. "I don't know Mary O'Shaunessy!" he cried. "And you cannot seize innocent citizens and drag them down to a police station."

"Actually, you are right. However, Judge Kinney is a personal friend of mine, so if I go directly to his home, now, I can have a warrant for your arrest filled out. I can return in one hour with several police officers, and then it will be official." He smiled. "I did forget to mention that if this scenario takes place, I will have to charge you with a crime. In this case, it would be murder."

Lincoln did not seem to breathe. And then his eyes turned impossibly cold. He gave Francesca such a cool and chilling glance that she started and was afraid. He turned an identical glance on Bragg. "Fine. I shall go downtown with you of my own accord. But I warn you, Commissioner, you are making a mistake. A vast one."

And Francesca thought, *That is what they all seem to say*.

As Francesca let herself into her own home—with a key, as the front door had been locked—she wondered if Bragg had managed to discover a link between Lincoln Stuart and all four friends. She also wondered if Maggie Kennedy was awake. Did she know Lincoln Stuart? Had she ever met him and would she recall him if she had?

And why did she now, after having left the Stuart home, have a strong feeling that Lincoln and Lydia were hiding something?

She kept thinking of a last glance that they had shared. Lincoln had remained cold and angry, Lydia had been pale and frightened, but there had been a silent communication there.

Suddenly Francesca stiffened in the act of removing her coat. *Lydia had not said one word on the subject of her husband having an affair with Mary O'Shaunessy. But she had had Mary's letter to him in her possession.*

Francesca felt, in every fiber of her being, that something was terribly wrong. Of course, Lydia had come to her in the first place to hire her to discover if her husband was unfaithful. But she had pointed the finger at Rebecca Hopper, not the second murder victim. Perhaps Lydia had not discovered his actual affair with Mary until that day, and perhaps, sensing his involvement in something far more dastardly, she had decided to keep his liaison to herself, in order to protect him.

She had tried to dismiss Francesca yesterday, had she not?

Francesca hung up her coat, as no servant was in sight, which was a bit unusual. When the entire family was out for a big evening, usually a doorman or two remained to take coats and lock up the house. Of course, she was early—it was not yet eleven and Julia had specifically said that no one would be back before midnight, at the earliest.

Francesca continued to work through the puzzle. If Lydia knew her husband was a murderer, then she was an accomplice of sort to his crimes, and that was a chilling prospect. As Francesca started upstairs, she decided that she would wait to speak with Maggie in the morning, as she had been sewing round-the-clock, and that while under a terrible strain. But she felt certain that Maggie knew Lincoln. Perhaps by now Bragg had already gotten a confession from him.

Francesca pushed open her bedroom door and halted in her tracks. Why hadn't a light been left on? No one had started a fire in the hearth, either. It was odd. More than odd. She did not move.

A tingle swept over her spine. *Something wasn't right. And where was the staff?*

Francesca reminded herself that Lincoln was on his way downtown and Mike O'Donnell remained in jail; still, she had an enemy now, and Gordino was out and about, perhaps plotting and planning revenge against her. And Sam Carter had once easily gotten into the house. No one knew where he was, even now.

Francesca opened her purse and slipped the tiny pistol into her palm. The five or six ounces of steel and pearl comforted her instantly as she strained to hear someone, something.

The house was stunningly silent.

Was it her imagination, or did her home always sound this way at the midnight hour—especially when everyone was out?

Francesca shivered. She could not recall it ever being this quiet, and everyone wasn't out. There were four children in the house between the ages of three and eleven, for God's sake. But they would have been sound asleep for hours and hours.

The hairs on her nape and arms stood up. She grew breathless.

Something wasn't right. . . . Her every instinct told her that. She had better go check on Maggie.

Suddenly Francesca was afraid of finding Maggie stabbed to death with a cross carved into her throat.

She ran from her room, suddenly thinking that the hall was hardly illuminated, and the fact that Julia only kept two wall sconces lit every night and it had never bothered Francesca before no longer mattered.

The house was too dark and too silent. Why wasn't a child crying out in his or her sleep? Why weren't servants in the kitchen, taking one last sip of tea?

She halted, panting. The stairs leading to the next floor were in utter darkness—and how could this happen? It was as if someone had passed this way extinguishing the lights.

Above her head, she heard a door slam violently closed. Or was it a window? What in God's name was that?

Maggie and the children were on the third floor. Francesca ran up the stairs, clutching the gun, trying not to recall Bragg's statement that it would be useless against a real thug. Lincoln was with Bragg; O'Donnell was also in custody. The litany was not reassuring. If Sam Carter was the murderer, he might very well be within the house, as he was brave and angry enough to do as he pleased.

Why hadn't they left a guard with Maggie and the children?

She reached the third-floor landing, which was also cast in darkness, and she heard a bloodcurdling scream.

For one moment, Francesca did not know what to do. A woman had screamed—and she knew it was Maggie. An image of the redhead being stabbed assailed her, and the next thing she knew, she fired her pistol into the air, an instinctive act to create a diversion and stop the Cross Murderer from doing his deed.

The sound was shockingly loud.

Francesca cringed, afraid the bullet would ricochet down and hit her, but it did not. However, a painting fell to the floor, almost at her feet.

"Don't move!" Lydia Stuart shouted from the open doorway of Maggie Kennedy's room. "If you move I'll cut her open the way we gutted fish when we were children!"

Francesca froze. Lydia had seized Maggie from behind and held a knife to her throat. Maggie was in her night-clothes; Lydia remained in her pale peach-colored evening gown. But there was nothing genteel about her now. In fact, even her speech was hard and guttural—as if she were someone else.

Maggie's frightened gaze went to Francesca's, and she saw the plea there even in the shadows of the hall. A banging began on another door down the hall, hard and angry.

"Don't fuckin' move," Lydia snarled, tightening her hold on Maggie.

It clicked then. But first, she had to think of the children. "Where are the children?"

Lydia smiled coldly. "They're locked in their room, Miz Cahill. You had to come along, didn't you, an' stick your little nose in the wrong place!"

Francesca inhaled, meeting Maggie's terrified gaze again. "Are you all right?"

Maggie nodded.

"But she won't be, for long, and now I have another problem, damn it," Lydia said harshly.

Francesca swallowed hard, understanding what the other woman—the Cross Murderer—was saying, only too well. She, Francesca, knew her identity now. "You will never get away with this. Bragg will quickly realize that Lincoln has been framed—by you."

"By the time he does that, you an' her will be stiff as boards. Drop the gun."

Francesca hesitated. This woman had killed her two friends, and now she would kill Maggie and probably Francesca, all the while intending for her husband to go to jail to take the rap for her.

"Drop the gun!" Lydia ordered, and Maggie gasped as the knife held to her throat cut into her skin.

Francesca dropped the gun. "Don't hurt her! I beg you. Just leave. I swear we will let you go . . . Lizzie."

Lizzie O'Brien smiled at her. "How clever you are."

"You have framed your own husband, didn't you?" Francesca whispered. "But why kill your two dearest friends? And why write the poems? Why carve the cross upon their throats?"

"I thought the poems very clever!" Lizzie exclaimed. "As Lincoln fancies himself a poet. He is always penning these stupid verses. I realized I must pretend to be a mad *man* to mislead the coppers. And it worked, didn't it?"

"It was very clever," Francesca said uneasily. Briefly she exchanged a glance with Maggie, who was as white as a ghost, her eyes terrified. "But I still don't understand *why*."

"I didn't *want* to kill anyone," Lydia said angrily. "I really didn't. But I knew I could not trust them! I knew that they would tell Lincoln the truth about me as soon as they discovered it." Her eyes turned black. "They were always so good. Growing up, it was always, 'Now isn't Kathleen such a good girl?' Or, 'See that sweet little Maggie. Now why can't you be as kind as her?' When I had my first boy my papa whipped me black-and-blue and told me I should be like sweet, pious Mary! She would never go with a boy, oh no!" Lizzie cried.

Francesca inhaled. "But she somehow met Lincoln—"

"And he fell for her!" Lizzie shouted. "We ran into each other a week ago, and I could not weasel out of a meeting, so I invited her home. Lincoln walked in and as always, Mary stole the day! Because she is so perfect and pure, so good! I saw the way he looked at her and I knew I had to end it, instantly. So I invited her back over for tea." Lizzie smiled, but then her expression changed, becoming feral.

Francesca shivered, ill. Mary must have realized how insane Lizzie was and that was why she had tried to approach Francesca before her death. Francesca realized they would never know what had changed her mind. "You invited her to your home to kill her. Did you follow her from the house? Kill her and then bury her elsewhere?"

"Yes, I did," Lizzie was defiant. "What else was I to do? She was going to tell Lincoln the truth, I am certain! And if Lincoln ever knew the truth, if he ever knew I was Lizzie O'Brien and not the oh, so sweet and genteel Lydia Danner, he would boot me out quicker than a man can spit! I have everything I want now, and if he goes to jail, should I care? I would have his house, his carriage, his money! I could not let my *dear* old friends destroy all that I have worked so hard for."

"So you simply set out to murder them all?" Francesca asked, chilled.

"As soon as I had Lincoln agreeing to an immediate marriage, I began to plan. How could I not? His mother lived in New York and he intended for us to return there. What should I have done? Married him and returned to the city and then have lived in constant fear of running into Kathleen, Mary, or Maggie? They are the only ones who could identify me." She smiled grimly. "I chose Kathleen to be the first. Because I made a mistake last year, well before I met Lincoln, of telling her my plans to masquerade as a genteel woman and marry rich. She was aghast." Lizzie laughed in disgust. "None of them ever had any brains. Or any balls."

"You are evil," Maggie whispered. "Disgustingly evil, mad!"

"Shut up!" Lizzie shouted, and the knife cut the skin at Maggie's throat.

"No!" Francesca screamed, starting forward.

"Stop!" Lizzie shouted, as a trickle of blood slid down Maggie's neck. She appeared ready to faint. "I am not evil, you fools! Why do you think I carved the cross on their throats? I wanted God to know that I am every bit as pious as they are! My whole life He has frowned down on me. But now, I can feel Him, finally, and He is smiling, He is pleased, because I have made peace with Him!"

Francesca met Maggie's gaze. She tried to warn her in a silent communication not to move, not to speak. Maggie seemed to understand, but there was a huge question in her eyes. Francesca had no answer. For the question was, *Now what?*

"Don't look at each other like that," Lizzie warned. "I am *clever.* Very clever, more so than anyone—and my life proves that. Why do you think that I hired you? I wanted

you to find the body. It was a part of my plan. To drop
clues like a trail of bread crumbs and lead you to Lincoln."

Francesca stared at her. She was a monster—and completely unhinged.

Francesca was appalled.

So was Maggie. She could not remain silent, apparently.
"You are horrid. None of us ever suspected you were such
a cold and evil creature. We thought you were wild, but
never did we dream you evil! Have you no remorse at all?"
She stopped, tears coming to her eyes.

"Shut up," Lizzie said. "But I will like killing you the
best! Saint Maggie! So pure—turnin' away all the men—
it's almost like you had four by immaculate conception!"

"That's not fair," Maggie said, twisting her head in spite
of the knife to look at the woman she had once thought to
be an old and real friend. "You know how much I loved
Joel's father."

Lizzie almost snarled. "I got to admit, he loved you,
too. I tried to get his pants off more than once and he
never caved in."

"God help me, I hate you," Maggie whispered, crying.
"You shall burn in hell for this."

"I ain't goin' nowhere except back to my fancy house
on the corner of Sixth Avenue," she said. She turned to
Francesca. "You got my confession now, don't you, clever
lady? But like hell you'll be able to use it. Get in the
room."

Francesca did not move. She did have Lizzie's confession, but it would not do anyone much good if she went
into that bedroom with Maggie, where Lizzie would kill
them both.

Joel.

He had ceased banging on the door.

He was a very clever boy, and had he been able to hear
their conversation from the other room? Francesca couldn't
be sure, as they stood in the middle of the hall, some dis-

tance from the children's room. But he was smart enough to know that they were locked in—and surely he had heard his mother's scream.

Her heart raced with hope.

"Come into Maggie's room, Miz Cahill," Lizzie said. "An' if you try anything, I am cutting her throat, right across the artery, an' that's the end of Maggie." Her eyes had somehow turned black; she meant her every word.

Francesca swallowed down a lump of fear, trying not to look at the gun at her feet. "Very well," she managed, slowly coming forward. Francesca and Maggie looked at each other. Maggie remained frightened, but she had calmed. There was a question in her eyes. *What should I do?* it said.

Francesca calculated that her parents might come home in another half an hour, and that amount of time now seemed like an eternity. And even if Bragg realized that he had the wrong man, he would not be able to get uptown much before that. They were on their own.

Except for Joel.

But she must not count on him, as he was locked in another bedroom.

Francesca entered the bedroom, which was lit with two small lamps, and Maggie and Lizzie moved inside behind her. Lizzie used her foot to kick the door closed.

Francesca said, "I will let you go, scot-free, now, if you release Maggie. You know that by the time the police arrive here you will be long since gone. You are very clever—I am certain you will find a way to escape the city safely."

"Oh, don't be stupid," Lizzie said. "I have no intention of being on the run for the rest of my life. I like living fancy and rich. Lincoln will have to go to prison for this. I am not about to lose my new home and my new place in life."

"I hate to tell you this, but Lincoln is with the police

right now, so they will know he did not kill Maggie or myself," Francesca said as evenly as possible.

Lizzie smiled. "Am I the stupid one?" she exclaimed. "I know that! I am going to have to get rid of both your bodies so they are never found—or make them such a mess that if they are found, no coroner will be able to figure out when you was both killed."

Francesca thought about what it meant to be stabbed. She was sick to her stomach, imagining what this woman meant. "You are mad."

"Maybe."

"Bragg will know I was killed after eleven!"

"But he'll release Lincoln for now. Because he really is innocent. And when they find your body and figure out it's you—if they ever do—he won't know whether you died tonight, tomorrow, or the next day. I am not stupid," Lizzie said.

"You are mad," Maggie whispered. "And evil!"

"You have always annoyed me," Lizzie said. "Because of all of us, you were the perfect one, the virtuous one, the saint." She stabbed her.

Francesca screamed and Maggie cried out, but the stab was in her side, a vicious and mean blow. "Stop!" Francesca screamed.

"I do believe little Sarah Channing likes me," Lizzie said, holding Maggie up, who had blanched impossibly. Blood blossomed on her ivory cotton nightgown, just above Lizzie's left hand. "I am sure she will console me when I weep on her shoulder over my husband having been found to be a murderer. I have a new friend!"

"You are despicable," Maggie whispered on a soft moan.

"No, I am rather brilliant, for a fishmonger's daughter."

Francesca thought, *It is now or never.* There was a small fire in the hearth. No flames were crackling, but the logs were glowing red. She would burn her hands terribly, but she would be able to set Lizzie's dress on fire, and if the other woman burned, she could not care.

Suddenly she felt a gaze upon her. It was Maggie's. Her eyes were wide—she had seen where Francesca was looking and clearly understood what she wished to do. Maggie shook her head slightly, and it was a plea for Francesca not to try something so dangerous and so drastic.

"What is it?" Lizzie jerked on Maggie and Maggie turned white—blood gushed from her wound.

Francesca dived for the fire.

Lizzie shouted at Francesca.

The window behind Francesca shattered.

As Francesca reached for a burning piece of wood, she thought it was a rock that had broken the window, and she knew it was Joel. But she did not stop, seizing the small glowing log.

The pain was immediate—stunning.

Lizzie shouted, "What is that! Hey—stop!"

The burning pain blinded her. Francesca hurled the wood at Lizzie's skirts, unable to see, blinded by tears.

But her vision was good enough for her to see the peach silk burst into flames, just as Joel came charging through the window like some dark-haired avenging angel. Lydia screamed as her entire dress went up in flames, releasing Maggie, dropping the knife, and running around the room. Seconds later, she hurled herself through the window.

Two police officers stood sentinel in the front hall beside the front door. Lizzie was unconscious and being carried out on a stretcher to a waiting ambulance wagon. Bragg and Newman were in the hall, overseeing her removal. She was badly burned, but she had put the fire out by jumping out of the window and into the snow.

Francesca sat on a sofa in the salon closest to the door, her hand covered with salves and heavily wrapped in a bandage. Although the burn had finally been treated by Dr.

Finney, her hand hurt terribly. She watched as Lizzie disappeared from her line of sight. Then she looked up at her parents.

Julia was close to tears. Francesca had never seen her mother cry—except after Connie had finally delivered her first child after an exceedingly long, difficult, and dangerous labor. When Neil had announced that it was a girl, Julia had wept.

She was sitting beside Francesca, holding her good hand, still in her royal blue evening gown, trying very hard to contain her emotions.

Andrew stood with his hands in the pockets of his black satin-trimmed trousers, his bow tie unhooked and dangling about his neck. His tuxedo jacket was tossed carelessly over the back of a chair. They had walked in about five minutes after Bragg and the police.

Francesca smiled gamely at Julia, who did not smile in return. She looked at her father, and he was awfully grim. Then she realized that Bragg had walked outside with Newman. She had briefly treated her hand with snow and ice after determining that Lizzie was not on fire and that she was unconscious and going nowhere. She had left her in the yard in the snow, rushing up to help Maggie with her wound. When Bragg had arrived on the scene, she had been placing a makeshift bandage on Maggie. She and Bragg had exchanged two sentences: she had told him that Lizzie O'Brien was the murderess, and he had said that he already knew. Dr. Finney was upstairs with Maggie now.

"Mama? Please, do not be so upset. It worries me to see you this way."

"You are my daughter!" Julia cried. "Dear God, Francesca, I last saw you at the ball, seated between Mr. Hart and Sarah, having what I thought was a very good time. And then we come home and find you with a badly burned hand, a woman unconscious in the yard—a murdering woman—and poor Mrs. Kennedy stabbed in the side! I just do not know what to do! For the first time in my life, I am at a loss!"

"My hand is not badly burned," Francesca said. "It is my fingertips which are burned, mostly, and in a week or so I shall be as good as new."

"No. Dr. Finney said he would change the dressing every day, to make sure no infection sets in. He said it is possible, but not probable, that you might be able to remove the bandage in a week. But he doubts it." Her eyes held Francesca's.

Francesca already knew all this; it might be several weeks before she had the full use of her right hand again. "I had to save Maggie's life."

"No. The police were responsible for Mrs. Kennedy's life. Not you," Julia said.

Andrew stood before them. "Francesca, no one admires you more than I do. You have made me proud, time and again. I thank God now that you were not hurt." He hesitated. "I am proud of you now, darling, for saving Mrs. Kennedy's life."

Julia gasped in a protest.

Francesca smiled a little, warmed as she always was when her father praised her. "Thank you, Papa."

Evan rushed into the room. "Good God! There are policemen everywhere, and I just saw an ambulance wagon leaving the house!" He stopped, eyes wide on Francesca and her heavily bandaged hand. "What happened?"

"I burned my hand and I am fine," Francesca said.

"She will be fine, in a few weeks," Andrew said to his son.

They had not been speaking recently, due to Evan's engagement; in fact, Evan had been ignoring Andrew, very much as an adolescent would. Now, however, he turned directly to his father. "What?"

"Apparently the Cross Murderer came here to do away with Mrs. Kennedy. Your sister saved the day, although she did burn her hand in the process," Andrew said.

Evan looked from Andrew to Fran. "Is Maggie all right?"

"She was stabbed, but she will be fine," Andrew began.

He did not have a chance to finish, because Evan rushed from the room.

And Francesca realized that Bragg was standing in the doorway. Her heart tightened and she met his eyes and wished they were alone. He said, "May I have a word briefly with Francesca?"

"Of course," Andrew said.

Julia squeezed Francesca's good hand one more time and said to her, "I will never allow you to be in danger again."

"I am all right, Mama," Francesca whispered.

More tears came to Julia's blue eyes. She made a disparaging sound. Andrew held out his hand to her, and she took it. They left the room.

Bragg closed both salon doors, and then he strode swiftly forward and sat down beside Francesca. He enclosed her left hand in both of his palms. "Are you all right?"

"You know I am," she said softly, their gazes locked.

"I know no such thing. Francesca, you could be gravely injured, stabbed like Maggie, or dead." He was anguished and the depth of his feelings was so evident that Francesca could not help but be thrilled.

"But I am not gravely injured, although I might have a scarred palm. Which I hardly care about."

"But I care," he said urgently.

"Bragg, she stabbed Maggie. She is an evil woman, and I did not know what else to do."

He lifted her good hand and kissed it deeply. Amazingly, his kiss stirred her the way their interlude in the Channing library had—but even more profoundly. She felt rocked by the very depth of her feelings. "I know," he said roughly. "You are a quick thinker and the bravest woman I know." He could not smile at her.

She suddenly realized that tears were shimmering on his dark brown lashes. "Are you crying?" she gasped.

"No." But he was clearly so distressed for her that he was almost in tears. "I am shaken. I do not know what to do to keep you out of danger."

"Well," she said, ready to cry now as well. "I cannot possibly sleuth for several weeks, as I do not care for the idea of confronting a criminal without the full use of my right hand."

"Thank God! There is a two- or three-week respite," he said almost savagely.

"Perhaps this was a bit dangerous," Francesca had to admit.

"Perhaps?" His golden eyes widened.

"Bragg?" She started to tremble. "I was really frightened."

His jaw flexed and, mindless of where they were and who was about the hall behind the closed doors, he lulled her into his arms. Francesca buried her face against his strong chest, and she felt safe. She refused to move. Her body seemed to melt into his.

She felt him cup the back of her head. Her hair had come loose ages ago, and it was a golden cape about her shoulders and back. His fingers moved through the strands, his entire hand covering her skull. It was vastly reassuring. She felt him kiss the top of her head.

"You will obey the doctor's orders?" he asked softly, kissing her crown again.

"Yes," she murmured, a tear seeping through her closed eyelids.

"Bed rest for the next few days. God forbid that hand gets infected, Francesca," he said.

She did not move, although she wanted to look at him. "If you continue to hold me like this, I shall agree with your every request." And she felt his smile, even though she could not see it.

"I see. Then no more sleuthing, not ever."

"Hmmm," she murmured.

He kissed her head one more time and drew away from her. She sat up and they met each other's regard. A moment passed.

"I had better go, even though I do not want to."

She knew what he meant. If Julia decided to check upon them, she would instantly understand the extent of their relationship and the depth of their feelings for each other. "Yes."

"I will call tomorrow," he said.

EIGHTEEN

Dr. Finney, whom Evan had known ever since they had moved to New York, was just exiting Maggie's bedroom as he came up to the threshold. Finney paused with a greeting, his black physician's satchel in hand, but Evan did not quite hear him. *Maggie had been stabbed.* He did not even look at Finney; he saw her instead, sitting propped against a heap of pillows on the bed, looking far too pale and somewhat bewildered. How fragile she seemed, yet he knew she was a very strong woman, as she was raising four fine young children alone. Her three youngest children sat on the bed by her feet. Joel stood by her side in his long sleeping gown.

She saw Evan and her eyes went wide.

"The wound is not deep, and nothing vital was penetrated," Finney was saying. He clasped Evan's arm. "She is a brave young woman, and a strong one, and I expect her to be hobbling about in a day or so." He smiled and left Evan standing there in the doorway.

Maggie struggled to sit upright, also fumbling with the covers as if to pull them to her chin. They were already well past her breasts, covering her completely. Instantly Joel began to help her.

Evan's alarm remained in spite of Finney's comments. "No, please, do not bestir yourself," he said from the doorway. "Mrs. Kennedy, I apologize for intruding. Are you all right?"

"I am fine," she said, avoiding his gaze, her hands becoming still. "Thank you, Mr. Cahill, for asking."

He did not feel relieved, not at all. Rather, he felt shocked and stunned. "What in God's name happened?" he asked. "And may I come in?"

She glanced at him, but briefly. "It is late," she said, and in spite of her condition, her words were firm, a definite and polite refusal.

He felt himself flush and of course he understood. But surely she knew he was not about to make advances, not now or ever. "I know it is late. But . . . I am concerned."

"Thank you." She reached for and took Joel's hand. Evan realized she was trembling. She was not half as composed as she pretended to be. He already admired her—how could he not? Her courage in the face of adversity was amazing; how did one survive, without a husband, with four young children, with only one's hands and skill at sewing the means of a livelihood?

"Can I at least put the children to bed?" he asked, now noticing how wide-eyed and alert they all were. Except for little four-year-old Lizzie, who was struggling to keep her eyes open and failing soundly at it. She was falling asleep while sitting up, propped as she was on Paddy, the only one of the lot who looked exactly like Maggie, with flaming red hair and bright blue eyes.

"That would be an imposition," Maggie said softly.

"Of course it is not an imposition." Evan did manage to smile, for he knew that he, at least, must not appear concerned or anxious. He strode into the room and scooped Lizzie up into his arms. She sighed, snuggling up against his chest. "Paddy, Matthew, your mother is fine," he said. "But she must get some sleep now, so she may be as good as new as quickly as possible. You, too, Joel," he said. "We are off to bed."

Joel didn't seem happy to leave his mother's side, and he glanced at Maggie, the question in his eyes.

"I am fine," she said softly to her oldest son. "And you are the hero of the day."

He didn't smile; clearly he knew the danger his mother had faced. "Miz Cahill is the hero. I can sleep in here on the floor."

Before Maggie could speak, Evan said, "You are a brave young man to think about protecting your mother, Joel. But two police officers remain downstairs, and I am right next door." It crossed his mind that even though this was the case and it appeared that the danger was over for the moment, he might spend the night in a guest bedroom. Discreetly, of course, and on this floor.

Joel sighed. "G'night, Mom."

She smiled a mother's smile, one filled with maternal love. Evan had to smile as he watched Joel receive his mother's good-night kiss. Maggie looked up and their eyes connected.

It was a very rare moment. Her eyes were extraordinary, and he could not look away.

She did not look away, either, as she usually did, and suddenly it became awkward. He felt himself flush. "They will be sound asleep in no time."

Her gaze now skittered away. "Thank you, Mr. Cahill."

"Evan, please," he said.

She did not answer and he took the children next door, tucking them all in, even Joel, who waited until last to get into bed. Evan patted Paddy's red head, ruffled Matthew's dark hair, and kissed Lizzie's smooth cheek. She, of course, was already asleep. "Shall I leave a night-light on?" he asked.

"Yes," both small boys chorused in unison.

He smiled a little, because he had stolen a peek at them last night when he had come in and they had all been sleeping with a night-light on. He turned it on and then paused beside Joel, who lay stiffly in bed, looking as if he would be awake all night, on guard against intruders. "The house is locked up. You are a growing young man; you need your sleep." Evan said, trying to be firm and fatherly at once.

Joel nodded slightly, and suddenly he appeared to be holding back tears.

"Nothing is going to happen to your mother," Evan whispered, so none of the other children could hear. "In fact, I am going to sleep in the room across the hall, just to make sure."

Joel brightened. "You'd do that? Fer her?"

"For all of you," Evan said with what he hoped was a reassuring smile. He still had not a clue as to what had happened; he needed all of the facts.

Joel hesitated. A sly light came into his eyes. "You want to be alone with her?" he asked.

Evan was startled, and then, as he straightened, he realized that he did. But it was not at all what Joel might be thinking, for there was nothing romantic about his feelings for Maggie Kennedy.

How could there be?

He was not like some of his friends, who dallied with showgirls and housemaids. Besides, while Maggie was a seamstress, she was clearly a woman of virtue. Of course, he knew that he found Maggie Kennedy attractive. He was a virile man with an eye for the ladies and in tune with his needs. Anyone could see that she was very pretty, with the most amazing blue eyes. But what difference could that make? There were women like his mistress, Grace Conway, and Bartolla Benevente for casual affairs.

No, there was nothing romantic in his wish to be alone with Maggie; it was an instance of his wanting to comfort her and make sure that she was really all right, as she was claiming to be. "Your mother is my friend," he told Joel seriously. "And I do wish a moment with her, to make sure she is comfortable for the night."

Joel smiled at him. "She's really pretty, isn't she?" he said.

Evan saw that the boy wished to be a matchmaker. He tousled his black hair. "Yes, she is very pretty, but don't go getting any ideas of romance. I am an engaged man, remember?" He tried not to scowl as he spoke of his engagement, but as always, the mere thought of it made him miserable and angry. It was not that he disliked Sarah. She was fine as a friend. But when he did marry, he had truly hoped to marry someone he desired and admired, someone he might actually love.

"Yeah," Joel said, his face falling with disappointment.

Evan hesitated, almost telling the boy that no one was more disappointed than he was. "Sleep tight," he said instead, and he slowly walked back to Maggie's room.

Maggie remained awake, gazing at the doorway. She avoided direct eye contact with him—as if he made her nervous. He already suspected that he did, although he could not imagine why.

"May I come in? Just for a moment?" he asked, forgetting that he had already asked that question and she had refused.

She hesitated.

"I don't bite," he said softly.

She nodded, glancing at the small fire.

He approached, but stopped when a good ten feet remained between him and the bed. "How are you feeling?" he asked gently.

She looked at him, this time for a moment longer. "Dr. Finney gave me a dose of laudanum. The pain has lessened and I am feeling sleepy."

"That's good," he said, his gaze sliding over her form under the bulky quilt. She had pulled the covers to her chin and it did amuse him. A quilt could not discourage his imagination; he was experienced enough and had seen her enough times to know that she was slim and perfectly curved. "Do you need anything? A cup of tea? A glass of milk? A brandy?"

"No, I am fine." But as she spoke, tears suddenly filled her eyes.

Unthinkingly he sat down by her hip and took her hands in his. He was astonished at how fragile they felt, because he knew her hands were strong and agile. "This has been a terrible night, Mrs. Kennedy. I do wish I could turn back the clock and make the world right again."

She pulled her hands free. "I am sorry. I am a bit over-wrought. I think I must get some sleep after all."

He shot to his feet. "Yes, you must. Tomorrow, in the light of day, you will feel better."

She suddenly met his gaze, very directly. "How can I?" she cried. "A woman I thought was my friend has turned out to be an evil and mad woman! She murdered my two dearest friends and tried to murder me!" A tear slid down her cheek.

He sat right back down, taking her hands, even though she tried to resist him. "It will take some time, I think, to get past this. I wish I could tell you how to move on, but I have never encountered a situation like this before," he said, feeling helpless. It was not a feeling he was used to having, and he simply did not know what to do when he truly wished to do something to make her feel better.

She smiled a little at him, through her tears, and this time she tugged her hands free. "You are so kind," she whispered.

"Who would not be compassionate in this instance?" he asked, a bit bewildered. She had called him kind before. Had she been so poorly treated by other men that she found him exceptional? He considered his behavior quite ordinary for a gentleman.

She shook her head. "Many."

He felt more sympathy for her welling up in him. "I do beg to differ with you."

"Your entire family is wonderful," Maggie said, appearing choked up with emotion. "You have all been so kind. Your mother, your father, and your sister, why, I would do anything for her!" she cried. "I only hope that the day comes when I can do something special for you all in return."

"You do not have to do a thing except get well," he said gently. And he smiled, because he saw her lids were beginning to droop, undoubtedly due to the effects of the laudanum.

"I don't know. My brain seems to be getting fuzzy," she murmured, her eyes rather closed.

"The laudanum is taking effect," he announced, and he stood up, somewhat reluctant to do so and aware of it. "Good night then, Mrs. Kennedy," he said.

Her lashes fluttered on her pale white skin, but she did not open her eyes, lift a finger, or say a word. He smiled at the sight of her finally asleep. Very careful not to make a sound, he tiptoed out.

And took a guest room across the hall for the night.

WEDNESDAY, FEBRUARY 12, 1902 — 10:00 A.M.
It had been such a lovely party, she thought, pen in hand. She felt dreamy and delicious all at once, and images of the evening before danced through her mind. In all of them she was the center of attention in her gold satin-and-lace ball gown, surrounded by attentive and smitten men.

She thought about Evan Cahill and felt her loins tighten. If his engagement was not broken, she wondered if he would have the courage to become her lover anyway, in spite of the fact that he was affianced to her cousin. But that must not happen, because he and Sarah were so ill-suited, while she and he made a wonderful match.

She had to remarry, sooner rather than later. No one knew that her despicable dead husband had tied up all of his wealth in railroads, electricity, and mines, willing it to his children from his first marriage. She had spent eight years with the old bastard, and all she had gotten in return was a few hundred thousand dollars. In Italy, everyone was laughing at her behind her back—and to her face—as one and all knew how the count had left her. Here, everyone thought her a wealthy widow, and it was the perfect place to find a wealthy husband.

Evan wasn't as wealthy as she would have liked, but when his father died, he would be. And the wait would be worth it, because he was young and handsome and she knew he would be wonderful in bed.

Bartolla sighed happily, because he hadn't really left her side the entire evening. In fact, quite a few guests had noticed their raging attraction to each other. Bartolla didn't have to be told—she was astute enough to know.

There was a soft knock upon her door.

Bartolla turned, still clothed in her peignoir, a concoction of sheer pastel green chiffon and handmade ivory lace. She pulled a heavier wrapper closed and called, "Enter!"

Sarah stepped in, beaming. "Was it not a wonderful night?" she cried, looking almost pretty, as she was so happy.

Bartolla laughed. "Yes, it was, and I know why you are so happy."

"Hart has said we should meet this afternoon to discuss the portrait and agree upon his purchase price!"

Bartolla had only seen Sarah this animated when she was in her study, painting in frenzy.

"Can you believe it?" Sarah rushed on. "One of my paintings will hang in his home, in his world-renowned collection!"

Bartolla laughed, happy that Sarah was happy, as she was truly fond of her. "But, dear, you might have a bit of a problem coaxing Francesca to agree to this. It is delicious, you must admit, Hart chasing Francesca, with her infatuated with the oh, so married Bragg—his very brother!"

Sarah's face instantly became sober. "He is chasing her? Oh, no, Bartolla, how wrong you are. I think they are just friends."

"Oh, Hart has no use for women friends." Bartolla waved dismissively, meaning her every word and knowing she was right. "Although perhaps he thinks to annoy Bragg, as he does despise him so." She knew Hart would love to ruin any love interest Bragg might have.

"I know Mr. Hart has quite the reputation for being rude, unkind, and self-serving, and of course everyone knows he is a terrible rogue when it comes to the ladies, but truly, Bartolla, he would not steal the love of his brother! He is genuinely fond of Francesca. It is rather obvious."

"It is rather obvious that he would love to ravish her in his bed," Bartolla mused.

Sarah appeared shocked. "I think not!"

Bartolla shrugged. How naive Sarah was. She did not add that Hart's "genuine interest" and his "fondness" would quickly wane once he had satisfied himself with Francesca. "Shall I advise you?" she asked.

Sarah sat down, nodding eagerly.

"Francesca cares for you, and if you press her, she will give in and sit for the portrait. It will give you a name in the art world, or at least give you an entrée and the attention of dealers and collectors, and she would never deny you that."

Sarah hesitated.

"Dear, it is convince Francesca to pose, or lose the commission and the entrée into the art world that it gives you."

Sarah stood. "I know. I shall convince Francesca to sit for the portrait, but not in the way you suggest. There is no harm in it! She is a beautiful woman, with an unmatched spirit, and the kind of selfless goodness that is just so rare these days. And clearly Hart sees that. The portrait will be my best work ever. How can she mind? Really? I am going to call on her in a bit, and I thought you might wish to join me."

As much as Bartolla liked Francesca—and she did—she hadn't liked her in that dark red dress, looking far too sensual and beautiful, all at once. The countess had had enough of Francesca for the moment and decided to encourage her in her sleuthing and her bluestocking ways—and mode of dress. "I shall lie about my rooms today, as I am very tired from last night."

Sarah's face fell, but she then brightened. "I suppose I should speak with her alone."

"Yes, you should." Bartolla thought about the triangle developing, and she chuckled and patted Sarah's hand. "It shall be an interesting winter," she said with a grin.

"Yes, it shall," Sarah said, animated once again. She jumped up. "Will you join me for breakfast, then? Oh—I see you are penning a letter."

"I think I shall take chocolate in my rooms," Bartolla said.

"Very well." Sarah kissed her cheek and left the room.

Bartolla reread what she had written thus far:

My dearest Leigh Anne,
   I hear you are presently in Boston, as your father is not well. First, may I offer my sincerest prayers on his behalf? I am thinking about you and your family daily.
   I am currently in New York and having a lovely time. Last night my cousin held a ball in my honor, and a few of us danced until dawn. I happened across your husband, and I can see, my dear, why you were first compelled by him. In some circles, he is already being highly acclaimed as a noble man of action, one capable of reforming this city's notoriously corrupt police department. Clearly he is a strong, intelligent, and determined man. But you never mentioned how intriguing his looks were! I hear he is half Indian, or some such thing. He

has been turning quite a few female heads, one in particular.

Francesca Cahill comes from one of the city's wealthiest
families; she is extremely beautiful, young, and unwed, and far
more intelligent than you or I. I have seen them together constantly, and I have only just been in town a week. At the ball last
night I found them in a private conversation, but I am sure they
were discussing police affairs. She is an amateur sleuth, and
she helped solve the Randall Killing, which I am sure you have
read about, as it has made all of the newspapers here.

The city is a whirl of fetes and dinner parties, balls and
musicales. The winter is a snowy one. We had four inches last
night! But that does not stop these gay New Yorkers, my dear.
Once your father recovers, you might consider joining me here.
I am sure you would love it, and we would have a wonderful
time. I intend to speak to my aunt about your staying with us
when you arrive. Do let me know if you can come.

                                                  Yours Truly,
                                                  Bartolla Benevente

Bartolla smiled, pleased with the letter, but then she had
an afterthought.

The post was so slow. She would have her letter hand-
delivered that very day.

Francesca knocked gently on Maggie's door. It was late—
noon—and she had only just awoken. Her hand continued
to throb, and in general, she felt miserable, as if she were
truly ill with the flu. She was also exhausted, but she had
managed to dress with Bessie's help, and she simply had
to check on Maggie.

There was a brief moment before Maggie responded to
her knock. Francesca stepped inside her room.

Maggie was in bed, and none of her children were present. She looked pale and wan, but she smiled at Francesca.
"You saved my life," she said.

Francesca smiled back at her and came to sit down beside her hip. "We saved each other," she said, not wanting
to recall the events of the prior evening. They were simply

too frightening and too gruesome, and the image of Lizzie O'Brien on fire and leaping out of the window was an image she hoped to forget—and knew she never would.

"How can I ever thank you for all that you have done?" Maggie asked, her eyes welling with moisture.

"You need not thank me any more than you have already done. Where are the children?"

Maggie glanced away. "Your brother has taken them on some sort of a drive. He is being terribly kind."

Francesca said truthfully, "He *is* terribly kind. It is his nature. How are you feeling?"

"My side hurts. But that is nothing compared to the sickness inside of my heart," she said.

Francesca reached for Maggie's hand with her left one. Her right one was heavily bandaged and impossible to use. Besides, even lifting it caused the pain to escalate. "I am so sorry. I am sorry you have lost two dear friends, and I am sorry Lizzie turned out to be what she had become."

Maggie nodded, apparently speechless. Then, "Will she live?"

"Oh, yes. But it may be some months before she has recovered sufficiently to stand trial," Francesca said.

Maggie sighed harshly. "We never knew. I mean, she was always rougher than the rest of us. Rougher, tougher, more frank. But we loved her, Miss Cahill. I was thirteen when I met her, twelve when I met Kathleen and Mary."

Francesca did not know what to say. "Perhaps she was always insane?"

"I just do not know. She was always wild, and careless of who knew. She would go with boys and flaunt it. She would laugh at the priests who tried to reason with her. She refused to go to confession. Sometimes she scoffed at us for being meek—for being devout. For Kathleen and Mary were very pious, and so am I. We were all a bit frightened for her," Maggie admitted. "Now I can see the signs so clearly. I knew she had chased after Mike

O'Donnell, even after he married Kathleen. But I didn't want to know, so I pretended not to. And I knew she flaunted herself in front of my Joseph. I trusted him, though, and I somehow pretended to myself that she did not really mean to entice him. Of course, she did."

"I am beginning to think she was so jealous of the three of you, for all of these years, and the envy ate at her, until she became so terribly twisted. Or maybe her charade as the genteel Mrs. Lincoln Stuart gave her an excuse to exercise her anger—and even her hatred. Do you think she secretly hated all of you for all of these years?"

"I am beginning to think so," Maggie whispered. "Maybe her attempts to seduce Joseph, maybe her love affair with Mike, were all about jealousy and hate." Maggie seemed paler now.

"We are being too morbid," Francesca whispered, patting her friend's hand. "I think this shall all come out in the trial. Lizzie is quite vocal."

Maggie nodded. "Do you know what is really frightening?"

"No."

"When we were young, I think, in a way, we admired her spirit. None of us would ever dare miss confession. None of us would ever swear, smoke, or drink. We were chaste until our wedding nights. She did all of those things, all that we were afraid to do. We knew we did not have her courage, so secretly, we were envious of her." Maggie was upset.

"Do not blame yourself now for trusting a lifelong friend!" Francesca cried. "Do not blame yourself for failing to realize how twisted her mind was—and is! And you have her courage a hundred times over, Maggie," she said flatly. "The way you have chosen to live, with virtue and pride, is no easy thing, and you do it with so much grace."

Maggie smiled a little. "You are being terribly nice to me, Miss Cahill."

"I am being truthful," Francesca said. "It is the only way I know how to be."

"I am coming to realize that."

"And will you ever call me Francesca?"

"I don't think so," she said.

They smiled at each other.

"Francesca? You have a caller. It's Hart."

Francesca was reclining in front of the fire in her room, trying to study but with little success, as her hand hurt and it had given her a headache. Outside, it was snowing again, this time heavily. She had remained in bed for half of the day and had lounged in her rooms all afternoon. Now, she was cross and irritable with the pain of her burn and debating taking a small dose of laudanum. It was perhaps five in the afternoon.

Francesca realized she had no choice. If he knew about her hand—and if he didn't already, he soon would—he would lecture her no end, and she was not up to self-defense. Or had he come to force her into submission on the subject of her posing for a portrait? Sarah had already convinced her that she must comply—as this was Sarah's chance to make a name for herself.

Francesca sighed. She walked into the bathroom and winced when she saw her reflection in the mirror. She looked horrible—ghostly. Her injury had turned her golden skin starkly pale, she had large circles under her eyes from the stress of pain, and her hair, which had been pulled loosely back so as to not aggravate her headache, was a mess. Francesca sighed again, more heavily, biting back a few tears of anguish. It was only a burn, she reminded herself. Dr. Finney had changed the dressing that afternoon, and there was no sign of infection. In a few days the pain would subside, or she could take the laudanum he had recommended.

But at least, when Hart saw her like this, he would no

longer think of annoying her with his proposition for a portrait. Surely he would cancel the commission.

In fact, he would hardly recognize her at all. She was not the seductive woman in the dark red dress from the evening before, oh no. She wasn't even her ordinary self. He would not look twice at her this way, and by damn, she was pleased.

He was pacing the smallest of the three salons with savage strides, as always, in a black suit. He whirled the moment she paused on the threshold, clearly vastly impatient. And he froze.

Unfortunately, her heart lurched wildly as she glimpsed him. Unease filled her. She could not look away.

He did not move. He stood so still he might have been a statue. His expression, which had appeared distinctly distressed for one bare instant, was now absolutely closed and impossible to read. Had she imagined his worry?

"Francesca. Are you all right?" he asked quietly.

She nodded, and then, to her horror, a tear slipped from one eye. "I am fine." Even her tone was hoarse from the ceaseless pain.

"I can see that you are in pain," he said, as quietly. He finally came forward, his gaze never leaving her face. "How badly is your hand burned?"

"Not that badly. I shall be rid of these bandages in a week or so, and in a few weeks I will have full use of my hand," she said, unable to tear her gaze free of his. It was extraordinarily intense, unwavering. Her unease increased, or was it her pulse rate? He had halted so close to her that their knees could almost touch. "Who told you? Bragg?"

Finally, she had a genuine expression from him, as real annoyance crossed his features. "Don't mention my brother now," he warned. He stalked past her and closed the door, which was absolutely inappropriate, but oddly, she did not object. She shivered, even though the room was very warm, with all the windows closed and the fire roaring in the hearth.

He turned, studying her closely. "Sarah told me. We had a meeting an hour ago. You were all she could talk about."

"I see," she said. Francesca had agreed not to mention the evening's work to anyone, but as Sarah was such a close friend and her brother's fiancée, she hadn't been able to lie to her when she had asked about the reason for the bandages on her hand.

"I am very concerned about you."

She softened, rather involuntarily, and she smiled at him. "That's nice of you, Hart. I take it you are no longer angry with me?" It was good to be friends again. How much it meant to her jolted her to her bones.

"I am very angry with you," he exploded, "and I am not being nice! Jesus Christ! You are practically in tears from the pain of that burn. How *could* you?" he demanded.

She could only stare, disbelieving. On the one hand, she did not like being shouted at or ordered about. But . . . did he really care so much? "Calder, Maggie's life was in jeopardy. I could think of nothing else to do."

"I want to hear what happened from beginning to end," he said darkly, "from your mouth, not Sarah's version of the events." He approached and took her arm, looping it so securely against his side that she tensed instinctively. What was he doing? What was he up to? she wondered, stealing a glance at his set profile.

He guided her to a small plush sofa. "But first, didn't the doctor give you laudanum for the pain?" His black eyes held hers again.

"Yes, but it makes me sleepy, and I cannot think," she said, aware of his having slid his entire arm around her, when she did not need his support. He was a very muscular man. He was taller than one thought, broader, more solid.

She suspected he had two inches on his brother and fifteen or twenty solid pounds.

"Sit down," he said.

She did not mind, in fact, she was relieved, because once he somewhat pushed her down onto the sofa, she was no longer so aware of his physicality. She watched him stride over to the bar cart and pour a glassful of scotch. The thought crossed her mind as she studied him that he was, in some ways, a frankly male animal. It was there in the way he moved, talked, gestured. Everything about him was aggressive, even uncivilized.

She shivered again and told herself that was not a fair judgment to make. Hart's mode of dress, his mansion, his coaches and staff, his art collection, why, all of it was very civilized indeed.

Then she amended her thoughts. A few of his paintings were not civilized, as they were too titillating and sensual to be so.

He returned and handed the glass to her. "Drink that. You are staring."

She felt herself flush. "You have always struck me as an interesting man."

He seemed startled, and then his eyes softened. "I have been called a lot of things, but never interesting."

"I am not trying to be rude."

"I know, Francesca. I know you far better than you think. Drink." He nodded at the glass.

"Calder, this is whiskey," she said.

He finally smiled just a little, mostly with his eyes. "You are the kind of woman who should love a good glass of scotch, Francesca. You may trust me on that."

She blinked at him, stunned. The idea was vastly appealing, as women did not drink anything other than wine, champagne, punch, or sherry. Julia would faint if she ever knew.

That did please Francesca, and she took a sip of scotch

and almost choked. Hart chuckled and slid his hand over her back, as if to pat her the way one did an infant. Instead, his hand did not move as the scotch burned its way down her throat and right to her belly. But there was something delicious about the fiery flavor on the tip of her tongue, just as there was something very disturbing about his hand on her back. She looked at him and tried another sip. "You might make me a drunkard," she tried lightly.

He watched her, his eyes hooded, not responding.

His palm burned her back the way the scotch unfurled its warmth deep inside of her. "This is rather good," she said somewhat huskily.

"It is." He did not say, "I told you," although his eyes expressed such a thought. "You are the kind of woman, Francesca, who would even enjoy a Havana cigar," he said softly.

She had taken a third sip of scotch. She somehow did not choke, vastly enjoying the flavor now, as he removed his hand from her spine. "Are you suggesting that I smoke?" she gasped.

His smile was faint, his gaze steady. "No."

"But you said," she began, wide-eyed.

"I have not a single doubt that in time you will enjoy a good cigar," he finished for her.

She was stunned. There were a few women who smoked cigarettes. But to smoke a cigar? Like a man? She met his eyes, breathless. "Am I mannish to you, Calder?"

He looked at her. "Hardly." His eyes changed.

She froze. She understood the glint there, for she had seen it last night, but last night she had appeared to be a temptress in a dark red dress, and today she was ill and in pain. Today there was simply no reason for him to look at her in such a speculative and predatory way.

He stood abruptly, and relief flooded her. "Tell me what happened, and do not think to omit any details."

It was a moment before she could speak, as her mind,

now a bit fuzzy from the scotch, was focused on him and his feral interest. What was this? And why did it bother her so? Other men had been interested in her, and she had not given a hoot or a single thought to them. Besides, Hart was her friend. He had even said he had no intentions toward her. She recalled the very obvious fact that he liked married women, divorcées, and prostitutes like Daisy and Rose, but the knowledge did not bring relief. She simply could not relax around him.

"Well? What happened?" he asked tersely.

His hands were on his narrow hips. He stood a few feet from her, which meant that he towered over her, as she was seated. Francesca gave up. She did not have the strength or the will to stand and confront him, and it was wonderful to have him play the protector, anyway.

"Do not badger me, Hart," she said lightly. She realized the scotch had done its job, as while her hand throbbed, it no longer was an effort to ignore it. "When I realized that a police officer had brought Bragg news, I left the Channing ball to go with him to search the Stuarts' house. He arrested Lincoln. We thought the case solved. I came home, only to find Maggie Kennedy being attacked. As there was a knife being held to her throat and as Lydia Stuart, who is really Lizzie O'Brien, had already killed her two other friends, I dared not take any chances. She made me drop my gun. When I realized she was about to kill Maggie, the only thing I could possibly do was seize a log from the fire and try to set her aflame."

He stared. His jaw was hard and it was a long moment before he spoke. "Francesca, only you would be so incredibly courageous."

She flushed with pleasure, unable to control it or deny it. "I like it when you compliment me, Calder."

He shot to his feet. "Don't flirt with me now!" he cried.

Had she been flirting? She blinked at him. She supposed that she had.

"I cannot believe that my brother allows you to involve yourself in his dangerous police work," he said flatly. "I suppose the time has come to beat some sense into him."

Awkwardly she stood up. His hand shot out, grabbing her elbow to steady her. "I am off balance," she said. Suddenly she realized that if Julia saw her now, she would never allow Hart close to her again. And Julia's absurd plans to match them romantically would fail.

"What are you smiling about?" he asked suspiciously.

And then they could return to being normal friends, without her worrying about anything else. "Am I smiling?"

He sighed, not releasing her. "I suppose the pain made the scotch go right to your head." He eyed her, not pleased.

"Wasn't that the point?"

"Yes, I suppose it was. But you are grinning at me. Your mother will not be pleased."

Her smile vanished and she felt it. "You are always so clever."

"What does that have to do with anything? In any case, I must insist that you give up this ridiculous sleuthing of yours."

She tried to pull her arm free and failed. All she did was stumble a bit. He righted her instantly. "Hart, you cannot insist upon anything where I am concerned."

He smiled, and it was dangerous. "Oh, really?"

Alarm bells went off. What would he do? He had no morals, no compunction, none! He might have a tête-à-tête with Bragg. And the two brothers could take sides against her. Worse, Hart might have such a discussion with Julia and/or Andrew. Francesca cringed inwardly at the thought. "I can hardly confront a criminal right now," she said breathlessly. "And I do resent your interference."

He was clearly exasperated. "I hardly care what you think of my so-called interference. Someone has to keep you in check. If Rick will not, then I shall do so, Francesca."

She was incredulous. "But why?"

"Why?" he exploded. "You are determined to put yourself in harm's way! Time and again! It is insufferable—unbelievable, actually! Why can't you behave like other innocent young girls?"

"I am not a young girl," she hissed, somehow pulling free of his hold at last. Her hands found her hips, and then pain shot through her burned palm, horridly, and she cried out, staggering blindly back.

He caught her in his embrace. "Jesus! See? You are suffering terribly!"

She fought the waves of pain, and she fought for control and composure. As the pain subsided, she realized he held her shoulders. She looked up. Tears filled her eyes, but still his face was but inches away and there was no mistaking the concern in his regard. "I am fine," she gasped. "Release me."

He hesitated.

"Please, Calder," she whispered. The urge to cry had changed. It was no longer physical.

He released her.

She inhaled and somehow sat down. She felt as if she had been beaten with a club. "I am very tired," she said, not looking up now.

"I apologize," he said instantly. "Please forgive me, Francesca."

She had to meet his eyes. "Yes."

He sat down beside her and took her good hand in both of his. Francesca stiffened as a searing recollection struck her—Bragg had held her hand while seated exactly this way yesterday night, but in the other room, on a different sofa. "I will call on you tomorrow," Hart said quietly. "I did not mean to cause you more pain."

She tried to smile at him and failed.

"But I shall continue to insist that your sleuthing end, Francesca," he warned. "As your friend, I must speak out."

She was too tired to argue with him. She felt resigned. "Insist as you will, Hart."

He tilted up her chin. "I can be a powerful ally, Francesca," he said.

She looked into his smoky eyes, simply stunned.

He smiled a little at her and stood. He stared down at her and she could only stare back.

A long and silent moment passed.

After several minutes, Julia walked into the room, and Francesca was instantly suspicious. Her mother had been eavesdropping outside of the door—she felt certain of it. "Mr. Hart, can I offer you any refreshments? A cup of coffee? A brandy?" She beamed at him.

He smiled back politely. "I am on my way out. But thank you, Mrs. Cahill."

Julia glanced briefly at Francesca and the scotch that sat on the low table by her knees. She smiled again at Hart. "My daughter can be too intelligent, and too headstrong, for her own good," she remarked, and Francesca knew she had overheard most of their conversation.

Defiantly she lifted the scotch and drank it.

"I am in complete agreement with you," Hart said easily, but there was laughter in his tone.

Francesca set the glass down loudly and saw them both watching her. "I am hardly in the other room," she said sourly.

Julia turned to Hart. "She needs a strong hand."

"I am hardly a horse," Francesca muttered, but if they heard her, they did not acknowledge her now.

"Yes, she does," Hart said calmly.

She scowled at him.

He bowed. "Good evening, Francesca. I will see you tomorrow."

She had the childish urge not to reply. Instead, she sighed. "Good night, Calder."

That seemed to please him, because the light flickered, changing, in his eyes.

"Let me walk you out," Julia said.

He accepted that, and as they turned, Julia said, "So, Mr. Hart, would you care to join us this Sunday for supper? It shall be a simple family affair, with Evan and Miss Channing, Lord and Lady Montrose, Francesca, and my husband and I," she said.

Francesca got awkwardly to her feet, disbelieving.

Hart halted. "I should be honored, Mrs. Cahill, to attend."

"Then we have a date," Julia said, pleased.

"Yes, we do, and I should not miss it for the world." Hart did not look at Francesca again, and he and Julia exited the room.

She stared after them and felt her mouth hanging open. She closed it. Panic came.

She knew what Julia was up to, but now she had a bad feeling indeed.

She did not like Hart taking sides with her mother, and even though she reassured herself that nothing would come of it, her senses screamed at her otherwise.

THURSDAY, FEBRUARY 13, 1902 — NOON

Francesca had come downstairs, as was her habit for breakfast. But still weak from the burn, she had lain down in the music room afterward and promptly fallen asleep. She was in the midst of a bizarre dream—in it, a crowd had gathered around her, whispering and speculating, and she could not understand why. Hart was there, too darkly virile for words, her parents were there, conspiring against her now, and Bragg was present, determined to save her from some threat she could not quite comprehend. But there were children, too, whispering, their tones hushed and curious.

"Dot! No!"

Fingers jabbed her cheek and mouth.

"Don't awaken her," Bragg said in her dream. "She is sick and she needs her rest."

"Frack! Frack! *Frack!*" Dot shrieked.

She wasn't dreaming, Francesca thought, blinking. And the first thing she saw was Dot's grinning face, an inch from her own. *"Frack!"* Dot screamed happily. "Wake!"

Francesca was fully awake but a bit groggy, and the pain of her burn was tolerable. She vaguely recalled her mother appearing at breakfast to insist that she take a dose of laudanum, and that she had fought over the amount of the medicine. She glanced past Dot and saw Bragg watching her anxiously. Behind him was Peter, holding onto Katie's shoulders as if she might run away. He had a clump of something green in his short blond hair.

"Francesca? I see you are awake. The commissioner insisted on seeing you, and clearly it is not an official visit," Julia intoned, not sounding pleased.

Francesca blinked and adjusted her vision and saw her mother on Bragg's left, almost out of her range of eyesight. She struggled to sit up.

Bragg replaced Dot, sliding his hands behind her. They were warm, strong, and terribly familiar. She met his golden gaze and felt her heart melt like too-warm chocolate. "Thank you," she whispered. "The children?"

He piled pillows behind her back and his hands seemed to linger. "Dot has been having tantrums, demanding to see Frack. I did not understand, but Peter appears to speak her language," he told her so softly she doubted anyone else could hear. "It was a good excuse to call on you, Francesca." His gaze was warm but worried. "How are you? Your mother says that you got up at eight today."

"Yes, I did, although I have no idea why," she said, overcome with the oddest relief. There was no one she needed more, she realized. And if only her mother would leave, she would take his hand and clasp it to her breast. "But the pain is gone. Mama insisted I take laudanum."

"You should. I hate seeing you in any pain whatsoever," he said as softly. Then he straightened to his full height. "Katie," he said sternly, "you may say hello to Francesca."

Katie glared at him and then smiled angelically at Francesca. There was a huge space where one of her two front teeth had been.

"Bragg! She has lost two teeth!" Francesca cried.

Katie slowly opened her mouth wider for an inspection.

"Yes, you have lost two teeth, and I do hope the good tooth fairy has left a penny beneath your pillow." Francesca smiled at her.

Bragg sighed. "I forgot."

"Bragg," she scolded, "how could you?'

He smiled at her. "Easily."

She forced her dazed mind to assimilate the innuendos there. "Has Lizzie confessed?"

His brows shot up. "You wish to discuss police affairs now? Francesca, all is under control. She shall be tried and found guilty; have no doubt about that."

Francesca relaxed against the pillows. She looked past Bragg at Peter. "Hello, Peter. How are you?"

He nodded. "Fine."

"He stopped asking me for a nanny, once he heard what happened to you," Bragg said.

She gripped his hand. "You aren't throwing the girls out, are you?" Dear God, she hadn't thought twice about a nanny or a foster home. She glanced from Dot to Katie. Katie was listening acutely to their every word. Francesca saw fear and anger in her eyes.

"Don't worry about it, not even once," Bragg said softly. "I am not throwing them out. They can stay a few more days. I have told Peter he can do the hiring himself."

"I can do it tomorrow," Francesca told him, hoping she would be up to the task.

"No, you cannot," Bragg said, "as you are confined to bed. I spoke with Finney myself, Francesca," he warned.

"The commissioner is right," Julia said firmly. "However, Rick, if you wish, I shall find you a nanny this afternoon."

Francesca gaped at her mother.

Bragg faced her. "That is very kind of you, Julia. I do not have the time to do so myself and—"

"Of course you do not. You are an extremely busy man." Julia smiled briskly at him, not fawning over him as she did over Hart. "Shall I give the girls some supper?" she asked.

"I do not want to impose upon you," Bragg said.

"Mama! That would be wonderful!" Francesca cried, truly grateful. "For it is certainly their supper time."

Julia smiled a bit at her. "I am hardly coldhearted, Francesca," she said softly.

"Katie doesn't eat," Francesca warned.

"Really?" Julia's brows lifted and she turned a firm stare on Katie. "Well, we shall have to change that, as she is thin as a rail. Peter, bring the girls and follow me." She marched out.

Peter came forward to scoop up Dot and he said, "I hope you feel better, Miss Cahill." He left with Katie following reluctantly—and casting backward glances at Francesca that were clearly anxious.

They were actually alone.

Francesca's pulse skipped a bit and she looked into Bragg's eyes and found him regarding her intently. "You do not have to worry so much," she said softly.

"It is impossible where you are concerned," he returned. He pulled up an ottoman and sat beside her. He moved a tendril of hair from her face. "I am having trouble concentrating, Francesca; I am so distraught with what has happened to you."

"Really?" She smiled, pleased. It was interesting, how naked one's emotions were when under the influence of a drug.

"Really, and do not be so pleased," he said flatly. "You are staring," he added somewhat darkly.

She sighed. "It is hard not to stare, and I do think you know why."

His eyes widened. He leaned forward. "I hardly know why, but keep in mind that we are in your mother's house and she isn't very fond of me right now."

"She likes you. But you are not available, so she wishes to keep an eye on us," Francesca said, rather amazed at her own bluntness.

He stared. "As well she should," he finally said.

"Are you now on her side?"

He hesitated, and nodded.

"What does that mean?" she cried, alarmed.

"It means that I have been sick with worry ever since I found you with your hand in a pail of snow," he said tersely. "It means I have genuinely realized the extent of my feelings for you—and it is frightening. I must be blunt. No good can come of this."

She did not move. She could hardly breathe. "I cannot believe you are speaking this way."

"Nor can I," he admitted then. "Because I cannot even begin to imagine life without you in it." He paused yet again. "Which is certainly the most sensible option that we have."

Dread filled her. She felt the intensity in him. "You do not mean that."

"I do, but I have come to a different decision entirely," he said.

She froze, almost paralyzed with fear. "What?"

"I am going to ask Leigh Anne for a divorce."

She reeled, speechless. It was a long moment before she could speak. *"What?"*

"You have heard me." He was terribly grim—and determination was carved all over his face.

"But . . ." She could not think straight, especially now, dosed on laudanum. They had met January 18, not even a month ago. And in so short a time he would change his life, discard his wife? And what about his future, his hopes, his dreams? "But . . . you aspire to the national Congress. It is your duty, your destiny!" she cried, remaining stunned.

"I begin to wonder if you are not my duty . . . and my destiny," he said.

It struck her then what this meant, what he intended. To give up everything, his wife, his responsibilities, his respectability, and his dreams of a future in the Senate, in order that they might be together. "Oh, my God," she heard herself say slowly. How could she let him do this?

Of course she could! This was *her* dream. Her most secret, private dream!

But his work as a public servant was so much more important than their own personal happiness.

He suddenly cupped her cheek with his calloused palm. She stared, meeting his gaze, wondering if he saw the fear in her soul that was surely reflected in her eyes.

"I should not have been so blunt. I haven't slept in days, thinking about this, arriving at my decision. Of course, your mother will fight tooth and nail against a divorced man—and a divorce might take years to attain. I would never ask you to wait, Francesca."

She was crying now. "I will wait. I will wait forever," she whispered, but in her heart she was now terrified, and it wasn't because Julia would never allow her to marry a divorced man. She was not his destiny. His destiny was the city and the state and the United States of America.

Oh, God. *What should she do?*

What *could* she do?

He hesitated, and she understood. The hesitation was not about the decision he had made; he was a man to hold to his course. So she reached up and held his nape, guiding him toward her. Their lips brushed, once, twice, three times.

It was bittersweet.

Tears whispered on the tips of her eyelashes.

Her mind shouted at her, again and again, *Do not let him do this!*

Suddenly he pulled her into his arms, but gently, clearly not wanting to hurt her. He looked past her eyes and, as if he understood her conflict, he stiffened.

"Don't worry," she said. She pressed her mouth to his.

He recovered, claiming her mouth with a stunning urgency, with panic, with desperation and his love. When the kiss finally ended, Francesca was not simply breathless; she was shaken to her core.

She loved him so much it was almost an impossible exaggeration of her emotions. She admired him more greatly—and believed in his statesmanship and the good he could do even more than that.

And in the same instant that she wrestled with the vast array of her feelings she realized that they were being watched, and so did he.

Bragg pulled away, whirling. Francesca looked past him at the doorway.

Dot stood there, beaming, oddly proud.

"We have a chaperone," he murmured, with relief that it was only the toddler.

"Yes, we do," Francesca returned as he turned back to her and their eyes met. They had to smile—Dot's interruption was timely.

"We should not set such a rude example," he began with a shake of his head.

"No, we should not," she agreed, still unsteady from their passion and still stunned by this latest turn of events.

Dot clapped her hands, shouting, "Kiss; kiss, Frack; kiss!"

Francesca winced, wondering at which moment Julia would rush into the room, comprehending everything.

"I think I am beginning to like her," Bragg murmured.

"I knew you would," she said, glancing at Dot. Dot grinned at her.

Francesca saw the puddle on the floor and realized why Dot was so proud. A hastily torn off diaper was beside it. "Uh-oh," she said, grabbing Bragg's hand and tugging on it, hoping to divert him.

But it was too late. He had seen the damage done. "I don't believe it!" he exclaimed, standing. "She tore off her diaper! The . . . brat!"

He moved away from her, calling sternly for Dot. She beamed happily at him but made no move to obey.

Francesca sighed; so much for their truce.

And when Dot finally edged forward, clearly aware that he was not in a pleasant mood, and as Bragg tried to grab her, unsuccessfully, as she dodged him, Francesca realized just how unpredictable life was.

She would not worry now about tomorrow, she decided firmly. She would not worry about Bragg giving up his future in order to divorce his wife, nor would she worry about the portrait Hart had commissioned or Julia's absurd plans. No, tomorrow was another day, and there was just no predicting what might happen—given the recent course of events. What she would do was rest and heal her hand, just in case another crime fell into her lap. She did smile at that thought.

At least her life was not dull, drab, or routine.

"She is running away from me!" Bragg exclaimed.
"That child has more nerve than two full-grown hooks and
crooks combined!"

She smiled serenely at him. "Dot! Do come here,
please, and show Bragg what a good girl you are."

Dot hesitated.

Bragg grabbed her hand. "There, I have caught you,"
he said sternly, but the little girl only laughed. He then
smiled at Francesca. "I shall return her to Peter's care, as
I am off for a one o'clock appointment with the mayor."

Francesca could not help having her curiosity piqued;
she wondered what issues they were addressing. "Good
luck," she said.

He smiled at her and walked out with Dot in tow. Francesca watched them until they had disappeared from sight,
and the moment they had, a new tension filled her. It was
impossible not to remain stunned over Bragg's assertion
that he would divorce his wife.

She heard the Daimler's engine roaring to life.

Francesca stood somewhat shakily and walked over to
a window, where she parted the draperies. The handsome
motorcar was already rolling down the drive, heading for
Fifth Avenue. She sighed.

"Miss Cahill?"

Francesca turned at the sound of a servant's voice. Bette
stood in the doorway, holding a small silver tray. Usually
a caller would place his or her card there, but now an
envelope lay upon it.

"This just came by hand, Miss Cahill," Bette said.

Francesca accepted the envelope. "Thank you, Bette."
Her name was written in a beautiful script upon the front,
and there was no name or return address on the back. This
was odd, she thought.

Francesca slit the envelope open with a letter opener. The note was also beautifully scripted, in the same hand. It was dated February 12. It read:

My dear Miss Cahill,
    I should be in New York City soon, and I wish to meet you at your convenience. I shall be staying at the Waldorf Astoria when I arrive. I look forward to making your acquaintance.

Yours Truly,
Mrs. Rick Bragg

[To Be Continued]

DEADLY PLEASURE

The moment she used the knocker, footsteps could be heard at a rapid pace in the hall beyond the door, hurrying to them. The door was thrust open immediately.

Francesca was greeted with the sight of a buxom woman in her early thirties, her dyed and curled red hair pinned up, clad in a well-made suit, although the jacket had been designed to show off an undue amount of cleavage. The woman was wearing large aquamarine drop earrings, a huge aquamarine-and-diamond pin in the shape of a butterfly, and three rings, all gems. Her face was pretty and quite made up. Instantly, Francesca knew she was not greeting a gentlewoman.

Francesca peered past the woman almost immediately and saw a wood-floored hall beyond the small entry, stairs that led upstairs just behind the woman. The door directly at the end of the hall was closed, but light spilled out beneath it. The hall itself was dimly lit.

"You came! Thank God, Miss Cahill—who's that?" Her tone changed, becoming one of abject suspicion as she stared down at Joel.

"I'm her assistant," Joel announced, slipping beneath the woman's arm as she held open the door and ducking into the entry.

Francesca made another mental note—Joel should know to let her do all the speaking. "Miss de Labouche?"

"Yes, yes, do come in!" the woman cried, indicating that she had indeed been the one to hand Francesca the note, but she faced Joel. "Stop right there, young man," she said sternly.

Joel slid his rag-clad hands into the pockets of his big wool coat and he shrugged. Georgette de Labouche shut the door behind Francesca. "Thank God you have come, but you should have come alone!"

The woman was in a panic. There was no mistaking the signs—panic was in her eyes and in her tone and written all over her face as well.

"Perhaps we should start from the beginning," Francesca said kindly.

"There is no time!"

Francesca began unbuttoning her fur-lined cloak. "Very well. Shall we sit down somewhere and begin?"

Georgette hesitated, glancing at Joel. Then, "We can go in there." She pointed at the closed door at the end of the hall, where light glared out from beneath it. Clearly the room beyond was brilliantly lit. "But the boy stays right here." She glared at Joel. "You don't move, buster. You got that?"

Joel made a funny face. "I got one boss and that's Miss Cahill."

"Don't talk back to me!" Georgette cried.

Francesca put a hand on her arm and smiled reassuringly. "I can see you are upset. We shall speak privately, have no fear." She looked at Joel. "Joel, your job is to assist me—when I need assistance. Right now, please stay here in the entry and wait for me until I ask you to do otherwise."

His gaze was searching. Francesca realized he was trying to decide what her words really meant—as if she were speaking in code.

"Stay right here," Francesca reiterated. She smiled at Georgette, who was wringing her bejeweled hands. The redhead looked close to tears. "He'll be fine," Francesca said, hoping she spoke the truth. While originally the idea

of Joel as an assistant had seemed wonderful, Francesca
wasn't quite sure she could trust him to do as she asked.
Which made him a loose cannon indeed. She did not want
to mismanage her first case because of the little boy.

Georgette led the way briskly down the hall.

Francesca asked, speaking to her rigid but small shoulders, "How did you know to contact me, Miss de Labouche?"

She glanced over her shoulder, her hand on the knob
of the closed door. "You gave me one of your cards outside of Tiffany's yesterday. It was an unusual card. I
tucked it away. But I never thought I'd have need of it,
and certainly not a day later!"

Francesca met her dark brown eyes. The woman was
crying. "It will be all right," she said softly.

Georgette turned and thrust the door somewhat open,
stepping inside. Instinct caused unease to assail Francesca,
and she hesitated for a moment before slipping past Georgette, who instantly slammed the door closed behind her—
locking it.

But Francesca only flinched at the sound of the lock
clicking, because directly in the middle of the room was a
man. A gentleman, by the looks of him. He was lying on
his abdomen, on the highly polished wood floor, his face
turned to one side, in a pool of dark red blood.

Francesca muffled her very own gasp. "Is he . . . ?"

"He's dead," Georgette said flatly. "And I need you to
help me get rid of the body."

FRIDAY, JANUARY 31, 1902—MIDNIGHT

Francesca gasped. Surely she had misheard Georgette de
Labouche. "What?"

"We must get rid of the body. You have to help me!
And the first thing we must do is send the boy away!"

Georgette cried, as if Francesca were a dolt.

Francesca could hardly believe her ears. This was her very first official case. And it was not just any case; it was a homicide, the gravest of crimes. A murder had been committed, and Francesca intended to get to the bottom of it. But this woman was asking her not to solve the crime, but help hide it. The situation might have been comical had a man not been murdered and lying there dead at their feet.

"Didn't you hear a word I said? If the police find him, they will throw me in the cooler for sure!" Georgette stabbed at the air, near hysteria.

Francesca took a deep, calming breath. She glanced once more at the dead man at their feet. Her stomach heaved. She had seen corpses before, of course, but they had been in their Sunday best and carefully arranged on the satin bed of a beautiful coffin. "Miss de Labouche? Who is this man? And . . . did you kill him?"

"See! Even you think I did it!" Georgette whirled, pacing, her bosom heaving.

Francesca tried to peer more closely at the dead man. "Is that a hole I see in the back of his head?" She wondered if she might retch. She must control the urge. "Was he shot? Or beaten with a stick?"

Georgette whirled. "I would never hurt Paul. He was a dear, dear friend."

Francesca was relieved as she faced Georgette, no longer studying the man. But she had seen right away that he was well dressed, right down to the tips of his shiny new Oxford shoes. She had noticed a gold watch fob in a gray vest where his dark wool jacket was open. The suit, the watch, and the shoes were all of a very fine quality indeed. "A dear, dear friend," Francesca repeated. "You are his mistress?"

Georgette did not flush. "Obviously," she snapped. "Will you or will you not help me dispose of the body?"

"So now you wish to *dispose* of the body?" Francesca

gaped. "Miss de Labouche, this man is not a mouse in a trap. He is a human being and the victim of a terrible crime. We must inform the police. A man has been murdered. In cold blood, I might add—from the look of things."

"Of course it was in cold blood!" Georgette cried, and she sank down on a red velvet chair, moaning and holding her face with her hands.

Francesca took another glance at the body. He had removed his overcoat and top hat; both items lay on another chair with a silver-tipped cane. She estimated his age as early fifties. Then she walked over to Georgette and laid her palm reassuringly on her plump but narrow shoulder. "I am sorry for your loss," she said softly.

Georgette did not speak. She moaned again and said, "I am going straight to the Tombs; I can see it now!"

"No one has accused you of any crime, Miss de Labouche. What happened?" Francesca knew she did not have a lot of time in which to ask questions. In fact, if she was a truly honorable citizen, she would rush off to call the police in that instant. But she preferred to ask some questions first—before the police began their investigation.

An image of Bragg flashed through her mind. They had worked quite closely together to solve the abduction of Jonny Burton. Something stirred in her heart. He had even admitted, once, reluctantly, how helpful she had been. She wondered if they would work together again, to solve this newer and even more dastardly crime.

Georgette looked up. "I was in my bath," she finally said. "Paul comes every Tuesday and Friday evening. His full name is Paul Randall," she added. "I heard him come in, or I thought I did. I expected him to come upstairs. I had a surprise waiting for him." Tears filled her eyes.

"A surprise?" Francesca asked, wishing she had a notepad. First thing tomorrow she would begin acquiring the tools of her new trade.

"I was in the bath, Miss Cahill. With champagne and other . . . things."

Francesca stiffened. "Oh." Things? Did she dare ask what those things were? She was dying of curiosity, and then she reminded herself that as a now-professional sleuth, of course she must ask. "What kind of things?"

Georgette blinked. "Toys. Devices. You know."

Francesca thought her heart had slowed. "Toys? You mean like rubber ducks?"

Georgette sighed in exasperation and shook her head, standing. "You gentlewomen are all the same! No wonder men like Paul come to women like me! Not rubber ducks, my dear. Toys. *Sex* toys. You know. Objects that bring extra pleasure. If you'd like, I can show them to you?" She stared rather coyly.

Francesca tried not to gasp as her cheeks flamed. She was stunned. She hadn't known that such objects existed, and in any case, what could they be and how were they used? She fought to get a grip. "I see." Her cheeks remained hot. Would Connie know anything about sex toys? Francesca doubted it, but she was the only person Francesca dared to ask. "So you were in the bath and then what happened?" She tried to sound brisk, professional.

"Many minutes passed as I lingered there, with the toys." She briefly smiled at Francesca, some kind of insinuation hanging there. Francesca did not quite know what she meant. "Of course he would come to find me; I know him so well. But he did not, and suddenly, I was concerned. And it was just at that point when I heard a sharp, loud crack. One sound. A crack. And I knew it was a gunshot."

Francesca had had an image of Georgette alone in the bath together with different-sized rubber ducks, the best her suddenly infertile imagination could do. She shoved that rather unwelcome image aside. "And?"

"And? I leaped up, put on a robe, and ran downstairs,

calling for Paul. I was praying that the sound I had heard meant something else. When I reached the entry, the door was wide open, so I closed it."

Francesca had a thought. "What about the staff?"

"I have no staff on Tuesday and Friday evenings, for obvious reasons, reasons of privacy."

"Of course," Francesca said.

"After I closed the door I turned, and the parlor door was wide open and I saw him. Oh, God! It was so horrid; you just cannot imagine how horrid it was!" She cried out, a soblike sound, and covered her face with her hands once again.

Francesca patted the woman's shoulder again. "I am so sorry."

Georgette looked up at her tearfully. "Are you?"

"Yes," Francesca said quietly, earnestly. "An innocent man is dead. This is a ghastly crime. I am terribly sorry, and I promise you, Miss de Labouche, that I will find out who perpetrated this deadly and foul deed."

Georgette said, "I only want to hide the body. Paul is dead. Finding whoever did this will not bring him back." Her mouth trembled again.

"We *must* tell the police," Francesca reiterated firmly. "So you ran to him? Was he still alive? Did he say anything?"

Georgette shook her head and briefly closed her eyes. "He was dead. His eyes were wide open, sightless, and there was so much blood!" She moaned and sank down again, but this time on the red brocade sofa.

Francesca looked at the dead man. His eyes were closed. "Did you touch him?"

Georgette nodded and whispered, "I closed his eyes, I just had to, but that is all."

Francesca nodded, folding her arms. She studied the dead man, Paul, for another moment, then glanced at Georgette, who remained motionless on the sofa, hunched

over in apparent misery. Francesca glanced around. "The
only way to enter this room is via that single door from
the hall?"

Georgette nodded.

"And you are certain you did not see anyone?"

She nodded again.

Francesca glanced at the clock on the mantel. It was a
quarter to midnight. Georgette had accosted her on the
street outside of Madison Square Garden at half past nine,
approximately. Perhaps it had even been fifteen or twenty
minutes past the hour. "At what time did the murder occur?
At what time did you enter your bath? How long were you
in it before you heard the shot?"

"It was six-thirty when I began to prepare to bathe. I
was expecting Paul at seven. He is usually prompt. He was
probably murdered a few moments past seven."

"Miss Labouche. This is very important. Did Mr. Randall have any enemies? Can you think of anyone who might
want him dead?"

"Only his wife," the redhead said, her regard sullen.

"I am in earnest," Francesca returned. "Are you?"

Georgette de Labouche grimaced. "He had no real enemies. He was not the type of man to provoke anyone,
Miss Cahill. He had retired from his position as manager
of a textile company five years ago. We met shortly afterward. He was a simple man. His life revolved around his
children and his wife, his golf, his club—and me."

Francesca was the one to nod, thoughtfully. Then she
sighed. "Well, I may have more questions for you, Miss
de Labouche, but for the moment, that is enough. I must
call the police. Do you have a telephone?"

Georgette looked at her. "They will think I am the one.
A murder like this is always blamed on the mistress."

"I do not think they will think you are the one," Francesca said, meaning it. "We must inform the police. We *must*."

"Fine," Georgette said, appearing very unhappy. "I do not have a telephone. While you go, I shall go upstairs and try to compose myself. Perhaps I shall lie down."

"I think that is a good idea," Francesca said. She hesitated. Bragg's house was only a few blocks away. Should she go out on the street and wave down a roundsman or go over to Bragg's? Eventually he would be informed of the murder anyway.

Of course she must go directly to Bragg. Otherwise there would be pointless questions and delay as she dealt with the patrolmen who would answer her call.

Of course, he had rebuffed her earlier, and she should not be pleased about their sharing another case. And she was not pleased—this was *her* case. She had found it first.

"I will see you to the door," Georgette said abruptly, standing.

There was something in the woman's tone that made Francesca start, and suspicion filled her. Georgette had said at least three times that she wanted to hide the body. Francesca realized she should stay and *guard* the body while sending Joel for help. Even though it was unlikely that the woman could remove and hide the body in the half hour or so that it would take the police commissioner to arrive.

"I am sending Joel round the block to the police commissioner's house," Francesca announced, watching her closely. "He is a personal friend of mine," she added.

Georgette blanched, and without a word—but looking even unhappier than before—she ran from the room.

As she did so, Joel fell into the room, clearly having had his ear pressed to the closed parlor door the entire time. "Hell!" he cried, eyes wide. "Look it that! Cold as a wagon tire, Miss Cahill, a real stiff for your first crime." He grinned at her. "An' a real to-do gent by the look of him."

"Yes, he appears to be a gentleman." Francesca was

stern. "Joel, if you are to be my assistant, eavesdropping is not allowed."

"Eavesdroppin'? Wut the hell is that?"

"It is spying," she said, coming forward. "You spied on a private conversation between myself and Miss de Labouche."

"I was lookin' out for you, lady," he said fiercely. "That's me job."

She looked into his almost-black eyes and melted. "You were?"

He nodded. Then, "Did you peek in his purse?"

She stiffened. "We are not stealing a dead man's purse!"

"Why not? He's dead. He can't use the spondulicks!"

"Spondulicks?" Sometimes conversing with Joel was like trying to comprehend a foreign language.

"He's dead. He can't spend a dime."

"We are not stealing from the corpse!" Francesca cried, meaning it. "Now listen carefully. Tomorrow we will sit down and go over some rules. Rules of your employment. But right now, I need you to go over to the police commissioner's house and tell him what has happened. If he is not there, tell Peter, his man." She hesitated, glancing behind her at the dead man. God, she would be alone with the corpse while Joel was gone. It was not a comforting thought.

Of course, Georgette was upstairs, so she would not really be alone.

"And you should hurry," Francesca added.

"Right," Joel said, turning to go.

"Wait!" She caught the shoulder of his jacket. "Do you know where you're going?"

Joel grinned at her. "Sure do. Madison and Twenty-fourth Street."

She stared. "How would you know where Bragg lives?"

He shrugged. "Whole world knows. Ain't no secret. Back in a flash." He hurried away.

Francesca stood very still, watching him leave the house. And then she felt truly alone.

She shivered.

The house was so quiet that she could hear the clock ticking on the mantel. It almost felt as if there were eyes trained on her back—the dead man's eyes. But of course, they were closed—and he was dead.

Fortunately, she did not believe in ghosts. Still, Francesca hurried down the dimly lit hall, wishing it were more brightly lit, relieved to leave the room with the corpse. She checked the front door. It was locked. That made her feel a bit better.

She cracked open the only other door on the hall, other than the parlor door, and glanced into a small dining room. It was cast in shadow. She vaguely made out an oak table and four chairs, a floral arrangement, and a sideboard with knickknacks. A kitchen had to be on the other side of the alcove. Francesca hesitated.

If there was a kitchen door that led to a garden out back or the street out front, she wanted to make sure it was locked. She was very nervous now. And why not? She was guarding the corpse of a man who had been murdered less than five hours ago.

Francesca looked up at the dark stairs. "Miss de Labouche?" she called.

There was no answer.

"Georgette?" she tried again, with the same lack of success.

Francesca glanced behind her. The parlor remained so brilliantly lit, and the dead body in the pool of blood remained a grotesquely eye-catching spectacle. Francesca realized just how nervous she was.

That was it. She dashed through the small dining alcove, trying not to consider that the murderer might still

be in the house—of course that made no sense—and she
found herself in the kitchen. This house did not have electricity, and it was a moment before Francesca turned on
one gaslight. There was a back door. It was locked.

She sighed in abject relief.

When she heard something.

Instinct caused Francesca to turn off the light and
crouch down beside the doorway to the dining alcove. She
had not closed the dining room door, and she could just
glimpse the hall beyond.

She heard something again. God damn it, but it was the
front door, she was certain of it, being carefully closed.

Francesca ducked completely behind the kitchen doorway, now perspiring madly. Joel had left about five
minutes ago. Maybe, maybe, he could run from here to
Bragg's in five minutes. But there was just no way that he
was already returning, alone or with Bragg, and anyway,
they would have to knock.

She trembled and heard a floorboard creak.

Someone had entered the house. Someone was in the
hall. Someone who was not announcing himself—someone who had a key.

She heard more soft footsteps.

Francesca went blank. But she had to know who the
intruder was. She thought he had walked past the dining
room doorway, but she wasn't sure. Keeping on all fours
now, she peered around the kitchen doorway and into the
dining room.

Just in time to glimpse a man's silhouette as he walked
past while in the hall.

Francesca ducked back. She heard the man halt. And
there was a very soft, barely audible expletive, followed
by absolute silence.

She imagined he had seen the body and that was what
had stopped him in his tracks and caused him to curse.
Was he staring at it now?

Suddenly she heard brisk footsteps returning. Francesca did not dare peer around the corner again, as much as she wanted to. She held her breath, afraid he might feel her presence, afraid he might change course and discover her hiding in the other room.

The front door opened and closed.

Francesca jumped up and ran into the dining room and shoved aside the draperies to peer onto the street, her pulse racing wildly. A very nice gig was pulling away from the curb, a single man its occupant—the driver. He was too far away for her to make out any features.

Francesca stared. Who in blazes had just walked into Georgette de Labouche's house in order to stare at her dead lover? Who would do such a thing, then turn around without a word and leave?

What in tarnation was going on?

DEADLY DESIRE

The Channings lived on the unfashionable West Side of the city. Sarah Channing was becoming a good friend, ever since her engagement to Francesca's brother, Evan. When her father had died, her mother, a rather frivolous and harmless socialite, had inherited his millions and promptly built their new house. As Francesca approached the mansion, which was quite new and horrendously gothic, she clutched her reticule as if she expected a cutpurse to appear and seize it.

Francesca was told by the doorman that Miss Channing was not receiving visitors.

"Would you care to leave your card?" the liveried doorman asked.

"Harold? Who is it?"

Francesca stepped forward at the sound of Mrs. Channing's voice. A not-quite-pretty woman with reddish-blond hair who was extremely well-dressed and somehow reminded one of a flighty, mindless bird was entering the foyer. "Why, Francesca! This is quite the surprise!" She clapped her beringed hands together in childish delight.

Francesca managed a smile. "Hello, Mrs. Channing. I am sorry to hear that Sarah is indisposed. I hope she is not too ill?"

Mrs. Channing's dark eyes widened. Then she put her arm around Francesca and leaned toward her, speaking in a conspiratorial whisper. "Perhaps this is a stroke of fate, indeed. That you should choose this very day to call!"

Francesca looked into her dramatically widened eyes—
as there was little else to do, with the other woman's face
a mere two inches from her own. "Whatever do you mean,
Mrs. Channing?"

"We are in the midst of a crisis," Mrs. Channing said.
Her breath was sweet, as if she had been eating raspberries
and chocolates.

Francesca was in no mood for a crisis other than her
own. "Perhaps I should leave word that I have called—
and come back at another time."

"Oh, no!" Mrs. Channing cried, finally releasing Francesca. "I *told* Sarah we should call for you! But she said
you were recovering from that horrid encounter with the
Cross Killer, and we mustn't disturb you! But you are a
sleuth, dearie, and we do need a sleuth now! Nor do I have
the foggiest of whom else to call upon in our time of
need!"

Francesca straightened. In spite of her worries, she
could not help being intrigued. "You have need of an investigator?" she asked, a familiar tingle now running up
and down her spine.

Mrs. Channing nodded eagerly.

"Why, what has happened?"

"Come with me!" Mrs. Channing exclaimed. And she
was already hurrying into the hall.

Francesca followed, not bothering to hand off her coat,
hat, and single glove. She quickly realized, as they moved
down one hall and then another, that they were heading in
the direction of Sarah's studio. She was perplexed.

Suddenly Mrs. Channing turned and placed her back
against the door of Sarah's studio, barring the way. "Prepare yourself," she warned, rather theatrically.

Francesca nodded, holding back a smile, more than intrigued now. What could be going on?

Mrs. Channing smiled, as if in satisfaction, and she
thrust open the door.

Francesca stepped inside. The room was all windows, and brilliantly lit. She cried out.

Someone had been on a rampage in the room.

Canvases, palettes, and jars were overturned. Paint was splattered across the floor and walls, the effect vivid, brilliant, and disturbing. Amidst the yellows, blues, and greens, there were slashes of black and dark, dark red. For an instant, Francesca thought the red was blood.

She rushed forward, kneeled, and dabbed her finger into a drying pool of dark red. It was paint, not blood.

Then she saw the canvas lying face up on the floor.

It had been slashed into ribbons.

"Sarah! I cannot believe what happened!" Francesca cried. She had been pacing in a huge, mostly gilded salon, which was as overdone as the outside of the house. A bear rug complete with head and fangs competed with the Orientals on the floor; chairs had hooves and claws for feet, and one lamp had a tusk for a pull cord. Mr. Channing, God rest his soul, had been a hunter and a collector of strange and exotic objects. Apparently his widow was continuing his hobby.

Sarah had just entered the room. She was a small and plain brunette, although her eyes were huge and pretty. Today, she was wearing a drab blue dress covered with splotches of paint. She appeared very pale, her nose and eyes red. Clearly, she had been weeping. "Francesca? What are you doing here?" she asked softly—brokenly.

Francesca forgot all about her own problems. She rushed forward and embraced her friend. "You poor dear! Who would do such a thing?"

Sarah trembled in her arms. "I told Mother not to call you! You have a badly burned hand and you are recuperating!"

Francesca stepped back. "Your mother did not telephone me. I called upon you, dear."

Their eyes met. Tears welled in Sarah's. "I did not want to bother you, not now, not after what happened on Tuesday," referring to the aftermath of the Channing ball.

Francesca took Sarah's hand with her own good one. "How could you *not* call me? I am your friend! Sarah, we must catch this miserable culprit! Have you called the police?" Her heart skipped madly. These days, the police and Rick Bragg were one and the same and never mind what Connie had said a few minutes ago.

"Not yet. I have been too devastated. I just found out this morning," Sarah said, and she was shaking visibly.

Mrs. Channing stepped into the room. "Sarah gets up before dawn. She takes a tea and goes directly into her studio. She will spend the entire day there, if I do not rescue her from her frenzy."

Francesca looked from mother to daughter. "So you found your studio that way when you went down this morning?" she asked.

Sarah nodded.

"Why don't you girls sit down? Francesca, have you had lunch?" Mrs. Channing asked.

"No, but I would like a moment alone with Sarah, if you don't mind, Mrs. Channing."

Mrs. Channing seemed taken aback.

Francesca smiled, politely but firmly. "Do you wish me to take—and solve—the case? If so, I need to interview your daughter."

"Oh, of course! My, Francesca, you are so professional." Then Mrs. Channing smiled. "I shall have a small meal put out anyway. Do as you shall, then, Francesca." She left, closing the door behind her.

"Francesca, how can you take my case now when you are hurt? Besides, didn't you promise to rest for a few weeks?" Sarah looked her directly in the eye.

She had, and she had mentioned her resolve to Sarah. "Never you mind, my hand is healing very well, Finny

said so himself. I would never let down a friend in need."
Francesca smiled and guided her to a couch, where they
both sat down. She leaned forward eagerly. "What time
did you first enter your studio?"

"It was five-fifteen. I get up at five on most mornings,
and go directly there." She smiled a little. "And I take
coffee, not tea, black with one sugar."

Francesca patted her hand. "And when were you last in
your studio? On Friday morning?"

Sarah nodded. "I worked there until about noon on Friday." Suddenly she covered her heart with her hand. "Francesca, I am so shocked. And worse, I feel ill. I feel . . .
raped, I suppose. Or I imagine that this is what being raped
feels like. I am shocked and sad and angry and I cannot
stop crying! Why would someone do this? Why?" she
cried, a tear sliding down her cheek.

Francesca sat up straighter. "I don't know. I have no
idea. But whoever it was, he got into this house to do his
deadly deed sometime between noon on Friday and five-
fifteen Saturday morning. I shall have to interview the entire household staff. Are there any new employees?"

"I don't know. Also, we were out last night," Sarah
said. "We went to the ballet. But still, there is a houseful
of servants, and a doorman is always on the front door."

"Still, a single doorman can fall asleep," Francesca
mused. "I shall have to speak to the doorman who was on
last night while you were out."

"That would be Harris," Sarah said. "He has been with
us forever, it seems."

"And when you are out, where is the rest of the staff?"

"In their rooms on the fourth floor," Sarah said. Suddenly she sighed, the sound filled with grief. "Why, Francesca? Why?"

"I don't know. But I shall find out. Sarah, do you have
any enemies?" And even as she asked, the question felt
ridiculous. Who would dislike, no, hate, Sarah Channing

enough to do something like this? She was a sweet young girl, and so reclusive that she hardly had any friends, much less enemies.

Sarah blinked at her. "I hardly think so. Why would someone hate *me*? There is nothing to be jealous of."

Francesca considered that. "I don't know. It is absurd. But you are a wealthy young woman, and you are engaged to my brother, who is quite the catch."

"I don't think either reason is sufficient for someone to break into this house and destroy my studio," Sarah said tersely. "Do you?"

"No, I do not. But people can be strange." She was reflective now. Her last three cases had certainly proven that, and more. She had learned there was a goodly share of insanity going about undetected. "Perhaps you turned a client down? Perhaps you portrayed a client in a way he or she did not care for?"

Sarah sighed again, heavily. "Francesca, I cannot recall anyone being angry with me for a painting. And—I do not have clients. I am hardly an artist. Everyone I have painted has agreed to sit for me, usually quite happily." Suddenly Sarah smiled. "Well, I do have one client." Her smile widened.

Francesca knew exactly whom she was talking about and tensed. "You mean Calder Hart?"

Sarah nodded, beaming. "He commissioned your portrait. Surely you haven't forgotten?"

"How could I?" Francesca said sourly. "I hate to disappoint you, but Hart only asked for my portrait because he was angry with me. We have patched things up, and he will hardly want my portrait now."

Sarah blinked at her. "Oh, I do think you are wrong. You are an amazing woman, and Hart sees that. He is very eager to have your portrait, I am certain of it."

Her tension—and dismay—increased. Francesca recalled the Channing ball, which for her, personally, had been a disaster—and the moment when Hart had looked at her in her disheveled state, a state induced by spending quite a few minutes upon a sofa in Bragg's arms. The look he had given her had been thoroughly unpleasant; he had known what she had been doing, and he had been quite clear that he did not approve of her interest in his *married* brother. (He had also, several times, admitted how perfect she and Bragg were for one another.) And then he had told Sarah that he wished to commission a portrait. Of Francesca—in her daring red dress, with her hair down, and her straps slipping, and her lips bee-stung.

Francesca flushed now. She hated recalling that nasty exchange. It was not Hart's business if she remained enamored of his half brother. In fact, she had told him so several times.

"Francesca, you aren't changing your mind, are you?" Sarah asked breathlessly.

Now it was Francesca's turn to sigh—almost. Instead, she muffled the sound. Sarah had begged her to sit for the portrait. This was her chance to gain a foothold in the world of art. It was, in fact, a huge coup to have Hart commission a portrait from her. "If he remains serious, of course I have not changed my mind," Francesca said, rather glumly. "I promised, and it would be the most stunning opportunity for you. But Sarah, do not be disappointed if Hart is no longer interested."

Sarah grinned. "Yesterday he dropped off a check. A deposit, if you will. He has paid me half of the commission in advance."

"Why, that's unheard of!" Francesca cried, stunned and furious.

Sarah lightly touched her arm. "You see, he is deadly serious."

Francesca stood, about to pace. Then she decided to dismiss Hart from her mind, as he had the knack of annoying her even when he was not present. "We have a case to solve. In fact, I shall go home, fetch Joel, and see if there is any word out on the street about the who or the why of this. Then I shall go down to Police Headquarters, as this is a crime, and it must be reported. First, however, I wish to interview Harris, the doorman." She wanted a head start on the case before the police became involved.

Sarah nodded. "I can see that, in spite of the unhappy circumstances, you are thrilled to be back at what you love most—sleuthing."

Francesca smiled a little. "I cannot seem to help myself, I guess. We are very alike, you and I."

"I realize that. Although no one would ever know it to look at us, as you are so beautiful and so full of life, while I am drab and shy."

"You are not drab! You are not shy!" Francesca rushed to her and hugged her.

"I do not mind being drab and shy. You know I do not care what others think. I only care about my art." Her eyes changed, glowing now, with anger. "I want to know who did this, Francesca, and I want to know why."

"I shall not let you down," Francesca vowed. And she meant it.

THE
CHASE

—

BRENDA JOYCE

NEW YORK TIMES BESTSELLING AUTHOR

CLAIRE HAYDEN has no idea that her world is about to be shattered: at the conclusion of her husband's fortieth birthday party, he is found murdered, his throat cut with a WWII thumb knife. He has no enemies, no one seeking revenge, no one who would want him dead. But the mysterious Ian Marshall, an acquaintance of her husband's, seems to know something. Because someone has been killing this way for decades. Someone whose crimes go back to WWII. Someone who has been a hunter . . . and the hunted. As Claire and Ian team up to find the killer, they can no longer deny the powerful feelings they have for one another. Then Ian makes a shocking revelation: the murderer may be someone close to her . . .

> **"Joyce excels at creating twists and turns in her characters' personal lives."**
> **—*Publishers Weekly***

ON SALE JULY 2002
FROM ST. MARTIN'S PRESS